The
Prophesy Gene

STUART D. SCHOOLER

Acknowledgements

Commercial real estate development can be lucrative and ruthless, so I would like to thank my first career for driving me to write the totally unrelated Prophesy Gene. Writers conferences are to real estate conventions as animal shelters are to the Westminster Kennel Club Dog Show. Sometimes you just need a place where everybody competing can be a winner. Even with the mutation of the publishing industry into something unrecognizable by literary luminaries of just twenty years ago, it is reassuring that the writer still does not have to check to see if his pen has been poisoned.

Twelve years ago, I first outlined The Prophesy Gene. After eight years, countless classes and conferences, I realized how very little an MBA/engineer/ part-time opinion page columnist knew about novel writing. I would like to thank Mindy Shedler for attempting to tell me sooner. There was no way to get that red pen out of her hand.

Within months of the finish line, a prominent literary agent expressed some concern that my manuscript might be perceived as "too literary" for a first novel, particularly one with "genre identity issues." He asked me if I could make it more commercial. I told him we were following the Paul McCartney rules on paperback writing and therefore, only one thing mattered. We agreed to talk literary fiction on the third or fourth novel. That is when I finally began to learn the trade, so anonymously, he should be acknowledged, too.

My wife, Marlene, reads a select few literary genres and The Prophesy Gene was never one of them. Yet, she edited relentlessly and after five children, I realized she wasn't going to quit on me over something as silly as my life's passion. Three outstanding authors read The Prophesy Gene starting from when it was garbage, through its literary phase, to where it is today. Howard Norman constructively critiqued an early draft and my instructors at UCLA, Caroline Leavitt and Lynn Hightower, helped me penetrate my characters' psyches and imbue them with texture and unique voices. Thank you all.

CHAPTER 1

An Environmental Cesspool. A Burrow.

Ever since the Aral Sea environmental disaster of the 1980s scientists and circus sideshow hunters had flocked to this remote corner of Central Asia, looking for freaks of nature. Other than the occasional three-legged frog and two-headed snake that didn't survive to adulthood, they had all come up empty. Until now.

"Evolution is far less plausible than science fiction," Michael said to his cousin.

Sarah Baskin focused on the single horn projecting from the center of the donkey's skull. She tugged on it gently, and the animal brayed in pain. "That's because the imagination is not nearly as creative as random chance."

"Tell Mr. Fuksenko that this is not a unicorn," she said, "but a deformity caused by all of the chemicals used here." With the assistance of a Russian-English dictionary, Michael translated to the Uzbek farmer.

"Michael, ask him if this mare was born with a horn and if she has had any foals yet."

The investigative journalist flipped through the dictionary and spoke in broken Russian. Fuksenko's leathery face was blank. Then Michael squatted his lanky six-foot-one-inch frame close to the mare's kick zone and made an expelling motion from her birth canal.

The man's eyes widened, and he erupted with an unexpected laugh. He spoke quickly, and Michael made him repeat himself more slowly. "Yes, she was born this way. Her foal was still-born and had no horn, and her mother was normal as well."

The environmental graduate student exhaled audibly. "Well, the dead foal was normal, so this horn's probably a birth defect rather than a genetic mutation."

The barrel-chested farmer furrowed his large forehead quizzically. He spoke slowly to Michael but kept glancing and leering at his fair-complexioned cousin.

Swirling a finger, the farmer exclaimed, "Yozhik," and motioned for the two cousins to follow him. His dog, a hip-high, twenty-kilogram shepherd mix, tagged along expectantly.

Michael flipped furiously through the dictionary as he dodged the cow dung. He looked at Sarah, puzzled. "Hedgehog?"

She shrugged.

They trailed the farmer to a dried streambed. The man motioned to indicate that the water ran heavily during the spring thaws and rains. He crab-clawed surefootedly down the steep stream bank as the dog and Sarah followed with equal grace. Michael slid down awkwardly on his butt, protecting the camera with his body.

On the embankment, they saw a large burrow partially screened by a web of exposed tree roots. The Uzbek grabbed a long stick and shoved it deep into the shadows while he turned a flashlight into the opening. An animal the size of an obese house cat and the angry brown color of a poked grizzly bear emerged in a high-pitched growl. It attacked the dog, who put up a brief fight and then retreated toward the barn. The large hedgehog gave pursuit. From the growling and snarling, it sounded as if the dog had decided to stand its ground. The fifty-something farmer chuckled and quickly crested the bank, with Sarah and Michael trailing.

The hedgehog had a pincushion of ivory-colored quills covering the entire length of its body. The dog had taken a painful noseful. Then the primitive mammal reared on its hind legs and, exposing razor-like teeth under its anteater snout, bit into the dog's breast. The animal's mouth wasn't large enough to do any serious damage, so it rolled onto its back and superficially lacerated the staggering dog's soft underbelly with sharp rear claws. The dog fell at once and was still before its master could reach it.

The hedgehog bounded off quickly in the opposite direction from its burrow.

"Come on, Michael, let's get back to its lair."

Sarah peered into the hole with the flashlight, inching slowly closer. Her light shone off the back wall. She saw shadowy motion and heard the tiny squeaks of multiple young. Moving quickly before the adult returned, she donned heavy elbow-length gloves and extracted one of the babies and several milky globules and quickly placed them in separate pouches.

Just in time. The hedgehog waddled back with blood on its snout, so Sarah and Michael retreated a safe distance from the burrow. Michael snapped high-definition digital photos from all angles. Then they scrambled to the top of the bank. It didn't make sense. The dog had suffered bites and scratches, but they were hardly life-threatening. Sarah stopped and directed her pale amber eyes into the sample container and gasped.

"We've got to find out if more of these genetic anomalies exist, fast. At first, I thought the animal *was* a hedgehog. But it couldn't kill a dog of that size even if it hit the jugular. Then I assumed it must be some sort of undiscovered giant water shrew, a distant relative of the hedgehog. They're one of only a few mammals that have venomous saliva, but their jaws can't penetrate the skin of large mammals."

"So?"

"It's neither. This is our worst nightmare. A new species formed by this ecological disaster could completely destroy the ecosystem. Predators like these soricomorphs," the taxonomic name that included all of the shrew's relatives, "can now leap frog over other animals in the food chain and start eating *them*. Bobcats that were the hedgehog's predators are now its lunch. We may have only weeks before this new species migrates into larger watersheds or kills curious children because they think it's a harmless hedgehog."

"Weeks? Isn't that being a little overly dramatic?"

"It's a reproduction machine with no natural enemies. There are eggs in the nest with live young. Mammals? Laying eggs? That's only monotremes. You know, platypuses? But the habitat and quills are more like a West Indies shrew. Its saliva is poisonous enough to kill a dog. And if you go backward up the taxonomy, you get to monotremes, whose rear claws are also poisonous."

"Shouldn't we destroy the ones in that nest?"

Sarah cast an awkward glance toward the farmer bent over his dog. "The farmer will take care of that. I'm just glad we got specimens first because nobody would have believed us. We don't even know if it's full grown."

Sarah said, "We need to go to the source of the stream." They followed the dried streambed into the beckoning mountains and their eyes met. They shuddered openly. As so often in their youth, they were thinking the same thing, whether or not they wanted to admit it.

"The shrew journeyed down here to get us to follow it up the mountain, didn't it?"

"What are you talking about? It lives here in the burrow. We need to go up there to see how far it propagated."

"Web-footed shrews live near water year around. The Aral Sea and this bed are dry. The water's in the mountains, Sarah, not here."

"As always, you are paranoid. It's a new species. It didn't know this area was only seasonally wet when it migrated down here last year."

Soviet planners had deliberately sacrificed the Aral Sea. The water from the two main rivers flowing into it, the Syr-Daria and Amu-Daria, was diverted for the irrigation of intensive cotton plantations. The Aral Sea continued to dry out year after year. The massive use of fertilizers and pesticides exacerbated soil exhaustion and sterilization. Runoff into the rivers, streams, and ground water that constituted the potable water of the rural residents resulted in an astounding number of bizarre congenital birth defects—extra limbs, missing lips, eyelids, and lower jawbones, and partially developed crania, but until now no evidence of anything that had propagated to the next generation, human or otherwise, advancement or deformity.

Sarah's graduate adviser had encouraged her to explore the Uzbek backcountry just south of the Aral Sea for genetic mutations that had reproduced viable offspring. Dr. Alexis Brankov, a tenured professor at the University of Chicago, had heard stories of rampant mutations in the valley from a colleague at St. Petersburg University in Russia and felt this could be the pinnacle of Sarah's research.

When Sarah had approached her parents about covering some of the trip cost, they had imposed one condition. She had to have a trustworthy companion. Several years ago, her brother Ethan had died from injuries sustained in Kiev, Ukraine while participating in a goodwill soccer tournament among college friendlies. The inconclusive investigation had left her parents overprotective of their remaining children. Oddly, though, it was not they who had suggested Michael, but Dr. Brankov. She had met

Michael several times and had suggested Sarah invite him as her scribe. He spoke some Russian, and as a male relative, he could escort her through this largely Muslim country. And Sarah had told her about Michael's desperate work situation.

Several recent, expensive dead-end leads had left Michael nearly unemployed. First, there was the twenty thousand dollars of the paper's money he spent in West Texas chasing a story about a newly identified uranium vein that turned out to be a buried truck load of stolen watches with radium dials. Then there was the time he went to the Texas City, Texas, ship channel to investigate illegal chemical plant effluent releases from an underwater discharge line, only to find out that the chemicals plant in question was the primary supplier of newsprint ink for his paper, and they had just switched to biodegradable soy-based inks. And finally, there was the mother of all disasters, a cover page story about a more energy-efficient manufacturing process that turned out to be a tax credit scam. He should have corroborated his facts, but instead he decided to sleep with the publicist, a rare opportunity for Michael. Sarah steadfastly stood by her cousin and was determined to repair his reputation. The ecosystem repercussions of Soviet neglect along the banks of the Aral Sea potentially rivaled the Chernobyl nuclear disaster.

All of Michael's missteps had occurred on his science editor's watch, so Michael knew that Neil would not share Sarah's enthusiasm for this trip. With little to lose, Michael had circumvented his boss and convinced the travel editor, who liked Michael's writing style and the "exotic vacation angle," to let him report on his adventures in north central Asia. He took the balance of his vacation and an extra week of leave without pay and prayed that Sarah's adviser had confirmed her facts better than he had done in Texas.

Until today, Michael's most intriguing, but as yet unwritten story from Uzbekistan was about an innkeeper who operated a brothel in his barn, but neutered himself because he couldn't resist the inventory. If only he could find the right audience.

Within hours, they had rented a pack burro from the hand-wringing farmer and were following the dry channel into the mountains. Michael was beginning to see the potential for a daily double. In addition to mutant killer hedgehogs ("The perfect movie title for the Sci-Fi Channel," he had told Sarah), the region to which they were now heading had experienced a mystifying number of confirmed UFO sightings in the 1990s. Unfortunately, he wasn't writing for the *National Enquirer.*

CHAPTER 2

High in the Mountains

They had covered nearly ten kilometers and come up empty. Nothing but indigenous species. Not surprising, because Sarah suspected that the animal was nocturnal. Michael kept one of Sarah's two cans of mace at the ready, even though there was little to be feared hiking a wilderness trail with a cousin who had made backwoods camping her weekend vacation condo.

As the afternoon shadows to their right lengthened, the gully grew damp. Puddles from the most recent rains clung to the sandy soil and formed a small pool of standing water that ran into the riverbed and disappeared over a distance of about two tractor-trailer lengths. The mountain stream cascaded with white water during the rainy season. At last, they were leaving the drought-plagued area. Grasses and willows struggled to take root along the banks of the stream, indicating groundwater just below the surface. They had risen about 150 meters in elevation.

All roads led to the smattering of remote villages in the foothills, the closest about twenty kilometers away. Unless they traveled through a pass separating the north from the south slope, they would always have the peaks in front of them, so there was little chance of getting lost. While Russian was still the most common second language for the Uzbeks, since the fall of the Soviet Union nearly all of the schools had switched to English so they could always ask for help. GPS didn't cover cart trails.

Sarah's stomach was rumbling loudly and Michael kept stealing handfuls of trail mix from the back of her pack. The surefooted burro had begun slipping on loose gravel. The pack animal had been loaded with Sarah's sample jars, syringes, and a foam-insulated stainless steel container packed with dry ice. It also had Michael's laptop, half a dozen spare batteries, and a bundle of reporters' notebooks, their only concessions to civilization.

Sarah was constantly conflicted between protecting the environment and the need for suitable research tools, like "disposable" polystyrene coolers, which were anything but. Michael was amazed that she could get four refills out of a single Starbucks cup.

Michael insisted that they move away from the hedgehog-infested riverbed before they make camp, so they found a thin eucalyptus grove next to a well-worn wagon trail several hundred meters away.

"I've got an idea," Michael said. "Let's water and feed the burro and stop for dinner."

Sarah looked closely at his bloodshot eyes. "Where did you find pot, Michael? And where did you smoke it? Do you want to spend your life in a Stalinist prison?" Sarah would have preferred diving off a fifteen-meter cliff into the ocean to getting incarcerated for smuggling drugs.

"You can't always be supervising me, *Mother*. Remember when I went downwind to relieve myself? And it's hash. You will absolutely not believe this. The farmer's son asked me if I wanted some hash. Of course, knowing that he could be some sort of Uzbek security agent, I said no. Well, when he took us back into the barn to get the burro, and while you were wandering around and scratching the necks of all of the barnyard critters, I found his drying room wide open, a crack. Unlocked, anyway. And certainly unguarded. I wasn't really even looking for it; I was just poking around the barn. I randomly picked just a few of the best specimens for us, so it wouldn't be noticeable."

"*Us?*"

"All right, for me. I don't have to share. We'll just give him a big tip when we return the burro. And then, to show that there are no hard feelings, we'll buy some more. This can't last more than a couple of nights."

"Not the way you smoke."

"I'll start burning the evidence," he said, and symbolically lit another joint.

They set up their tent and tethered the burro so he could munch on seasonal berries. As she took a deep drag on the hand-rolled joint, she rationalized. At least rotating hashish and cotton crops was better for the soil than the Soviet program was.

It was an intensely clear, moonless night, and the sky was a colander of stars. The moon wouldn't be rising for several hours, so they could watch the joint-enhanced images of the zodiac prance across the sky.

Michael serenely picked up his binoculars and scanned the horizon. As his eyes approached the foothills to the west, he noticed silvery clouds settling near the ground, shrouding the lowest hills with mist and leaving the higher peaks suspended in the sky. The clouds were not wispy near the edges, but had a sharply defined border. The heavens above them were slowly blackening and whitening in thick, alternating, vertical strands of primitive TV-test patterns until the stars slowly shimmered away.

"Sarah, what is in this hash?"

Sarah had curled up under her sleeping bag. "You're asking me? I don't know, but it's really good. Why?"

"Fog and mist don't form in arid climates, so maybe I'm hallucinating. And the clouds are eating the mountain."

Sarah came over with the sleeping bag draped around her body. Lightning had begun flowing across the ground in undulating waves and then discharging in bolts *into* the silky strands of clouds with increasing intensity, quite the opposite of the normal atmospheric phenomenon.

Streaks of light raced from the blackest holes in the heavens down to earth and exploded in a Fourth of July fireworks show. After nearly a minute, the streaks became interspersed with falling orbs of light that veered sharply right and left and then collided with the clouds and disappeared.

They stood transfixed. At first, the silence was broken only by a cricket's chirp, but as everything now directed itself toward the mysterious opaque cloud, even the crickets grew deferentially quiet. The wind disappeared.

Sarah whispered, "I don't like this. Give me the scientifically explainable any day."

"This is the best science page stuff there is. Just some atmospheric phenomenon," Michael said flippantly. "Get the cookies." She moved to grab a handful.

"No, I think we'll need both bags. I want to climb up the mountain and get a better view." He grabbed the day pack strapped to the burro.

Michael watched the burro slowly turn magnetically toward the cloud. Then it brayed loudly. It tugged on its tether, trying to free itself. Exasperated, it sat down camel-like on its knees and stared at the cloud unblinking.

They trekked toward the low-lying cloud. It was beginning to luminesce like a second moon and then pulsate like a twinkling star.

"Michael," Sarah began as she passed the joint back to him, "don't you think we ought to stop smoking this stuff? He probably grew it in the same stuff that mutated that soricomorph thing. We really could be hallucinating."

Sarah described the spooky balls of light headed toward the gauzy striped curtain just as Michael had seen them.

"Two people can't hallucinate identical images," Michael said.

"Aren't you scared of what's out there?"

"No, why?"

"What if the cloud's poisonous or possesses some high-voltage electric charge?"

"It's probably just a result of volatile pesticides evaporating from the cotton fields around the Aral Sea and ummm…reacting in the air with highly charged ions when hmm…the temperature elevates and the humidity falls to a certain level to form plasma which discharges into the clouds, making a great light show."

"You are stoned off your ass, and that is gibberish."

They giggled uncontrollably and plodded up the steepening hillside with the luminescing cloud lighting their way. Ahead of them, the scrub vegetation dotting either side of the path receded into the bleak terrain.

Michael pulled out the binoculars and looked back at their campground. It would have been lost in the moonless night had it not been for the glowing embers of their fire, illuminating the outline of their burro, still staring at the silky fluff that was their target.

As he handed Sarah the binoculars, another possibility occurred to her. She muttered under her breath, "Maybe it's not really there. Maybe someone is planting this stuff in our brains."

The wind kicked up and without warning, images exploded in their heads in a fireworks display of color. They pressed their hands over their ears and squeezed their eyes shut in a futile attempt to block out the sensory overload.

Sarah's eyes rolled up into her head. She saw herself on a land brimming with sub-Antarctic mammals and birds. Intuitively, though she had never been farther south than the Caribbean, she knew that it was an Antarctic shoreline on the Weddell Sea. She saw herself and Michael following a clearly marked path to a glacier. Through someone else's eyes, she could see that there was a woolly mammoth suspended in time deep within its thick cake of ice. And those eyes were sentient. Sarah knew that she and Michael were supposed to travel there together. But she did not know why or how.

She attempted to backtrack up the mental pathway from these images to identify their source or fill in the blanks, but it disappeared. She was caught in that split second between sleep and consciousness where attempts to interpret your dreams result in them slipping away forever.

When Michael attempted to focus on his cousin, his attention was drawn forcefully back to the images.

He was talking to himself. *How are we supposed to travel to Antarctica? What about the danger? And what's the significance of woolly mammoths?* And then his jaw muscles tightened on the penultimate question.

What are you? Humanity believes it is the supreme life form in the universe, and he had just realized that it may not even be the king of the 'hood.

As Michael's last thought popped into his head, the cloud shook tremulously as if laughing, but gave no answer.

The allegory and imagery continued.

In their minds' eye, they saw people looking up to the cloud. They prostrated themselves to the cloud and followed it everywhere. Some people simply evaporated, while others were absorbed into the cloud. Sarah and Michael's hearts raced as they sensed the tortured memories of their personification of evil within the cloud. But exactly whose memories were they? They couldn't identify them yet.

A new scene. This time it was a riddle. Being born on the same date, Sarah and Michael spun back into the wombs of their mothers together and traced their lineage through the common parents of Sarah's father and Michael's mother. But there was another unknown ancestral tree that led back through Sarah's matrilineage and Michael's patrilineage. When the two merged into common ancestors, both man and woman could communicate with the clue-giver that now invaded their minds.

An iceberg carrying a comet disappeared within an ice pack. Deep within a cavern under the ice, a tapestry of dark-skinned men and women, walruses and polar bears danced along the walls, engaging in their daily lives. In their minds' eyes, they saw a detailed map of the comet's location defined by images of the celestial sky and the azimuth of the sun, which only an astronomer could understand. The cloud sensed their bewilderment, and their minds went blank.

They saw millions of soricomorphs mutated into bipeds. Large crowds of humans were separated by an impassable yellow membrane from colorful caricatures of orange reptiles with golden eyes and monkey faces that, over time, evolved to communicate with the clue-giver cloud. The one-way membrane had run like an old window pane, distorting the image. On the opaque side of the partition, the humans could not see the raccoon-sized monkeys, but opposite them, the reptiles could study the smeared humans undetected. Lurking in the shadows behind the animal caricatures were tyrannosaurus rexes, brontosauruses and velociraptors.

When the humans discovered a tear in the membrane, the dinosaur images disappeared. The four-legged orange reptiles attempted to patch it before the hi-tech humans living in their modern cities noticed, but they failed. The humans poured through the opening and murdered the little golden-eyed animals until the membrane was patched and there were only a few left. The survivors contracted disease from the humans that left them unable to communicate with the clue-giver or reproduce. They grew old and then became extinct.

In a final vision, the sun rose and set 196 times at this exact spot, and the cloud returned. It was early September now, so six and one-half months later would be late March. Sarah and Michael appeared at that time for a future meeting at this same spot. If there were others with them when *It* sensed the others *It* destroyed them and then departed. The message was ominous, **either they came alone or they alone survived.** But, who was *It* protecting, *Itself,* or them?

For the first time since the vision started, they heard each other talking.

"*It* will protect us," Sarah said.

"*It's* going to get us both killed."

The silky cloud exploded in a dazzling green incendiary that seemed to dissolve their eyelids. They buried their heads in the dirt and collapsed into a thick sleep, repeatedly reliving each of their visions. Each time, the dreams burned more indelibly into their memories until integrated into their consciousness.

As the eastern sky grew orange, cool dew sprinkled the landscape and its sleeping inhabitants. The sun rose over the hills, burned through the haze, pulling Sarah into a groggy stupor.

She attempted to orient herself. Golden rays were flooding the plateau. Sarah's cousin was curled up in a fetal position a meter away. She roused him gently.

"Get up, asshole. We are going up to where that cloud was, okay?"

He opened his eyes and catapulted to his feet. The effects of the hashish had been expelled from his body. "I disclaim all my previous theories. Whether *It* was a product of the environmental damage here or ball lightning, *It's* going to kill us."

Sarah understood. Lay people didn't realize that soil contamination could release invisible, odorless, hallucinogenic gases directly into the thin layer of the atmosphere. Maybe the entertaining theories of a stoned journalist weren't just babbling after all.

"Michael, there was an exploding green light, and then we were in Antarctica with woolly mammoths. Did you get that, too?"

Their recollections and all of their sensory stimulation still matched exactly.

"What we saw and heard was real."

"Maybe. Or maybe somebody is playing a little game with us. I think the identical scene was injected into each of our minds. I don't even know if there were any silky, silvery, green cloud or yellow-white orbs out there. Maybe there was a meteor shower, but that's it."

"You think something paranormal or extraterrestrial implanted these images in our brains, Sarah?"

"You got a more plausible explanation?"

"That would be consistent with all of the UFO sightings here during the last decade. Unfortunately, neither a UFO in the sky nor the metaphysical being in our heads constitutes reportable journalism, particularly with the facts we have so far. No, that's not right. Both you and the burro will corroborate me for the *National Enquirer.* That's more than enough."

"What are we, *Men in Black,* getting our facts from the tabloids? Isn't that how you got into this mess at work to start with?"

"You have no sense of humor." He overcame his cowardice. "You're right. Let's look for some physical evidence. Then we'll get the hell out of here."

They resumed their upward trek, their silence broken only by profane outbursts as they tripped into the occasional jagged rock, tearing up their hands. They stopped to tend to their wounds on a smooth, picnic table-sized stone outcropping.

Michael finished the cookies, and Sarah grabbed the binoculars. She had barely put them in focus when they fell against her chest, caught by the neck strap. Her forehead was saturated with a sweaty sheen, and she gasped weakly. Her flawless features flushed like a rouged porcelain doll. Sarah rubber-banded her thick sweaty hair away from her face, regained her composure somewhat, and again picked up the binoculars.

"You're right. That wasn't just a movie in our heads. There was a live show, too."

Michael had been busy scribbling away in an attempt to recount the events of the night before. In the "who, what, why, where, when" of journalism, he was approximately sure of only where and when. He hadn't even noticed his cousin gasp.

He glanced up absently. "What?" She handed him the binoculars and turned his head in the direction of her discovery.

He peered through the lenses. "Jesus Christ. It's a massive animal slaughter."

Sarah moved to investigate, but Michael grabbed her firmly by the arm. He spoke softly. "Whatever killed those animals could be waiting to kill us."

"What do you suggest?"

"Run?"

"Was this my folks' idea of how you'd protect me? Michael, this could be the greatest story you will ever write."

"Yeah, and an environmental scientist has only a fleeting interest in this? Don't try to con me. Why am I the only one you do this to? You're real considerate of other people."

"I am trying to salvage your career, you idiot! If *It* wanted to kill us, we'd already be dead."

Michael had to concur with *that* reasoning.

Carrion-eaters were already picking at the raw exposed flesh. Buzzards beat at the lynx with their feathers as they competed with each other for chunks of Saiga antelope, already on the brink of extinction. The acrid bile and partially digested food burned their nostrils and overwhelmed the smell of death. As they slowly made their way toward the edge of the animal carcasses, they saw that some of the animals had exploded through their orifices. Stomachs lay on the ground still connected to mouths and grey matter popped out of eye sockets and ear canals. Entrails hung from the animals' rectums. Blood was splattered everywhere they looked—on trees, rocks, in the ground, high up in the native cypress.

As stomach acid backed into his throat, Michael gave ground. Away from the worst of the stench, he gave back his cookies until he gasped for breath.

When he looked up, he half-expected to find a vicious predator feasting on his cousin. Instead, it was eerily quiet amid the blue sky, spartan green trees, and multicolored wild flowers garnishing the taste of death. Butterflies fluttered around in dense clouds, alighting on the wildflowers.

He looked around for his cousin. This was her bailiwick, not his. She was standing in a pool of her own vomit four or five meters away, staring back at the killing field, glassy-eyed.

He smacked her gently on the butt. "You okay?" She nodded absently.

Anticipating her thoughts, he said, "We're alone. Look at the tracks."

The tracks were clearly defined in the thin topsoil. She walked purposefully about a third of the way around the circumference of the site, two-thirds the size of a baseball field. Outside its edges, there was no blood, no errant piece of animal tissue, nothing. Inside was a very sharply defined annulus of carnage.

Impossibly, there was no sign of struggle anywhere within the devastation. And not all of the animals were disemboweled. Some were just dead, with no sign of trauma.

"Something attracted them, and they headed willingly, oh, my God, toward their own demise," she said haltingly.

"Maybe like it did us?"

Sarah surveyed the scene again. "Michael, look carefully at the animals."

"I'd rather not."

"Look macroscopically then. What do you see? What species do you see?"

Michael ticked off a lengthy list. When he had gotten well into the amphibians and through the birds, he stopped suddenly.

"There's like every species indigenous to this region here, isn't there? Birds, reptiles, amphibians, rodents, great mammals, lesser mammals. I wouldn't be surprised if all of the insects and spiders were here, too." He thought for a moment. "How do you disembowel a spider?"

She grimaced. "Everything is here…but us."

Michael looked intently at the forensic evidence.

"The animals are lying here in approximately the same density through-out the affected area. Something attracted these animals equally from all directions. And where would that beacon had to have been to attract all of these animals this way?"

"In the center."

Goosebumps prickled on their backs. They wrapped bandannas around their noses and mouths and tiptoed their way around the carcasses toward second base.

It was like the cup on a golf green with the flag pulled. Once you spot-ted it, you couldn't lose it, but until then it appeared invisible. As they approached to within fifteen meters of the center, they saw a round hole about a meter in diameter. Within three meters of the hole, the animal carcasses cleared out in a rounded cone that pointed upwind, concentric to the graveyard. The carnivorous mammals hadn't started feasting this close to the center yet, just a very few small, cautious vultures that scattered quickly as they approached.

A breeze picked up, and clammy Sarah shivered. Michael's baseball cap blew off and was bounced around on the dust until it was snagged by a hoof, held erect by creeping rigor mortis.

Michael pulled a couple of sweatshirts out of the pack and handed one to his cousin. Within a meter of the hole they stopped and peered in warily with the flashlight. It was a vault of some sort that absorbed the light of the flashlight, reflecting nothing. They laid their bellies on the bit of virgin dirt next to the shaft and crawled close enough so that they could grab the rim and peer over the side.

They took turns throwing and dropping rocks in the pit. The rocks plinked as they landed in a dark invisible pool below. From the sound, the vault appeared four or five meters deep. When a rock hit the sidewall, either it ricocheted and sparked like flintrock, or made the sharp crack of a baseball bat on contact. Overwhelming fumes of rotten eggs forced them to pick up their heads every few seconds for precious gulps of fresh air.

Sarah and Michael lay about sixty degrees apart from each other and listened for signs of life in the vault. Their hearts pounded in unison into the hard dirt.

"Is it natural?" Michael said.

Sarah felt along the sidewalls. "Seems too smooth. Wait."

She slid her breasts just over the edge and fully extended her right arm down the side of the shaft, feeling its sides and banging periodically with a rock. Michael grabbed her by the waistband.

"Ow. Damn it." She jerked her left arm and looked at her fingertips. They festered and burned.

"Something alive?"

She hid her hand from the concern her mother would have expected of him. "Hand me the disposable gloves and the work gloves from the back-pack."

He did as instructed.

"Grab on tight."

She donned the latex gloves and put the work glove on only her left hand. She attached the flashlight to her forehead and slid down the hole to her pelvis while Michael wrapped his legs through a thorny bush and clamped his arms tightly around Sarah's muscular legs. Sarah saw a shimmering pool, like liquid mercury, only blacker. She stretched the full length of her body to reach it and it burned through her glove as soon as she touched it.

"Pull me out quickly." He pulled painfully against the thorns that were penetrating his jeans and puncturing his skin.

As soon as Sarah's body was out of the hole, the mental invasion of the previous night shattered their defenseless brains. Rocks exploded in a blinding flash and obliterated any evidence of the vault's presence. Flying shards of granite became lethal projectiles and flew in every direction, narrowly missing Michael's scalp. Panicked, they leapt up and ran for cover.

Sarah stopped under the protection of a hill that shielded her from the view of the circle of destruction. Her sweatshirt was covered with dirt, and the base of her skull throbbed from the glancing blow of one of the projectiles. She looked down at her double-gloved hand. Some sort of highly corrosive liquid had burned through both the latex and the leather. She flooded them with water.

Michael stood unscathed under the shadow of the overlook on the far side of the decaying animals from their campsite. He pulled the binoculars out to locate his cousin. She was squatting on the opposite side of the killing field, studying something on the ground. She appeared unharmed. He searched the area quickly for other signs of life and was surprised to find a shepherd girl moving along the ridge just above him. He waved to get her attention as he jogged up the hill toward her.

She whistled and a black and ginger, tiger-sized dog trotted to her side. A striking meld of Caucasian and Mongolian features set high cheekbones into a flat oval face. She was wearing heavy boots and a light gauze robe with a veil hanging from her hijab. Since traditional hijabs only cover the hair, the veil seemed to serve as a dust mask, rather than to promote modesty. She toted sandals on a belt cinched around a petite waist, quite unintentionally emphasizing well-developed, firm breasts. Her haughty air drew Michael magnetically.

A local to corroborate his facts might be perfect. Michael couldn't afford to screw up this time. When he was within five or six meters, he slowed his pace considerably, panting as much as the dog. The sheep-herding canine stood up and growled menacingly until she stroked its head gently. The dog sat down again, eyeing the stranger warily. Michael opened his pack in front of her and rummaged for food. Fortunately, he and not Sarah had packed, and instead of the usual granola bars and trail mix, he found an overlooked box of pop tarts as well as some beef jerky. He opened both and ate one of the pop tarts while he offered the girl the other. He handed her a strip of beef jerky, motioning to give it to the dog. The girl imperceptibly bowed her head gratefully, moving closer to Michael's space to take the pastry. The dog wagged its tail emphatically. He grabbed the jerky gently, now seeing Michael in a whole different light.

She dropped the veil, ate a piece of the pop tart, and with unconscious sensuality moistened her parched cracked lips with her tongue.

An urge arose in his pants, but he quickly dispensed with any romantic notions. The girl had to be in her mid-teens. Either Sarah, the girl's father, or the dog would certainly kill him.

"Well, the way to a girl's heart is through her dog." No sign of understanding. Michael pulled another piece of jerky out of the package, and she motioned for him to give it directly to the dog.

"Are you testing me or the dog?" he asked.

The dog tentatively sniffed the meat before soaking Michael's hand with a St. Bernard-like tongue.

"The dog tells me you are friend," she smiled coyly at Michael's embarrassment.

He recovered somewhat. "Russian, too?"

"English much better."

"Did you see what caused this?" He waved his arm expansively across the field of dead animals.

"No. Was here this morning. Animals wander up here from the valley and die all the time."

She finished the pop tart and was eyeing Michael's pack. Michael parted with the remainder of the box and all of the jerky. The dog then relocated to Michael's territory.

"Like this?"

"No. Never like this."

"Maybe something from the sky?" He pointed and looked upward.

She furrowed her brow for a moment.

"Out late last night. No. Nothing. Meteor…meteo*rite*? Clouds? They here almost every night, though. UFOs not so much." She radiated a flawless smile.

He stumbled helplessly. "My name's Michael. What's yours?"

"Sudecki, Michael." She pronounced it Mikhail.

"What do the UFOs look like?"

"Shimmering blue and yellow light. Streaks across the sky. Some bigger, some smaller. Every six or seven months sometimes. Not so different than meteors."

"Not last night?"

"No, Michael. Sorry."

"Have you seen any new animals here lately? Hedgehogs? Shrews?"

She wrinkled her nose in confusion.

"Tough vocabulary, sorry." He bulged his eyes and scurried along the dirt. "Strange little animals? Near water?"

She laughed teasingly, revealing a deep dimple in her right cheek. "Nothing around here." She pointed in the opposite direction of the Aral Sea and scowled ominously. "Strange animals sometimes at pool of rotten eggs, though. Maybe came here last night, Michael. Smelled rotten near here early this morning."

"Sulfur springs?"

She shrugged her shoulders and said, "Animals no one has ever seen before. Yellow, with feathers and fur. Walk on two feet and four feet. Carry things. Two, three, four together."

"No, these animals would be around here, near the water."

She shook her head and pointed off in the distance. "Girlfriend?"

He followed her finger. "Oh, shit. Sarah. She'll be pissed," he said sheepishly. "No. Cousin. Gee, thanks." He handed her a box of powdered juice and stirred with his finger. "Mix with water, okay?"

She pointed and said, "I live on back of that hill. You come visit me?"

He stopped and forced down the recurring urge. *What am I thinking? Focus. Focus.*

He ran down the hill yelling until he got Sarah's attention.

He heard Sudecki call after him, "I see you in your dreams, Michael."

He sensed that he'd see her again, but it wouldn't be in his dreams.

As they walked back to the campsite, Michael filled his cousin in on the conversation with the shepherd girl. "So, for sure, the dead animals are there, and while maybe the clouds and the meteorites were real, it doesn't really matter. Those images of comets on icebergs and mammoths were just in our heads. Oh, and while she hasn't seen any mutant soricomorphs, she does acknowledge that there are some strange animals running, swimming, and dying around here near some sulfur springs in the opposite direction of the Aral Sea. In fact, she says that a couple of them may have ventured out toward that black vault and all of that animal carnage early this morning. That would explain the rotten eggs smell in the vault. It's sour gas. Hydrogen sulfide from the springs. I wonder where they live?"

"I wonder if they are more mutants?" She knew he wouldn't respond, because he'd be afraid she'd want to investigate further. She self-consciously hid her hand and brooded. Hydrogen sulfide in high enough concentration could mean sulfuric acid strong enough to burn her hand. She decided not to share her musings with her cousin just yet.

They continued walking in awkward silence, each afraid to broach what was on the other's mind. Finally, Sarah spoke softly. "Do you think we had a vision from God last night?"

Michael looked askance. Neither of them were particularly spiritual, and he wasn't sure if he even believed in God, let alone what Sarah, the scientist, thought.

"Pardon me? What's God? Is it some alien life form that is so far beyond man's comprehension and power that *It* must be omnipotent and omniscient? Umm, then yeah, it was God."

"If it was God or wanted us to think it knew God, it would have identified itself. That's what beings do when they want to be in charge. They
either tell you they are God or his messenger," Sarah said.

"I don't know what God is calling itself these days. During biblical
times, an omnipotent and omniscient being made sense of the unexplainable. Now, I think if that same being were to reappear, it would be treated
as an enemy alien and humanity would attempt to destroy it first and ask
questions later."

"But we are not going to do that, are we, Michael?"

Before Michael could respond, they reached the campground.

Chance is perhaps the pseudonym of God when he did not want to sign.

--Thibault

CHAPTER 3

A Burro Hallucinates

Sarah breathed a sigh of relief. The burro was right where she left it. She fed the pack animal, who seemed unfazed by the previous night's events. She quizzed him. "Can't get spooked when there's nothing out there to see, can you? But then who disemboweled those animals?" It was no use. The burro only spoke Uzbek.

Her burro could easily have been among the carnage. The other animals came when they were called, but Sarah wasn't sure how strong the beacon was. Were they coming from a hundred meters away or hundreds of kilometers? This, at least, gave her some clue. If her burro had been summoned, it would have disappeared up the mountain with all of the others.

As she caressed the animal, she noticed a fresh, deep bridle cut in its nose. Then she remembered it braying at the cloud, just before they had climbed the mountain. The tether had saved him. Sarah took off its bridle and dressed the wound.

After breakfast, Sarah pulled out a couple of Tootsie Pops and handed one to her cousin.

There was trouble coming when Sarah pulled out something other than carob chips for dessert.

"C'mon, time to break camp." She began to pull down the tent.

"Are we going to find that mutant hedgehog or the animals near the sulfur springs?" Her cousin tried to sound casual.

"Neither. Without the proper equipment, they're a needle in a haystack. And we're not the right people anyway. You've got the story you came for, and I have DNA samples. Alexis will get local people on their trail."

"You think we're going to Antarctica, don't you? What happened to preventing the imminent destruction of whole ecosystems? Who said, 'This is our worst nightmare'?"

She spoke deliberately. "We saw the same vision yesterday, but I think it meant something entirely different to you. There has never been any physical evidence that woolly mammoths were indigenous to Antarctica, and we saw that mammoth through the eyes of a sentient, perceptive being. We know of only one sentient being at that time, a human ancestor. Either man or some other sentient animal was with that mammoth in a place that neither man nor mammoth were ever believed to have lived."

"That's almost newsworthy, even to the general public. Okay, we've got a story."

Sarah ignored his trivializing. "The laws of probability mean that if life flourished in one area that we thought was uninhabitable, then it has happened at other times and in other places throughout the universe as well. But we've got to prove it the first time."

"You're treating this vision like it's a statement of fact. Whether these images are real or not, that's a huge leap of faith."

"If someone ever had a personal manifestation of their calling yesterday, it was me. Did you see the part of the vision with those little yellow and black monkey reptile creatures hidden from the humans? What did that mean to you?"

Michael knew where this was going. "It means I am going to need a second Tootsie Pop quickly."

In the most serious conversation, he could always make her smile. "Anything else?"

"Assuming we saw the same thing, there are other creatures that communicate with our clue-giver that we don't know about. If we find them, we will kill them."

"Not we, well certainly not me," she glared at her cousin, "but humanity. And did you notice that those little yellow animals lived with the dinosaurs and were unknown to humanity until we found out about them?"

"Yeah?" He reached for the second Tootsie Pop.

"Do you know the genetic difference between a mutation and evolution?"

"Probably nothing?"

"Precisely. The difference is in human perceptions. Evolution is a mutation that improves the likelihood of survival and becomes more common in successive generations. Those monkey reptiles survived and evolved the ability to communicate with the clue-giver over tens of millions of years back to the time of the dinosaurs, until humans discovered them through a rift between the humans' habitat and the monkey reptiles' habitat and mankind just couldn't help but fuck with them." Her features hardened.

"Those peaceful little creatures had evolved so far beyond our comprehension that either recklessly, by mankind's arrogant aggression, or unknowingly by introducing new diseases to their habitat, humans disrupted natural evolution and replaced it with human selection. Every day in the lab, humans replace the science of evolution with genetic engineering."

"Sarah, there has got to be a dozen ways to interpret these visions and I can assure you, you are not following the scientific method. Do you also think that because we have hypothetically inherited telepathic powers which geneticists have never identified on humans that mankind will want to eradicate us?"

"It's not implausible, but now you're being difficult just for pleasure. How often did that shepherd girl say that celestial show occurred, every six to seven months? Like the next time we're supposed to return here? Would you rather see her again in your wet dreams, Michael, or when we get back here in six or seven months?"

"Why do you assume that all I ever think about is sex? Her name was Sudecki."

"Last night was only a teaser. Unfortunately, it was like finding an ancient treasure map. There's only so much authenticating we can do. I would have blown this all off as a bizarre hallucination if you hadn't seen all of the same things I did."

Her eyes were ablaze with the passion of her work. Michael decided he'd better back off a bit.

"Sarah, has it occurred to you that there is another explanation for all this?"

"All what? The visions? The night sky?"

"The whole thing. You suggested that something paranormal might have implanted all of these images in our brains. But what if we were drugged and when we woke up, we thought it had all really happened because someone had placed these animals around this pot in the ground."

"Drugged? By whom? The secret police, to hide the effects of the Aral Sea disaster from the world? It's way more likely that we started hallucinating together over some meteor shower and the power of suggestion caused us to each recall the same memories for about the thousandth time in our life. And the pesticides are what killed the animals as well. Your new girlfriend said so. That's way more plausible, but it still doesn't explain what attracted all of those animals."

"Sarah, you badly want to believe these images are real, and I know from personal experience how much trouble one can get into when one allows belief to suspend facts and reality."

They turned away from each other and focused quietly on getting to the Tootsie Roll center.

"You know, *It* had a name," he said.

"Yes, so I heard when the rock pile exploded three or four hours ago."

He picked up a stick and started writing in the dirt, outside her field of view. She did the same. Then they stood up and switched places and looked at each other's writing.

M'LOW CLOOM

"MC."

"Works for me. But, it also means we couldn't have been hallucinating if we both knew it. What the hell does it mean?"

"I guess that's one of the many things we'll have to find out."

Michael said, "Did you sense the omnipotence of that thing last night? *It* could protect us from anything, except maybe our own stupidity. I'm sure I'll be saying that again. Can drugs do that?"

"I've never knowingly tried those kinds of drugs—crack, heroin, ecstasy. Just grass and hash. I think that there's a subtle difference between how those drugs make you feel and how we felt last night. I didn't get the feeling that **I** was invincible at all. In fact, I felt very vulnerable. I was overwhelmed by this feeling that *It* would protect us. MC was invincible."

"Yeah, me too."

"Michael, MC made it really clear that if we don't do *Its* bidding in the next six and a half months, there's going to be violence, but not directed against us. We're protected."

"Suppose you go to Antarctica, Sarah. You can't go alone, you don't have money and *It* will kill anyone you involve in this."

"Except you. It's clear we are supposed to be a team. Otherwise, how do I know the difference between what's real and what's a hallucination?"

"I'm not sure you do now. But what about money?"

"We'll have to find some."

"I have an idea that may sound a tad opportunistic, but it does seem to address a lot of our problems. Let's trap some of these soricomorphs and find these little monkey reptiles, if they are real, of course, and sell them to a circus side show."

"The only reason you could possibly be serious is to get out of going to Antarctica."

"Sarah, things cost money. Trips to Uzbekistan, trips to Antarctica, weed."

"I have a slightly more ethical idea. Remember Peter Barber, professor of Paleontology and expert on Third Ice Age Epochs and senior professor at my school?"

"Of course. He can't write worth a shit."

"He had a rather lengthy passionate affair with Alexis and then dumped her when his wife became suspicious. These fossils are in his sweet spot. He'll love this stuff."

"Based on what evidence?"

"I'll come up with some."

"Like what?" And then, incredulously, "You think that's more ethical and less opportunistic? You're going to seduce him, aren't you?"

"I'll try, but only if there's no other alternative."

"That guy might as well be committed already. Sarah, you *reek* of sensuality. The only reason you don't make me all wobbly-kneed is that I slept and bathed with you until we were six, and I still get grossed out thinking about you peeing in the tub."

Michael and Sarah had very different problems with relationships. Michael had heard the stories from his friend Leo, an undergraduate classmate of his who was now at Chicago doing doctoral work and occasionally crossed

Sarah's path. Since her sophomore year in college, Sarah had only one brief, serious relationship. All of her family and friends loved the guy, but when he refused to get rid of his gas-guzzling Corvette, she dumped him, citing irreconcilable lifestyles. Her principles could only overlook so much in a relationship.

It was a shock for Sarah to hear those blunt words coming from someone whose sex life was a succession of painful failures. When Michael jabbered away about love interests and bar pick-ups, she generally just offered up consolation by giving him a woman's reassuring perspective that his failures were a result of the woman's shortcomings. Michael's ego was fragile enough and to him, she was one of the guys, someone you could spill your guts out to with complete confidentiality. She rarely made it across campus without being approached by men that most women would be more than receptive to, whether they were hunks or had hunks of money. There was nothing to be gained by throwing that in Michael's face.

"That doesn't really matter to this man, Michael. He treats female students with about as much feeling as he treats a disposable paper plate. It's going to take way more than sex."

"Sarah, you're not that promiscuous, and you're definitely not that devious."

"I have some other ideas, but right now, I am not that convinced either." Sarah jumped to her feet, "Oh, my God, we forgot about the video." They had left a video camera running when they hiked up the mountain the night before. It confirmed both of their suspicions. Outside of their heads, nothing out of the ordinary had happened. The sounds of the night in Uzbekistan were spectacular, and images of the sky brightening behind the mountains before the battery went dead would make a great visual for the travel article.

If they had spoken to God, for the moment at least, God was just up to his normal, scientifically explainable tricks, and if they were being set up, it was definitely being done by something far more intelligent than they were.

CHAPTER 4
Clear as a Cryptograph

Back in the States, Michael wrote a banal but well-received article on backpacking through the Tyan Shan mountains on twenty-five dollars a day. They scoured the web for reports on meteor showers, solar flares, unique meteorological events, UFOs, anything imaginable over Central Asia. Nothing unusual.

Several weeks later, Sarah received some startling news on the chromosomal abnormalities of their hedgehog. The animal was remarkably similar to the echidna, the only close genetic relative of the platypus. Probably some environmental contamination remaining from the Aral Sea disaster had reactivated dormant and unmapped sites on the DNA double helix that were common to the echidna and shrew, which caused it to secrete poison and lay eggs.

The animal they found had branched off from other mammals almost a hundred and twenty-five million years ago. While it was possible that it had survived and gone undiscovered in the backcountry for the past eighth of a billion years, it was much more likely that the mammal had reverted back to an extinct form of its ancestors.

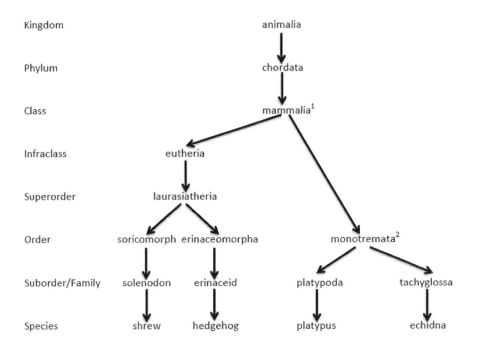

[1] Split about 150 million years ago
[2] Split 19-48 million years ago

Michael received a prestigious AAAS Science Journalism Award for his investigative work and Sarah's parents called to congratulate him as soon as she gave them the news.

"Michael, not only did you receive a very impressive award for your writing, you kept our Sarah alive and out of trouble. We are not only proud of you, but very grateful."

"Big deal," he said after the connection was broken. He was nothing more than Sarah's glorified personal reporter, yet she would have liked nothing more than for him to get all the kudos.

He had been her ghostwriter for years and she had deferred the credit and limelight to him whenever possible. In elementary school, Sarah was diagnosed with attention deficit disorder, problems with auditory processing and relatively mild learning disabilities manifested in difficulties with spelling and grammar, which she had overcome or hidden through tenacity, Michael's phenomenal ghost writing skills and other well-developed senses. Alexis Brankov was one of the very few at the university who knew of Sarah's secret.

Even fewer knew of Michael's secret. There was an old axiom in hockey. Big players had to prove that they couldn't skate. Little players had to prove that they could. Sarah asked for a favor and doors opened. Even women, because she was so unassuming, had trouble feeling threatened by her. Women took one look at him and then looked elsewhere. And he had already come to the brink of professional self-destruction, so men didn't take him seriously either. It was a superficial world.

There is always something to upset the most careful of human calculations.

— Ihara Saikaku

CHAPTER 5

Overcome by Fumes while Michael Fumes

Sarah's department had received a grant to study the surge in dead and dying sea mammals that had been washing ashore in the Pacific Northwest, and the head of the research team had invited her because she had a Class IV scuba license. It was mutually beneficial. A November swim in the North Pacific with lithe fishes was better than a week in the lab with awkward geeks, both of whom spent most of their time blowing bubbles.

The career benefits to Michael didn't justify the personal and professional risks of an expedition to Antarctica, so pressuring him was futile. He hadn't even responded when she sent him the customized four-foot-tall stuffed shrew with platypus-webbed feet. No sense of humor.

Her options were limited. She couldn't tell Alexis about their vision because Alexis would immediately suspect it was an auditory processing related problem and possibly say something to Barber, who would probably come to the same conclusion, eliminating the possibility of his cooperation. Michael was right. She wanted so badly to believe that genetic engineering, whether it was corn seed or human seed, was screwing things up that she just hallucinated it all.

Her group arrived at the study site with dawn creeping over the Pacific Northwest. With the exception of Michael's friend Leo, who had recommended Sarah to the study professor, she had only a nodding acquaintance with the other participants, and as usual, no one seemed interested in improving the relationship. They perceived her as aloof, and she lived up to her reputation. It was a common side effect of Sarah's learning disabilities, and while it was generally a misconception, with this group Sarah figured it was a benefit.

The shoreline was littered with sick and dying seals and sea lions, many barking and moaning weakly with vacant breaths. If it was a viral or bacterial condition which could affect a broad cross-section of marine mammals, then they would have to trap walruses and other related animals and test them, too. More likely, it was a shared ecosystem toxin, such as mercury.

The hundred or so yards of sandy beach were created by the tides in their relentless beating of imposing cliffs that gazed out over the ocean just beyond the shoreline. Bisecting the beach was a semi-natural jetty of impassable rocks that extended like a long toe from the cliff line westward into the water. At high tide, the jetty submerged about 275 yards out, and at low tide, it was another 300 to 350 yards.

The group had entered on the south side of the jetty by four-wheel drive. Travel to the north side by land was nearly impossible. The cliffs overhung the land below, so there were no footholds, making even rappelling perilous. Because there was so much animal activity on the other side of the jetty, the team leader decided to send Sarah to the north shore to look around.

Sarah donned her wetsuit and strapped on a precautionary emergency tank. A waterproof pouch held a walkie talkie, binoculars, a camera, and a flashlight. She followed the receding ocean out a couple of hours after high tide. The plan was to begin her return just before low tide so that when she rounded the end of the jetty, she wouldn't be fighting the tide all the way back in. The sound was teeming with anemones in fluorescent red and iridescent yellows and physically intimidating but timid barracudas and hammerhead sharks. A sea turtle weighing twice as much as Sarah swam by, but decided it was too difficult to remove the rubber packaging, so he meandered away.

She swam out to where the jetty submerged and continued until the outcropping was about six feet below the surface. Then she turned the corner to make it back to the western-facing shore. When the rocks again split the water, Sarah saw a sandy strip between the rocks and the water that was not visible from the other side. She pulled off her flippers and began walking along the cool, wet sand to avoid fighting the tide all the way to shore.

The sky filled with a cacophony of buzzards, gulls, and Pacific condors as Sarah neared the beach. Every major carrion-eating avian in the Pacific Northwest had arrived for the convention. The sand was hidden by a rush of black, grey, and dirty white feathers kicking and tugging in all directions at the feast before them.

Even with the cool air blowing over Sarah's saturated wetsuit, she broke into a hot sweat. Some of the hungry condors had wingspans longer than Sarah was tall, and she quickly sought refuge back in the water.

Sarah circled north beyond all of the activity and scrambled up along the craggy shore until she stood overlooking the birds by five or six feet. She heaved several small rocks and sufficient numbers scattered to afford her a clear view of several partially stripped sea lion carcasses. She filled the camera's memory card and moved in to get samples.

An overpowering combination of ammonia vapor from the guano and rotting flesh constricted each breath to sucking a thick milk shake through a straw. She fought to banish the haunting memories of Uzbekistan that flooded her mind. There was an organic explanation here, and she was thousands of miles from the Aral Sea.

Sarah grabbed her gear and ran for the safety of the barracuda infested waters. She couldn't slide down the cliff without tearing her wet suit, so she methodically descended to the water, which was almost seven feet below high tide at this time of the month. No sooner had the salt air cleared the ammonia from her lungs than she recognized a less familiar smell. Sulfur. The low tide had exposed a pungent tunnel leading back up into the cliffs from where she had just come.

Sarah left her flippers behind, unsheathed her knife, and pulled out the flashlight. She tossed her air tank and regulator in ahead of her and stuck the walkie talkie inside the tunnel's entrance. It was still getting a signal. She'd done stupider things, but they were all for science. This was neither the time nor the place, but Sarah wasn't about to let stupidity stop her. She slithered in with the flashlight ahead of her, and unexpectedly her head floated up to the stars in the hydrogen sulfide laden air above the sulfur pools. That was all she remembered until MC came to call.

A modest comet flamed through the atmosphere and crashed into pack ice, which broke off and floated into open waters, carrying the comet as its passenger. Then the vision picked up where it had left off in Uzbekistan. The iceberg began to melt as it moved toward the equator. Then it crossed into cold waters again and grew. Marauding light-skinned sailors boarded the iceberg and broke off blocks of it to cool their drinks and preserve their food. They took sick and landed in a port inhabited by people with darker skin. Many of the people living in the port died. It was a plague to which they had never been exposed and had no resistance. The ship cast off.

Something or someone pulled the iceberg and its passenger to its resting place somewhere deep within a frozen grave. Sarah could see that a map of primitive etchings that held clues to the comet's hiding place was hidden in Antarctica with the mammoth.

Sarah could see jets flying overhead. Deep within a cave, with ice melting all around it, were the remnants of the comet. Images of dark-skinned man and walruses and polar bears danced around its walls. Within the cave were mutations of microbes that had destroyed much life, leaving only the fittest to survive. Or in some cases, the mutations could immunize and save or even advance life. Sarah and Michael were immune to the effects of these microbes.

It seemed like MC wanted Michael and her to protect those organisms from mankind's uncontrollable desire to dissect and destroy things it didn't understand under the pretense of scientific research or defense of its own species. The cave's discovery by man was imminent. They had to beat them to the cave and protect its inhabitants, whatever they were.

Once again she saw those little yellow reptiles with golden eyes and monkey faces that were in her last vision, and they were communicating with MC. They were successfully repelling humans attacking their habitat by killing any that could not be trusted to hide their secret existence. But they were different from the last vision. **This time they were real and she was surrounded by them.**

Sarah's eyes flashed open, and she was taking in deep breaths through her mouthpiece. She was in the cave, and her flashlight was still shining its light, but she didn't remember turning on the regulator. Twenty or so feet into the cave and well above the high water line there was a flat plateau, and bubbles rose from the liquid residing within it. As Sarah got closer to it, the air became more acidic and her eyes began burning so badly that tears obscured her sight. She put her mask on, but the air inside the mask was also contaminated. It couldn't be effective unless she put it on in the fresh air. The water was lapping the entrance to the cave as she pulled herself outside. The gauge showed that the tank was more than half empty. How long had she been out? As she touched the knob to turn off the regulator, her skin quickly blistered, and she grimaced. It was the same acid burn she got from the vault in Uzbekistan. Sarah was beginning to assemble the clues, but she couldn't risk going back in or she wouldn't have any air left in the emergency tank for the return to her team.

The acid was burning through her wet suit, too. She dove into the cool surf, pulled on her flippers and swam so powerfully, she skimmed the surface as she put distance between herself and the shore. As she turned the corner of the ridge, a dorsal fin split the water, effortlessly accelerating up to Sarah's right arm and her heart skipped a beat. She gagged on a mouthful of salt water before the dolphin's head popped up. Giggling apologetically, it vigorously shook its head back and forth, splashing her in the face. It motioned over its shoulder, and she saw a second dolphin tailing them.

The first dolphin nudged her occasionally as it paced her. Upon reaching shallow water, the rear lifeguard fell behind and vanished. Then the dolphin next to her dove quickly and disappeared. The stroke of his powerful fluke churning the water under Sarah's belly lifted her out of the water.

Sarah's forty-five-minute dolphin escort was more than enough time to draw some conclusions. She could return with the research team and attempt to find the entrance to the simian lizards' lair, but it would be underwater, and she was the only diver. It was not more than a foot above low tide, which meant that on typical low tides, it would probably not even be exposed. Only when it was low-low tide, an event created by the moon and the sun both being on the opposite side of the earth from the cave at the same time, would it be visible. Even then, it was so toxic in there that nothing else could survive, including her. And those animals wanted it that way. If she did anything to betray their trust...Now she knew what that last vision meant.

Sarah reached the other side of the jetty, pulled off her flippers, stood up in shoulder deep water, and attempted to walk to shore. She called out but emitted nothing more than a feeble squeak. Leo and Sarah's other colleagues saw her head bobbing in the surf and quickly hauled her to shore.

She simply said, "Shark." The truth was unutterable.

These events were too well planned to be coincidental. It was a chilling reminder that they had not yet begun their quest to do the clue-giver's bidding. When Sarah saw the fluke approaching her, she believed that MC would soon make her entrails some marine carnivore's dinner. But once her bodyguards identified themselves, she realized that she had it all wrong. The dolphins were assurance that she would remain protected. There was no risk, but was there enough reward to convince Michael?

After a fitful nap in a rental van, Leo drove Sarah back to cell phone range. To her relief, Michael seemed pleased to hear from her.

She recounted her story, but left out the part about the simian reptiles killing anyone that didn't keep their existence a secret. After all, technically that wasn't a vision. She concluded by saying, "We were not set up. We have to go to Antarctica."

"Let me see if I understand this. You were sent out to study the pathology of diseased marine mammals and you find exactly what you are looking for. Based on that, you conclude that we should go to Antarctica?"

"I have no idea what killed those seals and sea lions, you fucking prick!" Sarcastically sweet, "I don't think that cave full of acid rain and simian reptiles saving my life was part of the plan, but it was part of the vision."

"Did you actually see these little yellow creatures?"

"No, they live in a toxic environment, but they saved my life. Michael, *It* knew we didn't understand everything in that first vision, so it was trying to help us."

"You were hallucinating again?"

"No dear, I only hallucinate when I'm with you. This was a vision."

"So you now know how to find that cave full of microbes that are waiting to destroy mankind?"

"I understand that we need to get to the mammoth to get directions to the cave. M'low Cloom doesn't have GPS, and sentient doesn't mean omniscient."

"How convenient is that? We have to go to Antarctica to get to the organisms and we have, what, a hundred fifty or a hundred sixty days to do both? And this mammoth is like a prehistoric cartoon Barney that teaches children about maps. Well, fortunately we don't repeat our stories to anyone else, so nobody thinks we are crazy, but it would be fun to get a third party's reaction to see if anyone thinks we are sane."

"Fun?"

"I have absolutely no reason to do this kind of daredevil reporting any more. Thanks to you and the echidna, my career has been salvaged and Neil and I have come to an understanding. He hates me and I mistrust him. But if I head off to Antarctica based on your sour gas induced hallucinations, assuming I survive, I will no longer have a job."

"Michael, recently we have achieved a modicum of success in salvaging your career. It's like sixth grade when you conned me into taking Scott down to the creek in my completely unfilled bikini top, so he'd miss the play tryouts. You got the part in the play opposite that Mandy girl you had a crush on. What did I get? A scraped knee fighting Scott off."

"Scott got a black eye, though."

"I am spending eight years getting a PhD so I can prove that Darwin was right. Natural evolution can fix all of the planet's problems faster than humans fucking with it. Out of the clear blue, pretty literally, this MC thing comes along and intimates the same thing to both of us. I'd kind of like to save thirty years of research and prove that hypothesis. Only one thing stands in the way."

"Money, credibility, dire threats?"

"You. For some reason MC thinks you should be involved in this. Maybe *It* feels sorry for you and wants to get you a Pulitzer."

"I think this is a slightly bigger favor than asking you to distract Scott for me."

The phone went dead. Sarah knew that if it was tough convincing her parents that she should go to Uzbekistan, then making this trip alone would give them both heart attacks. She could only hope that Peter Barber didn't find out how desperate she was.

CHAPTER 6
Science Sells

Sarah and Peter Barber had crossed paths a year or so earlier when he offered a conveniently scheduled graduate elective that was actually relevant to her research, a confluence of academic scheduling events rarer than snow at the equator. The class showed full on the computer, so Sarah had gone to see Dr. Barber in person. As she came down the hallway, his door had opened and a long-legged brunette with an hourglass figure had appeared.

She said, "Thank you, Dr. Barber. I am looking forward to working on this research project with you. It's too bad that the other student got himself over-committed and left you hanging."

"Hopefully, his loss will be your gain." As she walked down the hall away from Sarah, Barber stood in the doorway, indiscreetly panting like a lap dog.

During the last three years, Sarah had seen the brunette in the building almost every day. Her uniform was a sweatshirt and jeans, with her hair rubber-banded to the top of her head and her eyes peering myopically through thick coke bottles. Sarah turned around quickly and headed for the ladies' room. She had never met the man, and already he was living down to his reputation.

She took off her baggy sweater, revealing a thin tan top under which she was inconveniently braless. She brushed the soft brown waves down below her shoulders, added a pale pastel wet gloss to her lips, and then looked herself straight in the mirror. "I am a manipulative bitch no better than the rest of them."

"Come in," he lectured from his desk, and when she entered, he hadn't even bothered to look up.

She stood in front of the large, masculine walnut desk for nearly a minute before he acknowledged her presence. When he did, he gazed at her for a long moment as a poorly concealed mix of surprise and satisfaction pulled up the corners of his mouth and raised his eyebrows slightly. He darted around his desk to greet her.

"You are?"

"Sarah Baskin, Professor Barber."

"I see. And what can I do for you, Sarah?" He ushered her to an over-sized leather couch against the wall and sat down facing her.

"I need a graduate elective. You teach Paleontology five ten, and I have heard you are a stimulating lecturer." Sarah wondered what had caused her to select such an odd adjective.

He smiled at her. "Thank you, Sarah. Your, uh, name is well known around the environmental and life sciences department. I look forward to your enrollment in my class." He paused as if he forgot something. "But, you know, I believe the class is already full."

"Yes sir, I know. I can still enroll with your written permission. However, I understand. I'll register for it earlier next semester." She held out her hand as she rose to leave.

Barber grasped her hand, put his other hand on her shoulder, and gently pushed her back to the sofa. "Sarah, I can use someone with your technical writing skills to edit an article I'm writing and do two to three hours of research for me. I'll let you in if you'll help me out. Okay?"

"If you really need someone else, Professor."

"It turns out that I have just had a cancellation."

As she walked away from his office, she knew he was standing in the doorway staring at her derriere, and she was tempted to turn around suddenly. Unfortunately she desperately needed the class he seemed to lack.

Barber deftly generated half a dozen opportunities for intimate contact with Sarah. He attempted to drop off or pick up drafts at her apartment, schedule evening critiques in his office or at bars, and called her into his office to discuss her work in his class.

Sarah limited him to daytime meetings at the library and coffee shops. And she made sure that she owed him a critical draft of his article or culminating piece of research when tests or papers were due, in part because her cousin was doing all of the editing and he only worked on deadline for the paper. If she made herself indispensable to Barber's work, he would have to live with her wretched professionalism.

He ran into her right after grades were posted. "Sarah, my grammar stinks and your copyediting was flawless. Thank you for a phenomenal finished product." He wasn't thinking about the article. He was breathing audibly through his slightly open mouth.

"It was a pleasure, Professor Barber. I learned a great deal working with you. I would do it again, even if I didn't need special permission to get into one of your classes."

"You know, I had completely forgotten. We should collaborate on something in the future. You deserve a by-line, you know."

"Thank you for the endorsement. I'll keep that in mind." She again turned and walked out.

She heard him moving around behind his office door, so she rapped once, counted to one, and walked right in.

He looked up, startled, and hopefully, Sarah thought, off balance.

"Dr. Barber, I have an opportunity to make the greatest discovery of the last Ice Age, and by coincidence, I am studying for a PhD in Environmental Science at a school that has in residence perhaps the foremost expert on the biology of that epoch."

It was a misnomer, of course. *Ice age* is often used to mean a period in which there are ice sheets in the northern and southern hemispheres. By that definition earth is still in an ice age, because the Greenland and Antarctic ice sheets exist even though they have been retreating for about the last ten thousand years, known as the Holocene period. Most scientists commonly refer to that point in time as the end of the most recent ice age.

"What a pleasant surprise, Sarah. Who's endorsing whom?"

"Everyone needs a published by-line, Professor."

He straightened in his high-backed leather chair and fondled a paperweight that encased a distinguished scholar award that he had received several years earlier. "What have you got?"

What Sarah had was a pretty good imagination. She had all of the detail imaginable on how to find the woolly mammoths, but when he said, "Tell me what they, or it, looked like," she was a little vague. She did the best she could to sketch out a woolly mammoth hidden behind tons of ice and dirt, figuring she'd fix that before their next meeting, if they got that far.

Barber was skeptical. She leaned awkwardly across the desk from him in her scooped-neck, perfumed, tight pink spaghetti-strap top and said, "Let me take you to lunch and I'll show you everything I have." She couldn't afford dinner.

But fortunately, he could. "Meet me here for dinner at six. I'll buy. If you've got something, it will have been a bargain."

At dinner that night, Sarah described the shadowy form of a mammoth preserved in the belly of a glacier with its skin and fur intact in such vivid detail that Barber couldn't possibly doubt her recall. She also embellished on an actual Environmental Defense Quest trip during that time frame that she had found on the internet the week before. Peter staggered drunkenly between her hypnotic gaze and her shadowy cleavage.

Sarah refused the cocktail, declined to dance, and focused on everything she knew about the woolly mammoths. She almost cracked when the violin and flute ensemble came to the table and she let her newly manicured blood-red daggers linger a moment too long in a chance encounter with Barber's hand at the shared appetizer. In a delayed reaction, he heard what Sarah had said a minute earlier and shooed the music away to follow up with technical questions. For a change, Peter's relentless curiosity was actually competitive with his hormones.

Out in the parking lot, when he offered to give her a ride to her apartment, Sarah demurred and instead insisted on another meeting.

"What for?" he asked hopefully.

"I am willing to anoint you as the head of this research expedition and concede top billing to you. But I need money and your expertise to pull this off. And we need to move quickly before global warming makes this mammoth hideout as well-known as Times Square."

A cab had pulled up to drop someone off, and he ushered her into the back seat. "All right, then. Evening after tomorrow. We'll talk more."

She kissed him on the cheek and whispered, "Thanks, Peter."

Peter prepaid the driver, the cab drove off, and he ran shivering to his car, even though it was an unseasonably warm night.

A ten-minute ride back to Sarah's apartment wasn't nearly enough to sort through the evening's events.

The cab driver broke her concentration. "Hey, pretty lady, we're here already."

She opened the door to her apartment and quickly checked e-mail as she undressed.

For the first time in weeks, Michael was in her in-box.

Call me when you get in. She looked at her cell phone. There was a message waiting there as well.

Michael answered by saying, "Oh good, you haven't left for Antarctica yet? Gotten Peter Barber financially or sexually committed yet?"

"It might be the same thing, but it's a work in progress. If he was either, I wouldn't be calling you back, and I am sure that's not why you are calling me."

"I'm packed if you are."

The strong wine and events of the evening put Sarah into sensory overload.

"Pardon me?"

"I'm ready to go to Antarctica, but we are not going for the same reasons. Mankind destroying the planet with myopia is not news. It's not even on the Kids Page at the paper. You're ignoring the bigger story, and I want to get to the bottom of it. Who is M'low Cloom, and how and why is *It* communicating with *us*? So, I'm in for you if you're in for me. Oh, and I'm sorry I scoffed at the simian reptiles. If there are mammoths in Antarctica, I believe that MC will protect us, although it still sounds too much like a mafia setup to me."

Suspicion supplanted confusion. "Did you screw up again at work?"

"Thanks for the vote of confidence. No, nothing interesting has happened lately, at least at work."

"Well, you can't catapult a career on one big science award. They're always going to want to know what you've done for them lately. Even Edward R. Murrow followed up his rooftop reports on the London blitzkrieg with the McCarthy witch hunts. Wait a minute, that's not what this is about, is it? What do you mean, at least at work?"

He took a deep breath before continuing. "As you know, my modest celebrity status has improved my social life somewhat recently."

She snorted into her cell.

"Thank you. Please don't interrupt." He swallowed hard and delivered a funeral pastor's elegy. "Women hear about my escapades, and they presume that I am really spontaneous, adventurous and have big balls. Figuratively, of course. This woman Abby asked me if I wanted to go out in a glider with her yesterday. They tow them off a cliff about four hours west of here, usually with a small prop plane.

"We went up in a two-person glider. There were no luminescing orbs in the sky, and I wasn't stoned, but it was still pretty spectacular. We soared almost straight up three thousand feet, riding a warm updraft and then plunged that distance in less than a third the time.

"My stomach decided not to join us for the return trip. When we landed, I was too dizzy to walk. So they cleaned out the back seat, and she went up again with someone else."

Sarah struggled to suppress a giggle.

His voice cracked. "You really are only a bitch to me. This is not funny. Abby and I went out and got drunk the night before and we went back to my condo. I was showing off, and I'm afraid I told her everything about our trip to Uzbekistan."

"Everything?"

"I've got a big mouth, big enough to get her killed."

"How did she react to your story?"

"She made fun of me. She figured you and I were both stoned and seeing shadows and meteors and wild animals and a hail storm. All sorts of wacky stuff. Then we kind of got sidetracked, and she didn't say anything else about it until we were passing through some lacy threads of cirrus clouds in the sky the next day.

"She turned around to me and said, 'Michael, do you think it's easier to communicate with M'low Cloom up here, close to his home base?'

"I must have gotten all pasty-faced, because then she said, 'Geez, Michael, lighten up.'

"After we landed, the last thing she said to me before she went up, just to tease me a little was, 'I guess Tom and I will go up there and see if M'low Cloom will talk to just any couple, or if you have to be related.'

"I didn't really believe MC could or would do anything, or I wouldn't have spouted my mouth off when we got drunk, but suddenly I got scared, so I said to her, 'Don't tell Tom about this, Abby.'

"As she got into the cockpit, she stuck out her lower lip and said in her best West Texas accent, 'You poor boy, I'll do anything I want.' And she did.

"She went up, and I lay down in her car, and maybe five minutes later it hit me."

"What?"

"The same vision you had. Except for two things. Near the end of the scene, I could see jets flying overhead. Deep within a cave, with ice melting all around it, were the remnants of the comet. Images of dark-skinned men and walruses and polar bears danced around the cave. Within the cave were mutations of an organism that could still destroy life on earth…or save it. Inside the cave, we were invincible.

"They hit a thermocline and went almost out of sight. The altimeter pegged at twenty-three thousand feet—without oxygen. They came down like a meteor until the pilot leveled them off at a couple hundred feet and made a crash landing. The pilot was fine. He had blacked out at the top of the climb and not regained consciousness until they were in a tail spin. Abby's dead, Sarah. She didn't exactly explode, but it was close. Her eyes bulged out. Stuff oozed out of her ears. It was awful."

He spoke very quickly now. "I know what you're thinking, at that altitude and atmospheric pressure and with enough Gs squeezing you in free fall, it could happen to an astronaut if his space suit suddenly depressurized, but clearly it didn't happen to her pilot, and it wasn't one hundred thousand feet. It was twenty-three."

"I didn't see Abby die, but I did see the rest of your vision. You were being so cynical that I didn't have the nerve to tell you the last time we spoke."

"Well, I guess there goes the power of suggestion theory. The first thing Tom said when he could finally talk was that he thought the oxygen deprivation was getting to Abby because her last words to him were, 'Tom, do you believe in celestial visions?' Then, he said the plane caught the quick updraft, and he couldn't hear anything else. He blacked out just before it hit free fall."

"Coincidence?" said Sarah.

"Is it a coincidence that I am your editor again?"

"People focus on the most bizarre things. Michael, MC will protect us on *Its* quest, but finding out who *It* is and how *It* communicates with us is not part of *Its* agenda. We don't know how *It* will react."

"I know, but MC didn't tell us we *couldn't* know who *It* is. *It's* manipulating us for *Its* own agenda, and that's where the story is.

"There's one thing I don't understand. You've been pushing us to go to Antarctica since we met MC in Uzbekistan. How can you take orders from a presence you can't explain and not even care about that? And *It* appears to be able to murder at will. It would seem like with all of this power, *It* could take over the world or at least manipulate events without our help."

"But, *It* doesn't, does *It*?"

"Who or what could potentially have all of that unassailable power and not succumb to the urge for conquest and domination?"

"Certainly not something human. And if *It's* got that much self-control, it's more important to figure what *It's* trying to tell us about life on earth, rather than why or how."

"Well, agreeing to go is only one small step for mankind. We've got a lot of details to work out. Where are you with Barber?"

She brought him up to speed.

"Growing up, you wouldn't even take more than one free sample from the grocery store. Now, you are descending beneath inebriated, meaningless, lustful sex into something premeditated and manipulative. I guess they call that graduate school."

"This is not academic. It's business. Your job is much tougher. You have to convince your editor that you have *the* most phenomenal scoop of the century."

"Well, Neil's still a putz, but AAAS Science Journalism Awards aren't easy to come by, and at least today, I am the golden boy at the paper, thanks to the Aral Sea.

"I have one more question. Why do we have to go to Antarctica at all? The big story is those organisms that landed with the comet. That's the time-sensitive project, and we don't have all that much time left to find the comet, either."

"And therein lies the problem. We have absolutely no idea where to look for the damn comet. MC clearly wants us in Antarctica first, so I guess we are going to do that scavenger hunt thing and take this in order and hope that one clue leads to the next."

The next morning, Michael walked into the office of the science editor and said, "Neil, I have an unparalleled opportunity to chronicle one of the most amazing zoological finds of the twenty-first century."

"You've already given me one, and I think your cousin deserves all of the credit. I don't think you have a second one in you," Neil said.

"Edward R. Murrow didn't stop with the Battle of Britain. He went on fifteen years later to vilify Joe McCarthy."

"Wait a second. Are you comparing yourself to Edward R. Murrow?"

"Thanks, Sarah," he mumbled under his breath. "This time, my cousin has discovered perfectly preserved woolly mammoths frozen into the side of an Antarctic glacier."

"The same cousin? The one who sipped raw yak's milk straight from the udder and ate the pickled yak's balls? The one who called that shit, 'unparalleled delicacies'?"

Notwithstanding his great piece of journalism, Neil was giving Sarah the credit for *both* of the Uzbekistan articles. And he was going to give her credit for this trip to Antarctica, as well.

"The travel editor said it was a good piece. It didn't make *me* want to go there, but she was pleased. And your AAAS Award didn't even come out of my budget. You still don't have any vacation, you know."

"Neil, it's not coming out of your pocket. The paper got two articles from one trip, and most of it was on my vacation time."

"Rules are rules." Then, a supernova went off in Neil's head. "Wait a minute. There weren't any woolly mammoths in the southern hemisphere, were there?"

"We didn't *think* there were. She sighted them last year and kept it to herself until she had an opportunity to go with some experts. Dr. Peter Barber is accompanying us on this expedition."

"Top man in the field. All right, I'll sanction this. Get me first serial rights to whatever Barber gets published in the paleontological monthly science journal of science," he fumbled.

"I also want lots of pictures. Maybe Lois will want a sequel to places you don't want to go and our departments can split expenses. But, we can skip the local delicacies this time. How much time do you need?"

"About a month or five weeks."

"To do what? Take a penguin census? It sounds like three weeks to me."

"To keep expenses down, we have found free passage on a Seapeace boat and there's probably a story there, too. We couldn't afford a charter to Antarctica. What's my expense budget for this trip? I still have to buy supplies, food and air fare to meet the vessel." Then Michael added, "And, I will take LWOP, but only if I come back empty-handed."

"I am a Las Vegas gambler. You seem to like being manipulated by this very attracttive cousin of yours, who *I know* wandered in here once and was not introduced to me."

"My oversight. I thought you only liked women fifteen years younger than you who *didn't* know that you are married. Supplies are more than sixty thousand dollars, but Dr. Barber is getting a grant for well over half of it."

"Couple of nights in a hotel, cheap air fare, per diem and ten thousand dollars. That's it. And this is all unpaid leave, if you are unsuccessful, for what these expenses are costing me. This story had better make page one."

"I'll make sure it does, even if I have to make something up. And then you'll be able to fire me with cause, Neil."

"I don't need a reason," he said as he ushered him out the door.

All through the next day, Sarah agonized over the message. Business suit or clingy red cocktail dress? She spent less than an hour even thinking about clothes in a typical month, and she had been stressing out over the night's attire all morning. She was sure of one thing. She was only going to bed with him if it was necessary to close the deal. If she trusted Peter about anything, it was to let her know what his price was.

Perched on the roof of a skyscraper, the restaurant beheld a panoramic view of the twinkling boats cruising Lake Michigan on one side and Water Street in downtown Chicago on the other side. Access was via private staffed elevator. She ended up with a neutral business suit that revealed only the tip of a red sheer lace camisole.

Sarah had insisted that they meet at the restaurant, and as she rode the elevator to the top floor, it dawned on her that even if Peter bought into ponying up fifty thousand dollars or a hundred thousand dollars and kept it all business, she would still have to live with this man for the better part of the next month or so.

Peter looked trim and distinguished, the abundant grey flecks in his temples and sideburns contrasting with his predominantly black hair and navy blue sport coat. He grasped her hand and then took her by the small of her waist and directed her to their window table in a secluded corner of the restaurant.

He ordered wine, shooed the waiter away, and led with a blunt question.

"Sarah, what are you going to do if I don't get behind you?"

"I'll go to *National Geographic*, the *Discovery Channel*, *Animal Planet*, and Dr. Lazarus."

He cringed. Lazarus was an unscrupulous rival at a university in the Pacific Northwest.

"You risk more if I succeed with them than if I fail with you. How will you explain to the Chancellor of the University that I came to you first and you let this opportunity get away?"

If Sarah saw what she said she saw, then any leverage Barber had to get her into bed had just evaporated. It was extremely unlikely that all of the other contacts on her list would reject her because everyone knew that Lazarus was hornier than Barber was and Lazarus wasn't even married.

She slid back from the table, crossed her legs, and took a long slow sip of wine before she responded. Her long lashes fell to the lipstick on her glass, and then she locked her eyes on his. He tried, but he couldn't look away.

"Peter, the summers in Antarctica aren't that long. The EDQ, Seapeace, Australians, Argentineans, and a whole globe of scientists are overrunning the place. If we don't leave in three weeks, someone else will grab this opportunity. I have a ticket to Seattle the day after tomorrow, and I will be in DC five days after that. Decide now. *You* are my first choice. If nothing else, it will be good for a university that's been pretty good to both of us."

Peter knew where the *Discovery Channel* and *National Geographic* were headquartered. He had never been this thoroughly outmaneuvered. The worst part was, he didn't even mind.

"I'm in."

"Peter, there is a small peripherally related problem that I could use your help with."

"Alexis Brankov?"

"How...?" She recovered quickly. "Yes. I have to provide some sort of alibi for this time off. She knows nothing about the EDQ or this discovery and..."

Peter let her squirm for a moment. "And you are wondering how she is going to react to this trip?"

Sarah reddened. "I don't really know why she would care at all."

"The faculty and graduate staff of this, or I suppose any university, is one big rumor mill. I would be naive to think that you have not heard the rumors. After all, I know you are extremely thorough in your research." He tipped his glass to her. "I will go to your department head and describe a research expedition of mine that needs an assistant with your exacting qualifications and ask him who he recommends. Then, I will get him to ask Dr. Brankov for permission to have you accompany me."

Sarah relaxed visibly. "You'll let me know how she responds, won't you?"

"What are her choices? It's good for your career and frankly, I out-rank her and outpublish her. If she calls you, please remind her that we've worked together before, and it was strictly business then and will be strictly business now."

"That's very reassuring. Thank you, Peter."

He attempted to hide his disappointment.

They moved past the gambits that had marked their relationship. They had much in common. They both enjoyed science fiction, sailing Lake Michigan, mindless children's cartoons, expensive vodka shots, good red wine, and an overarching need to believe in the implausible. Even though the food was overrated, dinner turned out to be excellent. This time, Sarah relented and let him take her home.

In the car, she said, "Peter, did you ever read those articles about my trip to Uzbekistan?"

"Sure, it was great research. Your cousin's an excellent writer. I looked online and saw that he was writing a book about the trip. You two travel together often?"

"We're very close. We even share the same birth date. Did you know that it was Alexis' idea that he come with me to Uzbekistan?" Her pouty-lipped vulnerability led him to the obvious conclusion.

"He's joining us, isn't he?"

She nodded guiltily.

Peter's insides churned. He looked soberly into Sarah's face, attempting to impose himself on what was encoded behind those nearly transparent golden eyes. The reaction was startling. It had been years since something spoke to his soul, rather than his lust. *She* was seeing into *him*.

"And if I object?"

"As a result of his series on Uzbekistan, the *Chronicle's* putting up some of the money for this trip as well. They had an option. You'd have to put up their share and then buy them out of their option."

"I see." He did, but he still objected.

When they got to her apartment, he parked the car and they got out. The weather had turned noticeably cooler since they last met. He took off his cashmere sport coat and wrapped it around her shivering body.

"Peter, what are you doing?" She asked presumptively.

"I'm walking you to the door, Sarah. Haven't you ever gone to dinner with a gentleman before? Besides, this isn't the greatest neighborhood, or haven't you looked up long enough to notice?"

"Thank you, Peter." She left him at the security entrance to her high rise and promised to stop by his office the morning after next.

As she hung up her outfit for the evening, she noticed her cocktail dress still hanging in the closet, usurped for the evening by her cunning.

When she came by with his freshly cleaned sport coat several days later, he pulled out his wallet.

She was embarrassed. "Peter, really. I couldn't take money from you."

He handed her a folded piece of paper. "That's not what you said at dinner."

She unfolded a check made out to Antarctic Mammoths, LLC for sixty thousand dollars and gasped.

"Find someone to form an LLC in that name, open a checking account that requires your signature and mine, and we're off. I am looking forward to working with you again."

Her professionalism collapsed and she ran around the desk and threw her arms around him as he attempted to rise and then almost fell back over his chair.

As she walked out, he found himself attempting to calm his quickened pulse. Peter's skin was tingling from Sarah's spontaneous embrace. He was also jealous of a man he had never met, who gave him no reason to feel threatened and whom he knew from his previous work had the literary ability to take this expedition, if it was successful, to a heretofore unattainable mass exposure audience. But, what really bothered him was that he had never felt threatened by any man before, so why this punk?

Peter didn't meet Michael until Sarah and he arrived at Houston Intercontinental for the connecting flight to Buenos Aires, just two and a half weeks after Sarah convinced Peter to join them and twenty-five days after a sulfuric acid pool and the soaring death of Michael's date convinced them that they had few alternatives and limited time before disaster struck again.

Peter mulled Michael and the relationship over as the cousins embraced and caught up. Sarah told Michael that his wardrobe improved substantially since women started taking an interest in him, and he asked her if she ordered the vegan meal on the plane. Any disinterested observer would have assumed it was typical sibling banter.

"Sarah keeps reminding me how fortunate we are that Chicago has in residence one of the world's foremost authorities on the last Ice Age Epoch. I hope that I can do your talents justice in my chronicles."

Peter returned the compliment, "That mutant echidna piece was excellent. You corroborated thoroughly and cited dissenting views to Sarah's findings, yet it was simple enough to fascinate any layperson. I personally preferred the travel article. It sounds to me like the better part of that story was what went *un*published."

From Buenos Aires, it was a puddle jumper to Cape Horn, Argentina and after a couple of taxi rides, they found themselves walking up the gangway to board the Seapeace interdiction vessel, *Sea Coral*.

Michael, of course, tripped on the foot treads in the catwalk.

Waiting on deck to greet them was the ship's master, Captain Ralph Quicksilver. They had signed on as volunteers in exchange for taxi service to a cove in the Weddell Sea. Sarah's explanation was plausible enough, an environmentalist on a return trip to Antarctica after a maiden voyage last winter with the EDQ, accompanied by a science reporter cousin who wished to chronicle a journey to the bottom of the earth. What they expected to find, if anything, was not to be disclosed to the captain or crew until they reached the Weddell Sea. Peter Barber's background, though not his identity, was kept a secret.

The skeptical captain took one look at them and said, "You are much too delicate to have been to the Antarctic, Ms. Baskin, and you Mr. Seagal, will not survive this trip as a working hand." He immediately sized up the Barber-Baskin relationship, as well. He knew exactly what was attracting Peter to the Antarctic at the end of summer aboard a boat like the *Sea Coral*, regardless of their real mission.

Listen my children and you shall hear
Of the midnight ride of Paul Revere.
Hang a lantern aloft in the belfry arch
Of the North Church tower as a signal light—
One if by land, and two if by sea;
And lo! as he looks, on the belfry's height
A glimmer, and then a gleam of light!
He springs to the saddle, the bridle he turns,
But lingers and gazes, till full on his sight
A second lamp in the belfry burns.

—Henry Wadsworth Longfellow

CHAPTER 7

Cast Adrift among the Suspicions

Paul Revere and Peter both had a two-light disaster in progress. It had been a month since Peter had cut his deal with Sarah back on land at the university, and now, here at sea, their relationship was still platonic. At least he had negotiated a much better deal on the credits and royalties with his intellectual head in charge of the decision-making.

Initially, Peter had excused himself from the most menial shipboard chores, but to the apparent delight of Ralph Quicksilver, Sarah had goaded him into pitching in with increasing frequency.

When the captain found Sarah and the professor swabbing the deck after the necropsy of a shark caught in an oil slick, Ralph couldn't contain himself. He waited until Sarah was out of earshot. "You handle a mop quite well, Dr. Barber. You do this work at home?"

"Hardly. At home I have a cleaning woman. I do this here to show solidarity with the crew." Quicksilver conspicuously ogled Sarah's muscular Lycra-painted hips moving rhythmically with the ship.

"Really? What would it take to get you to work alongside your cleaning woman?"

Barber slopped shark blood on the captain's feet.

Michael was like an eight-year-old at an amusement park. The ship's '60s-era diesel engines required regular tweaking, and Michael had developed a fair understanding of diesel engine mechanics while working a part-time job in high school repairing big rigs.

Peter had assisted the chief engineer with some minor overhaul on the bilge pumps, which keep water from collecting in the lowest holds of the ship. When they finished, Michael relieved them for the overnight engine watch. He lay on the cot with his head propped against the wall and began making log entries into his laptop and working on a story line for the first installment of his travel article. The engine heat and rocking of the mother ship swaddled him like a newborn. In minutes, he was snoring with the engine and the laptop slid off of his stomach and onto the cot.

Michael woke up in a pool of his own sweat, coughing and gagging from an oil fire burning in the rag pile. It was spreading rapidly toward the diesel feed line. His eyes watered from the bluish smoke, and the ceiling was lost in the haze. He assessed the priorities. Notify the crew, contain the fire, shut off the diesel line, save the laptop, exhaust the engine room. There would be only three other people awake at this time of night.

He dropped his laptop over the knee-knocker threshold as he screamed for help. Then he tied a clean rag over his mouth and nose. It smelled of old motor oil, but it prevented his lungs from burning with each increasingly spasmodic breath. He felt for the fire extinguisher and scorched his hand on the metal handle, instinctively stuffing it into his mouth.

"Shit!"

His hand had knocked something warm and fuzzy off of the fire extinguisher. The image registered and he felt on the metal deck for the asbestos gloves. Precious seconds were slipping away and the flames were feeding on the combustible lead deck paint.

Michael pulled the gloves on and aimed the fire extinguisher through the haze. He hit the base of the fire and then moved toward the diesel line and doused it with chemicals. The fire was skipping from one oily spot on the floor to another and had nearly reached the pile of old newspapers under the fuel line. It was now hot enough to ignite the diesel fuel and blow the engine room. He shut the fuel feed valve. Hopefully the engine would suck the remaining fuel out of the line before it ignited.

A leg on a wooden table was smoldering. He doused the table, and then dragging it under the emergency exhaust fan, he clambered onto the table and hit the switch. He heard its motor whirr as the table collapsed. Everything went dark.

Peter was passing the engine room and saw smoke escaping and hit the alarm. Two of the crew arrived quickly and killed the fire, while a third donned the portable oxygen tank and mask and dragged an unconscious Michael out of the room, his breathing shallow and vapid. A tennis ball-sized lump protruded from the back of his head. Hair was burned away from both arms, and his forearm had peeled like an onion. One of the crew summoned Sparks, the radio control woman and physician's assistant. Peter went to get Sarah while the other rescuer gave Michael oxygen.

A pimply, grave-faced volunteer arrived with a stretcher and they gingerly transported him to the single-bed infirmary. Ralph was waiting at the door.

Ace, the shift duty officer from Chattanooga drawled, "As best as we can tell, Cap'n, a fire started in the engine room. Michael got it under control and then fell off that old table in there when he was reaching up to direct the big exhaust fan. He's got some burns and a nasty lump on the noggin."

"Engine's stopped, Ace." In the tumult, no one had noticed that the ship had gone silent and was drifting.

"Oh, right. He must have shut the fuel line off. Good thinking." Ace directed someone to inspect and reopen the fuel line and then sprinted to the control room to restart the engines.

Peter returned to the infirmary with Sarah. She touched Michael's hand, and tears streaked his charred arm and blackened face.

Sparks completed her preliminary exam and hooked him up to supplemental oxygen and an intravenous line.

"Heart rate and blood pressure are low but within normal ranges. His pupils are significantly dilated. Maybe a mild concussion."

She was interrupted as Michael attempted to lift his head up but collapsed on the pillow. "Did we hit an iceberg with my head? Is this the *Titanic*?" Then he saw the IV attached to his arm.

"What happened to me?" Sarah squeezed his hand. "It is so rare when pretty girls hold my hand. It figures. We're related, aren't we?"

"You almost burned up the ship."

"It almost burned me up. Stalemate."

Sparks ushered everyone out but Sarah and the captain.

"What happened, Michael?" the captain asked.

"Oily rags caught fire. No idea how. Sorry for killing the engines. All I remember."

"Well done. Could've been a lot worse. Get some rest." The captain's bear paws gave the shoulder of Michael's unburnt arm a fatherly squeeze.

Michael turned his head slightly and whispered, "If this is how M'low Cloom protects us, what's going to happen when *It* gets mad at us?" He held her hand tight and closed his eyes.

Sarah looked at Sparks. "I think he's fine, Sarah. Some minor burns on his right arm above the cuff of the glove. Thank God he had the presence of mind to put them on. We'll need to monitor him in sick bay for several days before we put him back to work." Sparks stroked his cheek gently and mussed his hair a bit. "Doesn't seem like there's any serious damage to his lungs. A little smoke inhalation. I'll check his blood oxygen levels a little later and we'll know more. My guess is he'll be fine by the time we get to your drop-off point. He's a lot sturdier than when he boarded, you know." She grabbed a large tube of topical benzocaine and a pill bottle of morphine.

"A little morphine, Michael?"

His eyes widened.

They laughed. "Once."

"Geez, all my mom would do was kiss it."

Sarah said, "Your mom knew you couldn't be trusted with drugs."

Sarah thanked Sparks, kissed her cousin on the forehead, and turned to leave the room.

Michael said to Sparks, "Could you give Sarah and me a moment in private, please? She'll keep an eye on the drugs."

Sparks winked at Sarah and left the room.

Michael grabbed one of Sarah's triceps and pulled her toward him. He said in a low voice. "This was no accident, Sarah."

"Somebody *set* the fire?"

"I don't think anybody was trying to get anybody killed or destroy the ship, just get me incapacitated. You know who was in the engine room right before me, don't you?"

She shook her head.

"The personification of evil."

She was confused for a second and then scowled. Telling Michael that Peter had discovered the fire would just make matters worse. "Why would Peter want you out of the way? You're no threat to him."

"No, but as you've noticed, he's not exactly a team player. He trails behind you like a lovesick puppy dog and views me as an obstruction or an expendable parasite, depending on where you are at the moment."

"Is that all men ever keep track of, who other men are lusting for?"

"The secret's out."

His breathing was becoming labored. "We'll just keep an eye on each other's tails, okay?" She kissed him again and walked out of the infirmary to Sparks and Barber waiting in the corridor.

"He said that he wants to rest for a while, Sparks."

"I'll call you if he asks for you."

She nodded and turned to Peter. "C'mon, let's get me a drink." He wrapped a blanket and his arm around her and ushered her back to his cabin.

They sat in the spare steel grey room. It contained a bunk with an upper and lower berth, a chair, a small built-in writing desk, a porthole through which the sun already streamed in at three am, and a built-in closet with doors over several shelves to keep their contents from sliding to the floor as the ship rolled.

Peter reached under his desk and pulled out a bottle of twenty-five-year-old scotch. It was nearly full. He got two paper cups from the sink and poured. Sarah sat on the edge of the metal bed, her lips pressed determinedly together. She took the cup and calmed herself with the oak and caramel notes of the golden brown liquid. Peter touched his cup to hers, sat down with his hip pressed against hers and sipped. Michael was right. She had been deluding herself into believing that she could keep him at bay for the duration of this trip. She threw the hard liquor down her throat and winced. Peter squirmed.

Even if Michael was wrong, he was still right. They had to maintain control over their third partner, and if she kept him at arm's-length he was capable of almost anything. She wondered what men did in this situation. It was still a sexist world.

"I don't have family like that, Sarah. I barely talk to my brother. He's too rich, I'm too famous, and my sister is too drunk much of the time."

"We grew up as fraternal twins, two blocks away and born four and a half hours apart. We get as much pleasure from each other's successes as our own." She knew it was a lie, at least on Michael's end, but it was a small one. "Sometimes, we're just there to help each other see ourselves as others see us."

She took the bottle off of the metal shelf and poured four ounces. She filled his half-empty cup.

Peter smiled.

She drank the glass down without pausing. Peter followed suit.

Sarah slowly licked her lips with the tip of her tongue and looked at Peter through half-closed eyes. She put her cup and his down on the desk and slid her hands and arms inside his coat and rubbed his back. Her thick brown waves fell across her face and she let it tickle Peter's cheeks, taunting him.

She slid one arm out from his coat, put another shot in the glass, and swallowed quickly. Then she ran her hand through his hair and pulled him toward her. His lips parted quickly and she kissed him deeply while he slid his hand under the back of her sweatshirt.

She pulled away and softly cupped his head in her palms and caressed his cheeks with her thumbs. "I attempted to keep this professional since I first met you. I've failed." She pushed him down by the shoulders onto the lower bunk, pulled up his sweater, and exposed his torso. Then she did the same to herself and pressed her taut, partially naked body directly on his. His eyes closed, and he moaned involuntarily. His pants were already building with anticipation.

He put his hands under her sweatshirt and onto her bare back.

"They're cold, Peter."

She gently moved his hands to her crotch to warm them.

Michael was out on deck three days after his injuries. He had suffered second-degree burns on one patch of his arm just above the cuff line and first degree burns on most of the rest of the arm. It was still slightly blistered. Right now it was bandaged and covered with a parka.

Even though there was a warming sun hovering low over the horizon of an ice-blue sky, the wind took frigid bites from their faces. Foam peaks atop seven-and-a-half-foot swells caused the ship to sway like a pendulum. Sarah and Michael leaned over the deck rail as she broke the news to him.

"You fuckin' slept with him?"

"You gave me no choice, dear."

"Pardon me? I don't remember being in the cabin holding you down."

"Sometimes, you are too crude and disgusting even for me." She conceded, "You were right. We'll have better control over him if I'm sleeping with him. He can't screw you if he wants to keep screwing me."

"Until when?"

She paused and scowled her eyebrows together. The question hadn't occurred to her. Michael was usually the one who lacked an exit strategy. "Probably until we get back from Antarctica and everybody lives up to their end of the bargain. I won't use him, Michael. Right now, we are both benefitting."

"I don't think he'd be so sensitive if he was using you, Sarah." He took a deep breath of the cold salt air and a cough sent his body into spastic convulsions.

"You okay?"

"Yeah. Sparks says it'll hurt, but I need to take progressively deeper breaths to regain lung capacity before I have to confront the mammoths." He changed the subject. "Did they confirm the cause of the fire, Sarah?"

"Oily rags next to the heater spontaneously combusted. It was a low flash point cleaning oil."

"It fits. Couldn't you have slept with him a couple of weeks ago and saved my arm hairs?"

She touched his bandaged arm. There was something else on his mind. "Sarah, you know we are in way over our heads."

She looked at her cousin intently. He seemed to have aged considerably on the trip, and it wasn't just from the engine room incident. His forehead was now deeply furrowed; his spoiled city boy hands heavily calloused. The wave of his chestnut hair had even begun to show a few stray signs of graying at the temples, but at least his soft lanky frame had finally developed some ripped muscular definition. On the whole, she thought the effect wasn't bad.

"How quickly we lose our faith." It was a clear reference to M'low Cloom. "What's your point?"

"Point?" He spat out the word as the ship suddenly lurched heavily forward. "Ralph Quicksilver is highly suspicious of us landlubbers. As we first walked up the gangway, he noticed how little a print journalist and an environmental science student know about the sea and, if I might add without insulting you too much, environmental science. The point is, MC or no MC, we are going to get killed out there. I didn't see M'low Cloom putting out the fire in the engine room, and I don't see him stopping Peter Barber while we are at his mercy in the remote reaches of Antarctica."

"If we said to the captain, 'We were just kidding, we don't have to go ashore anymore,' what do you think he would do, make us walk the plank?"

"Sarah, if Ralph Quicksilver is the swashbuckling Errol Flynn, then that must make me Gilligan and you MaryAnn."

Sometimes good analogies were worth ignoring. "We've been much closer to death before. Remember when we were eight and our parents told us to go play in my basement during that cocktail party they were having upstairs? And we were mad because they wouldn't let us hang out with the adults and eat the hors d'oeuvres? We decided that we would teach them a lesson by turning off all the power in the house, so we found our way to the electrical panel boxes and nearly electrocuted ourselves."

"Yes, but we did swipe the hors d'oeuvres while it was dark. I have no idea why we survived then, just so we can freeze to death in Antarctica. But I do know why we survived Uzbekistan."

Without warning, the sea became tranquil, and they reflected its mood. The white peaks disappeared. Unlike hearing and sight, the more rarely used human sense of equilibrium evoked a purely instinctive reassurance that renewed some of the irrational invincibility that they had felt in Uzbekistan.

"Sarah, everybody doubts that we will find these woolly mammoths, including our parents and a man who is hopelessly obsessed with you. And they think you've seen them before! Why are we so confident?"

"Because we have an identical road map leading to these woolly mammoths implanted in our brain. MC has convinced us that we will succeed in our quest and *It* will protect us."

"As long as MC doesn't stand for Mistaken Conclusions. Do you feel it, Sarah?"

"Yes, Michael, I do. I am glad you do, too," she said with relief. "MC will assure our success *and* our survival."

"Even when I was getting torched in the engine room, I suppose I knew that nothing serious would happen to me." He coughed again and continued.

"It's going to come up, probably real shortly, so are we clear in our minds where we are going?"

"Yes. I'll recognize every inch of that coast. It has been burned into my brain. Isn't it the same way with you?"

"Yes, but I am supposed to play dumb. If Peter and Ralph realize that we have exactly the same memories of your 'last voyage', which neither of us took, Captain Quicksilver and Dr. Barber will, as the gangsters say, 'be on to us' and MC will be on to them."

They were interrupted by a sempiternal, "Land Ho!" from the iceberg watch. At the same time, Barber found them, and tension once again permeated their little corner of the ocean.

Barber stared at Sarah for a long, withering moment until he seemed to make a decision. "You're on deck, Miss Baskin, and tomorrow our ship sails if you'll pardon the double entendre. Something has been puzzling me that I should have asked a month ago. You were working a winter break internship with the Environmental Defense Quest last year, studying the effects of global warming. You believe that global warming exposed an entombed woolly mammoth. If it was me, I wouldn't have been able to contain myself."

When Sarah offered only a puzzled expression, he continued.

"You, on the other hand, just kept your mouth shut. Why?"

"The people on that EDQ ship either would not have comprehended what we had, or if there was a brain among them, they would have brought in their own people, taken full credit for this, and I would have lost control over what may be the biggest find of the new century. You on the other hand immediately grasped the paleontological significance and had said you would let me be published right alongside you even though it's outside my core research.

"Michael and I have been taking misadventures together since we were in diapers. I have no track record, we have no money, and I'd rather be fucked by somebody qualified on all counts than by those EDQ idiots."

Michael covered his involuntary guffaw with a voluntarily contrived cough.

Two nights earlier, as Sarah and Peter lay sleeping with her head resting softly on his chest, he was the alpha male. His patience had paid off and now he had leverage. Michael and Sarah hadn't been adequately deferential to his money and his name, and once he had stepped onto the *Sea Coral*, they knew that he couldn't back out. Confronting them over the unlikely source of their information about these woolly mammoths was supposed to be payback and put them back in their place. Somehow, it had all just backfired.

"I guess I'll take that as a compliment." He smiled fraudulently and retreated to the port side.

Michael said, "You are really good."

Her eyes lacerated him. "What am I supposed to do? Let MC kill him? Let him screw us? I hate myself."

"The ambitions of the moral and the amoral are equally blind. So, don't be so fast to judge *me*. Wait a minute. That's not it at all. You really care about him, don't you?"

"Yes, no, I mean yes, I care that he doesn't get killed and no, I don't care about him emotionally. I had no trouble rationalizing my manipulative behavior when I saw him as nothing more than a self-serving lecher."

"But, that's not the case anymore, is it?"

Silence.

"This is way more than infatuation or lust. He's in love with you, isn't he?"

Ralph's rapid approach saved Sarah from answering.

Michael looked back and forth between Ralph and Peter and made a decision. "Wait up, Peter."

Ralph was an odd agglomeration of the old sea and the Seapeace philosophy of activist environmental interdiction. Half Delaware Indian, more or less, he had grown up around the water and had attended the US Merchant Marine Academy in Kings Point, New York, on full scholarship. After that, he had progressed rapidly along a career path that put him in command of some of the most massive oceangoing container ships in the world. A chance proximate encounter with the aftershocks of the Exxon Valdez ecological disaster had reconnected him to his ancestors' symbiotic view of life on planet earth. From there it was straight to Seapeace's door. He was overqualified for this assignment, a blessing if you were dependent on him for your safety, a big problem if you had some ignorance of the seas to hide.

"The show's about to begin, Sarah. Do you have any idea what you are doing?"

"We think we do, Ralph, but we're still relying heavily on you." A distant crack of lightning and then the roll of thunder near the mountain range cut short the conversation. They held onto the railing and stared out at the looming mountains. Clouds were gathering around them, quickly obscuring the peaks from view. It was unlikely the clouds would amount to much in the semi-arid climate of the Antarctic continent. They still could not make out the contours of the distant shoreline with the naked eye.

Not five hundred meters off of their port bow, they were distracted by the sea rising into the sky, accompanied by a fountain of spray. The merest glimpse took their breath away. Sarah clutched the railing and the blood drained from her face. "What is that?"

In a few short seconds, it was obvious to everyone. "You never saw a blue whale on your last trip? Did you see any whales? Do you know what a whale looks like?"

"We saw whales. Sperm and fin whales, but no blue whales. They're no comparison to this."

The great cetacean lifted itself to the surface of the sea, some five thousand meters deep at that point. The mammal would go no higher. Unlike most whales, the enormous mass of a blue whale prevents it from breeching the surface of the water. Its barnacled undersides remain a cloaked mystery, visible only from below. It was easily four times the length of the boat and nearly twice as high as the con. The boat's wake spread out for hundreds of meters behind them. The leviathan effortlessly paced the twenty knots now being maintained by the *Sea Coral* while leaving barely a streak on the ocean's glassy surface. All hands leaned over the railing for a view of the largest mammal ever to roam the earth.

They were mesmerized. The impressive Peter Barber had spent his life chasing the fossils of animals like these. But in the flesh, they were impressive; he, small and insignificant. For Sarah and the crew, this was the essence of their life's work, to protect these endangered species that once safely swam almost as far north as the Tropic of Capricorn. One eye, the size of a trash can top, looked at them sadly in surrender. After some minutes, it proffered a discernable wink and veered to ram them amidship. At the last possible second, it dove deeply under the bow and vanished. As the astonished crew gasped, her forty-ton calf rose up and then dove alongside her beneath the ship.

When they looked again to shore, the mountains had grown dramatically larger, and they could just make out the shoreline of the coast of the Weddell Sea. They would need to be ever wary now of icebergs and calving glaciers.

The *Sea Coral* was a well-equipped icebreaker. However, far larger ships than the *Sea Coral*, the *Titanic* being the most notorious, had been done in by undetected icebergs or the mini-tsunamis of a calving glacier. Periodically, chunks of glaciers the size of the Empire State Building would shear off in an ear-splitting roar and come crashing into the ocean below. The force of the newly formed iceberg on rare occasions could generate tsunamis twenty-five meters high or more, capsizing nearly any seagoing vessel. According to many scientists, the effects of global warming on the polar ice caps had caused the formation of icebergs and the calving of glaciers to increase rapidly in frequency. Rarity or not, the captain doubled the eyes on watch.

Sarah and Michael stared intently at the mountains and the shoreline from different ends of the ship. Very shortly, either she could direct the captain to their disembarkation point, or they would be exposed as frauds.

"Captain, I think you need to go a kilometer or two to the right. There's a little finger, peninsula, uh, thing that juts out into the sea, and we want to pass well to the right of it." At this distance, the peninsula was invisible. They could make out a massive peak in the background and what appeared to be three smaller peaks in a separate range in the foreground.

A smile replaced Quicksilver's stone-faced skepticism. He was familiar with the targeted land mass. "Well, let's go up to the control room, pull out the maps, and see how good your memory really is." His tone was less ominous now. In the last ten minutes, the weather had transformed yet again and exploded into another brilliant cloudless sky. The two climbed the steep metal stairs, leaving Barber and Michael alone on the main deck. At the top of the stairs Sarah turned anxiously. Her eyes and her memories met her cousin's.

Barber lit his pipe and slowly exhaled the aromatic tobacco into the gusting wind.

"We've got a lot of money into this, Michael."

"There's a lot more at stake than that, Peter. You have a reputation to protect. I've got one to establish. Young investigative reporters only get to pursue a very limited number of expensive hunches on the newspaper's time and expense account, before they are doomed to high school science fairs and soap box derbies."

Peter pursed his lips and blew smoke forcefully into the wind.

"Had Bob Woodward and Carl Bernstein not found their 'deep throat' and done such a great investigative job they would still have been slogging away on the beat. They needed ability *and* a big break, before a big break down. One more failure, I'm done, a big success and I'm a superstar."

"And don't you think that Woodward and Bernstein worked real hard to get that source for information, Michael?"

"No harder than I am working."

"They were investigating and exposing a plot to manipulate the results of a presidential election by breaking and entering. In the science world, if someone makes a significantly newsworthy discovery, then we or our institutions issue press releases about our findings and while we write our scholarly works, we might grant interviews to the media. We are the Woodwards and the Bernsteins doing the investigating and your cousin is a damn good writer, which means you should be calling my secretary for an appointment."

Michael didn't know if the extreme satisfaction of busting Peter in the mouth was worth the pain to his burned arm. Revealing the truth, at least for now, was out of the question.

"I am also here to cover the personal story. You know, how far will a renowned paleontologist go for the three f's—fame, fortune and a good fuck? And how much will his wife tolerate, just to bask in his shadow? Peter, I am one hundred percent sure that we will find what Sarah says, and she needs one partner she can completely trust. Unlike you, I won't commit arson or manslaughter to achieve success. I suspect you know who left those oily rags near the boiler to spontaneously combust while I was sleeping, don't you?"

Peter's teeth cracked his pipe stem like a pistachio shell. "I don't even know what spontaneous combustion is. Listen to me, punk. If I were you, I wouldn't threaten anyone right before I stepped onto a lawless continent with nobody covering my ass."

"I have somebody who I can trust covering my ass, Peter, which is much safer than having somebody sleeping with it."

"Why are you so confident? Do you know something that I don't know? Because if you do, then you should be getting a lot more of the credit here. Why would someone almost as hungry as me for the limelight be deferring to someone who doesn't even care? What's she got on you?"

"You couldn't even begin to understand, and frankly Peter, it's better for both of us that you don't or you could end up in worse shape than I'm in." He proffered his burnt arm.

"Is that a threat?"

"Not from me, Dr. Barber." He walked away before Barber could quiz him further.

Peter watched Michael's backside and fumed. He turned and projected himself to the shoreline through the binoculars that had been dangling around his neck. To the naked eye it had appeared barren, belying a whole ecosystem of activity. Four-ton southern elephant seals and penguins lingered along the shore and specks of green were clearly visible on the naked portions of the shoreline that gave up their snow and ice cover for a few short months.

Michael looked at Peter from across the bow. He appeared almost ten years younger than his forty-seven years. It was no surprise that he had so much success with women twenty or twenty-five years his junior. Michael felt a twinge of jealousy for a man who seemed to experience nothing but success with both his career and with women.

Only Sarah knew all of the incriminating details of Michael's Texas Gulf Coast co-generation debacle. Process and manufacturing plants would use steam in the manufacturing process and the leftover heat that wasn't used in the process could generate electricity or heat other buildings, rather than being released into the air and wasted. The inefficiency in Texas is that the weather is too mild to use much of the waste heat directly for heating.

A large industrial manufacturer had proposed a novel reverse co-generation process for the air conditioning season. It would preheat its water used to make steam by removing heat from the cooling water used in the air conditioner, which reduced energy costs in both processes. There were hundreds of thousands of dollars in tax credits and savings at stake and during demonstrations by Ellen Nesbit, the company's public affairs officer, the measured energy savings exceeded expectations. However, there was a branch left off the energy balance. Her company was precooling its water by running it through massive heat exchangers under its docks on the ship channel. The result was that the air conditioning energy savings always looked larger than they really were, overstating the amount qualifying for tax credits.

Michael had run the whole process by his college chemical engineering roommate who told him that these kinds of energy efficiencies were unheard of. By that time, he had already published the lead story in the three-part series. When he confronted Ellen, they had already been sleeping together regularly. Soon after the third installment, Ellen received a promotion, dumped Michael, and hooked up with her boss. Another paper exposed the fraud four months later, based on the information in Michael's series. The company pleaded nolo contendere to tax fraud, Ellen was either the perpetrator or the scapegoat, Michael never found out which, and they paid a seven-figure fine.

The *Chronicle* never blamed Michael formally, although that didn't stop Neil from berating Michael for his stupid rookie mistake of not corroborating the facts. Michael knew that appearing inexperienced was more forgivable than ignoring evidence and letting a personal relationship color your objectivity, so as a personal favor, Michael's roommate kept his mouth shut about the whole affair.

In the cramped control room, Sarah and Ralph painstakingly reviewed the map and the plan for the next seventy-two hours. Sarah and Michael had hand drawn the map from their combined recollections and she had scanned it in to the computer at the university, so they could overlay it to an existing base map which would allow them to further manipulate their drawing. Most of their markings were not map symbols, but landmarks and visual aids necessary to direct them to their target.

Quicksilver had questioned Sarah and studied her map carefully before they had cast off from Argentina and had concluded that she knew where she was going. But, there were limitations. He had no way of knowing if the inland landmarks and distances were authentic or accurate. She had even shown the approximate path of the sun across the mountain ranges at the time of year Sarah had supposedly last been here, as well as some rough lunar risings and phases. While she could have collected that information from meteorological data and solar and lunar charts, it was a lot of extra work just to gain passage to a frozen desert to perpetrate a fraud.

Growing up streetwise in a small town on the Delmarva Peninsula, Quicksilver had learned to rely on his instincts about people just to survive. He knew something was wrong here, but he couldn't put his finger on it. Sarah and Michael weren't devious, but they were hiding something. Once you feel the icy wind of Antarctica and see the seven-meter swells, even in the middle of the summer, you never forget them. And Sarah seemed completely overwhelmed when she experienced them on board the *Sea Coral.*

"Well there're the three peaks in front of the single larger one, exactly as you show on your relief map, and here is approximately where the shoreline ice melts away in the summer. The small plateau overlook, which doesn't show up on any of our own maps is here," and he peered through the telescope mounted to the deck. "We will put you ashore in the five-meter skiff about a couple of kilometers from shore when the sun turns back up tomorrow. That will be about three am local time. You shouldn't need much more than an hour to get to shore and another two hours to unload your snowmobiles and be off. With a little luck, you say it's about fifteen kilometers inland, you'll make camp at your destination that night.

"Stay in touch with the satellite phone. It's real unreliable here, between the Aurora, the location of the geosynchronous satellite and the weather. We will see you two or three days after that, max. I don't want to be here any longer than that, and given your experience and skill level, you shouldn't be either. We can't be coming ashore to rescue you. We have a rendezvous with an illegal whaling ship that I really don't want to miss." Quicksilver gave a small smirk of anticipation, revealing yellow-stained teeth.

"Now that I have lived up to my end of the bargain, it's time you lived up to at least a portion of yours. What do you expect to find here?"

Did they *expect* to find something here or had she found it already? As Ralph and she reviewed each step of their journey inland, Sarah's mind's eye was revisiting a memory. She squinted from the bright sun reflecting off of the mirror-like ice; her nostrils tingled from the cold, clean air.

Her pulse had jumped as she and Ralph discussed a hairpin turn through the mountain pass. Why? Was there some danger in that cleft in the mountains that she had experienced before? No, it wasn't deja vu or clairvoyance, it was a real cognitive memory. She *saw* animals roaming around the icy tundra and then suddenly, the memory went blank.

If she said too much, she had to worry about keeping her stories straight, in case Peter and Ralph compared notes. If she revealed too little, she wouldn't be credible.

"When I put to shore here with the EDQ, I found a woolly mammoth frozen in a wall of ice and snow. Maybe several woolly mammoths. It was particularly unexpected because this is a traversed and studied portion of the continent. I believe that an inordinate amount of melting exposed it or them. I suppose that you know that woolly mammoths are not exactly indigenous to Antarctica?"

He nodded.

"So, how did they get here? And, what will we find buried with them? For that piece, I needed a paleontologist, which is why I invited Peter Barber. The rest, I think, you kind of know."

"And Clark Kent is here to chronicle this?"

When they were younger and she was being picked on, it was Michael defending her. She was the oldest in her family, and he, the youngest in his. Until her teens, there was no winning. Boys made fun of her ungainly appearance, and she wasn't quite tough enough or big enough to take them on. Girls made fun of her because of her unusual interests and her learning disabilities. She seemed to share nothing in common with them.

"Yes, Michael is an award-winning science writer and he can document that even the most controversial of us, that would be Seapeace, Ralph, are courageous heroes fighting to preserve our planet as we know it."

"We haven't let adverse public opinion affect our agenda thus far, but I can't imagine how some positive press wouldn't help, eh?"

CHAPTER 8

A Summer Cruise

The winch slowly lowered the massive powerboat over the side of the mother vessel. This was the *Sea Coral's* lifeboat, but Seapeace also used it to create havoc for fishing vessels engaged in illegal or unethical fishing or whaling.

Beneath its weathered grey paint were six-inch-thick welded steel plates and an ice-breaker bow, powered by twin three-hundred-horsepower Volvo inboards, more than adequate to outrun angry Japanese and Norwegian whaling boats, sperm whales and icebergs. They would need every inch of steel protection as they headed for the unstable frozen coast.

Lines had been lashed to the sides of the skiff and held loosely by a couple of men on the deck of the mother vessel. If the boat tipped heavily to either side as it was being lowered, it would be their job to keep the supplies and equipment from reaching the sea ahead of the boat. The small craft landed with a hard smack against the water. The cables slackened at the impact and were quickly pulled taut again until Sarah, Michael, and Peter cast off.

The sun was now well above the horizon and the winds had subsided. It might reach fifty-five degrees Fahrenheit at midday, but only in direct sunlight. By early February, the sun would make its first big plunge below the horizon at about two am, leaving a few minutes of gray twilight. Thereafter, the amount of darkness would increase very quickly, growing to twelve hours worldwide on March 21, the southern hemisphere's autumnal equinox.

They checked their wireless headsets and other equipment. Screaming in this weather would dry out the vocal cords faster than a December Packers game in Green Bay, Wisconsin.

The captain gave Barber's hand a quick squeeze, then he grasped Michael's elbow and reached to shake his hand. "Michael, I expect you to make me look good in this article. If you want to write me in to this portion of the trip, I won't deny it."

Recovering from the unexpected humanity, Michael grasped the captain's hand with both of his.

Then Ralph pulled Sarah into a big bear hug and whispered in her ear. "Manmade dangers are a lot more common than natural disasters. You want to be famous, not posthumous." Worry lines appeared under the bill of his Arizona Diamondbacks baseball cap.

Before they departed, Ralph gave them a stern lecture on the dangers of frostbite. When the sun neared the horizon and the wind whipped up, any body part could suffer severe frostbite in minutes. The risks of relieving one's self in such conditions caused the males to unconsciously clamp their legs tightly together.

The three descended a Jacob's ladder tethered along the hull, and Peter took the wheel. Most of Peter's sailing experience was aboard his thirty-six-foot powerboat on Lake Michigan, quite a different operation but still more experience than Sarah and Michael had combined.

Barber's mind wandered as he maneuvered the craft toward shore, dodging chunks of ice and an occasional leopard seal out penguin hunting. This was the riskiest trip he had ever undertaken. The climate was hostile and unforgiving. They had fewer lifelines in the event of disaster and he never had less evidence that they would find what they were seeking. He attempted to rationalize his impulsive behavior. The thrills and dangers of the quest invigorated him and he didn't know how much longer he could physically endure a trip like this. This would be the most spectacular find of the century and interpreting the ramifications of it would all fall upon him and Sarah. His knees were turning to jelly.

"Sarah, you ready to jump out?" Michael called to her.

"Peter, pay attention." Michael spoke sharply, pulling Peter back to reality.

They eyed each other warily. Peter revved the engine, and the sea foam kicked up from the shallow propeller. The speed increased by four or five knots, and then the bow slammed into the shore. Peter kept the throttle up while Sarah and Michael anchored the port and starboard bow lines. Michael tapped the stakes into the soft top soil to start them, but when he heaved the sixteen-pound sledge over his head to break into the permafrost, he nearly fell over backward.

Sarah said, "Have you ever considered taking up power lifting?"

When Peter lowered the bow door to push out the snowmobiles, a gaggle of enthusiastic penguins attacked Sarah and Michael, attempting to overrun them and make off with the dried fish and meat rations on the boat. Sarah dispersed them with snowballs while Peter chased after them, swinging a propane torch. "Barbequed chickens, anyone?" They hissed and flapped raucously, but kept their distance. Their boots slogged through the slippery bird guano and the caustic ammonia corroded their nostrils.

They set up solar panels and dry cell batteries at a makeshift base camp and departed. Sarah was driving the lead snowmobile, with Michael holding on behind her. Peter drove the second, with the balance of the supplies being towed behind. Michael turned the power down on his headset, so only Sarah could receive him. They could compare their memories of the landmarks that would lead them to the icy tomb.

"Michael, when Ralph and I were going over the map you and I made, there were *emotions* attached to my memories. Does that make sense to you?"

"I suppose. Every time you think back to the death of your brother, the moment you learned of his death is associated with the despondency of the moment. People don't just remember sights and sounds and smells. They remember emotions, as well, and they're all tied together."

"Do you have emotions attached to these memories that MC has implanted in our brains?"

"Yeah, but as I delve more deeply into them, I find myself surprised. I don't really think that I would have felt that way in that situation, but yet, that's what I am associating."

They hit the hairpin turn in their memories and slowed down considerably, forcing Peter, who was traveling behind, to do the same. Their path sloped away on the outside of the turn to a treacherous thirty-meter shear drop that glistened with a kaleidoscope of lethal ice shards along its entire slope. The rough ice of the inside of the turn hid in the shadows, while the outside had been bathed in sun, causing it to melt and then refreeze into a slick bobsled chute. The snowmobile fishtailed on the ice and slid to the edge of the embankment.

Michael started to slide off the back right side of the snowmobile, and the sudden shift of his weight caused it to begin to tip over the side. He grabbed wildly with both hands and latched onto the strap across the seat, his inertia pulling the snowmobile to the edge of the precipice. He desperately pulled his center of gravity over the inside drive track to force the snowmobile back onto the ground. He yelled to Sarah to give the tracks more power. The treads caught and pulled them through the ice and back onto the snow.

Peter saw what was transpiring. He hugged the snowy inside of the turn, and followed Sarah's lead.

It was enough excitement for the day. They stopped on a snow-packed area sheltered from the wind and turned in immediately after dinner.

Peter tossed in his sleeping bag in a futile attempt to cope with the land of the midnight sun and honking seals. He missed his wife's aristocratic disgust of the great outdoors and he worried about keeping his philandering secret. In the past, whenever he had been exposed, they played that game where he'd promise eternal fidelity and spend fifteen thousand dollars on jewelry. It always seemed to coincide with money being wired into his account after he hosted a documentary on a little-watched education channel. But this was a different game. This time he'd have to pick a door and live with it.

The next morning, they attempted unsuccessfully to contact the *Sea Coral*. There was electromagnetic interference from the Aurora Australis, ghost signals reflected off the pass and the *Sea Coral* had its own mission to fulfill. Staying in touch with them came second.

The going was much easier on the second day. On the far side of the pass was a plateau a few football fields in width, set between two hilly ranges of ice. In three hours, they had crossed to the far end and the mountainous area on their right had begun to recede to a frozen plain facing the South Pole. On the left, just beyond the back side of an obstructing glacier was the ocean.

Suddenly, Michael yelled so loudly into the microphone, that even Peter, who was riding close by, heard him over the lawn mower din of the engines.

"This is it! Pull over!" Sarah's body went taut as she recognized the recesses of the craggily ice.

Peter motioned everyone to turn up their mikes. "Michael, how did you know? Who's giving directions?"

It had not occurred to Michael or Sarah that Peter might actually hear them without the headsets, particularly since yelling was taboo. "Sarah's sketches were so realistic that I immediately recognized the fissure at the face of the wall and the terrain. I just reacted."

They dismounted. They were a football field away and they could make out nothing more than windshield streaks of dirt and minerals mixed with packed snow, covered by a thinning cap of grey ice.

While Sarah and Peter unloaded, Michael called Ralph. Sparks admonished them for being late and maternally berated Michael for his persistent cough. He promised her to have Sarah change his dressing daily. Ralph was adamant that they avoid the satellite phone dead zones during the designated call-in hours.

Quicksilver then reluctantly spoke to Peter. "Ralph, they know exactly where they are going. I know that we were both skeptical, but we're driving along when suddenly Michael let out a shriek, and here we are!"

"Really? Michael?"

"Yeah. He had been studying the renderings that Sarah had provided some time ago, and he spotted her fissure before she did. I may have been entirely wrong about his value here."

Ralph finished the conversation quickly. After Peter, Michael and Sarah had departed, Ralph had turned his attention to Japanese shark fishing. The bastards amputated the tails, dorsal fins and other exotic parts highly prized as aphrodisiacs and miracle cures and then threw the carcasses, sometimes with gills still pulsating with life, back into the sea to save space for more of the high-priced bounty. They had a great deal of ocean to cover to rendezvous and interdict the targeted fishing trawler.

Ralph was convinced that Sarah knew where she was going, but had never been there before. She was the only one of the three who had been given an outer berth for a portion of the trip, and she had trouble sleeping at night because she didn't bring anything along to cover her eyes. She claimed she had seen Antarctic fur seals, but they were hunted almost to extinction in the last century and were now confined to the rocky islands off of the western shore. An odd mistake for an environmental scientist.

Ralph made a phone call to an old friend. He was already gone for the day, but Ralph hoped to have his answers by morning.

CHAPTER 9
Can Mammoths Body Surf?

Sarah felt like she was heading into the mouth of Class Five rapids in the New River Gorge. Her breathing was short and fast and her pulse quickened. Their dreams had not been some diabolical subterfuge, but a time portal into the earth's past and she was about to enter.

Michael unloaded the excavating, paleontological, and photographic tools, while the others began searching the glacier. There was a chance of light snow or an ice storm overnight.

When Peter tapped him on the shoulder, he turned and froze.

In a fuzzy shadowy blur, beyond the ice, grime, and time, was the unmistakable outline of a woolly mammoth lying on its side. Even in death and separated by pack ice, it was an imposing figure. Peter fumbled for the propane torch and began melting away sections of the snow and ice to clear up the picture. Sarah picked up a second torch and they continued in this manner for some minutes until the remaining ice, less thick and dirty, framed a picture straight into this perfectly preserved icy tomb.

"Michael, get the tools out first so we can make some progress before the temperature falls. Then while Sarah and I are working to expose the animals, you can set up camp."

"Not a problem. Can I bring you a cappuccino before I get started?"

Michael almost immediately regretted the words. Peter was a pompous aristocrat, but Michael had to figure out a way to coexist with him a while longer. "Peter? I, ummm, regret the accusation on the ship. I was jumping to conclusions without all of the facts. It was unprofessional."

"It wasn't only unprofessional, it was highly circumstantial, Michael. But, I think I am equally guilty. You bring a lot more to the table than your portfolio. Let's hope we get you some of the credit you deserve."

An odd comment coming from Peter. Was it that obvious? Michael shared Sarah's palpitations over the mammoth. He felt like he did the first time he saw his by-line on the front page.

Sarah had melted a one-and-one-half-meter outline around the torso of the animal, from about head high, down to her knees. Michael had started the cooking stove and brought over hot drinks. He checked the video and then started asking informational questions on camera.

"So, what are we doing here?" he asked Barber.

Absorbed in his work, Barber looked up incredulous and straight into the camera. He immediately recovered and assumed his professorial demeanor. "We have identified what we expect to be a woolly mammoth species buried in the side of this glacier. It appears to be in excellent condition, and while we would like to remove it in one piece, our capacity to transport such a large creature is limited. So, we are going to attempt to remotely retrieve some samples from the fossil, if indeed that's what it is, and conduct further research and analysis back in our lab."

"What do you mean, 'if indeed that's what it is,' Professor?"

"Well, that's a good question, Michael. You will be getting extra class participation points. A fossil is the remains or impression of a pre-historic plant or animal embedded in rock and preserved in petrified form. This is more like cryogenic preservation. The Antarctic climate seems to have preserved this body in its approximate condition at the time of death.

"We believed we knew quite a bit about these animals, but finding them this far from what we thought was their sole natural habitat in the northern hemisphere raises enormous questions that might be answered because of this specimen's condition. We might also learn what type of cataclysmic event resulted in these animals dying on their feet."

"Dr. Barber, do we even know that they are dead? You mentioned cryogenic preservation."

Now Peter looked really pleased. "No, we don't know if they're dead. We just assume that because there is no evidence that you can freeze mammals alive at this temperature and then resuscitate them ten thousand years later. But it does make for a good science fiction movie premise." He added pedantically, "Animal cells explode at this temperature."

Sarah had been blurry background motion and now walked fully into focus. She had been melting ice with the torch, so perspiration had left a moist sheen on her face. Her parka was slightly unzipped. She appeared oblivious to the chatter and the cameras. At least the boys were learning to behave symbiotically.

"I've set some small test charges around the perimeter of the hole and wired the detonators together. We are ready to blast here."

Michael turned his attention to his cousin. "Sarah, what sub-species do we think we have here?"

"We don't know really. We know four subspecies of woolly mammoths walked the earth up to about four thousand years ago. This may be a fifth. It may not have lived contemporaneously with the others, but could be an ancestor, a descendent, or some earlier branch off of the evolutionary line altogether. Through carbon dating of the tissues, we would hope to determine approximately when this animal lived and its age at death.

"Dr. Barber alludes to several more fascinating questions. How did this animal get here? None of this genus ever lived south of the equator and there is a lot of hot weather to hike through to get here from Siberia to which all of the other sub-species were indigenous. This is like finding a penguin colony living at the North Pole. It would seem impossible.

"Finally, how did we even come to find these woolly mammoths? These creatures were buried between hundreds of feet of snow, soil, and silt. What caused them to suddenly be exposed to the greedy eyes of humanity? Was it global warming or some sort of tectonic upheaval?"

Peter motioned them behind the protection of a small outcropping for the blast. The small puff of ice and dust sheared away a footlocker-thick slab of ice. The picture window into the life and death of the mammoth became a bit clearer.

The work became more delicate as they chipped closer to the mammoth's protective tomb. Michael suggested that they lay a heating wire inside the waist-high ledge created by the blast and let it slice through a section of ice down to the ground. Then they could connect the cut away block of ice to the back of the snowmobile and extract the whole chunk.

While the heat did its work, they finished setting up camp and checked in with the *Sea Coral*.

Several hours later, they had a large refrigerator-sized opening into the glacier. Seven or more meters of packed snow, ice and dirt stood over their heads. As best as they could guess, they were still more than a meter away from the mammoths, although it now appeared to be only one mammoth and some other animal in the background. The roof of the ice vestibule could come crashing down on them without warning, so they took turns working within the cramped quarters.

With the reverberations of a small explosion, the ice creaked like a submarine crushed by water pressure at the sea bottom. A crack spread quickly from one of the inside corners of their ice cave toward the mammoth. The roof splintered and sprayed onto their heads. The crack stabilized. They exhaled.

Sparks received a return call for the captain from the Executive Vice President of the Environmental Defense Quest. Like Quicksilver, John Newlanding was of mostly Native North American descent. The two men had connected early in their careers. They were part of a large number of Native Americans working within or on the periphery of the system, proselytizing the Native American's view of the symbiotic relationship with Mother Earth.

Quicksilver took the call in his naked cabin. It was an incongruous act for a man that was never secretive, though his explanations were usually limited to a few sparse words.

Back on the bridge, he extracted a rarely used, personally carved rosewood pipe from the recesses of his hooded parka and wandered the main deck for some time, blowing smoke sculptures of birds that took flight or dissipated into the Antarctic air.

Newlanding had confirmed Quicksilver's suspicions. While there *was* an EDQ science expedition to Antarctica last summer, there was no Sarah on that or any EDQ boat down south last summer.

However, Sarah Baskin was a small donor and member of the Environmental Defense Quest. She did appear in their database as having requested information to support her research from time to time. He had the right woman.

"It's like these volunteers are joining the French Foreign Legion. The interviewer writes, 'Likes the environment. Hates multinational fishing industry. Enjoys water. Swam with dolphins. Will work for food. Hired.' It's free labor in exchange for anonymity.

"If she hasn't been here before, then why create such an incredible story to get here? Why cover up the source? Maybe Michael is the one hiding something."

"Great imagination, Ralph. Try again."

With Ralph talking to himself, Ace had approached undetected. He had sailed with Ralph dozens of times stretching back to Ralph's commercial shipping days and Ralph's Ozark mountains deck hand turned first officer knew his commanding officer well.

Ralph reddened slightly and walked aft as quickly as he could. *No*, he mumbled to himself, *Barber says they are standing in front of a woolly mammoth. He is definitely the love-lost fool thinking with his dick, who has let his heart and his crotch tell his brain what to do. I've checked his credentials, at least the professional ones. Maybe they're planning an unfortunate accident for him right after they finish their work. No, they're not killers. And they will get more mileage out of flanking Peter at the press conferences or reporting his story than they would if they took all of the credit in tribute to Peter's memory. Besides, this is only peripherally in Sarah's or Michael's professional field, if you believe what they said about their fields of expertise.*

His conversation with himself continued. *They knew about these woolly mammoths somehow and someone has been here before and seen them, even if it was aliens visiting from another planet.* He pulled off the grimy Arizona Diamondbacks cap, tightened the rubber band on his salt and pepper ponytail, and replaced it.

Ralph sat down on a built-in rusted metal bench running alongside the diesel exhaust stack. The bare steel was cold on his ass. *Michael and Sarah have the same knowledge. Why would they hide that? Did Michael have an informant that he's trying to protect by giving Sarah credit for the discovery? No, it has to be something more obvious.*

What's the crime? A couple of frauds make a big discovery. If they have stolen someone's thunder, when the word gets out, that person will probably yell foul, and the lawyers will get involved.

At least he was sure of a couple of things. They didn't steal anything from Seapeace or the EDQ and Barber was getting more than he deserved, on all fronts. And the discovery was real, so Seapeace was coming out way ahead.

Ralph had given himself a colossal headache. If he was still drinking, he would have taken a couple right now, but eco-command and drinking didn't mix. The captain's thoughts were involuntarily refocused on his duties by a distant bolt of lightning electrifying a dull grey sky, followed seconds later by an explosion of thunder that shook the ship. The tranquil sea had ended.

Sarah, Michael, and Peter felt the rumble of thunder under their feet, as well. Was the ice cracking again or were their runaway imaginations kicking into higher gear? They unconsciously quickened their pace. They were now within a couple of feet of the woolly mammoth, when Sarah abruptly grabbed the drill from Peter's hands.

"We can't get any closer, guys!"

"Why not?" Peter asked.

Hands on her hips like a six-year-old, she lectured them. "We aren't just uncovering the story of the woolly mammoths and their extinction. This is the pristine condition of the planet's atmosphere ten, maybe twenty thousand years ago. The air and the foliage were instantaneously frozen. If you want to find out why this mammoth was intact, you have to bring it back the way you found it, in the ice."

Peter was a paleontologist, not an environmentalist. The condition of the air and the water five thousand or twenty million years ago was intriguing, but not on his radar screen. It would only get in the way of his work.

"Sarah, this ice could have collected in layers over thousands of years. It could be a result of an avalanche. The discovery here is the woolly mammoth." Without warning, he transformed to a cornered pit bull. "That, you conniving bitch, is how you got me down here, and before I freeze my ass off tonight, I am going to get to this thing."

Michael had moved inside their little ice box with his digital camera to get some pictures. With the help of multiple refractory filters, the shadows behind the hairy mammal finally began to come into focus. For Peter and Sarah, so had each other's motives.

"Hey! Conniving bitch and Peter, come here quickly! It just got more interesting." The three squatted precariously within the opening. As they did, the sky lit up again, followed almost immediately by an even larger crash that bounced them off of the walls of their tomb. Michael rubbed the bottom left corner of the ice window quickly, until his body heat and friction had melted it smooth.

"Before a cave-in kills us all, I am going out. Get down on your hands and knees and look beyond the mammoth's right front foreleg and tell me what you see." Sarah squatted and stared for a long time and said nothing. Then she backed away to let Peter in. He tilted his head at all different angles and kept polishing the window with his hand. Finally, he pressed his nose and forehand right up against the ice.

"Oh, my Lord! It's a man!"

"Typical sexist pig comment. No, it's a human. We have no idea whether it's a man or a woman. No, no. I'm sorry. You probably know. If it was a woman, you'd have an erection by now."

Another crunch of cracking ice silenced them quickly. They were enervated.

Sarah said, "Bright ideas, Professor?"

Peter was blubbering. "We need samples. We need to carefully remove the specimen. We need pictures…"

"We need more supplies, more people, and a couple of more months of summer," Michael interrupted. "We don't have those, so let's do the best we can and return next year with a larger research team."

"When does winter start here, anyway?"

"In about two weeks. Autumn's tomorrow and maybe the day after."

"All right, boys. Here is what we are going to do. We are going to melt the ice down to get the best pictures that we possibly can. Then we will core drill the remaining distance to the woolly mammoth and the human, so we can get some body samples. We'll do it when the temperature is falling, so that as soon as we get our samples we can fill in the hole with water to minimize foreign contamination. Either way, Michael will try to get the best pictures that he can and then we are out of here tomorrow."

Outnumbered, Peter acquiesced.

They worked through the night and well into the next morning before Michael was forced to prepare for their departure. Sarah continued tenaciously. Lacking the stamina of his younger partners, Peter conceded his body a few hours of rest in the tent.

Sarah went into the tent to wake Peter. He snored like an unoiled chain saw. She shook him slightly, but there was no response. She saw his toiletries kit open next to him with a prescription bottle slightly exposed.

She quietly plucked the bottle out of the bag. It made no sound because it was empty.

"Ativan?" She whispered to herself.

She replaced the bottle and went out of the tent to grab Michael to help her wake Barber.

As Michael followed, he said, "I don't know what's more unstable, that block of ice or our expert. Either one of them could crack at any moment." Sarah said nothing.

Sarah woke Peter who gazed at them glassy-eyed. Michael said, "We couldn't sample the human, but there is a small chance that we can tell you what the sex is, Peter."

Michael pulled out his camera. "Fiber optic lens. We drilled all the way across the mammoth's body and took pictures as we went. We think we got as far as the human. When we can get these pictures on a bigger screen, we might be able to make out the body of the human and the mammoth's mammary glands, if it has any."

They broke camp almost twelve hours past their departure window. The Aurora and the deteriorating weather crackled static in their headsets. Peter was ashen-faced and lethargic, so Sarah and Michael drove. After a four-hour roller coaster ride, they pitched their tents just below the pass, protected from the wind and the elements. Unfortunately, though, there was no satellite reception.

While the sun hovered near the horizon, the icy glaze became a house of mirrors, with lightning continuing to reflect back and forth into oblivion, casting prehistoric shadows in every direction.

Sarah slept between the two men. Only Michael seemed to nod off quickly. Sarah lay wide-eyed in her bag, listening to the stillness.

Occasionally the lightning would bathe everyone in the eerie purplish hue of the tent and the hills would glow with life. As she finally dozed off, a particularly loud crack jolted her and her heart pounded. She wriggled closer to Peter. For comfort or to keep track of him? When the next crack came, his eyes sprung open as well and, even in the sub-freezing temperatures, sweat beaded on Peter's brow.

"You ever experience this before, Sarah?" His whispers were punctuated by shallow gasps for breath.

"When?"

"During your last trip here, dearie."

Sarah's head bounced on his thumping chest. "No, but even if I had, I don't think I'd be any less afraid. Aren't you worried?"

"I've survived some rougher spots than this over the years, but I guess I'm still a coward."

Sarah was thankful for the uncharacteristically honest display of emotion. She drew closer and drifted off to sleep.

Peter smiled silently in his bag.

Michael woke up fully refreshed. He bounced to his feet and immediately set about packing up. Bedraggled Peter said, "Michael, how the hell could you sleep through that?"

"In college, there were nights when my roommate's stereo was so loud that they would call us from the building across the quad to turn it off. And you know what? I didn't hear that phone ring at four am, either. Anyway, what's the difference? Sarah will wake up if she hears a bud burst. She'll let me know if there's a problem."

They emerged from the tent into the gloom of the new day. The sky was heavily overcast and the wind had died down. The absolute stillness between the growing rolls of thunder and the spine-tingling cracks of lightning strikes against the mountain ice was most ominous. There was no jet traffic overhead, no whoosh of the air conditioner, no rattle of the dishwasher and the animals had taken all of their voices with them—and disappeared.

As they started to pack up, Michael pointed back toward their earlier campsite near the mammoth's entombment. "Is it my imagination, or is that mountain moving?" A crack was growing along its side.

"I think we are headed for a landslide," Peter said. They abandoned the tents and raced the snowmobiles toward the base camp bouncing precariously with each rupture of the rock and ice seam.

The wood-splitting sound of shearing ice was a commonplace occurrence near the glacial coasts, like the taxi horn in midtown Manhattan. But this was something much more foreboding.

As they came into view of the shore, the rapid concussing of mortar blasts shook the ground, tossing the snowmobiles like tricycles. Peter, an Army Reserve veteran, yelled over the cannon fire into his headset. "This is no landslide."

Peter was staring at the glacier behind. As Michael and Sarah raced the snowmobiles to the boat, penguins and Weddell seals fled the shoreline for higher ground. Sarah screamed back, "Avalanche?"

Michael shot back, "Couldn't be. An avalanche is instantaneous. It would either reach critical mass or die off quickly. This is more like a developing hurricane!"

The roar and shaking subsided just a bit. Peter stared behind them and now turned and spoke a bit more calmly. "Our glacier is calving."

Michael couldn't see Peter. But he saw the quizzical look in Sarah's eyes. She shouted into the headset, "Calving? You mean like making little baby glaciers and shearing off into the sea?"

"I'm afraid so."

Motioning to each other, Sarah and Michael pulled their snowmobiles to a stop under the cover of a nearby outcropping. As the ledge above them began to disintegrate, they quickly pulled the snowmobiles out to open ground to avoid being buried alive. Unable to control the vehicles against the seismic vibrations, they abandoned them and ran in the direction of the boat and their tent, still over two kilometers away.

Sarah knew that over the years of evolution, humans had lost much of their instinct for dealing with natural disasters.

"Follow the animals." She redirected her companions away from both the glacier and the beach and to higher ground. At what seemed like a safe elevation, they stopped to catch their breath. Michael extracted the portable digital video from his parka and started shooting. An early twentieth-century vessel, long shipwrecked near the foot of the crack, disappeared into the growing abyss. A digestive crunch quickly followed.

The crack forming at the top of the glacier they had been excavating just a day before now began to widen quickly toward the bottom and the new iceberg peeled like a banana from the hillside.

They were like new parents experiencing their first childbirth. In slow motion, the iceberg calf slid down the mountain and crashed into the sea below. First came the whooshing and sucking sound as gravity pulled the iceberg underwater and it bobbed quickly to the surface. White-breasted majestic cape petrels, with wingspans of nearly a meter in length, skuas and horny-beaked giant petrels, usually found in more tropical waters all frantically soared toward higher elevations, in a turmoil of stray feathers and down, as the wind, ice and dust particles kicked up into the sky from a geologic cataclysm rivaling its meteorologic cousin in the Sahara.

"There goes our next clue," said Michael.

Now awareness dawned. Sarah said, "We've got bigger worries. A tsunami's coming."

Peter nodded while Michael looked around feverishly. "We are not high enough. We'll be swept away."

It was nearly a sixty-degree ascent on the icy ocean-sprayed rocks. Weakly rooted bushes and insubstantial footholds was all they had to grip as they raced to stay ahead of the soon-to-be rising water. Sarah pointed up about twelve meters.

"There seems to be a ledge there that looks large enough to hold us all. If we can reach it, we should be safe and," she added wryly, "Michael can get a good camera angle."

Michael motioned off to the left some five or ten meters. He shouted over the surf, "There's an animal path."

Sun and wind-burned, they safely made their way to the outcropping up the mountainside.

A wall of water nearly twenty meters high rose up from the sea. Because of the narrowness of the calf from side to side, the angle of the fall toward the Weddell Sea and the steep slope of the sea's floor, the wall of water was barely thirty meters wide and moved almost parallel to the shoreline rather than crashing into it with maximum destructive force.

Even at an oblique angle, the tsunami climbed the shore, broke a hundred meters inland, and in one great crush, their base camp was annihilated and swept out to sea.

The boat, which had been pulled up to the shore and anchored securely into the sand and frozen soil beneath it, was like a kite freed from a child's hands by a sudden gust of wind. It surfed the crest until it was deposited by the breaking wave a kilometer down the shoreline. Then the wave continued out to sea, taking their tent and supplies with it. One of the snowmobiles survived, but the other was swept away in the torrent, bobbed on the surface momentarily, and then was crushed and buried under the second wave of ice and snow.

The backside of the wave foamed like a rabid animal. It was not the brown, acrid suds that stagnated around factory discharges, but delicate white-on-green fluff bubbles that camouflaged its destructive power. The water crested just below their sanctuary, loosening rocks around the opening and making their perch more unstable as water lapped at the entrance before receding quickly.

Out to sea, Ace and Sparks listened and watched with increasing anxiety. Both were old hands at childbirth.

Until now, they had been right on time for their rendezvous. Through powerful binoculars, the captain could see that the three had not yet returned to the base camp. He wasn't surprised. And knowing the problems with communications, he wasn't concerned about the lack of contact. He was concerned about survival, theirs and his.

The captain remained stoic. He gave orders to put back out to sea at full speed, which would put him a half day behind schedule. A number of the deck hands kept watch at the stern. Even for those that had made the trip a number of times before, viewing the calving of a glacier was a rare event to be viewed strictly as a spectator sport.

"Where ya' think they are, Ralph?" Ace asked.

"Wherever they are, they've got a good view. I'm guessing that they're pretty far inland, maybe at the pass because they missed the call-in and got so far behind schedule. We'll wait it out."

Every few minutes, Michael's journalistic curiosity would overcome his fears and he would move to the edge of the ledge where he had the best view. Mortal danger was an acceptable business risk for reporting a front-page exclusive, particularly when there was no way to avoid it.

For Peter, the water rising to consume him was the fulfillment of a statistical certainty. You go on enough expeditions and eventually the risks catch up with you. The same was also true of adultery. He wondered what the gossip columns would say. For a fleeting moment he considered throwing himself from the cliff and ending the speculation.

Sarah was the only imperturbable one in the bunch, because she knew that their presence here wasn't her idea. MC would not have sent them here if *It* could not protect them. Right now, she had to believe like she had never believed anything else in her life. If M'low Cloom wasn't real, they were dead.

In the water wall's rearview mirror, it pulled with it the tidal swell, the way waves recede back into the ocean, washing ashore driftwood, animal carcasses, and pieces of ancient wreckage from ill-founded voyages.

They had lost all track of time. The waters returned to their monotonous drumming and a few of the penguins and seals made a cautious return, listening rather than talking.

The path was washed away, leaving an impassable clutter of wet rocks, ice and sand. Rappelling made the most sense, but they lacked both equipment and skill.

In the distance they spotted the remains of the one snowmobile. Whatever it contained was all they had left. Their satellite phones were there and if they worked, they might be saved, if the *Sea Coral* had survived.

Peter said, "A real estate developer friend of mine said you always need an exit strategy. I wonder if he would have been thinking of that on the way up here."

"What goes up, must come down." Sarah pointed up the still dry hillside above them to the remains of the animal path. "It's got to lead somewhere."

Michael said, "Yeah, to the South Pole."

"We could slide down on our asses."

"Peter, I like my ass and I know how fond you are of Sarah's. You do it." Normally, she would have kicked her cousin in the balls after a remark like that in front of someone else, but right now it was the perfect tonic.

Ace and the captain had watched the wave inundate the rendezvous point and then head out to sea. Ralph knew that swells and generally unpredictable surf followed a tsunami and the attendant surge. Under other circumstances, the old sea hands would rapturously watch Mother Nature assert her control over mankind. He waited another four hours for massive riptides to pass before he returned to shore. Sparks continued unsuccessfully to raise the three on their phone.

Ralph walked around the deck, again talking to himself, with Ace trailing inconspicuously behind, amused. "They're not only liars, they're idiots. I wonder if they had the sense to reach higher ground? No, no, perhaps they thought that if they took their boat out into the water they could go around the wave. More likely, they just lost or forgot their phone and the batteries went dead and then they drowned.

"Now, the selfish bastards will distract from *my* day of paleontological fame by getting themselves killed." At some point, Ralph realized that he would have to radio back to his base to explain the situation. But not yet.

"You're not worried, are you, Ralph?" Ace asked innocently.

"Huh? Oh no, Ace. It's those idiots."

"But, they found the woolly mammoths, didn't they Ralph?"

Ralph looked askance and then nodded, his eyes brightening. It was impossible to keep secrets aboard a ship of this size. "Yeah, they found them. But they're probably at the bottom of the sea with them after this."

They had hiked up the narrowing path for over an hour and a half, making the drop-off seaward increasingly hazardous. Peter's lips had begun to turn purple.

Sarah said, "We don't want to be here when the temperature drops again. I think we ought to risk climbing down." The slope was still more than fifty degrees. Anything short of a smooth ride and gentle landing would put Peter into shock.

Michael said, "You want me to go up ahead while you rest?"

"Yeah, go around the bend and see if it gets worse or better. We need to make a decision soon." Sarah sat Peter down and put her arm around him.

Michael was gone for less than a half hour and when he returned his despondent look told the whole story. Peter was asleep with his head in Sarah's lap.

"The path goes on for probably four or five kilometers, at least."

"And then what? He can't make that hike."

"Well, just up ahead it becomes a gentle decline all the way back to the sea, so if we have to, we'll just roll him back to the shore."

"Who would go out with you?"

"Who would go to Uzbekistan and Antarctica with you?"

They reached the shore and the snowmobile late in the afternoon. From there they could see their capsized boat sticking out from behind some rocks several hundred meters away. The radio and the phone were dead, but dry.

One of the sleeping bags had survived in a watertight pouch lashed to the snowmobile. They wrapped Peter in it. He sat up and watched Sarah work. Even though it was cloudy, Sarah set up the one workable PV panel.

"Is this a priority?" Peter asked.

"This will only take five minutes and it's going to get sunny eventually. The sooner we get electricity, the better." He obviously was feeling well enough to second-guess her. "You and Michael want to see what other provisions we have left?"

They collected small amounts of driftwood and old wreckage and using a remaining Sterno container as an igniter, quickly had a wet, smoky fire going.

"Sarah, don't talk to me about the hole in the ozone layer over Antarctica right now. I don't want to hear it."

The men plucked the surviving supplies from the snowmobile, and then Sarah insisted Peter stay by the fire and attempt to heat some of their remaining food while Michael and she headed to the boat. He agreed without protest.

The boat's bow had snagged on some rocks, which kept it from being pulled back to sea. Sarah slithered underneath and found that some of the still attached supplies were intact, their waterproof covering secure.

They were almost a kilometer from Peter, yet they could easily see the smoke rising from the fire. They walked past a chunk of ice that had been left by the receding swell. It was nearly the size of a FedEx delivery truck.

Sarah passed into its shadow and screamed for her cousin. "Michael! Oh my God, quick, you've got to see this. I don't believe it. It's our woolly mammoth, with a spear hanging over its ear. It's huge; it's intact. We're taking it back."

Michael had been lagging behind and now came racing along Sarah's side. His lucky video camera was rolling in no time. And there it was. The water had washed away some of the thousands of years of dirt that was layer-caked into the ice with each passing season and climatological event. This view displayed an erect mammoth as seen from overhead and suspended above its right ear was a long black spear with a crudely sharpened stone tip of some sort. Human-like fingers grasped the spear's shaft and the arm led to a barely visible human which, from this view, appeared to be lying under the animal's belly, meaning the ice block was rotated ninety degrees from the way they found it.

"Sarah," Michael said, as he was filming, "You know, of course, that we are filthy rich. We will make millions on the interviews, millions on the book and movie rights. We'll write the book, the screenplay, we'll get to be the executive producers, we'll..."

He was cut off by an elbow to the mid-section. "That's enough, Jacques Cousteau. Your video camera is picking up all that audio. Are you forgetting how we came to be here? And how do you think we will get this two hundred metric ton ice sarcophagus out to sea, onto the boat and back to civilization still frozen? We are several hundred meters from the shore and we don't know if we even have a boat to hail, Mary."

"I'm not the one who just announced we are taking it back, you moron!" As if to make a point, he pushed heavily at the block of ice. It went nowhere.

They tied a coil of rope they found with the boat to a large rock and heaved the rock over the ice block to the other side. Sarah grabbed the rope and with Michael holding on at the opposite side, she scaled the ice tomb and Michael threw her a flare gun and a couple of flares salvaged from the boat, along with his camera. She pointed the flare gun in the air to shoot.

"Wait. Don't fire yet. Do you see any other clues to our next MC destination?"

She quickly scanned the ghostly images underneath her. "Nothing, but even from here there's a lot that's obscured."

She looked up from her perch and saw Peter limping over. "Peter's coming."

"Well, shoot the flare then."

She pointed the flare gun into the sky and said, "Don't worry, I am not leaving this mammoth's side until we find our next clue."

"I see you've stumbled across our discovery. What were you doing, signaling the *Sea Coral* so that you could make a quick rendezvous and leave me for dead and frozen?"

Michael said, "Peter, if we wanted you dead and frozen, you fuckin' idiot, we would have killed you in your sleep or shoved you off the ledge into the oncoming tsunami. As horrible as this sounds, you and your credibility are worth more to us alive than splitting the proceeds two ways. I did an Internet search when Sarah suggested you lead this team. And you know what I found? You've never had to share the limelight before. This is an entirely new experience for you."

The smoke from Peter's fire was picked up by the Sea Coral as they steamed back to their rendezvous. Captain Quicksilver grabbed the binoculars and surveyed the scene. He could make out a small figure moving near the burning campfire.

Sparks and Ace flanked him, waiting for orders.

"Well," he said, "at least one of them is all right, but where are the others?"

He scanned around the campfire. Ace was squinting toward the shore-line and he could make out a massive object reflected in the sun, just short of the tidal line. When Sarah popped the flare, Ace and Sparks' sharper eyes saw it, but it was missed in Quicksilver's binocular view.

"Ralph, someone just shot a flare off of a mass of ice on the shoreline."

Quicksilver redirected his sights. "I think it's Sarah! She's on top of that mound. Ace, send a boat out after them. Sparks, try to get them on the satellite phone or those walkie talkies."

Michael realized that one walkie talkie was worthless between them, but for ship-to-shore, it might have value, if only the *Sea Coral* was monitoring it. He found Sparks on the emergency frequency.

"Everyone's fine. Just a little cold and wet, Sparks."

"We saw the flare, Michael, and thought we could make out Sarah standing on top of that slab of ice."

"That's no slab."

"It's not?"

"It's a new mascot. Let's first figure out how to rendezvous and then I'll explain." Michael knew that his cousin would definitely have taken the agenda in a different order.

"Ace and a couple of other guys are leaving in about five minutes in the other boat. They'll head toward the flare shot."

"Thanks. That's great. Some of our gear survived higher up the mountainside. We'll retrieve it and meet you. Can you get Ralph, Sparks?"

"Sure. Michael, we're glad you're fine, regardless of what Ralph says," she glared.

"Ralph, you know that slab of ice that Sarah is standing on?"

"Yeah?" He grunted.

"There's a woolly mammoth in there that's waiting to get out and Sarah's keeping it prisoner."

"What?"

"She says there's ten or fifteen thousand years of environmental and evolutionary history locked in that ice and she wants to bring it back that way. I don't see how, though."

Ralph was confused. "You brought the mammoth with you in the ice?"

"No, no Ralph. Well, not exactly. The calving glacier and the tsunami deposited the ice tomb containing the woolly mammoth on our doorstep. We just want to take it home and adopt it."

"Unbelievable. How are we going to do that, particularly the way Sarah wants to do it?"

"I'm just a reporter. Although this is going to make a great sidebar to the story. You and my cousin are the environmental geeks. You figure it out."

"And as a bonus, you survived. We'll call you back on this in a couple of minutes. I want to make some phone calls."

They didn't have a lot of time. A cold front was coming in and the ceiling would be dropping shortly after that. The forecast called for snow in the next forty-eight hours. It was going to be dangerous because they could lose the mammoth entirely, but there were few alternatives. The ice block would eventually melt sitting on the shore in the summer and then treasure hunters or carnivorous predators would be on the first meat that peeked out from the ice.

They had to be ready by the next high tide, about seven hours away. Under Ace and Michael's direction, the crew lashed and grappled hooks to the block of ice, and connected them with cables back to a small power-boat with Ace at the helm. They connected another, somewhat longer line between the damaged, but still seaworthy skiff and winching motors on the *Sea Coral*. When the tide was all the way in, Ralph brought the *Sea Coral* to within a meter of beaching her. Then he towed the righted skiff back out to the water, running the *Sea Coral*'s engines in reverse, rather than using the winching lines, so as not to beach the big ship.

They aligned the skiff between the *Sea Coral* at sea and the block of ice on land. Next, they transferred the grappling line holding the mammoth from Ace's craft through rings sitting atop rods aligned lengthwise over the formerly beached skiff and then the *Sea Coral* pulled the mammoth ice block back into the water. Once it was completely afloat, the *Sea Coral* towed the mammoth and the skiff out to sea while the skiff dropped its bow door and revved its engine to maneuver the craft toward the mammoth. The skiff went toward the mammoth while the *Sea Coral* pulled the mammoth back into the open bow doors of the skiff. It fit like a square peg in a square hole. They towed their prize toward Cape Horn where it met up with a waiting pair of Huey helicopters and a refrigerated C-130 transport back to the States.

CHAPTER 10
Conflicting Agendas

The *Chronicle* had first exclusive rights to report the story and the right to reprint or excerpt the article from whatever science journal published it. The tsunami, the near death of the team and rumors of extra-marital affairs made movie rights and a best-selling book a distinct possibility. The involvement of an animal and environmental vigilante group added further to the intrigue. Neil would have to go back and reread his contract.

Anything that took place on a Seapeace ship was Seapeace's intellectual property, and the skiff was part of the ship. It would take the soon-to-be arriving attorneys years to sort out who owned what.

A press conference was scheduled for eleven o'clock the second morning back, to coincide with the evening news back in the States. Michael's paper had put them up in the George Christchurch, one of the most opulent hotels in all of the South Pacific.

The Ship's Master had scheduled an early breakfast with the discoverers hours before the circus was set to begin.

"Congratulations, Sarah and Michael, your success has secured the silence of anyone, including Seapeace, who might want to expose your subterfuge."

Peter nodded vigorously.

"In deference to those of us who know the truth, I thought we might come to an understanding."

Sarah and Michael exchanged hooded looks.

"Yes, now we are getting to my agenda," he said, as if reading their minds. "But, I promise that it will catapult your careers.

"If woolly mammoths lived in Antarctica, what else is hidden there? How do we know that those prehistoric humans are extinct? They could be living underground with an ice roof over their heads letting the sun in six months of the year. If we found them, we'd probably put them on a reservation or breed them as subhuman slaves. Sorry, I'm digressing. Convert your credibility into some hard research funding and do some genuine good with it. Sarah made the prescient observation that Seapeace might get some positive press for a change. We may even see a pop in donations."

His coal-black eyes penetrated Michael. "Award-winning investigative journalism requires that you ask the right questions to start with." Quicksilver was a good judge of character and he had done some research on Peter and Michael. He knew where Michael was vulnerable. Peter was irreparably corrupted, but he had one weakness, and she was sitting next to him.

"Mankind will destroy the scientific evidence of life's origins dating back millions of years, while spending millions to preserve a four-hundred-year-old building." They smiled at him. He smiled, too. "Humans. Sorry, digressing again. You either need to bring these bigger issues to the forefront at the press conference, or I will ask how you became aware of these iced carcasses. Sarah, I know that you were never in the Antarctic with the Environmental Defense Quest and Michael and you are co-conspirators. If you were with the EDQ when you found this mammoth, then they'd have a decent legal claim on this whole sordid affair, and I haven't heard from them yet."

There was no longer a question that Ralph would be in grave danger from MC if he attempted to follow the trail back to Uzbekistan.

Peter's blue eyes peeked through narrow slits, and he rhythmically clenched and relaxed his right fist. He unclenched out of cadence and said, "Michael, you had a major role in our success and our survival. At the press conference, I would appreciate it if you would speak to some of the points that Ralph has made."

Michael had been focusing on the all-you-can-eat breakfast buffet. He was sympathetic to the arguments, but left the passion to his cousin. It was just entertainment, so far. "What? Me?"

"Michael, the role of the press is changing as they occasionally become part of the news, but you can still report on this objectively. You're the least controversial person here. Hell, you can even show off your war wounds."

"What about Sarah? This is her discovery."

"Exactly. If she does nothing, she gets most of the credit. Right now, all you get is a by-line. That doesn't seem adequate, does it?"

The press conference rambled. Peter controlled much of the question and answer period. He was experienced at this sort of thing, he was the expedition's expert, he was articulate, and he was in his element. He drew Michael in early and gave him full credit for initially spotting the prehistoric human and brought him to the podium when they got to the calving of the glacier. Thereafter, Michael needed no help. He took credit for moving them to higher ground and of course, their rescue and the rescue of the mammoth. Michael returned to his seat behind the moderator, the plump bespectacled curator of the local museum.

She asked, "Any more questions?"

As the curator surveyed the silent audience, the captain rose reluctantly from his seat near the back of the platform and moved unevenly toward the lectern. At first, it went unnoticed by the curator. Sarah saw him make his move and bolted to the podium to nonchalantly cut him off, almost body blocking Ralph to the floor. He paused awkwardly, retraced his steps, sat back down, and licked his suddenly dry lips.

The last thing on Sarah's mind when she walked up the gangplank three weeks ago was business suit attire for a press conference. Michael was in the same position, but for him it was simply a matter of getting his jeans washed and making Sarah pick out a turtleneck and blazer for him off the rack. At that, she had to coordinate the colors for him. She had planned on deferring the limelight to those with greater self-confidence and better oratory skills, but now, here she was in khakis and a funky one-piece Shetland wool top with a collar that tied in the front and hung down like a necktie. She froze in front of the camera, and all she could think of was, *I look like Annie Hall without the stupid hat.*

She began tentatively. "I would like to make a couple of closing remarks." They were also her introductory remarks. A palpable silence was broken by the soft whoosh of the room's air handler.

She explained that she had been on a trip to Antarctica the previous year as a guest of a group that wished to remain anonymous because this was not their field. At the time, she was unsure of what she had found but had resolved to find a way to return to Antarctica the next summer for further exploration. Seapeace had cooperated, and here she was.

"We have now found proof that man and higher order mammals either lived in or migrated to Antarctica in the last ten thousand years. The implications for the story of life on earth are enormous. Species long thought extinct on this planet have been flourishing tens of thousands of years after they were presumed to have died out and in places where we never even thought they existed. We know that other life forms have also survived in those very few unexploited and unexplored corners of the world. The coelacanth is perhaps the most prominent example in recent times.

"This is irrefutable evidence that we should look for other such hidden marvels in the world. A relative of the extinct woolly mammoth and of modern humans was entombed in the ice and went undiscovered for heaven knows how long. Why? First, it's hard to go looking for something that you never thought existed. And second, global warming, most directly affecting the ozone layer over Antarctica, has caused the protective ice around these precious windows into the past to melt. As more of our history is revealed, do not be surprised to find carnivores feasting on them before we find them, since those animals' habitats are rapidly being destroyed by human civilization. Once exposed to mankind's greed, we should expect the evidence to disappear into someone's private collection or some shark's belly.

"Some of those discoveries will be flourishing in hostile temperatures, pressures, and even fluids that in our narrow view of what supports life we would have thought impossible. Life-giving water and air may be poison to others. This adventure should prove that earth does not belong to man. We are simply its miserable stewards and whatever self-inflicted wounds we may wreak on our planet will probably one day lead to our own extinction."

As Sarah walked back to her seat, she noticed a slightly wrinkled Native American, grinning from ear to ear. This time it was worth the stage fright.

Peter had to leave town the day after the press conference to quell a domestic rebellion and begin his write-up. He ran into the captain in the hotel lobby as he was departing for the airport. "Captain, how do you suppose they found out about those woolly mammoths?"

"You're the one who's screwing the guide. Hasn't it ever come up in pillow talk?"

Peter confessed, "I didn't do a lot of checking before I agreed to this trip, and when I finally asked, I got double-talk. You got what you wanted at the press conference. I guess I'll just have to wait until I have a little more leverage before I ask again."

"Yeah, like that's going to happen."

"Sometimes the balance of power shifts in mysterious ways, Ralph."

CHAPTER 11
February 1, The Next Night

Sarah and Michael returned to the oil masterpieces and crystal chande-liers of the George Christchurch several hours before dawn. They had spent the evening celebrating with Kiwis and Aussies at a bar that charged twenty American dollars for local call drinks, but tonight they were celebri-ties and someone else was paying. Michael had his choice of women. Several attempted to move things into the direction of their hotel room, but Sarah interceded. The heavy petting and face-sucking on the dance floor with alternating women would not have looked good on the front page of the tabloids next to the frozen mammoth. Michael pouted the whole cab ride back to the hotel.

Sarah had originally planned on a quiet evening sampling New Zealand's world-renowned, grass-fed, open-range mutton. Under any circumstances it would have been a treat because she only had red meat three times a year. But there was something even more irresistible about these men with the beefy biceps, their "far corner of the globe" anonymity and earth tone accents. They were as gregarious as penguins. She thrilled to the light-hearted bump and grind, because after weeks at sea with Peter Barber, she needed some release from the predatory sexual possessiveness. On the other hand, if some racy pictures made it back on the internet, it would be an easy, albeit cowardly way to end their relationship. She wasn't ready to inflict that kind of pain.

They sat in the lobby, waiting for the roller coaster ride in their heads to end.

"So, Sarah, what shall we do next? Dive to the bottom of the Pacific and find the remains of a marine mammal that dwarfs the blue whale? You know deepwater fossils are the most impossible to retrieve and they preserve well in the depths of the ocean. I don't think we will need to beg for money anymore," Michael lowered his voice.

"And you won't have to seduce any more old men to secure the necessary credentials." Even in his drunken stupor, Michael immediately regretted the words.

"I am sorry. I didn't mean that."

"You did. You're incapable of lying when you're drunk. What choice did I have? I knew *you* weren't going to seduce anybody into fronting us sixty thousand dollars."

The lobby's silence was unbroken but for the gentle whip, whip of the ceiling fans. When Sarah glanced up, the hotel staff immediately became keenly interested in the wallpaper and the logo on the blank hotel stationery. "Let's go down to the beach."

As they approached the rental car, Sarah held her hand out. "I had three drinks hours ago, and you're still sloshing."

She parked at the edge of the public beach area. They slung their shoes into the Japanese SUV and bared their feet on the cool pearly sand. The deserted beach was decorated by strands of seaweed, pink and blue shells, and flopping and rotting fish. The gulls called out to each other over the gently lapping waves of the turquoise South Pacific. Each receding wave deposited sparkling sea foam, which glinted delicately in a moonlight bath until it was absorbed into the sand.

"Ready for the next step?"

"Pardon me?"

"You're not that drunk."

Michael said, "We have demonstrated the resourcefulness to lie our way onto a ship to Antarctica, deceive people into fronting nearly a hundred thousand dollars and putting their lives on the line, and we've emerged as celebrities. I deserve a break."

"Which one of us are you attempting to con? Next year, Peter Barber and all of the talk show hosts will be saying what have you done for me lately? Those hot-looking birds that were hitting on you tonight will again be treating you like the geek reporter that you are, and this will be just one for the scrapbooks. If we don't want people to believe that this is the 'immaculate deception,' we need a repeat performance."

Michael's dilated pupils peered from bloodshot eyes. "As always, you make much more sense than me. Did you know that I already had a call from an agent who wants to represent me to write a movie documentary on the undiscovered mysteries of the South Seas? They are lining up at our door."

"I don't want to put up with two Peters. God, I didn't want to put up with one. That press conference and that well-written, self-serving piece of journalistic puffery you filed sounded like Michael single-handedly discovered a prehistoric man and woolly mammoth, aided by his loyal assistants, Peter Barber and Sarah Baskin. Think about that for just a moment. You were ostensibly brought on this trip to chronicle a discovery and along the way, you became part of an adventure story. Who is going to give you any technical credit here? You were a scribe. You didn't dive into the icy waters of the Weddell Sea and pull out Sarah, Peter and prehistoric man and revive us. You are no more a hero than any of us is. You had no clue what that tsunami was going to do to us. At least Peter had some common sense."

"Yeah, he had enough common sense to recognize that I made a critical contribution, which is more than I can say for you. And he doesn't even know that I did all of your copyediting for him a couple of years ago. Maybe he should be our partner. Maybe he should be my partner."

"Michael, this isn't an ego game, and you certainly aren't the head coach. You don't get to decide who plays. This is reality. We do not want to get more people killed and we are running out of time. MC has a deadline."

"That's it. This is just a reality show. Sorry for the mixed metaphor." She knew how that stuff bothered him. "All the pieces of the scavenger hunt are there, but carefully hidden. And the head coach and the studio, in our case MC, is guaranteeing our safety. Our job is simply to find all of the pieces, take the credit and collect first prize. This was only the first piece. We have to rendezvous with MC, but first we have one more adventure. What do you remember?"

Michael seemed to be dozing off. Suddenly, he bolted upright and said, "What's M'low Cloom?"

"I don't think we know yet, Michael."

"I do. M'low Cloom is first prize. We find all of the pieces and we know who or what M'low Cloom is."

Patronizingly, "That's for your agenda. At least now we have the first piece."

"It's a warm sunny day in a cold wasteland. So, it's spring or summer. There's a huge damp, dark room, probably a cavern. In it, there is something that killed a lot of people, who in our visions were dressed like they were living in the Middle Ages. So, it was probably the fourteenth century. Maybe the black plague? It's mutated, disappeared and reinfected various parts of Europe in nearly every century, so I could be off on the timing."

Sarah continued with the images that were etched in her mind as well, just as they had been on the trip to Antarctica. She was recalling a repressed, vivid nightmare. "It's not just people. Animals, mostly unrecognizable marine mammals, are also infected. They're caught and eaten by the humans and other animals up the food chain. Somehow, maybe through insects, I don't know, the disease is transmitted to the human population."

"And then the sickness and disease stopped for some unexplainable reason, temporarily for the lighter skinned people, and permanently for the darker skinned people. There has to have been some explanation, either a developed immunity or the microbe mutated to some harmless form, right?"

"Right after that, MC tried to implant this confusing celestial roadmap. *It* could tell that it made no sense to us, so that's why I think *It* decided to put it in writing and bury it in Antarctica forcing us to go there."

"I wonder if *It* intended to do that at the outset."

"Probably not, but after sixty seconds in your head, *It* realized that you would have tried to skip step one and take the short cut to step two. Michael, think harder, think back to what *It* said and the images in our mind. We have to make this next trip in less than six weeks."

"Hold it right there, buddy girl, I think you and I are focusing on different things."

She looked puzzled.

"Remember how you convinced me that this trip would resuscitate my career? Well, based on one day's feedback, I would say you deserve a 'ten' for clairvoyance. And my greatest fear, that I would now be dead, has proven barely unfounded. But, what about my agenda? Who is M'low Cloom and how does *It* know about these organisms in a cave and humanoids in the ice? You care only about fitting well-hidden messages to your hypothesis that mankind's snuffing out evolution by replacing normal mutations with genetic engineering. But, what if there aren't any hidden messages? Global warming exposing unknown animals in the polar ice caps isn't news. It's not even a surprise."

Michael was beginning to sober up. They walked along the beach in silence, the ocean plain bathed in the long shimmering wash of the full moon. Even though the sand slid coolly through their toes, both had dug their heels in.

Michael stopped in his tracks and muttered something inaudible over the waves.

"What?"

"Remember in Uzbekistan when you said that we saw that mammoth through the eyes of a sentient being because it was communicating with MC?"

"Yeah?"

"Look at the clues on these first two quests. MC knew exactly where the woolly mammoth was. How? *It* sees things through people and maybe even animals, I don't know. Remember, MC didn't tell us that there was a humanoid hidden in the ice, just the mammoths. MC knew that the woolly mammoth was where it was because that primitive man knew where it was. The last sentient being that saw the comet saw it while it was still moving. That's why the next set of clues is so cryptic. *It* doesn't know where the remnants of the comet are either."

The sun was beginning to brighten the eastern sky and the stars slowly faded from view. The coming dawn woke the gulls and they dive-bombed for fish approaching the surface to feed.

Sarah leaned back with her hands behind her resting on the sand, her elbows locked straight, staring out into the ocean. "You think *It's* communicating with us in the same way as that human ancestor we discovered?"

"No way to know, really. But *It's* only sharing information with us from beings that are already dead. Maybe that's all *It* has. I think that's been going on for a long, long time when you recall some of the other things we've been seeing when we communicate with *It*."

"So, *It* can't see into the future."

"*It* can't even see into the present. You know, if you had the wisdom of ten million years, that would give you some good cosmic insight into how things might play out in the future under similar conditions because it probably already played out that way somewhere in the past. Even though it seems like history repeats itself, that's not the same as prognosticating."

"But, why did MC pick *us* to go on these quests?"

A couple of hours ago her cousin couldn't even navigate a curb.

"I don't know if it did. That reconnection of the DNA from both sides of our families has given us some genetic trait that permits us to communicate with M'low Cloom. In the first vision, our common ancestors' memories were part of MC, but maybe they never had the chance to communicate with *It*."

"And why now? Maybe that is the bigger question."

"Maybe *It* wasn't around here until now, but I have no idea where *It* goes when *It's* not around. Or, *It* may not have had any reason to communicate with us until now, which would make these quests even more significant."

"There's a third possibility. We may not have had the ability to communicate with *It* before now. You know some markers on the DNA code turn off or on as a person ages, like reaching puberty. We may not have reached telepathic puberty until recently."

Just then, Michael's cell phone rang. At first, neither of them made the connection. Sarah came back to reality first. "It's your phone, dear. I try not to carry mine 24/7."

Michael fished around in his back pocket. "Hello? Oh, hi, Aunt Sheryl." He grimaced at Sarah who returned the expression. "It's about five am, I think. She's standing right here. No, we weren't sleeping. We are actually walking along the beach. No, she doesn't have her cell phone. Yes, it's here with her. She just doesn't have it now. She could have used mine to call you when she got in, but she's just an irresponsible, selfish daughter who doesn't care how much you must be worrying about her. Hold on, I'll give her the phone as soon as she detaches herself from the young man she's with."

"Liar!" Sarah screamed, at the top of her voice.

"It's your mother. You don't call anymore because you're too famous. She saw the press conference on AOL news and wants to tell you that your tie was crooked."

CHAPTER 12

Apparently Apparel

Sarah's nightmare haunted her several nights a week. She woke curled in a fetal position with her fingers cold and blue. The tsunami had reached up to the rocks and plucked her and her two partners like rose petals, delivering them to the fathoms below. But her companions were not Michael and Peter.

When they went their separate ways after returning from New Zealand, they agreed to reconvene the day after they received the woolly mammoth analysis to review the results and see if it provided any further insight into the motives or identity of M'low Cloom. Sarah wanted them to start the research on the location of their second destination as soon as they returned, but they were unprepared for the overarching impact the publicity had on their lives.

Between the television interviews and the *National Geographic* documentary, the autobiography requests and Michael's prize-winning series on the most recent trip, it was nearly impossible to continue being an anonymous science reporter or graduate student. Michael's aspirations had finally become reality, and Sarah didn't want to impede his success, but they had a much more urgent agenda, and MC had proven to be very impatient.

Peter Barber called daily, alternating between a crazed lover and a mistrusting business partner. Unfortunately, the only one she could confide in about her MC and Peter nightmares was too distracted right now to care. In the three weeks since they returned from New Zealand, they had IMed once, on their birthday.

The evening after the preliminary woolly mammoth lab analysis came in, Sarah arrived unannounced on Michael's front doorstep. There was no answer, but Michael's security access code was a poorly kept secret. She found organic fruits and vegetables in the crisper, carob chip cookies in the pantry and free-range chicken in the fridge. Perhaps her cousin's diet was improving. She helped herself and began researching their second expedition. The Houston weather was already in the upper sixties, which was summer time compared to the wind chill near zero that she had just left in Chicago. She changed into skimpy shorts and a midriff t-shirt with the bottom six inches torn off. Michael would show up eventually.

Sometime after two in the morning, Michael and his boisterous retinue tromped down the hallway. Sarah waited inside the doorway. Michael opened the door and all conversation abruptly ceased. Sarah thrust out her hand and introduced herself to the group. The other male and the two women, both wearing too much eye shadow, ogled and glared respectively as she introduced herself.

"Hi, didn't Michael tell you I was coming here today? He probably forgot himself. I'm his cousin, Sarah Baskin."

Michael's friend, Headley, smiled broadly. His gaze immediately rested discreetly on the shadows lurking just beneath her clingy t-shirt. Headley's girlfriend grabbed his arm and pulled sharply.

After an awkward moment, Michael looked at his cousin and said, "Sarah, isn't there something else you can wear?"

Sarah looked at him sheepishly and grabbed a sweatshirt. "I am sorry. I was working at my laptop, and I didn't know when to expect you."

"At my apartment? And I was expecting *you*?"

Headley's date had steered him to the couch, and now the wild stallion broke free.

"Michael has told us so much about you, and we have enjoyed watching you on the talk shows."

He glanced to her laptop.

"Planning another trip?"

"Oh, another reporter?" Sarah had closed her online connection when she heard them coming down the hall.

"Yes," said Headley, missing the sarcasm. "Has Michael mentioned me?"

Headley's date inserted herself into the conversation. "You know, Sarah, it's really been a pleasure meeting you. We were just stopping by here to pick up a second car, so Headley and Michael could take LeeAnn and me," she motioned with her chin to the other woman, "home."

Her companion, a synthetically well-proportioned platinum blonde made-up to hide years rather than highlight cheek bones, felt less sexually threatened than intellectually overwhelmed. Her original plans for the evening had been unexpectedly crimped.

She conceded the evening to salvage a future rendezvous. "We don't need separate cars now, Michelle, because Michael and his cousin obviously have a lot of catching up to do. Headley, can you drop me off at home?"

Michael attempted to protest, but Sarah cut him off. "That's really sweet of you. Perhaps the three of us can have dinner tomorrow night?"

"Yeah, sure." LeeAnn's tone frosted the windows.

Michael was working for the same reclamation company. "I'll walk down to the car with you."

He exploded upon his return. "Can't I even go on one stinking date without you messing it up? Did I ruin your good time with Peter Barber? What are you doing here, anyway? I don't need this intrusion. I am the hottest science journalist in the whole country. I am being courted by *Animal Planet*, the *Discovery Channel*, you name it. Have you seen my calendar? Have you seen the offers we got?"

"We also have procrastinated on our offer from M'low Cloom."

"Procrastinated? Remember when we thought we were being set-up?"

"That was yesterday," she said dismissively. "*It* will kill us if we don't meet *Its* one-hundred-ninety-six-day deadline, of which we have only about what, forty-five days left? You're the one who said there were too many questions unanswered. We know a little more than before, but we have less time to get the rest of our answers."

"What do you mean?"

"I got the mammoth report. Only it's not a mammoth."

"What is it?"

"I received the carbon dating and DNA analysis of the primitive human and the woolly mammoth. It's not one of the four or five mammoth species we are familiar with because they are all its evolutionary *descendants*. That means this species dates back to the late Tertiary Period. It didn't migrate to Antarctica via an ice bridge, but the other way around, with the more modern mammoths and even the mastodons of the La Brea tar pits originating in Antarctica and then spreading north before this ancestor got stranded."

"Same story with the hunter. It's an ancestor of Cro-Magnon man that came to Antarctica for the food supply, and when some migrated north, evolved, and then became extinct, this one and the mastodon-mammoth ancestor survived even with the harsh change in climate until these particular individuals died *five hundred years ago*."

"Oh, my God. How is that possible?"

"Modern man's exploration of Antarctica only goes back about one hundred years. These guys were just left alone. We don't conclusively know what flourished in Antarctica five hundred years ago, but one thing we know for sure from the mammoth's stomach was that there wasn't much plant life left."

"And why do we think M'low Cloom wanted us to find this?" She had him hooked better than LeeAnn.

"Humans and animals find a way to survive symbiotically and what affects one, *either one*, can kill the other one. That biped's spear didn't kill that animal, one of three unrelated natural events did. Mammoths were vegetarians, and by the time it died, there was little low-lying grasses and ground cover vegetation left on Antarctica, which also meant that the carbon dioxide levels were probably a lot higher. Either the mammoth suffocated from the lack of oxygen in the air, or it simply starved to death, and being the primary source of food and maybe pelts for these prehistoric humans, they just died out, too. There's an interesting corollary to that point, but if you're sentient it's pretty scary."

"Scare me."

"Global climate change occurs pretty frequently without human influence. Excessive vegetation, particularly tree-like vegetation that consumes carbon dioxide and releases oxygen can drastically change what kind of life the planet supports. A large meteor crashing on earth and kicking up enough dust to blot out the sun or unleashing a virus can do the same thing. Even prehistoric continental forest fires can have the same effect. Global climate change is a pendulum, and when it reaches an extreme, it swings back. However, by the time it does, species like us become extinct because the planet has for too long become uninhabitable for them."

"You said three unrelated natural events. What's the third?"

Her amber eyes glowed. "I found the map to our second discovery, but it was pretty worn."

Michael cocked his head and Sarah pulled out an artist's portfolio case full of pictures.

"He was wearing it on his mammoth-skin vest."

She laid out a series of photos on the kitchen table and brought up their digital versions on her laptop screen.

By burning into the leather and using plant dyes, three pictures were woven together to form a story. In the first picture, a flaming ball landed on an icy shore. In the second picture, one done completely through burn marks of various depths and strokes, the same ball, now frozen over, was surrounded by men, women, and dead mammoths. In the third picture, honed by more subtle shading of bright yellow and red dyes, the ball, now part of a large iceberg had broken from shore and drifted into the ocean with gaunt men and women waving happily and throwing spears as it drifted into the sun.

"That's great. What did we learn from that? Some comet landed in Antarctica and drifted out to sea. And where did it go? This isn't a clue; it's not even art. It's nothing."

Almost inaudibly, "It's all we have. Except for this." She now pulled out a flat stone about two inches thick and laid it on the table. On one surface of the stone were streaks of unpolished silver with embedded iridescent blue flecks. When examined in bright light, it had a completely matte finish. In indirect light, it twinkled and glowed like a radium dial. Visible on the edge, around perhaps 120 degrees of its circumference were one-sixteenth-inch-thin wafers sandwiched between thick outer layers. Some were flecked with blue and others were gritty brown and yellow. It was no more than eight inches in diameter.

"I found it in a pouch slung over his shoulder and swiped it. It really belonged to us anyway."

"I'll be right back."

When Michael returned from his bedroom, he was no longer wearing his two-hundred-fifty-dollar Diesel jeans, but was happily barefoot and zipping up his faded Levis.

"Sarah, there was something waiting in my in-box when I returned to work after Antarctica that was a little disturbing."

"Mmm, hmm."

"Look at me. MC's not killing us or anyone else."

She turned in his direction and her fingers froze on the keyboard. "I got the coroner's report. Apparently, the more expensive gliders have black boxes like the ones they recover from commercial airline crashes. The plane got to thirty-nine thousand feet, not twenty-three thousand! Abby suffered the equivalent of the bends and she had some sort of undiagnosed vascular disorder which causes the venal and capillary walls to thin. Her death really *was* accidental. If I had known that before we went to Antarctica, I guarantee you I wouldn't have gone to Antarctica."

She stood up slowly and her shoulders drooped. "So, we are not going hunting for a cave that would have probably killed us anyway?"

They had come this far for each other, and so far Michael had come out ahead. He had romance, and he was on the career fast track. Michael realized that validation of an absurd theory about the future evolution of life on earth was a little more lofty aspiration. But everyone had a right to pursue their dreams. And what good was family, if it wasn't there to support them?

"No, we just need to look for more plausible explanations before we assume the supernatural."

"Double-checking our sources and research. I deserved that. Touché."

Michael pulled up a second chair to the laptop.

"Sarah, what do you remember from the vision about the comet's direction of travel?"

"Nothing. I remember the comet drifting in the ocean like on the mammoth skin vest."

"Which way was it drifting?"

"To the right. Clockwise."

"The Coriolis effect. Must have been heading to the northern hemisphere. And remember those murals in the vision? No penguins. But plenty of polar bears. Arctic circle probably."

"It has to have either beached on a shoreline or sunk at sea. I don't see us lying our way onto a submarine to find it at the bottom of the ocean, so let's assume it beached on a shoreline sometime since the black plague, which is when we think it broke free from the Antarctic ice sheet."

"The comet beached near a cave that was accessible by people that were able to make these story books on the walls. So, maybe there are legends from indigenous peoples about caves with miracle cures. Let's look online."

"Damn it, my computer crashed." She rebooted. "I've got a virus. The operating system is gone! I've got to recover it."

"Let me see."

They both stared at the blank screen. Michael said, "Your hard drive is completely blank and unformatted. That's not a virus." He proffered a puzzled look and sprinted into his bedroom closet, returning several expletives and a minute later with a small device that resembled an electrician's voltmeter.

"All journalism majors have to minor in something. Do you remember what I minored in?"

"I don't know. Drugs? Physics?"

"A little more specific, but close. Magnetism. This is a gauss meter and it shows that the magnetic field created by this stone is incredibly powerful, powerful enough to completely erase your hard disk. It would also be a very valuable trinket for primitive man, conjuring up all sorts of magic if he found some ferrous metals laying about. Strong magnets even attract some birds and insects. My guess is he plucked it off the comet. The comet was magnetized all along and it was strongly attracted to magnetic north, which is, by the way, a magnetic field south pole, to *attract* a north pole, which makes the comet just the opposite. The comet crashed into the Antarctic ice pack and was repelled by the South Pole and attracted to the North Pole. It finally broke off and headed north. It got as close to magnetic north as the Arctic polar ice cap would let it. And then it just sat there."

"Until when?"

"Until magnetic north left the ice cap and moved out into open waters. Then it followed it at sea until it got beached on land again somewhere near this underground amphitheater that was inhabited by humans."

"Wonderful. So how do we find this amphitheater in our vision?"

"Well, for starters, it looks like you're going to have to use my computer. Start after fifteen hundred, more or less. You just have to figure out the relationship between magnetic north, the amphitheater, the comet, and viruses because it's almost five am, and I am going to sleep."

"Could you possibly be a bigger asshole?" She shook her head in surrender. The biggest incompatibility between the two cousins was that she could stay up all night and talk or study and he was worthless after midnight. But, at least when they went camping, he was the first one up to start the campfire. She gave up and went to sleep.

When Michael returned from work late the next evening with vegan Chinese, he found Sarah on his computer, much as he had left her. Magnetic North had crossed the North Pole around 1500, hit Greenland around 1600, and since the late 1700s had migrated around what was now the Nunavut territory of Canada and its territorial waters. He looked over her shoulder while they ate.

"See if there's anything in Inuit folklore that seems like a relevant reference," Michael said and then he turned around and went to bed.

Sarah hit pay dirt less than an hour later. She yelled to him in the bedroom. "This is why you think Peter's right. You do five minutes of work and think you deserve all of the credit. I'll let you know when I'm finished."

On a website maintained by the Nunavut territorial government, she found the Inuit legend of the lost cave that cured all diseases. She printed out all of the old drawings and maps and fables she could find, but the cave had been lost for nearly two hundred years. When the white man came looking for the Northwest Passage, they shared all their designer diseases. The Inuit had no antidotes, immunities, or prophylaxis of any kind. Many were wiped out before the cave saved them. When the Europeans heard about the miracle cave that cured all diseases, they wanted to steal it for themselves, so the entrances were hidden and then lost to history.

But, the cave wasn't a panacea to cure all diseases. The microbe that the comet stocked it with possibly killed off the mammoth population, which meant that something in there was probably still dangerous enough to animal life that it could wipe out other species as well. Perhaps that explained why there were no mammoths or mastodons left in North America. But, there was something even more curious in the legend and she knew only one person who could decipher it.

"Michael, wake up. I know where we are going." They were back in her aunt's basement. Three steps and a flying leap landed her obliquely on his chest.

"Ooof! We aren't eight anymore."

"Get your ass out of bed." She pulled him up by the rear of his boxer shorts.

"Please. I need those."

"You made some offhand comment that some insects and birds are attracted to a magnetic field. What did you mean?"

"In the States, many birds and monarch butterflies navigate via the earth's magnetic fields using tiny amounts of magnetite in their brains."

"Listen to this." She read from the screen. "Encased in the ice around the cave were well-preserved specimens of many birds and butterflies of species that were unknown to the Inuit."

He was suddenly wide awake. He read the sentence several times for himself. "The comet confused the butterflies and the migratory birds. The field was so strong that they thought they were heading South and then they must have really gotten confused when they followed it all the way to the North Pole and froze."

"Remember the butterflies flitting around all of the dead animals in Uzbekistan? Could that possibly be related?"

"Don't some animals primitively communicate or hunt by sending out or monitoring neural electrical fields?"

She nodded. "Platypuses for one."

That stopped him. Michael concluded, "That's for another time. Don't get me sidetracked. All electrical fields induce a magnetic field, sometimes a very powerful one. If our communication from MC was via the kind of electrical signals within your brain, but thousands of times more powerful, it could have induced a magnetic field where we had the vision, which would explain the presence of those butterflies."

"I minored in magnetism," she mimicked.

They were interrupted by a loud rap at Michael's front door. The building was a gated, garden-style affair, common in the Houston area. It had been a rental project, recently renovated and converted to condominiums. The walls were thin.

Michael said, "I guess we were being too loud. I'll go and apologize." He looked through the peep hole.

He turned to Sarah, "Shit! It's Peter Barber! What's he doing here?"

"How do I know? I didn't tell anybody I was leaving town! Oh my God, I didn't tell anybody I was leaving town! He's probably wondering what happened to me."

"Michael? Sarah? Open up, please. It's raining, and I can hear you yelling at each other," Peter said.

Michael motioned to Sarah to hide all of their work.

"Coming, Peter. The apartment is bigger than it looks from the front door."

"I'm sure. Take a taxi and hurry."

Michael opened the door and found Peter's hair pasted to his forehead and openly suspicious. His blue eyes burned. Michael handed him a towel. "Peter, come in, but we were just leaving for a late-night toddy. Care to join us? What brings you into town anyway? Are you speaking at some sort of obscure top secret science colloquia?"

Peter surveyed the scene, his eyes stopping at Michael in his boxer shorts and then lingering on Sarah, bra-less under a t-shirt. "I often wondered why a lovely woman like you has had no known relationships with men in what, four years? This would explain a lot, but certainly you can do better. I needed to speak with Sarah privately."

"You chased her all the way to Houston? I thought chasing graduate students was an intramural sport. Going national now?"

Sarah knew that Peter had been prying into her private life, but confronting him now would clearly accomplish nothing. "Michael, please put some pants on. He was asleep, Peter. I've been up doing research." She kissed Peter wetly on the lips. "Pick a bar, boys."

"I'll wait until you put something on, either over or under that t-shirt."

Barber had left a message on Sarah's cell phone just after she left Chicago. Sarah had ignored it, as had become her habit. Peter's twinges of jealousy had grown into ulcers. They had slept together only a few times since their return, and he felt a growing emotional detachment by Sarah during their lovemaking. He had turned to a private investigator, one who had turned up nothing.

After Michael made some offhand remarks about a sequel adventure in a TV news magazine interview, Peter had become convinced that Michael and Sarah were scheming to cut him out of any future research expeditions.

Peter wanted in, if not professionally, then as an investor. After he took so much of the financial risk on a long shot in Antarctica, he wanted payback on a sure thing. And a chance to bring another long shot in. Sarah.

They found a quiet corner booth at the back of a noisy country-western bar where they wouldn't be recognized and ordered a round of long necks. To the regular patrons, a woolly mammoth might as well have been slang for a fat hairy whore.

Sarah began, "So when I didn't call you back, you just assumed that I came to Houston to visit my cousin? That's pretty presumptuous of you, isn't it, Peter?"

"Where else would you go unexpectedly without telling me? Your old roommate was clueless, and you only told Alexis that you had a family emergency. Michael didn't know about any family emergency, and he hadn't heard from you in a while. He did say that the two of you had notes you needed to review, so it wouldn't surprise him if you were on your way down here. So, I took a chance. We are part of a team, aren't we, Sarah? Michael?"

When Michael nodded agreeably, Sarah said, "I don't know what Michael's thinking, but we *had* a good team, Peter. The league's been disbanded. We're retired now."

"You don't expect me to believe that crap, do you?"

"I appreciate you calling Michael to let him know of my impending arrival so I could have free-range chicken and organic vegetables waiting for me."

She turned to her cousin. "You set me up."

"I didn't like LeeAnn anyway."

Sarah continued, "Regardless, there isn't anything else brewing, neither professionally, nor intimately. We stopped taking baths together nineteen years ago."

"I am not some gullible fool. It is obvious to me that you are planning another expedition. I heard you in your apartment before I knocked on the door. I want in. I put up with your amateurish antics the first time around. I even funded the goddamn thing. Either that, or I expose you. Quicksilver and I know that you," he looked directly at Sarah, "have never been to Antarctica before. Somehow you became aware of this woolly mammoth. Something crooked is going on here, perhaps through one of Michael's journalistic connections. He knew when we were on top of that mammoth's tomb. Maybe he deserves all the credit."

"I want to thank you for that, Peter, because getting me in front of that press conference got me kudos from the paper, the media, and three girls whom I have since fucked. Suppose for just a second you're right. Once you were to make such a preposterous allegation, your marriage would be over, your relationship with Sarah would be over, and if your allegations were not proved in a court of law, your tenured position would be finished and you'd have to answer for slander. The only one who would come out ahead is me. That sucks for the two of you."

Peter leaned into Michael's face. "You're going to tell my wife about this?"

"Gentlemen..." The music had stopped playing, but the two men had become so embroiled in their argument, they were oblivious to everything.

"Is she that stupid? The woolly mammoth could see you were having an affair with Sarah. And it's been dead for five hundred years!"

The bouncers moved into position.

Sarah fumbled quickly in her purse, produced a fifty-dollar bill, threw it on the table, and said quietly, "Let's get out of here."

There was a real irony in their return to the car. Michael and Peter walked four or five steps ahead of Sarah in animated conversation, that in less than ten minutes had gone from fist threatening to backslapping. Sarah knew she should be pleased by the sudden turn of events, but she also knew better. In her entire post-pubescent life, a man had never become close to her who didn't have an ulterior motive. It wasn't always sex, but coed softball pitcher and organic chemistry tutor was a short list. Now she was watching the one man she completely trusted cozy up to the one man she trusted least. Sure, Michael had ulterior motives, but he was always transparent. You couldn't get more transparent than Peter this evening, so what was Michael up to?

Michael was as emotionally stable as an Irish Setter, while Peter was mercurial, at his best. At his worst he was clinically bipolar. When she returned from Antarctica, she had checked on Peter's empty prescription bottle. Ativan was a common treatment for bipolarism. But, it wasn't the depression that worried Sarah the most. Alexis believed that Peter suffered from occasional bouts of paranoid schizophrenia as well. When he remained medicated and avoided severe emotional trauma, he functioned normally.

In the car, Michael said to Sarah, "I think Peter has a point here. We owe him one, and just one more quest. The next time, if there is a next time, we ought to include him."

"Are you out of your mind? This is completely inconsistent with everything you've said."

Michael said, "Peter, where are you staying?"

"Nowhere, yet."

Michael's fingers blurred the cell phone's keypad. "Peter, stay at the Galleria. I'll drop you off at your car, and we'll catch up with you sometime tomorrow. I am sorry about the threats."

"I got a little carried away, too, Michael, Sarah. We've been through a lot together. But I still insist on being a part of your next trip, no matter what I have to do."

He got out of Michael's car and walked to his rental.

Michael turned to Sarah and said, "He doesn't seem real stable. Was that a threat? Should we be concerned?"

She didn't answer.

They went up to Michael's apartment. They put on music and Michael's white noise machine that he used when he was conducting confidential phone interviews.

Michael began, "I think we should tell him the truth and include him."

"I do not understand you. Peter won't stop here and you know that. He wants to know where all of these completely disconnected leads are coming from. He will insist on joining us on our next M'low Cloom visit."

"His contacts and his experience would be incredibly useful. There's no downside. You know he can't blackmail us, and this is your fault anyway."

"My fault?"

"If you had dumped the guy the day we got back, this wouldn't be happening."

"Who told him where we were? And who wanted me to sleep with him to start with, Michael?"

They were interrupted by a knock at the door. It was Peter again. He was slurring drunkenly at the door. "Who the hell is MC?" he screamed.

Sarah whispered, "What do we do? How did he overhear our conversation?"

"I don't know, but we can't let him stay out there screaming. Let him in."

Peter fell through the doorway spewing epithets and splashing scotch out of a pint.

Sarah tried to calm him. "Peter, I don't know what you heard, but you don't understand. You would be in very grave danger. MC has more power than any of us. *It's, It's…*"

"You are a lying slut, Sarah Baskin. I am going to expose you for the charlatan that you are. After that, no one will even finance your purchase of a used car."

"Peter, we are trying to protect you. Come with us to the North Pole, but you cannot ask how we learned about what we are going to find there because the truth is, we don't even really know the answer. Let's sober you up and then I will fill you in on all of the details. We are leaving in two days." She ran her fingers through his hair and kissed him softly with full lips. He froze briefly and then the liquor overcame his resistance.

"Michael, I am going back to the hotel with Peter. I'll call you in the morning."

THE HOUSTON GALLERIA HOTEL
JUST BEFORE NOON THE NEXT DAY

"Michael, I am coming over alone. Peter caught the first plane up north this morning. He's probably getting in about now. His wife called at about three this morning. She found out that I was down here and put two-and-two together. She is at their cabin in Northern Wisconsin. Peter was petrified, which is great. He's says he's going to try to catch up with us in Canada, but I don't think he is ready to walk away from his marriage yet. I found an empty prescription bottle of his in Antarctica. Alexis confirmed that he's being treated for bipolarism and probably paranoid schizophrenia. We got back to the hotel, and he went into a rage. He refuses to believe that you and I are not casual lovers. I'm coming over."

"Well, I guess his wife solved our problem for us."

Sarah's cell phone rang just as she walked into Michael's apartment. It was Dr. Brankov. On Peter's way to the family cabin, his limo had swerved in dense fog to avoid hitting a bull moose and had run off a bridge where the guardrails were undergoing repair. Peter had somehow managed to escape the vehicle after it hit the river, only to go over a waterfall and be impaled on a jagged rock eighty feet below. The limo had hung up on a tree before it hit the falls. The driver had escaped with minor injuries.

CHAPTER 13

Road Trip!

Sarah's perpetually rosy lips lost their color. She sat for a while, in a chair located in another world, before the amber eyes refocused. When she spoke, there was an aggressive edge.

"What did you and Peter talk about last night when the two of you were walking back to the car?"

"He was telling me how critical I was to our expeditions and how he thought I deserved more of the credit."

"That makes sense. You wanted him to come along again. He was your big rah, rah man."

"It's not un-deserved, Sarah. I ghost wrote that piece for him a year ago, remember."

"How can I forget? What else?"

"He told me that he had thrown some of those oily rags out when he was in the engine room right before me because, as hot as that room was, he didn't want them to catch fire."

"Spontaneous combustion."

Michael nodded. "He lied. The room smelled a lot oilier than the day before, and it was hotter, too."

"You called his wife, didn't you?"

He nodded again.

"And you knew about the pills."

The bobblehead continued.

"You couldn't lose, could you?"

"Well, I would have gotten more press time with his help, but no, *we* couldn't lose. The irony is that I really did nothing wrong, and the man tried to blackmail us. By calling his wife, I was just imposing my morality on someone else. Remember, Sarah, the moral and the immoral are equally blind."

"Still, it was probably nothing more than an accident."

"A moose in the middle of a bridge? Hitting the guard rail right where there was no guard rail? Escaping the car only to have the car and driver survive? Sounds like a lot of sordid coincidences to me. I wonder what their altitude was?"

"Sarah, I don't know what 'come alone or survive alone' means because I don't think MC can really kill people. Or animals for that matter. Or, just benefit from coincidences. I think typically, I'm the fatalistic one, but when it comes to MC, you'll accept almost anything as part of MC's plan and I'm the skeptic. Is that because MC is, what did you call *It*, a personal manifestation of your calling?"

"Michael, whether or not MC can kill people doesn't change the end result. If Peter hadn't followed me down here, he'd still be alive."

"And if he hadn't tried to maim me, he might be on his way to Canada, eh?"

"I am not going back to campus right now to deal with the recriminations. Get packed. We're leaving from here. Now. "

In less than four hours, they were headed anonymously north. Soon, the spring in south Texas gave way to winter in the plains states and then the pristine snow-covered farm fields of Canada's prairie provinces which seemed to stretch all the way to the Arctic Circle.

They took turns checking into hotel rooms, single occupancy, hoping to maintain their anonymity. Each night they continued looking for a better link to the lost cave and its entrance.

North of four corners Canada, the common boundary of Manitoba, Saskatchewan, the Northwest Territories and the Nunavut Territory, they tentatively crossed their first ice bridge, a ferry crossing in the summer that froze over and was striped for highway traffic in the winter. In Arviat, on the western shore of Hudson Bay they abandoned their car at the airport.

"Don't you think Texas tags look a little conspicuous here, Michael?"

"It'll be all right," he shrugged.

"There's only eleven cars in the parking lot."

He threw mud and ice over his tags. "See? Car looks like it belongs here."

BOOTHIA PENINSULA - TALURQJUAK

The town of Talurqjuak was located on the edge of Resolute Bay and was home to about two hundred or so indigenous Inuits, as well as moose, the rare grey wolf in the summer and polar bear. They welcomed the visitors warmly, albeit suspiciously. Tourist season, for everybody but polar bears and puffins, was usually in May. By then, there was already more than eighteen hours of daylight. Sarah and Michael were acclimated to this weather.

In a restaurant bar in Talurqjuak, a couple of men sat drinking quietly at the bar, watching the Toronto Maple Leafs of the National Hockey League playing even-up against the Phoenix Coyotes. In the far north, satellite TV was the most common means of obtaining news from the outside world. In the corner of the room two women played pool and listened to '80s hard rock.

There were eight tables in the dimly lit room. Sarah and Michael picked the least grimy of the lot. The bartender, a tall Inuit with broad shoulders and long pig-tails came over to take their order.

He recognized them almost immediately. "Baskin and Seagal! I heard you two were in town. Let me get you a plate of barbequed venison strips. On the house."

"Well, that's not bad. We made it to our destination this time before we were recognized. We've got to work on clandestine operations."

"Next trip, Sarah."

He hurried away and returned with the strips. He took their orders and several seconds later, the Leafs–Coyotes game had been preempted by the replay of a newscast featuring Captain Quicksilver and the shots of the woolly mammoth locked in glacier ice storage.

The bartender called over to them, "Many of the locals here made a copy of this broadcast. You know why, eh? Aren't many natives who will say nice things about white Americans. In public, I mean."

One of the men at the bar looked up at the screen and screamed at the bartender, "Moose, what happened to the hockey game? I don't need to see white predators, excuse me, I mean white *people,* stealing more shit. I want to see the hockey game."

Moose squirmed. "Darwin, I don't think Captain Quicksilver is a white man. And the white predators are sitting right behind you, so please show some manners."

"He's a paid chauffeur and a traitor, just like my father and all the rest of them."

Sarah jumped up. Michael tried to restrain her, but she was too quick.

She got within an inch of Darwin's face and, recoiling at his combustible breath, said, "You are a clueless drunk. Captain Quicksilver is a Delaware Indian who has dedicated his life to protecting marine mammals. He's a damn good sea captain and he risked the safety of his ship to retrieve evidence that even from six thousand miles away, the white man is destroying the earth's last unspoiled patch of frozen land."

Darwin was taken aback. "You're feisty. And you're cute."

The bar door slammed open, and a woman stood momentarily in the doorway, scanned the room, and then moved belligerently toward Darwin. She took a quick look at Sarah and shoved her back three steps with her forearm. "Out of my way."

She grabbed Darwin by the arm and jerked him off of the bar stool.

"Get up, you drunken slob. It's time to go home. Your father isn't feeling well." She turned to the bartender, and her expression changed from ice to butter.

"We'll square up tomorrow, Moose, okay?"

The bartender nodded and the couple left the restaurant.

He sheepishly turned to Sarah and Michael, "Sorry. That had nothing to do with you. Happens a couple times a month. You'd never know they're really quite in love."

A roadhouse not far from Talurqjuak had ten shanty hotel rooms with a bathroom between each pair and a small bar and sandwich shop overlooking a snow-packed parking lot. A poorly heated rear corridor providing shelter from the frigid winds led from each of the rooms to the bar. With their planted memories and tracking maps for magnetic north over the last several hundred years, they deployed from their base to look for someone familiar with the Inuit legend.

On the evening of the third day, they were completing a futile ten-hour drive back down the west coast of the Boothia Peninsula on snow-packed roads in their rented high-ground-clearance SUV. Michael had been complaining about his sore shoulders all day and Sarah had started eating candy bars. The arcing of the northern lights across the evening sky lifted their spirits. Streaks of fluorescent greens and iridescent orange-reds waved ionized gases low across the night sky. It was understandable why ancient peoples on either side of the globe, from the Norwegians to the Aborigines of Australia had attributed mystical powers to something so ethereal and unexplainable, even though they had guessed right the first time. Charged particles streamed away from the sun god, more commonly known as the sun and interacted with the earth's magnetosphere where it was strongest, near the surface of the magnetic poles, emitting light waves and colors in the visible light spectrum and beyond.

"One of the men I spoke to today was with the Geological Survey of Canada. They are the ones charged with keeping track of the magnetic north pole. Before you get too excited, he doesn't know anything more about its location in the seventeen and eighteen hundreds than we already do, although apparently if you suspect it was somewhere for a while, you can prove it by testing the soils to see if ferrous minerals became magnetized. He just happened to say that the Aurora was going to be pretty spectacular tonight because we are in the peak of solar flare activity on the sun and that largely determines the intensity of the Borealis. He said that it gets even better the farther north you go."

"How far north?"

"I don't know."

"I think I do. Let's have dinner at the bar where you beat up that drunk. They have wireless."

Michael jumped on the laptop while Sarah paced back and forth with a beer and pretzels.

"Look at this."

One of the most dramatic occurrences of the Northern Lights was recorded during the third week of June in 1791 almost directly over the west coast of the Boothia Peninsula. Tourists traveled from five hundred miles away to view the brilliant display in the upper elevations. The aurora borealis was visible at lower latitudes as far away as Quebec City, PQ, Fairbanks, AK, Greenland, and Norway. Researchers believe that the light show was a result of an extremely rare combination of events. Magnetic North was directly under the western edge of the Peninsula land mass and regularly recurring solar activity had reached its highest level in several hundred years.

Sarah said, "Do a search for earthquakes around that same time."

"Why? They don't have anything to do with Northern Lights or magnetic north."

"You said that I had to put all of the pieces together." He shrugged and winced. "I'll rub your sore shoulders. Keep searching."

"Here it is. Son of a bitch."

Near the location of magnetic north a slight tremor was felt during the night. In the morning residents found a new land mass nearly eighty feet high had erupted from tectonic upheaval along the shoreline. It was apparently part of a bigger eruption that had broken through the pack ice leaving an exposed ellipse in the melting channel nearly one hundred miles long. The remainder of the land mass had sunk back into the channel between King William Island and the west coast by morning.

"That was the comet. Right before we left I read where extreme solar flare activity can cause the magnetic poles to move in an elliptical motion up to eighty kilometers in one day. The comet got caught up in all of that flare activity and went swirling around the channel with magnetic north. It's just like metal filings being moved around a piece of paper from a magnet underneath. Print that stuff out. Now all we have to do is find the comet land mass, if it's still there, and we'll find the cave," she said.

"I don't know why I didn't think of this back at my apartment. Do you ever read publications like *Science* or *Nature* or the *Geophysical Journal?*"

"No, I have my own trade rags to read. Why?"

"They are forecasting record levels of solar flare activity to occur in the next thirty days."

"That's why MC wants us to finds the comet. Magnetic north could move maybe a hundred kilometers, even temporarily, and the microbes could follow the magnetic field out into open waters or daylight and get released to the surface. Whole animal species could go extinct," she said urgently. "We don't have much time to find the cave."

If whatever was in the cave caused the demise of the remaining mammoths on earth, then its release could spell the end for elephants and their relatives.

"There's a real inconsistency here, dear. Originally, you thought MC was concerned about the microbes being discovered and destroyed by humanity. Now, we're speculating that the microbes could be released and cause a pandemic around the globe. Why do you think MC didn't tell us about this threat? Seems like *It* would have known. I think there's only one possibility. *It* didn't care, Sarah. Doesn't that bother you?"

"*It* seems to be pretty obsessed with natural selection, doesn't *It*?"

Understanding the urgency in either case didn't change their luck any. Almost two weeks after leaving Houston, they found themselves in a cabin on the Boothia ice pack, their diet reduced to smoked venison, cured whale meat, and dried fish. Steaming mugs of chocolate caribou milk sat between them.

Michael said, "Scientific research is easy. Making sense of folklore, now that's impossible."

"Yes, well…I am giving this search one more day and then I think we should head straight back to Uzbekistan."

They had done their best to find the cave and *It* would know that. Another vision would give them more clues and they could return before the solar flare activity kicked up.

They headed north at sunrise. Halfway up the coast they become stranded in white-out conditions. With no road, no viable maps and too many thawing rivers and glacial lakes to navigate, the southerners attempted to turn around, but the accumulating snow had already reached the SUV's bumper. They were stuck. Michael opened the door and watched his tire tracks disappear in seconds. They had only a few hours before darkness fell.

They had a blanket, a full tank of gas and a spare fifty liters in a can in the back. If they kept the engine on all night just to run the heater, they would probably make it until morning. After that, they would freeze to death huddled together in the cabin of an SUV lost in a late winter storm in northern Canada.

The XM satellite radio proclaimed this the worst March storm in over twenty years. Sarah and Michael had figured that out for themselves.

"We'll find our cave all right. We could be sitting on top of it right now. Maybe we should start digging through the floor boards."

They huddled together, and Sarah fell asleep on her cousin's chest. For the first time since this whole M'low Cloom fiasco began, it was Michael, normally the more taciturn, who spent the night jerking awake to be sure that the engine hadn't stalled or the snow blanket hadn't so thoroughly insulated the car that they suffocated from carbon monoxide poisoning and never knew what hit them. Anxiety was not the same thing as fear.

Michael finally fell into a deep sleep as morning arrived silently. They awoke with a start to a silvery gray coating in their sound-proofed cocoon.

"It's really peaceful up here, Michael. You need to get a digital watch." The ticking of Michael's analog watch reverberated throughout the cabin of the vehicle.

Michael yawned and then his eyes popped open. "That's because the engine's not running."

The gas needle was on the wrong side of *E*. Sarah grabbed the key. Michael stopped her.

"Don't bother. It's empty, and we can't afford to run down the battery in this weather. We need to dig out the emergency tank as quickly as possible. If the engine and battery cooled down too much, we won't be able to restart the car."

Their doors would not open, even with a combined effort. Sarah opened her window and an avalanche of snow cascaded on top of her. She crawled out of the window into the nearly chest-deep snow and began burrowing toward the ground with her mittened hands. It took twenty minutes to extricate herself from the snow hole into which she had fallen and make a trench to the gas can. Every time she poked her head up out of the hole, the wind flayed her face with icy noodles.

"Get out here and help me!" She saw the stunned look on his face.

"You have a problem with manual labor in the frigid Arctic?"

A voice behind her said. "No, I think he's surprised to see me."

Just about a meter behind her stood a leather-skinned Inuit man on snowshoes, accompanied by a husky malamute mix heeling by his side.

"Can I give you a hand?" Crow's feet popped through the top of his ski mask and he pulled out a small snow shovel. Wearing snowshoes that kept him on top of the fresh powder, his chest stood above the roof of the SUV. His face was trimmed by the moose fur of his hooded parka, exposing a small oval from the bridge of his nose to his eyebrows. He was a cross between a gorilla and the abominable snowman.

Briefly, Sarah thought she was face-to-face with M'low Cloom.

She fell into the snow laughing. Not more than thirty meters over the man's shoulder was a small wooden house connected to an igloo addition. She hadn't even noticed the house behind her or the man approaching the car, his snowshoe steps muffled by the snow and carried away on the wind.

He pulled Michael out through the window, slipped the two of them into extra pairs of snowshoes that were slung on his back and led them toward the house. As they entered the yard, sled dogs barked enthusiastically from the door of their shed. An inside dog launched his front paws onto them in the vestibule as an elderly man peered at them curiously through the house window.

They pulled off their heavy outerwear inside the doorway. Sarah faced the doorway with her back to their rescuer. She hung her jacket and mittens on a nearby peg, turned and gasped.

"Darwin!"

He smiled sheepishly. "I was hoping you wouldn't recognize me, Sarah. It was kind of embarrassing. I didn't really mean a lot of those things I said. I don't remember a lot of them, either."

Michael shook Darwin's hand as the older man emerged from the shadows.

Darwin's father, Sam, had the same broad face, wide-set eyes and full hairline, but his age was difficult to estimate. His wrinkled skin was a thickened brown stew, which hinted at a more serious health condition. It contrasted sharply with the twinkling eyes and expressive bushy eyebrows.

Darwin's wife entered the room. She had a somewhat fairer complexion and blushed a burnt copper when she saw Sarah and Michael, but recovered quickly.

"I guess you saw the two of us at our worst," she said amiably and pushed an invigorating liquid that frothed of caramel and hazelnut into their hands.

The patriarch said little and after some uncomfortable small talk about the weather and the riff raff at Moose's Bar, Sam asked if they had found the caves they were seeking. They stared into their mugs.

Sam said, "There are no secrets among the Inuit. Let me see your drawings." Sarah looked at Michael and shrugged. On a table, she laid the sketches of Inuit scenes in the caves and the maps of magnetic north, along with their recent acquired knowledge of the land mass created by the 1791 earthquake.

The man mused over the drawings for a long while, occasionally grunting and pursing his lips tightly. Every five minutes or so he would ask a question and then grow quiet until a heavy congested cough rattled his body. He wheezed slightly and then with soft, wrinkled hands, stroked his stubbled beard and repeatedly cleared his throat.

"I will take you to this spot tomorrow," he said, in a low, raspy Canadian accent. "There are many legends told by our ancestors about this place. It held miraculous healing powers for my people. They would disappear in these caverns for weeks. When the white man came, many Inuit were rumored to have gotten sick. But, those who had contact with these caves never fell ill. The cave is not far from here, but the entrance has been lost for generations."

He led them down a long, dimly lit hallway. Coarse canvas wall coverings mated with layers of earth-toned pelts to form a tapestry. Animal skins had been painstakingly fitted together to form wall-to-wall carpet. A fire reflecting off the glistening hallway beckoned them into the round ice house that they had seen from the outside, the smoke being drawn magically through a narrow slit in the center of the domed roof. In the center of the room, away from the cold walls, were two beds covered with animal skins and wool blankets.

"Sleep here. There's wood for the fire." He motioned to the pile in the corner. "I'll look in on you later."

The sun returned about noon the next day, but the roads were impassable. As Sam looked out the window, his frail countenance withered.

Darwin said, "Father, the truck's snowed in. Give it another day."

Sam shook his head vigorously. "No, there's no time. They said they have to leave tomorrow. We'll take the dogs."

"You're in no condition, Father."

Sam excused himself and his son. When they returned from a back room, he was smiling.

The father clapped his hands together and exclaimed, "Well, let's get at it."

They loaded up two sleds. Darwin drove one and Sam mushed the other with Sarah and Michael as passengers. Engulfed in animal furs, the bumpy ride was slightly moldy, but warm. The dogs slogged ahead for a couple of hours or so, before Sam, in the lead sled, pulled them up. Sarah was relieved. She had been banging into something cold and hard under her right leg for the last half hour.

Sam was coughing fitfully, and after Sarah jumped off the sled, Darwin pulled an oxygen cylinder from Sarah's sled and handed his father a mask. Sam sat on the sled petting the dogs and inhaled for several minutes as Darwin erected a small tent and fired up a propane heater. Sam crawled inside on a fur floor.

Thick clouds of condensing breath surrounded the cousins' excited conversation. A projection of snow-covered land into the ice-packed channel would be completely invisible from the ground or from the air in the winter, recognizable by air only during the summer melt. Even then you had to know exactly where to look and what to be looking for. From the shoreline the mass rose thirty or forty meters and projected an equal distance into the channel. Along the shore, geothermal geysers belched and spit steam that kept much of the area protected from the surrounding permafrost. Burgundy, calf-high, prickly shrubs had managed to take root in the soft soil.

Darwin said, "Lots of iron in the soil here. Look how it's reddened the shrubs. There are even a couple of scrub pines. I wonder how deep that root system will get before it hits the permafrost and its growth is stunted. We're hundreds of kilometers from the tree line."

Permafrost was the rule this close to the Arctic Circle. About a meter of soil melted every spring and summer, but there was never enough heat to warm the soil farther down. Below the permafrost line, the soil stayed frozen the year around. Sam nodded thoughtfully while Darwin glared.

They released the dogs and the four adults wandered around the area chipping away at the ground with picks. More than once, Michael and Sarah found remains of birds and clusters of monarch butterflies frozen within the ice. They were on top of the comet, but they couldn't find the doorway. They noticed Sam studying the invasive animals frozen thousands of kilometers from home, but he said nothing.

Sam sat down near one of the steam holes and breathed in the pink-tinged steam tainted with the odor of rotten eggs. The cousins could hear him muttering under his breath. "My people were here before. I can feel it." He left the search only to take oxygen in the small tent and feed the dogs.

As twilight fell and the Northern Lights shimmered across the sky, they packed up to go. Sam taunted them gently.

"What do you expect to find in this cave?"

"We are not antiquities robbers. We just want to find the cave. Whatever is in there is the property of the Inuit people."

"You are the first white people to come here with knowledge of this hole in the earth in hundreds of years. I believe that it existed long before the Europeans came here seeking the Northwest Passage and exporting their religion."

Sam ruminated a long moment. "Five hundred or more years ago, we lived as tribes around the Arctic Circle, subsisting on whale meat, walrus, and reindeer. Legend has it that there was a mystic spiritual cave. It was little more than a place to get out of the cold and wind back then. Our people would go down to the cave and suck on the icicles. It was full of minerals, dissolved calcium deposits, sulfur, lots of iron. It tasted putrid, but they believed it cured all illnesses.

"After the earthquake, our people continued coming to the cave, but it was no longer a medicine man's placebo. It now imparted miraculous curative properties to our people through the air and the water. It was a prophylactic as well. We were no longer susceptible to many diseases that the white man brought, or that we ourselves had previously contracted. We passed these immunities to our children but then the cave started filling up with steam, and the air and the water became acrid, so we stopped going to the caves. There was no need anyway, and when Inuit finally returned to confirm the legend, the entrance was gone."

"How come most of this story is missing from the online references?"

"Until the territorial referendum was passed in nineteen ninety-two, nobody cared. This was an overlooked, inaccessible part of the Northwest Territories. It was just oral history being retold by semi-literate drunks like the ones that hang out in the bar with Darwin."

Sarah and Michael reddened, while Sam chuckled. He slapped his son on the back. "He's got an MS in forestry and a good mind, both of which he could make better use of, but sometimes he just likes hanging out with his buddies, many of whom fit the stereotype and live off of the old ways and survive retelling folk tales."

"You've conned us." Sarah pointed her finger at him accusingly.

"I am a graduate of the University of Toronto, an immunologist who spent my career at the Royal Academy of Sciences doing research on infectious diseases. I retired to my native Nunavut ten or twelve years ago. And you, Sarah Baskin, are not just here to go spelunking."

Sarah expelled a melting laugh into the frozen air, "Sam, I was a little suspicious of you from the moment your son introduced himself as Darwin."

"That's a give-away. You almost missed me. I was in Arizona the last three months. Just got back last week. We Native Americans aren't really this dark, you know." He gave a toothy grin. "Let's go back to the house and see if we can divine a cave entrance."

Sam continued to probe on the way back to the house. He didn't seem as concerned about how they found out about the legend of the cave as he was about what they expected to find there. Sarah confided that she had heard rumors that there were ancient viruses and bacteria and perhaps cures all still lurking in the lost cave.

Between Darwin's drunken indiscretions at the bar exposing deep-seated hostilities toward the white man and Sam's obsession with a quarry that until now had just been a native legend, Michael fretted to Sarah that they could be double-crossed at any moment. Their bodies would be hidden forever under the Arctic ice pack because Peter Barber, the one person who knew they were here, had become MC's most recent victim.

Darwin had a call waiting when he returned and had to catch an early morning flight to the Northwest Territories, so Sam, Michael, and Sarah told stories and drank local moonshine until late in the night.

CHAPTER 14

Smoke Signals from the Nunavut Territory

It was the profound stillness that woke Michael long after the dogs had given up all hope. They were alone. Michael shook Sarah vigorously. "He's gone, Sarah. They're all gone. Why would a man leave perfect strangers alone in his house?"

They followed Sam's pick-up truck tracks back to the frozen shoreline. A dog's snout poked expectantly through a crack in the cab's fogged windows, but Sam was nowhere to be found. The vehicle was unlocked.

"What do you think now, Sarah?"

"He left us a map, for chrissake. For some reason, he just wanted a head start." She let the dog out and scratched behind his ears. "Hello, Mendl."

"Mendl?"

"If he named his son Darwin, it only seemed logical that he would name his house dog after the father of genetics. Oh okay, he told me yesterday."

Sarah's cell phone beeped and buzzed with an old text message just coming through.

"Who's it from?"

She looked at the message, smiled, and ignored her cousin. "Find Sam, Mendl. We are not the only ones who search the internet."

Sam's upper body was immersed in a hole he had made next to the reddish scrub pines, leaving only his trousers and boots exposed. Mendl clamped down on the seat of Sam's pants and tugged until he emerged. Mud plastered his hair and neck, and his skin had assumed the same burgundy radiance as the bushes. He hopped to his feet.

"It's beautiful. I returned this morning as soon as my son left. That native brew you drank last night was one hundred forty proof. We call it the Northern

Lights Out. When Darwin spotted the pines, I sent a message ahead and had Darwin called out of town. You'd think that a man with an MS in forestry would realize that pines don't ever grow in permafrost frozen ground, which means that something is keeping the ground below above freezing.

"Emphysema's a tough thing to live with. I needed to see if the curative properties in the legend were true, and I didn't want anyone stopping me." He resolutely kicked the oxygen cylinder and then he grabbed his toe as he winced. "This weather is the absolute worst. Until today, this probably would have been my last winter in Canada.

"Last night, I got to wondering how an old location of magnetic north would help you find an Inuit cave. I, too, know that magnetic north magnetizes ferrous metals in the soil. But you didn't add that together with the burgundy color of those pines needles. They are laden with iron. And when magnetic north was here, it somehow confused those birds and butterflies into following it. That part I haven't figured out yet. Fortunately, Darwin didn't either, or he would have exposed himself and the planet to whatever's lurking underground in his haste to protect his precious Inuit history from the white man. He's a good man, but I trust your judgment more than my own son's. That's why I had him called out of town.

"So, what's so exciting down there, you two? And it's not Native American wall etchings that protect people against all sorts of diseases."

Sarah showed Sam her reproductions of the leather designs on the Antarctic man's clothing and Michael described the intricately fashioned highly magnetized stone, both leaving out any references to MC.

Sam said, "That explains how you learned of the comet and how it happened to be heading toward the North Pole, but how did you tie that in with the Inuit legend?"

Sarah produced her printouts of the newspaper accounts of the 1791 northern lights and the information she found through the territorial website.

"And the two of you put all of this together and decided that the comet must have somehow been responsible for the curative and prophylactic properties of The Cave of Legends, so they must be in the same location, at magnetic north. And the birds and the butterflies homed you in because they were somehow also attracted to magnetic north?"

The cousins shuffled uneasily on their feet. "Exactly. Well, let's start digging." Michael moved toward the truck, but Sam wasn't quite finished yet.

"And how did you say you knew where those mammoths were to start with?"

"Sarah sighted them when she was on an expedition the year before and didn't tell anybody because she wanted to return later with some real expertise."

"And she and the head of that first expedition felt comfortable with an urban Yankee wandering around Antarctica, kilometers away from her 'tour group,' all by herself?" Sam questioned. The same Yankee, I might add, who almost froze to death in a spring Canadian snowstorm."

Even Mendl cocked his head skeptically.

They were digging themselves into a hole from which they might never emerge. Sarah had had enough. "Sam, you know that's ridiculous. This is not the right time, just as yesterday was not the right time to tell us you had emphysema."

"Fair enough. I'll accept that for now, but the right time will come. How dangerous is what's down there?"

Sarah said, "We don't think it's dangerous at all to the three of us. However, as you surmised, it could be pandemic to humans and other plant and animal life. It could wipe out whole species."

Michael said, "It's possible that whatever is down there was attracted to magnetic north the same way that the monarch butterflies and birds were. If magnetic north were to move strongly in a direction that would point those microbes to an exit door to the surface, we could have an epidemic."

"It's been here hundreds of years, what's the urgency now?"

"Astrogeophysicists are forecasting record levels of solar flare activity in the next twenty days or so. It could be powerful enough to break the comet off from this land mass, or just to cause the migration of these microbes to the surface. No way to tell."

"Twenty-five to thirty days? Not a lot of time to figure out what's down there and decide whether to destroy it, warn people, or develop an antidote."

"Or protect it," Sarah said.

Sam turned away and stared into the hole. When he looked at them again, his eyes had welled with tears. "Sometimes book learning causes one to forget the more important lessons. We don't understand something, so we want to kill it or defend ourselves from it even though it protected my ancestors from all sorts of diseases. Well, you can't protect what you can't find. Let's get down that hole."

They pulled shovels and picks from the truck and within an hour, they had an opening large enough to wriggle through into the cavern below. Sam returned to the truck and came back with an olive green foot locker of Army surplus materials.

"Motion detectors and infrared sensors." He connected them with wire which he then dropped down the hole. The immunologist continued to surprise them.

They dropped a ladder through the hole to the ground about three meters below and descended. Sarah and Sam climbed in and Michael lowered packs of supplies and sample containers before following them in. They pulled the ladder down the hole behind them. Sarah and Michael attached reels of heavy nylon fishing line to the backs of their waists like the mythical Theseus who used Ariadne's ball of thread as a crude GPS to find his way out of the maze after he had slain the Minotaur. The line was tethered to the ladder.

As they moved into the tunnel ahead, their flashlight beams bounced off the fog and sprayed light everywhere but on the bogged ground below. They were eyeless fish, advancing into the net of an unknown and possibly invisible life form. They held onto each other and the walls to keep from losing their footing until they left the cloaking steam of the geothermal mist seeping from the ground. The path turned icy and slippery, and their pace slowed to a shuffle.

As the temperature started to rise, the air cleared and they loosened their parkas. The floor thawed again, providing surer footing. Their flashlights now illuminated smooth nondescript walls and ragged ceilings dripping with stalactites poked through billowy clouds in the ceiling. The cave widened into a large amphitheater just as the ceiling went below the levels of permafrost and they redirected their light to a barrel-shaped cloudless vault some fifteen or more meters above. The room was nearly a hundred meters long and almost as wide. Crystals encrusting the ceiling refracted reds, greens, and indigos around the room like a discotheque ball.

Sam spoke softly and an echo reverberated throughout the rotunda. "They spoke of this in the legends. The cave of a thousand voices."

Deposits of cobalt and manganese had been used as chalk to make murals of hunters in Hudson Bay tracking seals and sharks, whales, and polar bears. Aboriginal lives and rituals were depicted in storyboards around the great room.

In one crude storyboard, a sallow-faced preteen girl was being carried into the cave. In the next scene she was laid in the great rotunda near one of the exits. Chalky ethereal spirits emerged from the exit tunnel and caressed her body, drawing it down the tube. Finally, she walked out of the tunnel, apparently cured.

"It appears that my ancestors knew which tunnel possessed the healing vapors. Look," he said, pointing to another mural.

Underfoot, the floor was rough and porous, like sea coral. Not too many years ago, the permafrost had extended to these depths. Streaks of pale manganese oxide, dark green molybdenum chloride, cobalt, gold, and silver wove through the dominant calcium carbonate rock running through the middle of the floor, creating intricate floor patterns that shimmered in the light and came alive in the dark.

They followed the rough directions in the mural toward the left from their point of entry until they came to a single opening. About ten meters inside the hole, it split into two tubes. Other dark arched tubes were at least seventy-five degrees around the circumference from them. They examined the adjacent branches carefully, from floor to ceiling. It seemed impossible to tell to which one the mural was referring. They split up to explore the tunnels separately and agreed to reconvene in two hours at the entrance point. That gave them an hour to explore and another to return.

Sam entered the tunnel on the right. Sarah and Michael went through the opening on the left and found smaller branch tunnels that the early natives had used to relieve themselves and others where they had left pelts for warmth. Little organic matter of any kind was left. Empty stone lanterns, once fueled by whale oil were scattered on the tunnel's floor. In another tunnel, the stillness was shattered by water dripping from the ceiling and crashing onto a stone floor, where it trickled through an opening to a mysterious splash below. A natural cistern? Their voices reverberated so they kept them to a whisper.

There was no visible evidence of life and there were no human remains either. Apparently, if anyone died here, they were removed to the surface or interred in some undiscovered chamber.

Michael said, "We don't have any idea what we are looking for, do we? We could think we found nothing, return to the surface, and be dead four hours later."

With resurgent M'low Cloomian faith, Sarah said, "I think we'll know it when we find it."

Several hours later, they returned to the rendezvous point. A half hour passed and Sam did not return. "Seems like he found something," Sarah said. "Or vice versa." They ventured into the doctor's steep labyrinth. After about a kilometer, Michael's compass needle began to jerk up and down. The comet's powerful magnetic north field was directly ahead of them, down Sam's path. Their walkie talkies generated only static.

"Sam has chosen correctly," said Michael.

"I wonder if that was a random choice," Sarah mused aloud.

They pulled on Sam's lifeline. It offered no resistance. They moved more quickly, calling Sam's name and following his line. Deeper into the labyrinth, the ground transformed again, the coarse dry surface became covered with a nearly opaque, cold grey, viscous fluid that penetrated their bones up to their thighs. They shuffled along grabbing for hand holds along the walls, while wading through a rapidly deepening puddle that rose to consume them.

The reel counter latched to the rear of Sarah's belt indicated that they had already traveled more than ten kilometers. As they descended, the ringing in their ears and the air pressure increased dramatically. Sam had the manometer, from that they could make a good estimate of depth—if they could find Sam.

Michael had been leading the way with his flashlight until he dropped it into the soup and it blinked out. They should have been thrust into sudden blackness, but the moisture-laden air was charged with red and orange streaks that careened from the wall to the floor, passing through their bodies. There was an oily odor of soft tar on a stifling summer day.

"What the hell is this?" Sarah said, as Michael grabbed her hand.

His sweaty palm crushed Sarah's hand as he picked up the flashlight with his other hand. "Static electricity? Don't ask me what's causing it. It's usually generated by friction in the *absence* of humidity. This is really spooky. I guess there's one good thing about it, though."

"What's that?"

"No methane gas, or we'd be wall covering by now."

"So that means no decaying plants or animals?"

"I guess not, but then I don't know what this smell is from. Not my area of expertise. I guess it's not yours either, eh?"

Michael attempted to relight the flashlight. The streaks were dancing all around it and shooting through its case, shorting out the batteries.

Sparks arced from the wall to their heads, and their hair spiked in all directions. They couldn't ground or discharge themselves. When they attempted to touch the wall, or each other, there was no inadvertent recoil and "ouch" as when static electricity discharges from your finger to a grounded surface.

Michael changed the batteries and turned the flashlight on again. Almost immediately, it started to blink and flicker. The temperature had now risen to nearly fifteen degrees celsius, or about sixty degrees fahrenheit, warm on the surface here, even in June.

When he yelled out for Sam at the top of his voice, not only was there no echo, his voice came out in a whisper. They were now up to their knees in the liquid fog.

They moved over to the sidewall for a frame of reference if their flashlights went out again. The wall was no longer solid, but had a leathery, pebbled skin that receded to the touch, like a timid house pet. Michael leaned against the wall and this time it engulfed his hand like a beanbag and quickly consumed his arm.

"Sarah," his voice cracked, "it's got hold of me and won't let go. Help me get my hand out."

Sarah's feet were slowly sinking into the floor as well, but she hadn't yet penetrated the floor's skin. When they were walking in the middle of the tunnel, it felt like they were still treading on the coarse, calcium carbonate rock, so Sarah stuck the flashlight in her waistband and leaned toward the center floor. When she ducked her head into the opaque fluid nothing happened. She felt like she was moving through very thick air. She could breathe easily and painlessly, but her body told her that she wasn't getting any oxygen. She stuck her head above the clouds, took a deep breath, and dove in. The floor was just irregularly shaped enough for her fingers to grasp the jagged surface. Her arms fully extended and her nails buried into the rock, she dragged her feet from the death grip of the perimeter floor to the coarse hard center path. Her neoprene shoes had disappeared.

The harder Michael struggled, the closer his nose edged to the wall and the stronger the tar smell became. He couldn't pick his feet up without leaning farther forward, and he couldn't see them either.

"Stop struggling," Sarah screamed, but her voice was barely audible six feet away.

He whimpered, "Please get me out of here. It's eaten through the cuff of my jacket."

"Is it burning?"

"No, it's just warm. I can move my fingers a little bit."

"What do you think it is?"

"Now's not the time to dissect it. Pull me out."

Sarah didn't see how it would be possible, but she didn't want Michael to panic. She looked in her knapsack for something—for anything—to try and to give her time to think without revealing her fear to Michael. She had duct tape, a cooler, food, matches, sample jars, and batteries. In her pockets she had chemical hand warmers, a knife, Canadian coins, and a magnifying glass.

She lit a couple of matches, and as soon as they flickered she threw them against the wall. They were out before they hit the side and immediately absorbed by the wall.

Inside the cooler were several chunks of dry ice. She put her gloves back on, grabbed one and touched it to the floor. At first, nothing seemed to happen, and then it just disappeared from between her tongs.

"Did you realize that you were putting frozen carbon dioxide into a carbon dioxide bath?"

A soundless shriek escaped her lips. Sam and his voice had changed in the last six hours. His complexion had the radiance of a teenage girl, and he was as frisky as a puppy. He spoke with the timbre of an opera baritone.

"What the hell are you talking about?"

"We are several kilometers below the surface. At this pressure, carbon dioxide has the density of a liquid, but the diffusivity of a gas. You are standing in pure liquid carbon dioxide."

Michael said, "This is all very interesting, but can we talk about this later? *You* seem to be feeling better, but my condition has deteriorated somewhat."

He smiled calmly, "Let's get Michael out of there and I'll explain."

Sam's yoga master serenity calmed the desperation the cousins had been trying to suppress. What did he know that they didn't?

"We need to take these core sampling plugs apart at the seams and put them around Michael's arms." The core samplers were galvanized steel tubes about the length of an adult shoe with a handle across the end. One simply pushed it into the ground with their hand or foot and pulled out a round cylinder of sample.

Sam and Sarah split the two samplers and put them over Michael's arms like metal cuffs and then popped the seams back together.

"We pop these over Michael's arms and then push them into the wall to form a barrier between his skin and the wall. I believe he's being attacked by some sort of fungus that consumes organic material and carbon dioxide." He turned around to show that the back of his parka was completely gone. "Once it gets a taste of this steel, it should stop sucking on Michael's arms. I don't think it would really eat him anyway. He's still alive."

It took nearly a minute before the fungus spit him out. Then Sarah and Sam were able to each grab an arm and extricate his legs from the pudding with a large thwack that landed him on the hard center floor.

Sarah borrowed the forearm cuffs, dove into the carbon dioxide, and managed to retrieve what was left of her boots.

The doctor paced nervously. "You were 'sucked in' a little sooner than I was. Infectious diseases aren't just viruses and bacteria. There's foot and genital fungi and the wall fungus living on the liquid carbon dioxide in this cave system. They may have survived on it out in space, too, where it would have been a solid. I used the portable air analyzer. The overall oxygen levels in the air are about normal, but the carbon dioxide is extraordinarily high, much higher than we would find on the surface, so there's less nitrogen down here. Liquid carbon dioxide doesn't even exist on the earth's surface. At atmospheric pressure it goes straight from a solid to a gas. Sarah, I'm surprised you didn't put all of that together."

Sarah had been sitting on the hard path in the center of the tunnel. When she looked up into the doctor's eyes, he saw tear streaks washing the grime from her cheeks. "You're right. Sorry." She looked at her cousin. "I was a little preoccupied."

The doctor squatted down in front of her and spoke softly. "What would you like to do now?"

The question forced Sarah to leave her emotions behind and return to the mission. "We'll take samples. Fungi are one of the very few multi-celled organisms that can survive out in space. This fungus cannot live on the earth's surface because it consumes liquid carbon dioxide and other organic material and then seems to sequester the carbon as calcium carbonate and magnesium carbonate. Life really can flourish anywhere, and we don't even recognize it." As Sarah uttered those last words, recognition dawned.

"I thought you were keeping way too much scientific equipment next to an igloo in Talurqjuak. Sam, what's your last name?"

Now it was Sam's turn to be embarrassed. "I think you know the answer already."

"You shared the Nobel Prize for Medicine in 1988. Why didn't you tell us?"

"The last expert you took with you died and right before we came down here, you told me that you didn't want to share a discovery with a bunch of neophytes in Antarctica. What would you have done?"

Michael said, "You are a wily man, Sam. You must be one tenacious research scientist."

Sarah said, "What happened to you in the tunnel, Sam?"

"I walked along this branch of the tunnel for about a half kilometer or so past here. I stayed near the center of the path initially. Abruptly the path dropped off steeply and became very slippery. I attempted to get a hand hold on the walls, but the floor caught hold of my feet. I screamed, and well you know where that went.

"I was oozed away in some oily coating on top of this stuff. I had taken off my pack to take samples, so it was left lying on the stone portion of the cave floor. The floor was quite comfortable, though. As you probably noticed, Michael, it's kind of warm beneath its surface. As soon as I realized that struggling only made it worse, I lay perfectly still and floated downstream like a log on a waterfall. As I cascaded over a sheer drop-off, my body was ejected in a slippery mess into a pool of water below. I got knocked around a bit, but I ended up with nothing more than a bad headache in exchange for complete remission of my emphysema symptoms. Not a bad trade-off, wouldn't you say?"

Sarah said, "Because of the pressure down here, I think the fungus is absorbing the water and releasing some sort of hydrocarbon with an oxygen by-product or vice-versa, which explains the smell."

"You notice the very carefully orchestrated changes in color and frequency and intensity of the light in here? Sometimes it turns the whole cave system red. It's almost impossible to see through it at times," Sam responded.

"No. Where did you see it, at the bottom of the waterfall?" she asked.

"Yes, and right here, too. That's odd. Are you both color blind?"

Sam turned to start collecting samples so he couldn't see the puzzled looks shared by Michael and Sarah. Sarah mouthed, "I'm not color blind."

Michael shook his head.

With the sample bags in tow, it took nearly eight hours to make it back to the entrance.

In the main rotunda, Sam opened up one of the large cases that had been too cumbersome to lug down the tunnel. "Ever see one of these, Sarah?"

"Never that small. It's a portable mass spectrometer, isn't it?"

"It's configured for an assortment of volatile organic compounds and heavy metals."

Sam had taken a pair of identical samples at several points during their exploration. Now he tested one each of four of the identical pairs. If the mass spectrometer was given a large range of compounds to seek, it would identify the specific compound found and its relative presence in the sample.

Sarah leaned over his shoulder as the machine displayed its chemically encoded results.

"Sam, isn't that almost exactly the composition of low sulfur crude oil?"

"It would seem that we or the comet have somehow stumbled across fungus either living in oil reserves here in the Arctic tundra or producing them. It's going to be a lot tougher to keep this secret."

"Well, given all of the toxins, diseases, and infections originating from fungi, it may already know how to protect itself," Sarah said.

On the surface, it was nighttime. Sam pulled a sheet of plywood and a saw from the back of the pick-up truck. They fashioned a cover over the opening to the cave, heaped mud and snow over it, prayed for some fresh powder and departed.

They drove without a break to the airstrip where Sarah and Michael had first arrived. The immunologist was on the phone for nearly an hour before he emerged from the cinder block control tower. Michael texted Neil to tell him that he had to hold his story due to preemptive public health concerns. Neil gave the public forty-eight hours to get safe. He wanted his story before the *Toronto Mail* broke it.

Sam spoke loudly to be heard over a turboprop engine warming up on the tarmac. "I contacted the head of the Canadian Royal Academy of

Sciences. They are expecting snow here in the next forty-eight hours. It should be enough to cover our tracks. The site is on Nunavut territorial land. We don't know exactly how far we traveled underground, so they'll have their solicitors deal with the property rights issues.

"The Royal Canadian Mounted Police will provide twenty-four-hour air surveillance until the site is thoroughly investigated and sample analysis is complete. I am taking everything to Toronto now," he concluded, motioning to the large twin-engine DeHavilland Dash-8 with the territorial government's crest on its wings.

"Doctor, I have an obligation to my university. I would like to participate in some of the studies," Sarah yelled over the fluttering of the propellers at start-up.

"Understood. You two will get full credit for this discovery. And you will have a major role in the research." He puzzled a moment. "Aren't you coming along?"

"Sure," Michael said.

Sarah glared at Michael. "We can go with you to Toronto for a couple of days, but then Michael has to file a story, and I need to return to school to finish a project that I've had six and a half months to do and it's due in a week. We'll be back after I hand it in."

"Michael, I am sure that your editor is pushing for a story. Please defer identification of the site until we can secure the location. You seem to do great travel pieces. Why don't you open your first installment with how you decided to come here? I know I'd find that fascinating."

CHAPTER 15
Conflict and Confrontation

"You've already bought us tickets to Uzbekistan, didn't you?" Sarah wrung her hands as she paced. "Michael, we are out of time. One hundred ninety-six days, remember? We have four days. Then…"

"Then, what? MC won't harm us. It needs us to do *Its* bidding."

"This isn't about harm, you moron. It's about an urgent need for answers. We need to find out why MC appears to care more about protecting microbes, rather than preventing a pandemic, so that we might possibly provide some cogent advice to the Canadian government before magnetic north moves in the next three weeks and it's too late. Does MC care about nothing other than letting evolution take its course? Not only do we have a responsibility to, I don't know, maybe our fellow humans, we have to find out why MC came up with this deadline. Hasn't it occurred to you that maybe there is some other threat out there?"

Sarah knew that Michael understood the stakes as well as she did, if not better. While the questions were different, Michael had an even more urgent need for answers. She could take decades understanding why MC cared about humanity plundering the planet. But, MC's identity, and why *It* was communicating with them was critical to both their immediate survival and Michael's career.

When Michael had accused her of being difficult just for the pleasure, Sarah knew that the treatment was mutual. It was an integral part of their relationship. But, this time, he wasn't being obdurate just for enjoyment. He wanted something.

"All right, out with it. What do you want?"

He reddened slightly. "If I ever get married and my wife knows me as well as you do, I am in big trouble."

"You already are, because I intend to tell her everything."

"Business class. We travel separately. And I have some equipment I want us to take and I don't think a reporter will be able to make it through customs," Michael said.

She fired back. "We leave tomorrow and meet up in Tashkent. You arrive first. No one will know where we are going, except M'low Cloom, of course, and maybe the State Department. Hopefully, it will take the Feds a little longer to figure out where we are going, if we leave from Canada."

"Visas?"

"You pick up yours at the American Embassy in Athens."

"Very thorough. What part of this did I just negotiate for, that you didn't have planned already?" He dropped his shoulders in surrender. "Okay, I'll get us transportation while I'm waiting for your arrival. Speed is important. I have to file this story."

"Understood. Please be invisible. We really need to avoid attracting attention to ourselves."

TASHKENT, UZBEKISTAN - TWO DAYS LATER

Sarah connected in Frankfurt where she was to pick up her visa at the US Consular Office there and then arrive at Tashkent about eight hours after Michael.

German security was as efficient as during the Third Reich, though much more even-handed and courteous. As part of their deal, Michael had convinced Sarah to be the courier for a highly sophisticated array of sensing and monitoring equipment to better unlock the mystery of M'low Cloom.

Unfortunately, much of the hi-tech equipment was also ideally suited for terrorist activities. After twenty-four hours of interrogation and several encrypted conversations with the FBI and Interpol, German security conferred and Sarah was released.

Sarah vacillated between perplexed and rabid. What was her cousin hiding when he insisted that she bring the equipment along? He had her so worn down that she hadn't bothered to interrogate *him* further when he insisted she bring the equipment. Either the shmuck knew that whoever had the equipment would get waylaid and searched and he wanted a couple of days to party, or he was just incredibly lazy.

She finally resumed her trip two days behind schedule. There was no longer any margin for error, but at least none of the most critical electronics had been waylaid at an impoundment facility in Frankfurt. Michael sounded unconcerned when she spoke to him just before her departure. He assured her that he would make expedited travel arrangements, recover the lost time, and sidetrack the media hounds if they showed themselves. She still wasn't happy with him, but she had no time to dwell on her own emotions.

Michael returned to the airport and was directed to a corrugated metal shack the size of a basketball court in an isolated corner of the air freight terminal. On a makeshift pad sat a recently painted black market Russian military chopper, its rotors glinting fresh gold paint.

Sitting on a threadbare couch sat a matching man. The pilot had an angry jagged scar over his right eyebrow, a gold front tooth, and patched jeans. Days of salt and pepper stubble covered a pock-marked complexion. He wore an olive flight jacket that appeared to have been strafed along the sleeve.

Michael ran a hand over a half dozen grey hairs in his unshaven chin, shoved both hands roughly into his jacket pockets and swaggered through the door menacingly until he flinched at a spider that had dropped by its silky thread right in front of his face. He nonchalantly studied a model of a MiG-25 Foxbat interceptor jet capable of altitudes of 120,000 feet, early AK-47 semi-automatic rifles and an Mi-24 single rotor helicopter with a glass house cockpit that exactly matched the one on the tarmac, while developing a plausible story. The pilot grew impatient, stuck his head out the door, and spat on the black tarmac. Then he walked toward the journalist and extended a deeply scarred hand with mutilated ring and pinky fingers. With the other hand he fondled the fine brown suede of Michael's jacket.

"Very, very nice. Where you need to go?" he said in a thickly accented Turkic rasp. Before Michael could respond, the man played out his resume. Oishkipeh had served briefly in the Soviet Army, played mercenary for a while, and now ran a helicopter tourist service, shuttling international corporate executives to manufacturing facilities or remote mines and mining offices. Michael's request that Oishkipeh take him and a female companion just beyond a remote mountain pass and then pick them up two days later was a little off the tourist route.

Journalist Michael wasn't accustomed to being the "interogatee." No, he told Oishkipeh, he was not a corporate executive. Yes, he was here on kind-of a vacation and he realized that his destination wasn't a tourist hot spot. He confided that he was a travel reporter and very quickly flashed his press credentials before the pilot could read them. He was writing an article about exotic vacation destinations for discreet executives to visit with special companions that needed to keep their identities private.

Michael's readers were accustomed to sightseeing first class, he explained. A helicopter tour of the mountains would suit them well and his photographer wanted to be inserted into the mountains for a night or two to photograph the local wildlife to accompany his article. Oishkipeh agreed to take Michael and his photographer on their brief junket. Michael bartered briefly over the fare and lost. There was only one private helicopter in town.

Michael casually mentioned that he had a night to kill until the photographer arrived. The pilot winked knowingly and made some recommendations, which Michael thought, along with the suggestions of the concierge, ought to keep him busy until Sarah arrived.

Sarah headed straight from the airport to her restaurant rendezvous with Michael. He did not immediately acknowledge her arrival. Michael had scheduled a lunch date with his Russian beauty of the evening before and now he would have to diplomatically jettison her.

He sauntered over to Sarah at the bar and began talking softly.

"So, how was your trip? Act excited to have me pick you up," Michael suggested.

"I'm excited," she monotoned. "The flight was great. Are you a member of the mile high club, too?" She unbuttoned the top button of her top to expose some cleavage.

She glanced over her cousin's shoulder. "You think I'm excited? You should see the woman you just dumped." She motioned with her eyes to the woman behind Michael's back.

"Oh, I, uh, met her just a little while ago and told her that I was meeting a business associate. I probably forgot to tell her that you were attractive."

"Right. And she forgot to tell you that she was Uzbek secret service?"

"You are paranoid."

"And you are stupid, because she is either much too good looking for you or desperate to latch onto an American. What is she doing in a bar at lunch time? This isn't the local watering hole of the metro Tashkent office district."

Michael decided not to press the issue. He had spent the night at an ecstasy party and his cousin had spent the night in an airport after a night in interrogation.

They found a table next to a window overlooking dilapidated grey buildings and broken asphalt. The menu boasted an exotic selection of smoked goat and spiced lamb's organs. Michael expected Sarah to be relieved that he had booked the helicopter to save time.

"That's not exactly clandestine, but after my interrogation by Interpol in Frankfurt, what difference does it make?"

"Sarah, we haven't talked since we left Nunavut. Maybe we got it all wrong at magnetic north. Remember the glow in the cave that Sam was telling us about that we never really did see and that bullshit about us being color blind? I think that when we finish our analysis, we are going to find that Sam and maybe all Inuit can see farther into the infrared spectrum than most other people. Kind of equivalent to dogs hearing sounds above the range of most humans."

"I did some research. Carbon dioxide emits infrared radiation at a wavelength of 4.26 micrometers, which is just below visible red light in the infrared spectrum. That's what Sam was seeing. I think MC was communicating with that fungus somehow. Otherwise, how would *It* have known what those cave murals looked like? If the Inuit were telepathic, they would have communicated with *It* hundreds of years ago, but the comet wasn't there back then."

"According to your theory, MC is going to want that fungus protected because it communicates with *It*. According to my theory, *It's* going to want not just that fungus, but everything in the cave protected because it doesn't want a bunch of scientists and politicians monkeying with natural evolution, even if it could unleash a plague on the planet. The logical conclusion is still the same, though. MC doesn't care about humanity."

Sarah refused to speculate. "We'll find out soon enough, either when the lab results come in or when we rendezvous tomorrow night. Let's go to the airstrip and get some answers." One day left.

Oishkipeh eyed Sarah lasciviously and then quickly donned a mask of hospitality. Sarah decided some casual flirting could only make Oishkipeh more cooperative.

As the helicopter took off, Sarah felt the gentle g-forces press her into her seat cushion.

"Your first flight in a helicopter, Ann?" Oishkipeh asked over the whomp, whomp, whomp of the blades as they cut the air. Neither of them had obtained passports with forged identities, but here, the American dollar was still king. If Sarah wanted to identify herself as Ann, no one would ask any questions.

"Yes," she said tentatively. Her eyes immediately shot to Michael, giving him a quizzical look.

The pilot handed her the joystick. "Here, it's easy. Just wiggle. It goes where you want to go."

She took the phallic symbol confidently and stroked it purposefully with her thumb and forefinger. Then she smiled at Oishkipeh outside of Michael's field of vision. Michael, or Mark, was distracted anyway. He had never been in a helicopter either and the sensation of continuously leaning out of his seat when they moved forward wasn't any better than his one trip in a glider. He began scanning the approaching rocks and hillside very carefully. This was a unique opportunity to see their meeting place from above, if he could find it.

In late March, the higher elevations were still covered in a deep snow pack. Only scrubs of pine and rocks jutted up from the mountainsides and peaks. From the air, very little of the ground was exposed. Michael motioned to Oishkipeh.

"Where's the pass?" he yelled over the engine.

Oishkipeh pointed to a cleft in the mountains. From the air, it was indistinguishable from the surrounding sea of white.

"I can't see anything," Michael yelled back.

"Of course not. It's blocked. You didn't know? I thought that's why you hired me to bring you here. Stupid Americans."

Michael shrugged. "When does it clear out?"

"Hard to say. If there's no more snow this season, I would guess maybe two to three weeks it might be warm enough to get through. The weather has been warm the last several days. Maybe sooner than two weeks."

"Where you say you come from, Ann?"

"Chicago, Illinois. Ever heard of it?"

"Sure, it's in central part of America. Central America?"

She chuckled disarmingly. "No, those are countries just south of Mexico and north of South America. You'd probably call this Midwestern America."

"Okay. What you do there?"

"I am a student at a college there."

"Is that where you meet Mark?"

"Yes."

"But you live in different cities now, no?"

"Mark gets around. We see each other pretty often."

Michael grunted and motioned to Sarah with his eyes. She looked down. From the sky the meeting point appeared to be a plateau scattered with scrub trees in the early stages of budding. For the most part, it was covered with snow, hiding the animal massacre that lay beneath, but in some spots it was thin to bare. To the more casual observer, it was nothing more than snow-covered scrub and fallen branches. If you knew what you were looking for, you could see bumps and bulges in the snow, barely covering rib cages and carcasses.

"What's that, Oishkipeh?" Sarah pointed off in the opposite direction as she jerked the joystick up and in the direction she was pointing. The chopper quickly rose several hundred feet. The jolt gave her an excuse to grab Oishkipeh's thigh for balance. It lingered long enough to be a distraction. She relaxed. Now the gruesome graveyard of baked bones was to their rear, as was Michael's lunch.

A pristine waterfall cascaded over a cliff foaming into a narrow river in a ravine below. Wary antelope were drinking at its base, with an ear and nostril open for predators. Sarah thought the field was near their campsite, but the waterfall was new.

"It flows only in the spring. It usually starts later, but like I said, it's been warm just the last several days and we had a lot of snow this winter. It's generally dry by late summer."

Michael interjected. "Put us down anywhere around here, please."

Oishkipeh took back the controls and brought the helicopter in smoothly.

Michael had advanced him fifty dollars before they started and the pilot had agreed to put them down within 350 miles of the starting point.

Michael now paid him two hundred dollars and the balance of two hundred fifty dollars was due when he picked them up and returned them back to the airport late the next day. If they could reach him via satellite phone or e-mail, then they could adjust their plans.

Sarah walked ahead while Michael squared up. The pilot grabbed Michael's arm and said in Russian, "If I had known this was what you were waiting for, I would have sent you to much classier women. I would pay for this one."

"Money can't pay her price," and he ran to catch up with Sarah who was already in wilderness mode. They set up camp for the night after Oishkipeh was well out of view. The next night was their meeting with MC.

Oishkipeh stopped by the hotel to visit his concierge friend as soon as he landed. Josef recalled that Mark always dressed in jeans and tipped in American money. Late the night before, he had come back to the hotel with one of the local high-class prostitutes.

The pilot slipped Josef ten dollars. He found the whore the next day in the restaurant where Michael and Sarah had met for lunch. For another twenty dollars, he learned that she and Mark had partied the night before and she stole money from his wallet. She also came across his press credentials. She didn't claim to remember his name, but didn't think it was Mark. She didn't care. Most men lied to her. Another ten dollars, and she remembered the name Michael Seagal. She also described his lunch date.

An internet search produced names and pictures of the two cousins, as well as their escapades with a woolly mammoth, a dead man, and a tsunami. At least it explained why a beautiful woman would be camping in the Uzbek back-country in March with a man like Michael. Oishkipeh was scheduled to pick them up at three o'clock the next day.

Sarah and Michael hiked up the snow-covered path on autopilot. At nightfall, they waited. The weather dipped below freezing, but it was still balmier than sub-Arctic Canada. The sky grew partly overcast, blotting out the moon, and a northerly wind ushered in a cold front. They lit a large fire. Dawn emerged through a cloudy sky, but M'low Cloom did not.

Sarah's doubts were growing. Had MC ever been there to start with? Perhaps the organic theory really did line up better with the facts on the ground. The hydrogen sulfide gas knocked them out, caused them to hallucinate and somebody, some real person who didn't want to take the risks themselves, brainwashed them into believing all of these clues that they had planted in their brains. Michael just made up the vision at the glider site to be supportive of his ditzy cousin's senseless expeditions to save the world.

Sarah was also puzzled by Michael's behavior. There were none of his usual rants about returning home or what an idiot he was for letting her talk him into this. She didn't want to ask him what he thought about MC's absence because she knew she'd have to listen to the I-told-you-so's and he'd insist on abandoning the quest. But, if he never believed any of this MC nonsense to start with, that would explain his taciturn behavior. She'd give it one more day and then take her lumps. She needed to buy some time. She asked if they should contact the pilot and delay their return a day while she went with him to the farmer's barn and got him some more hash.

"I already have. Contacted the pilot, that is. He'll be here at ten o'clock tomorrow morning." He said nothing else about MC's tardiness after that.

The extra day was all that Oishkipeh needed. He flew in low to avoid detection and landed a day's hike from where he had deposited Sarah and Michael. He rented a burro to take him to the drop point. It would be weeks before the writer and the scientist would publicize whatever they found. They would have research, papers, contracts, many things to do. The online stories said they were very secretive about their expeditions. Just today, Oishkipeh saw rumors that they had returned from a great discovery in Northern Canada only to immediately disappear again. Their whereabouts were a mystery.

Oishkipeh spotted them at their camp near dusk. He hid the burro behind some rocks and branches, pulled a bandolier of cartridges off his shoulder, and slung it over the neck of the burro. He crouched near the ground and focused his binoculars. They seemed to be doing nothing. There was no fancy equipment there, just pots, pans and…nothing. He looked several hundred meters past their campsite and saw the stripped carcasses and bleached bones of hundreds of animals strewn around a large field, peeking out from the snow cover.

"I have heard legends of these things," he muttered to himself. "In Africa or India, elephants all migrate to a central graveyard to die. I wonder how they found this place?"

CHAPTER 16

The Pilot

Immediately after sunset, a California Candle of flames shot up into the black sky from a small crack between two hills to the west. The cloudy orange and purple waves on the horizon distorted its distance. Sarah and Michael grabbed their heads. An unfamiliar androgynous voice bellowed, "I am here."

The mental reverberations knocked them off their feet, slamming them into the ground. Was the sound all within their heads or exploding around them?

M'low Cloom commanded them to travel to the source of a spewing volcano of fire. They heeded *Its* call like zombies. They had traveled around the world, slept in the bitter cold, and waited an extra day for the return of M'low Cloom and when *It* arrived they were instantly renewed.

On *Its* first visit, *It* had projected flat images without emotion. This time, MC took Sarah and Michael on a roller coaster ride with their own feelings at the helm. Rage shook Sarah, and she was blinded by tears of despair for her planet. She prostrated herself at the boots of her superiors, groveling for mercy. For a moment, MC seemed to be an omniscient extraterrestrial that predicted the future of their world. Then, their consciousness and their emotions melded with MC, and *It* was nothing but a collection of selected memories from around the universe.

By contrast, Michael felt a surge of empathy toward MC that dissipated his anger toward the unidentified intelligence. As different as his feelings were from Sarah's, the result was the same. He and MC were emoting as one.

The voice said, "No. You are one of the very few that will not see hell!"

Sarah did not hear, imagine or feel Michael's thoughts, but felt MC's response. MC again sensed their confusion.

They continued to move toward the volcanic flames. Sparks and molten rock flew hundreds of feet into the air and oozed down the mountain side. Trees crackled in flames as they were touched by the scalding liquid rock. The snow briefly became rivulets before it vaporized. Miraculously, the cousins remained unscathed by the heat and the spitting lava. Their cauldron of emotions slowly came into focus. MC's anger was palpable, yet forgiving.

"Why," *It* wanted to know, "did you wait more than three months before traveling to Antarctica? And then, after you found the animals in the ice, why did you delay traveling to the comet?"

Michael said in his mind, *How can It be so stupid? Doesn't It understand the mess It has gotten us into?*

Sarah understood. The androgynous voice was a blend of hers and Michael's, created by *It* and projected into their heads. *It* was only asking questions that either Sarah or Michael were asking themselves or each other.

In their minds, the vision turned to Sarah and responded. "If mankind encounters life forms from the comet, it will destroy them, even though they are not a threat to the planet, but an evolutionary advancement."

It directed itself to Michael. "Still you doubt me." And then a tapestry of millions of societies fading into oblivion. "We do not measure days in rotations of the earth, or years in trips around the sun; we measure time as the galaxy grows." They sensed M'low Cloom's humor. "It takes an uneven number of earth rotations for the earth to revolve around the sun."

What is It talking about? They thought as one.

From a great distance, they could see the earth moving to a precise spot in its orbit around the sun. When the earth started its journey, it was night in Uzbekistan. When it finished it was daytime. They both knew the earth took 365 and one-quarter days to orbit the sun. M'low Cloom was a day late because of *a rounding error*. It was part of the same problem *It* had with pinpointing a location for the cave. Latitude was easy, because it is a celestial and geometric concept, but longitude is strictly a manmade concept, an abstract notion to MC.

MC was manipulating their thoughts, but not by extortion, deception, or mind control. MC was simply using superior logic to win a debate with them. *It* had won Sarah over, but Michael was not yet convinced.

But, MC's tardiness and *Its* celestial view of time, rather than in terms of the earth's rotation raised a question that Michael was not going to let go unanswered. *MC, where do you communicate with us from?*

MC was perplexed. *It* did not exist at a particular place or time. MC somehow controlled a great deal of electromagnetic energy. The energy was similar to the electromagnetic radiation emitted from the sun, but *It* released *Its* energy in discrete waves and packets and intensities that actually communicated something. Like the supernova destruction of a star viewed on earth hundreds of light years later, the energy released dissipated and grew fuzzy over great distances. MC's communications with anything, including Sarah and Michael, grew weak and staticky as the distance increased.

M'low Cloom showed Sarah and Michael dangerous weapons that were possessed by people that would not or could not use them. They were naturally occurring bacteria or viruses, harnessed by man for their power to destroy other men. They posed a greater, unknown danger to other life on the planet, with grave indirect consequences to mankind as well. They had to destroy the weapons, and this time the vision had showed them a detailed map leading them straight to their prize–or to their doom.

Through another's eyes, they were peering into a jungle cave guarded by African soldiers. Then their M'low Cloomian conduit was thrown into the cave with innocent young men, boy soldiers really, who in the vision, died from exposure to the weapon and were then heaped into a mass grave and burned beyond recognition. Sarah and Michael were heading into the middle of a civil war in Sudan and they had 212 days from their first rendezvous with MC to accomplish their mission. Within days thereafter, MC knew that people with whom *It* communicated would retrieve the weapons and use them to destroy nearly all of the telepathic people remaining on the planet, including Sarah and Michael.

They were in earth's future now. Animals evolved into new species, some as different from those on earth today as the dinosaurs were to modern man. A few were evolutions of existing marine mammals and primates that developed to rival man.

The flourishing new species were resistant to naturally occurring viruses and bacteria. Those that weren't had died out. In isolated ecosystems, people were mutating, adapting and proliferating.

Some of the changes were superficial and physical. Bald men and saggy-breasted women were nearly extinct. Other changes were invisible, yet more significant, like an improved olfactory sense. And completely new senses were propagating through the population, telepathic senses like the ability to communicate with MC and electromagnetic senses like Sam's or a monarch butterfly's. MC was making a prognostication of likely results of natural selection based on *Its* past experience. Humanity as Michael and Sarah knew it, had been medically and genetically repaired for so long that their species had been leap-frogged over by those that benefitted from natural selection. Homo sapiens, as they knew them today, was becoming extinct.

Oishkipeh watched the cousins leave the camp. Now, he could barely see the forms of Sarah and Michael at the top of the hill. He did not see a fountain illuminating the sky, just two people wandering around a wide cleft in the mountains with a volcanic crater-like hill as a backdrop. He attempted to pick up their conversation with his directional listening equipment. Their lips were moving, but they were saying nothing.

"This is not a scientist and a journalist doing research. These are a couple of nuts," he muttered aloud.

The light fluffy powder of snow muffled Oishkipeh's movements up to Sarah and Michael's site. The brush rustled softly, yet the air was still. He pulled his pistol from his waistband and crouched at the back side of their tent. Clearly visible in the snow were new cat tracks. Oishkipeh smelled rotten meat and then felt the warm moist breath breathing on his left shoulder. He turned his head slowly to face the charcoal streaks on the yellow fangs of a mountain lion. The yellow eyes locked onto their target and then one hundred kilograms of muscle sprung through the air. Oishkipeh saw bits of raw flesh between the fangs heading toward his throat. He shot wildly, grazing the cat. It turned to run, trailing blood. Oishkipeh shot again at the animal's tail as it ran across the field and back into the heavy bramble. The cracks of his 9mm Glock echoed through the canyon. His chest heaving through his coat, Oishkipeh sat for only a few moments before returning to his tracking of Sarah and Michael. He was not going to let a wild animal distract him. If they spotted him, he had an alibi at the ready.

Michael seized an opportunity to horse trade. *M'low Cloom, we will do as you ask, but who are you and why are you here communicating with us?*

Sarah posed two questions. *M'low Cloom, are you able to communicate only with us, and what is the significance of these discoveries to you?*

MC confirmed Michael's hypothesis. They had inherited telepathy and there were a number of others who communicated with MC at different levels. MC offered an allegory of a man living on an island and teaching another man and his dog to fish to survive. Soon the dog's descendants fished better than the humans did. The humans perished but the dog flourished.

Why did the dog's skill quickly outpace the human? Sarah asked, but as soon as she did so, she knew the answer. The dog had been allowed to evolve naturally.

Unheard by Sarah and Michael, two shots echoed through the canyon and their trances were broken by an intense charge of what? Static electricity? Lightning? It crackled and snapped as it hit the ground far below them, standing their hair on end.

MC's last transmission was a charred human at their campsite and several sunrises that would pass before they could see him with their own eyes. Then everything went dark.

Sarah and Michael waved their arms in chaotic windmills calling out to each other. The warmth that had radiated from the vision departed as instantaneously as it had appeared. The chill of the air returned.

"Sarah?"

She sensed his fear and moved quickly to his voice, tripping and falling into him, knocking him over.

"I'm scared."

"You should be, Michael. You pissed *It* off."

"I pissed *It* off? Well, if you didn't piss *It* off, then why are you blind, too?"

"Who said I was blind?"

Michael said, "Okay, then lead the way back to camp and stop feeling my face."

"In my mind's eye, I can still see everything."

"Great, but your mind and butt are still attached. A lot of good your clairvoyance will do if you are frozen solid."

They laughed until tears chapped their faces.

"Michael, let's see if we can feel around and collect something to start a fire. You have matches, don't you?"

"Do I have matches? I have hash, too."

"Great, we'll burn that to keep us warm."

"I've got a little flask of Russian vodka."

They each took a swig and started feeling around on the ground. "Shit. Oww," said Sarah.

"What happened?"

"I twisted my ankle when I tripped into you. It hurts to put weight on it."

"How fortunate. I don't think we have anywhere to go for awhile."

She paused for a long moment, "Do you think *It* knows that you have a different agenda?"

"*It* doesn't care, Sarah. *It* has its own agenda, and *It* needs both of us to execute it. *It* doesn't care what my agenda is. *It's* keeping us around because we can communicate with *It*. If MC really needed us, *It* would have left us dinner."

"We are blind and stranded in the Uzbek wilderness and all you can think about is food? Ummm, Michael?"

"Yeah."

"There's an animal here. It's got a hoof. It's got at least two hooves. It's got hair, not really fur and a body. It's got bags on its back and a bandolier of bullets around its neck. It's got pointed ears and a bridle." And then it nuzzled her and she smiled. "And it's got a scar on its nose, Michael. It's the burro we rented on our last trip."

"You're crazy."

"I may be, but there's a burro hallucinating on my leg. Oh, look. Or, don't look. There is food, a little propane stove and a bedroll in the burro's pack. What did you want MC to leave us?"

She fed the animal from the food slung across his back. Then she tied him to a tree and Michael found wood for a fire. Sarah and Michael stuffed themselves into the single sleeping bag and draped their coats over some sticks, making a little tent for their faces. Michael tossed and turned.

"Now what?"

"This isn't some God awful camping trip of yours, Sarah. As you said, we are blind and stranded in the outback of a foreign country. There are wild animals. We have guns, but unfortunately we are blind, so we can only use them to whack at the animals, which means we'll probably hit each other. At the end of our vision, MC charred something or someone. That burro belonged to someone."

"We are traveling with very little of value, mostly your laptop and a bunch of batteries. If someone finds us before Oishkipeh gets here, we'll offer them money if they get us back to civilization. Oishkipeh already knows we are worth more if he gets us back to Tashkent. Stay up all night and stoke the fire, if you're worried about being eaten alive."

"Then it would be just like camping at home."

"Very funny. That's mosquitoes. It's too cold."

Michael and the burro moved methodically around the campsite collecting more loose wood for their fire, orienting themselves periodically by the fire's warmth and Sarah's voice.

He sat on a stump, listening to wolves howling in the distance. Were they getting closer?

"Fuck it. Either they eat me or MC will protect me or I'll get lucky." He drifted off with embers dancing high into the sky where they metamorphosed into shooting orbs and the wolves' howls became MC's tremulous voice until their muzzles exploded in a splatter of blood and guts.

"Even in your dreams, you are lucky, Michael." He woke with a start. She put a finger over his lips. "Shhh. You will wake your cousin."

He turned to her voice and put a hand up to her face. "Sudecki?"

"You recognize me."

"I recognize the myrrh and lilacs. And the dimple. We are blind, Sudecki."

"Blind?"

"We can't see. Just for a little while."

"How, Michael?"

"There was an explosion. Do my eyes look all right?"

"Most of you filthy, but your eyes are beautiful green, Michael."

His cheeks burned. "What time is it?"

"It's early. Sun in maybe one hour. I saw smoke from your fire. I am happy I found you."

She took his hand and gently stood him up. Most of her nails were broken and her palms calloused, but even the backs of her hands, supple and secure, aroused him. He caressed them and she lightly massaged his palm with her thumb. "Come, I will feed and clean you."

She led him down the hill toward the water where she washed his face and tended to his cuts and bruises. "Now your face is cold. I am sorry."

He felt the warmth of her cheek pressed on his before her lips softly parted his, and then his mouth was on fire. She pushed him down to the ground. If he could be this aroused and debilitated from the tenderness of her breasts, then sight was hopelessly overrated.

She guided him inside her, and their fantasies merged into an erotic rhythm. Michael melded with her, body and soul. She screamed and Michael moaned simultaneously as they climaxed, or so he thought.

"Michael, there's a body over there in the bushes."

She helped him back into his pants and led him to the bushes.

Michael heard Sudecki rustling around the body. "Oh my God, Michael, here's his identification card. He's with the secret police. Someone is going to come looking for him. We have to get out of here."

"How long has he been dead?"

"Not even hours. Blood from his mouth still wet. Birds circling overhead."

Sarah was awakened by the burro's icy nose and the radiant warmth of the sun. She bolted up disoriented until the previous day's events flooded her memory. She stroked the animal's nose and slithered out of the sleeping bag.

"Michael? Michael, wake up," she called. "Fine fire man you turned out to be."

She grabbed the burro's bridle and hoisted herself on its back. "Kismet, find Michael."

It moved purposefully down toward the stream. She called for her cousin as they moved.

"We're over here."

A puzzled look. "We? I've got the burro."

Michael and Sudecki were holding hands tightly. "Sudecki, meet my cousin Sarah."

Her voice quavered. "Hello, Sarah," and then a pause. "You are very beautiful."

"And I can tell from the tone in my cousin's voice that you must be as well."

Michael scrambled to help Sarah dismount. He took her hand and guided it. "Whaddya think?" He touched her hand lightly to the body. She recoiled and then groped carefully.

"What is she doing, Michael?"

"Sudecki, I'm blind, I don't know, but it's probably something very clinical."

"I am feeling in his mouth."

"I told you."

"He's missing a front tooth. How hot would it have to be to melt gold?"

"About a thousand degrees Celsius, I think. Good catch. Sarah, Oishkipeh had Uzbek Secret Service ID on him. We need to get out of here."

"Sudecki, we're really glad you came along. How'd you find us?"

"I dreamed that Michael was here, so I came looking. Fire. Smoke. Not hard. Nobody else around."

Sarah felt around a little further. His exposed hair had disappeared leaving not flesh, but rare meat seared on a grill. She asked Sudecki to describe the scene.

She described the scene anxiously and then said, "We must leave now. Talk later."

They packed quickly and scoured the area for evidence of their presence.

As they walked off, they heard the stillness broken behind them. The pungence of human decay was in the wind. "The animals have taken his body."

Sudecki held Michael's hand and pulled Kismet, ridden by Sarah and lagging behind, with the other hand.

"Michael, you marry your cousin?"

"No, they don't do that in America, at least not in most of America. But the real reason is that Sarah and I are more like twins. We have the same birthday and everything."

"If I looked like her, I don't think it would stop even my brother. She must love you very much to come all the way to Uzbekistan with you."

"Actually, it was her idea, not mine."

The awkwardness must have shown on Michael's face because Sudecki stroked his cheek with the back of her hand and said nothing.

"Michael, I saw your little furry animal. Shrew?" She made little shrew motions and chuckled. "Sorry, forget you can't see."

"Animal fishing in stream leading into Abu Daria. Stream very clear. Shrew would close eyes and ears. Swim very fast with mouth closed. Then suddenly it dive into very still mud and scoop up shells? Shellfish and other animals. Over and over."

"That's odd. Sudecki repeat this to Sarah. Sarah, catch up," he called behind him.

"What can that woman possibly know?"

"Sudecki, she's my cousin, my best friend, and a scientist. We don't share a sleeping bag, not figuratively anyway."

"Only because you too smart for her."

"No, only because she can do a lot better than me. And because we are just friends."

Sudecki sharply jerked the animal's tether, so that it lurched forward, almost throwing Sarah.

"Come Sarah. Michael call you." As soon as Sarah bounced forward on Kismet, she dismounted, and Sudecki repeated her story.

"Electroreception, Michael. Most monotremes, like the platypus have little sensors in their brains or their bills that detect the electrical impulses that their prey's brain sends to its muscles. That's how platypuses hunt. They don't see, hear, or smell underwater."

The magnetism minor said, "Sarah, sometimes every twenty-two years, when solar flares reach the peak of their cycle, they expel so much electromagnetic energy that they can power telephone lines, knock out power lines, disrupt satellite communications and change weather patterns. Do you think it's possible for a being to generate a powerful enough electrical current from electrolocation to electrocute a human?"

"At very close range electrical eels can generate 500 volts and 1 amp of current, which is enough to kill a human under the right circumstances. They also use their electric current to communicate and navigate. From the last vision, I'd say MC is not omnipotent, but at close range, *It's* a really lethal shot."

"I don't understand, Michael," Sudecki interjected. In their blindness, they had completely forgotten Sudecki was along for the ride.

"We're just trying to figure out what caused that man to die, Sudecki."

"What is electro, electro...?"

Sarah said, "Certain animals hunt by sensing little tiny electrical impulses in other animals' brains. Some animals actually send out electrical signals or even communicate with other animals by electrical impulses."

"What's MC, Michael?"

"Shit. MC is Myopic Cardiopia, which explains how we saw all of that stuff in the sky. It's kind of like seeing with special glasses, and we lost them when we were blinded."

Sarah said, "You just make it up as you go along, don't you?"

Sudecki gave the tether more slack so that Sarah fell behind again.

"Sudecki, it's getting late. Where are we going?"

"We can't go to my home. Family ask questions and if secret police find you there, my mother and I get raped, my younger brother get beaten and my father and older brother end up in slave labor camp. Need to get as far from Oishkipeh as possible. Take you near town, and I must leave you. Nobody can see us together."

"We need to return the burro first, Sudecki."

"Where?"

"Pull him up ahead and let him lead us. I think he'll head for home. Donkeys are good at that. They're like little butterflies with a homing device."

Sudecki missed the joke, but she did as Michael asked and tugged abruptly on Kismet's lead. It charged ahead of the pack with Sarah holding on tightly to its mane and then slowed to a walk. As Sarah passed them, Sudecki mumbled something in Russian.

Another hour passed and the burro veered off of the main road onto a twin-rut wagon path that led well away from the road. The sun had fallen behind some clouds hovering near the horizon. Michael's teeth chattered.

Sudecki pulled them to a stop under a small cluster of trees that overhung the ground leaving a large swath of dirt bereft of snow. "Camp here. Water nearby."

She helped them get their tent up, light a fire and prepare dinner. Then she took Michael down to the stream. Sarah fell asleep in the tent before they returned.

CHAPTER 17

Assorted Natural Disasters

Whn she awoke the next day, the sky was blue, Michael was curled up next to her and Sudecki was gone.

"I freeze alone in the tent and you're humping in the woods. Where'd she go?"

"Back to her herd."

"So you came crawling back to exploit my body heat?" She favored her left leg as she pulled herself out of the tent and attempted to orient herself. There was fifteen or twenty centimeters of snow in the fields, but the ruts were clear from regular use. She recognized the small cleft in the hillside which hid the farmer's house from view. "Kismet did a good job. We should get to his house by nightfall if we hurry."

"Can you walk on your ankle?"

"Kismet can carry me a little longer. The burro's real loyal. It's not thinking with its dick."

Michael squatted down and studied the burro. "That's because it's been gelded."

"That girl really resented me, Michael."

"She felt threatened by you. These people marry their first cousins."

"She must have noticed the sexual tension between us."

Michael ignored the sarcasm. "The first time I saw her on the hill, she said she saw me in her dreams. Then she really did. I think she is a carrier of that same gene that allows us to communicate with MC. And somehow, biologically, it's attracting us to each other. It's like telling us to breed more telepathic humans. Is that possible?"

"Mapping the human genome is not the same as understanding the human genome, although there are some people who think we can get there from here. What did she say in Russian when she pulled Kismet and me past you yesterday?"

"She said, 'She is your blood, but I am your dreams.'"

"If she only knew."

Michael said, "MC knew exactly where those cylinders were, so *It* must have communicated with whomever put them there or is guarding them. But why can't whomever is guarding those cylinders use them, and if they can't use them, why don't they destroy them?"

"I guess we'll find out. What do you think 'you will never see hell' means?"

"I think *It* plucked that from our memories. *It* interprets hell as an afterlife concept that is the antithesis of heaven or God. That would either imply the absence of an afterlife according to MC, or that if there is one, MC knows we won't be part of hell as MC saw it in our minds."

"Whoa—Oh shit, Kismet. Michael, we are in big trouble."

"Again? Does this have something to do with going to hell?"

"The pass is blocked, you idiot! We're stranded until it melts!"

The burro led the way sure-footedly. The sun, reflected off the snow, began burning their necks and faces. They plopped lumps of melting snow on their foreheads and cheeks to keep cool. By afternoon, clouds came rolling in rapidly and the heat of the sun was displaced by a frigid breeze. Kismet steadfastly kept his pace and sense of direction, reaching the farmer's house just as the sun dipped below the horizon.

The lights were out when they knocked on the farmhouse door. Sarah and Michael identified themselves loudly, alternating between Russian and English until the farmer's shotgun answered the door. The farmer pulled them through the door, disappeared in the back room, and quickly returned waving a newspaper featuring the story about his hedgehog. His broad face smiled from the front page and he proudly held a cage containing one of the venomous soricomorphs.

His squat wife shuffled into the room, stuffing her hair under her kerchief. When she saw the two, she began speaking rapidly to the farmer in Uzbek, her voice rising. The shotgun had been hanging limply at his side, and he now raised it menacingly in their direction.

"Why are you here?" he said to Michael in Russian. Sarah pulled the man outside and pointed to Kismet.

"She found us in the mountains."

"Where is Oishkipeh?"

"We don't know," Michael said.

The man looked at them nervously. "He is dead?"

Michael repeated, "We don't know. We haven't seen him."

"But you know him?" the farmer asked.

Michael spoke to Sarah in English. "He wants to know if we know him."

"I think you need to tell the truth, because Oishkipeh may have said something to him when he rented Kismet."

He turned back to the farmer. "He was supposed to pick us up in his helicopter, but he never came." Michael made hand motions for the helicopter because his dictionary was on the burro.

The farmer responded, "The helicopter landed. He rented the burro. That night, the helicopter was hit by lightning and exploded near the pass. Very bad. The police will come looking."

He went to the burro. His hand started to shake as he went through the side bags and saw the high-powered rifle and semi-automatic weapons.

"These belong to Oishkipeh?"

"They are not ours."

He nodded and pointed to the rifle. "Security police guns. You sleep here and leave early in the morning. I will take you to the path over the mountain. Leave everything with me. Say nothing to anyone about this."

"How long will the trip take?" asked Michael.

"A couple days to Tashkent. I give you food."

Suddenly, he put the shotgun on the table and broke into his deep belly laugh.

"You want more hashish for this trip, too?"

"You knew?"

"It's okay. You only took a little, and I overcharged you for the burro." He again pulled out the picture in the paper and said proudly in English, "I celebrity!"

Sarah and Michael tossed and squirmed on straw mattresses in the unheated bunk house, with the wind whistling through every crack in the five-square-meter building. Sarah said, "Michael, why would Oishkipeh have landed his helicopter here? He knew where he was supposed to meet us, didn't he?"

"Sure. We agreed to meet at the drop point, which was right near our campsite. I don't know why we weren't thinking about it earlier. Didn't you wonder where his helicopter was when your sight returned?"

"No. I was happy to have my sight back, and he was already dead, so I didn't even think about the helicopter. All I thought about was hightailing it back through the pass."

"Me too, but I think Oishkipeh landed here early and hiked in with the burro so he could ambush us."

"Maybe, but I doubt it. We were probably easy shots up on the mountain, particularly with that high-powered rifle. I think he had something else in mind."

"What?" Michael responded.

"Oishkipeh figured out who we were. He was going to steal our discovery and then probably kill us. With the assumed name thing, he may have figured nobody knew we were here."

"I hope you're right, because then they may not know he is missing until we are out of the country."

"We'll see in the morning. I think you were a little overly optimistic about MC helping us make up for lost time."

She was answered by her cousin's snoring.

A dishwater grey fog enshrouded the farmhouse the next morning. The temperature had remained steady overnight just above freezing and the melting snow saturated the air with moisture.

A second clap of thunder and the building and ground shook around them, growing in intensity, tsunami-like, spilling Sarah out of bed. The roaring and shaking continued for another five minutes and then slowly subsided.

The farmer came in a few moments later. "Dress quickly. We need to leave soon. Avalanche last night."

Within ten minutes they were in the bed of a horse-drawn sleigh covered with woolen and goat-skin blankets. The blankets itched and smelled of barn straw and damp wool. The farmer motioned for them to keep out of sight.

"Road busy this time of day."

Soon they heard the clip-clop of hooves ahead.

"Down," he hissed.

A short conversation ensued.

As the clopping receded, Michael whispered, "Oishkipeh's helicopter was spotted near the pass."

The spit and belch of an Iron-Curtain-era diesel tractor grew in volume as they continued on the path. The engine throttled down to a noisy snore and their driver exchanged pleasantries with an old peasant woman and man, apparently using the vehicle as their primary means of transportation.

"Now what?" said Sarah.

"Because the pass is blocked, the people are coming from this side of the mountain to investigate the helicopter, rather than the village, which is inaccessible by car right now."

The tractor backfired as it drove away, shaking up the horses. They bolted briefly, slamming Michael's head into the tailgate.

"Ow."

"Quiet," said the farmer, "until we leave the road. It will get a little bumpier. Can't be helped."

For the next hour or so, they bounced up and down like the wave at a football game.

Then the farmer stopped and tapped them on their feet. They sat up and followed his finger to the glinting steel of Oishkipeh's helicopter blade barely visible on the road below them, about a kilometer away. It was all that remained uncovered from the avalanche.

"Three, maybe four days before they dig out helicopter. Probably think he's inside. You get out of Uzbekistan."

Circumventing the pass had led them to an overlook of the village below and a narrow, straight path that was a forty-five-degree drop, merging halfway down the mountain with the road on the other side of the pass. The avalanche had exposed too steep a slope for the horses to restrain the sleigh.

The farmer stopped at the crest. Then he made a decision. "Out."

He extracted an old wooden toboggan strapped under the sleigh.

Sarah grabbed Michael's jacket before he could run. Ruefully to Sarah, "No fucking way am I going down the mountain in that thing. I'll take my chances with M'low Cloom and the Uzbek police."

"You're exaggerating. When you want to calm stupid horses to take them out of a burning barn, you cover their eyes." She pulled out her bandana.

Michael backed away quickly. "Don't even think about it or you'll be limping on both legs."

"You are being a weenie again. Weren't you the one who said, 'I think this will all work out, Sarah. MC knows the urgency here. You just have to have some faith'?" She mimicked.

The farmer gave them a small sack of food, pointed to the toboggan and said, "Don't tell anybody where you got this from."

Sarah handed the farmer all of the Uzbek money they had and a couple hundred euros.

She slid into the front of the toboggan and stuck her feet under the curl in the front. She peered down the narrow bobsled run, peppered with pinball bumper trees at every turn and her heart began pounding. She loved roller coasters but Michael detested them. There was only a steering rope and side straps for control.

Michael stood his ground. "Can I have a joint?"

"You need to keep your wits about you. This is not the time."

"Why do you get to drive?"

"The front end of the plane crashes first."

"Hurry," said the farmer.

He pressed Michael into the toboggan behind Sarah and his arms and legs wrapped around her chest and waist like a vise.

"Close your eyes. I obviously don't need to tell you to hold on to me, but you have to let go of my arms. It's making it kind of hard to steer, dear."

The farmer exhaled deeply. Sarah looked up at him, winked, and nodded her head. The farmer got behind the sleigh and gave Michael a gentle push on the back which transferred through to Sarah's feet pressed against the curve in the front.

They started slowly at first, and Sarah had just enough time to say, "See this isn't so bad, just lean with me to steer. Are you paying attention?"

A muffled response warmed her back.

Trees and rocks blurred as they picked up speed. They bounced off mounds of snow on either side, but stayed on course. The village grew quickly ahead of them. Near the bottom of the hill they catapulted over a mogul and became airborne, heading straight to a dilapidated house. They landed on the edge of its wood fence with the crack and splintering of toboggan and pickets, and continued more erratically toward the center of town. A clump of trees approached quickly on their left, just before the next building.

"Lean right, Michael."

They both leaned, but to no avail. Too late they started to turn away from the trees. They spilled over the side of the toboggan and scraped to a halt in someone's front yard. A boy of about ten looked at them curiously. The toboggan was resting at the foot of the trees, next to his house.

Sarah grabbed her cousin and their packs. She put her finger over her lips. If the little boy could keep a secret, the toboggan was his. Miraculously, it had suffered only minor damage. The boy smiled, helped them collect their things, and scampered after his prize. Sarah and Michael were on their way back to the States in less than twenty-four hours.

CHAPTER 18

Michael's Expendable. Sarah's Indispensable.

On the first day back from Uzbekistan, Neil the asshole called Michael into his office. Michael assumed it was to inquire about his most recent unexpected disappearance. Neil was still looking for an excuse to fire him but short of turpitude, which in the newsprint industry was really limited to plagiarizing and fabricating sources, or perhaps an obsolescence of the print media, they didn't do that sort of thing. Michael never even padded his expenses. Losers accompanied birdwatchers in their search for extinct woodpeckers until they smashed their own heads against a tree and resigned. Neil used every single deadend to persecute Michael. When he spent $25,000 chasing the uranium vein story, Neil tried to take some of it out of Michael's pay, until the HR department killed that idea. When Michael exposed the chemicals plant for illegally discharging untreated biodegradable newsprint ink, Neil accused him, in his own gutter-mouthed way, of acting like a dog chasing a bitch in heat, which Michael vigorously denied. That was one of the other problems Michael had with working for a lecher like Neil. *That* lie he could see right through. But now, Michael had Neil where he wanted him. Michael was the rising star at the paper, and it was Neil's job to keep him happy.

Michael expected Neil to be acting like a combination of Spiderman's boss and the guy at the *Daily Planet*, but he was all smiles. A woman in her early thirties was sitting in his office wearing a well-tailored business suit with a Freedom of Information Act skirt. It appeared that they were having a private meeting, but when Neil saw Michael, he beckoned him in pleasantly.

As Michael had told Sarah before they went their separate ways from New Zealand, "Pleasant is to Neil as Seapeace is to the American Petroleum

Institute." He entered warily, convincing himself he could at least get a better look at what the skirt seemed only too happy to reveal.

"Michael, this is Lindsey Light. She is a literary agent. She thinks that you have a hell of an autobiographical story to tell, for print or the silver DVD. However, it turns out that a number of people and institutions might compete for a claim to that story, including your employer. We are happy to permit you to take a leave of absence to chronicle your adventures, as long as you don't take any time off with pay and we get the benefit of first serial rights to everything newsworthy that you are doing under our employ anyway. Don't you have a contract?"

Ms. Light rose to shake Michael's hand as he turned to Neil. "No, I don't. And your tentacles don't extend that far."

Lindsey slowly and deliberately crossed her legs and made a futile attempt to cover her upper thighs. Her low-cut tailored grey silk blouse affirmed a perfectly proportioned, taut body. Frumpy Neil, with his protruding gut, wore an adolescent smile. Michael wasn't exactly miserable.

"Michael, our agency would like to represent you in the negotiation of book and movie rights to your story. Your writing skills are very highly regarded and this story is sensational. But others can write this story as told to them by your cousin. We would like to represent both you and Ms. Baskin."

"I don't speak for Ms. Baskin, Lindsey." Michael knew that if this had been a joint decision between Neil and him, instead of with Sarah, he would have signed up already.

"Yes, of course, we understand that. We have approached you first to solicit your assistance in consummating a deal with both you and your cousin."

"Why me first? Every professional views Sarah as a much more valuable commodity than me. In fact, most of them think that I am some sort of parasite living off of my cousin's successes."

Neil blurted out, "Yes, Michael, but you're *our* parasite. We're the beneficiaries."

Lindsey said, "Perhaps some would view it that way, but to us, you are by far the more valuable. Your remarkable expository skills can bring this story to life."

She paused, hoping that the gratuitous compliment would be sufficient. Michael was an expert at the interview game. An awkward silence passed before Lindsey realized that she was going to have to continue.

"Well, there are other reasons. We have a pre-existing relationship with your paper. The educational imprints have better access to her through the university, so if we go through her, we lose. And we expected that you would probably be more approachable, from a business perspective, as well."

"So, you checked, realized you couldn't cut me out entirely and then decided to see if you could use me to get to my cousin and tie us both up?"

She cleared her throat and rearranged her already perfect skirt. "We have surmised that it would be more difficult to financially influence her, and she will not discuss Peter Barber or your friend, Sudecki."

These people knew no limits. "Meaning, I could be bought easier and I'd be more likely to divulge the tabloid side of the story?"

She nodded resignedly. "That's a rather exploitative way to look at it."

"Thank you. We understand each other. I will only arrange the meeting. You have to sell her. If you're successful, I am in. It's a fifty/fifty deal between her and me for all of the economics, the term, the options, everything. But, there is one thing that is not fifty/fifty. We'll discuss it after I talk to Sarah and after we have an agreement."

Neil smiled wanly. "He's a pig, but he's not a scoundrel." Neil was, of course, both of those things and he couldn't understand why the whole world didn't operate that way.

"I suppose you'll need yet another couple of days off for this, Michael?"

So, courtesy of the Falk Agency, Michael boarded yet another plane to Chicago. A year ago, he was scraping together money for ski trips. Now, he had more frequent flyer miles than he could use and he always traveled business class.

Lindsey Light was going to meet the cousins in Chicago after stopping in Los Angeles. The package of book and movie rights that she was proposing would be worth more than five million dollars to Michael alone. One million up front to each of them and then the balance when the movie rights were sold. If they kept producing, she had options which paid them twice that. Of course, that meant more contact with M'low Cloom and pushing Michael's mortality to its limits.

Surprise visits to Sarah's apartment weren't nearly as much fun for Michael as they used to be. When they were both poor nobodies, Sarah had a roommate who had a line on wild parties at least four nights a week while Sarah was in her lab. Sarah was a loner, and as soon as she had a little money, she moved into a place of her own. If she was hooking up with somebody regularly, Michael didn't know about it. She was way too disciplined with her time to enjoy it by having sex and partying three or four nights a week.

Michael found her in her grad student office. She seemed to be expecting him. He offered to take her to lunch and she delivered an ultimatum in return.

"I hope you are packed and ready to go."

"Absolutely. But there's even better news. I have raised the money and I'm looking forward to this trip, *enthusiastically.*"

She turned back to her computer screen as she spoke. "So, you found the wizard?"

"What wizard?"

"The wizard that gave the lion his courage."

"Very funny. I have enough money and still have enough trepidation for both of us. The way I see the images created by our most recent mind meld with MC, this is like a covert military action, and we still don't do that so well. We make Inspector Clouseau look like a super-agent."

"We are dealing with ruthless, unscrupulous people, Michael."

"But, why should we be afraid of them? Did Lindsey call you already?"

"Who's Lindsey?"

"Some woman who is using me to get to you. Not important. Whom are you talking about?"

"Insurgents in Sudan."

"Oh, them. They won't bother us. MC will give him visions of our invincibility, and he'll cooperate and protect us."

"That's ludicrous."

"Why? Because I am beginning to sound a little like you? Would it renew your belief in my self-serving duplicity if I told you that the real reason I came here was to tell you that Lindsey Light wants to be our agent? She is offering us each a million dollars for our story, *so far*, and maybe another eight million if she sells the movie rights and we keep producing. We can buy a lot of protection with that money."

It took several seconds. "That *would* restore my faith in your pre-emptive greed. I assume you told her that your cousin, the bitch, would never agree?"

"I would have, but somehow, she knew that already, which is why she came to me first. We are supposed to meet her for dinner at The Peninsula, whatever that is."

"Beneath this blue jeans facade, Michael, is a classy dame that likes five star restaurants."

"Yeah, it's probably a lot better than that inn we ate at in Uzbekistan. What was that, one star?"

"Only on an extremely clear night."

Suddenly somber, Michael said, "There's another reason we have to make this trip to Sudan. There is a way to possess MC's knowledge and the memories of those *It* communicates with. MC is the server on a network of sentient life. The directions to Antarctica and to the comet came from dead people that knew the whereabouts of that mammoth and the lost Inuit rotunda. There's a living human out there that gave MC directions to this cave which *It* was able to pass on to us. How? The secrets to MC's existence must be in Sudan. And that's what I've always been in this for."

"Michael, we don't personally know anyone who communicates with MC, do we?"

"Only each other."

"Exactly. If we want to figure out how MC communicates with us, we need to know the gene for telepathic communication. Our DNA is probably too similar. We need the DNA of that person in Sudan who knows where these weapons are. And if we don't hurry, those weapons are going to get used and, according to our vision, all of the people with whom MC communicates, including presumably us, will be destroyed."

"Will you do me a favor? When we get those answers, can I get top billing? All you care about is natural selection and the human destruction of our planet anyway."

"As long as you don't get us both killed. I care about our destruction, as well."

Michael expected the meeting would be entirely unproductive, but he wasn't one to turn down a free meal at a first class restaurant. He liked to think of himself as an unrequited bohemian connoisseur of fine foods. The only time he experienced epicurean delights was on someone else's expense account, even if it was the *Chronicle's*, which today it wasn't, because Neil wouldn't have approved it.

He couldn't decide if the company enhanced his image or made him look even more out of place than usual. Sarah had her hair professionally styled and wore a backless black cocktail dress that was tailored to her gracefully sculpted body. Lindsey was adorned in a clingy black and red frock with an angled slit on one side that went nearly up to the top of her left thigh. The cleavage was substantial, but diplomatic, until she leaned over. As Michael expected, all of the men in the restaurant, except himself, were staring at Sarah, even though it was Lindsey that slipped the maître d' twenty dollars for a table with a view of Lake Michigan.

Lindsey had a brother who worked for a big-time Chicago-based hedge fund and venture capital firm. As soon as the trio sat down, Lindsey saw him at the bar with a man about five years older than herself. She needlessly reapplied more lip gloss at the table and said, "Excuse me, I see my brother over there with his boss. I think I'll just go over and say hello." It was an odd coincidence for somebody who lived in LA.

She sauntered over and engaged the two men in conversation for a couple of minutes and then the older man went over to say hello to someone else he knew at the restaurant. Lindsey and her brother became animated and Michael thought she was going to slug him. When the boss came back, Lindsey was all smiles again.

Michael leaned over to Sarah and said, "Twenty bucks for a view of Lake Michigan?"

"It was a fifty. I came here with Peter six months ago. She's in the hunt for him big time."

"Who, the boss?"

"No, her brother. Who do you think? Her brother looks familiar, though. Have we met him before?"

"I haven't. But, I know who he looks like."

"Who? He's cute."

"Your brother, Ethan." Ethan was Sarah's brother who had died in Kiev.

Michael and Sarah shut up when the three of them headed over to the table where the cousins were seated.

"Sarah Baskin, Michael Seagal, this is my baby brother, Ethan, and the Managing Partner of West Shore Investments, Alex Langhorne. Mr. Langhorne recognized you from the news stories, and apparently he's quite the amateur paleontologist."

Michael was sure that Alex Langhorne knew nothing about paleontology. When he took Sarah's hand in his, Michael looked at Lindsey and knew that it was going to be a claws-out cat-fight and Lindsey was going to end up with her tail between her legs. He also saw Sarah's hand go limp. He quickly explained her reaction to the group.

Sarah took Ethan's hand and said, "Well, it seems like I almost have my brother back again."

Ethan attempted to strike up a more pleasant conversation, describing his management of a seed fund that was investing in a computerized ancestry search engine and even though Lindsey was encouraging him to continue, when the younger Light saw his boss' reaction, he made a quick choice between money and blood and redirected himself to a conversation with Michael.

Michael feigned interest in Ethan's business, but all of his attention was directed to his seat on the sidelines. When it was clear that Ethan was doing the same, with a subtle head jerk in Langhorne's direction, they dropped their pretenses so they could continue their discreet eavesdropping.

Everything about Lindsey was flawless and professional, but Sarah's complexion had an incredible backwoods hiking glow framing a disarming smile of moonlight white teeth between frosted full lips. Langhorne couldn't take his eyes off of any of it and Lindsey couldn't take her eyes off of him.

They carried on polite conversation for a few minutes until Ethan said, "Alex, I believe the maître d' is motioning that our table is ready."

Alex Langhorne pressed his card into Sarah's hand. "These stories can be profitable. One of our venture capital funds may be interested in financing your work and underwriting a film production. You're in Chicago, give me a call and we can discuss it further."

Michael thought that if he had said "discuss it further over dinner," Lindsey's complexion would have matched her hair.

Sarah wrote down her e-mail address for him.

As soon as Ethan and Alex turned away, the sommelier presented the wine to Sarah for inspection. Michael recognized it immediately from his class in the stewardship of fine wines."That's an exceptional wine, Lindsey. Complex bouquet and one of the top three vintages."

"I didn't order wine yet."

"Yes, ma'am," the sommelier said. And then undiplomatically turning back to Sarah, he said, "the older of the two gentlemen you were just speaking with sent it over."

Sarah smiled at Alex across the room and he nodded to her. Michael recalled that the bottle was about three hundred dollars at the "Wine Chat Toe" in Houston, so he guessed that it had to be six hundred to a thousand dollars here.

After dinner, as they walked through the lobby and out of the plush restaurant furnished in authentic Louis XVI era furnishings, Sarah casually pulled Alex's card out of her clutch.

"Alex Langhorne, Managing Director. Angel Funding. Mezzanine Equity."

Lindsey muttered, "Even my own brother would steal business from me." Then she looked up stunned, as she realized that she'd spoken aloud and said, "Sarah, do you mind if I copy Alex's e-mail address? I may have some other business for him."

Sarah said, "It's probably the same format as your brother's e-mail address, Lindsey, but why don't you just take the card? I don't need it. He's got my e-mail address if he ever wants to find me."

The next morning, Sarah called her attorney and instructed him to cut a deal and get each of them no less than a five hundred thousand dollar advance. They would take a two-month leave of absence to an undisclosed location and pull together all of their notes, including their escapades in Uzbekistan. They were to check in at least once a week and send progress reports.

The balance of a total of four million was to come after the agency's review of the first draft of something. But, always thinking, Sarah told the Falk attorney that they got no options. She made it clear to them that they didn't need what could be another five million or more.

Michael wasn't sure how people with less than seventy million could *not* need another five million. Sarah promised to explain it all to him later, but he suspected it had something to do with Alex Langhorne.

CHAPTER 19

On the Lam

Michael was only partly correct. It had more to do with a modest venture capital investment made by Lake Shore Investments. Soon after Sarah spoke to her attorney, she received an e-mail from Ethan Light. Her first reaction was to send it to junk mail, because in the aftermath of the Peter Barber affair, she was repulsed by the thought of entering into another relationship right now. And, based on what Michael had told her, she didn't see Ethan hitting on her if Alex was interested. But, the subject line was the best hook she had ever seen.

Sarah, I think we are related.

Lake Shore's genealogy investment had led Ethan to an almost impossible relationship deep in the rural Portuguese countryside. But, if Ethan's theory about being related was true, it would explain almost everything. She decided to adjust her plans accordingly.

Sarah and Michael checked into an extended stay accommodation in Rio de Janeiro, Brazil, and prepaid for twenty-one days. Michael hooked up an answering machine to the hotel phone and tested the remote call forwarding system. Comfortable that it would function properly from his satellite phone, they hung the Portuguese **Do Not Disturb** sign from the doorknob and slipped unnoticed out of the hotel. Several blocks away, they caught a cab to the airport and flew non-stop to Lisbon, Portugal, where they paid cash for another flight to Rabat, Morocco.

Both Michael and Sarah were surprised by Sarah's ability to make out the language of the locals in both Lisbon and Rabat when all she had in her linguistic arsenal was four years of Spanish. Sarah picked it up from her father's parents when she was very young, as best as she could figure. They spoke some dialect that was akin to Spanish with a little bit of Arabic thrown in, mostly with her Aunt Rachel. She made a mental note to ask her father about it when she got home.

They still needed to devise a game plan to enter and escape Sudan safely. Sarah waited for Michael to fall asleep and then methodically began her online search. Nearly all of northeast Africa was three hours ahead of Greenwich Mean Time, local time for Rabat. By four in the morning GMT, northeast Africa would be going about their business.

The visions of ruthless and unscrupulous people had been puzzling Sarah. In their séance with MC, they had both seen another person with whom MC communicated. He was an African stranger who spoke English with an unfamiliar accent. Sarah knew that when the time came, she would recognize him. According to MC, Sarah or Michael shared a common acquaintance with him and she needed to find that person.

Sarah picked up the mattress and turned its contents onto the plush pile carpeting of the Rabat Sheraton floor.

"Get dressed. If you are permitted to sleep while I do the work, then I decide how to wake you. I corresponded with a colleague at the University of Alexandria a year or so ago about freshwater dolphins that ply the Nile River. I found him online early this morning. We are meeting him in Alexandria. You know that vision we had about someone else, someone very dark and speaking heavily accented English? Remember the common acquaintance we shared?"

Michael nodded uncertainly.

Sarah was pleased. It was rare that she absorbed more from an MC mind transfer than Michael. "I may have found him. My colleague and his Sudanese friend are picking us up at the Alexandria airport. Maybe he can get us into Sudan and perhaps his fellow tribesmen can garner us safe passage."

"That's a stretch, Sarah."

"He's got contacts with the rebels and we are going into their territory. There has got to be a way for him to get us into Sudan without getting discovered. Regardless, it's just a next step. We aren't flying from here straight to Darfur. Did you do any better investigative work in your sleep, reporter boy?"

As they passed through customs in Cairo, they noticed the usual throng hanging over barricades and straining anxiously for glimpses of friends, lovers and family members. A few were dressed in khaffiyas and traditional robes, but most wore American t-shirts and jeans, with political, commercial, and sexual advertisements shouting from their chests. Eight neatly groomed men and one woman stood apart from the people greeting their parties. The men wore open-collared white dress shirts and pressed black trousers that wilted in the stifling heat, while floor fans made an unsuccessful attempt to stir up the stale air in the concourse. Only the woman appeared powdered and cool in a loose-fitting bone blouse and royal A-line silk skirt that extended just below her knees. Sarah's fair complexion and luminescent eyes attracted unabashed looks from the men, while Michael's swarthy skin and chestnut hair immediately lost him among the residents of the most industrialized and educated population in North Africa.

Held high in front of them was a large banner that read:

THE UNIVERSITY OF ALEXANDRIA
Welcomes Renowned Environmental Scientist
PROFESSOR SARAH BASKIN
and Science Reporter Michael Seagal

The cousins scowled. As they walked into view, Sarah in khaki shorts and Michael in faded jeans, flashing cameras captured Michael's disdain, and Sarah's muted smile as she waved to her friend.

Mounir Elfar and Sarah shook hands and then Mounir enveloped her in a spontaneous hug as if reuniting with a long lost friend, rather than first meeting an e-mail correspondent.

The woman interceded and bowed her head apologetically. "I am Professor Scheinin. Among other things, it is my job to keep the gentlemen in line."

"Men are the same everywhere, Professor. I assure you, it's fine."

"Thank you, Miss Baskin."

In the customized livery vehicle provided courtesy of the university, Sarah and Michael met Mounir's Sudanese colleague. Professor Scheinin sat in the front with the driver. The rest of the welcoming party had piled into a second car to form a short caravan. The guests studied Mounir's colleague carefully to see if he matched any of the images in their MC vision. Sarah and Michael's eyes met and confirmed their mutual disappointment.

After they exchanged pleasantries, Mounir asked in British flavored English, "Sarah, please tell us how we may be of service to you."

Cutting off Sarah, Michael said, "We have reason to believe that we may be able to find remains of the prophet Joseph," using the more locally accepted Islamic reference to the biblical son of Jacob, "in South Central Sudan."

Sarah attempted to retain a mask of professionalism, "Yes, of course…"

He finished, "Sarah could have told you before we arrived, but she signed a confidentiality agreement with my paper over this lead she is helping me follow up on and you know how conscientious she is."

"…about pulling your ass out of a fire," she mumbled.

The Sudanese national studied them. According to Mounir's e-mail, Ali Aswari was fluent in English. Ali said, "Joseph's bones? In Darfur?"

Michael's mouth opened, but nothing came out. Sarah weighed the risks before her cousin could jump back in. Whispering so that even Ali had to strain to hear, she answered, "Yes. We have been led to each of our discoveries by visions."

Ali responded in the same tone, "Then I know who will be expecting you."

Sarah continued normally, "Do not tell anyone about this, Mounir. You may be putting our lives in danger."

Mounir spoke solemnly. "The Bible says that Joseph's bones were brought with Moses out of the land of Egypt at the time of the Exodus." Then he laughed heartily. "But, those are only fables. Based on what I have read about you and Miss Baskin so far, it does not seem so preposterous."

"And you want my assistance to gain safe passage to and from a lawless area controlled by ruthless people?" Ali asked.

"We," she gestured to Michael, "are worth much more alive and free than kidnapped or dead to the secessionists, if our success advances their cause. And we have no agenda. We are completely apolitical. The world will witness their humanity and desire to protect a global treasure."

Ali said, "They will let you find your treasure and then hold both you and it for ransom, particularly with the current popularity of Americans. Whether you fail or succeed, you will never leave alive."

The limousine dropped them off at the hotel to freshen up and relax. Their room at the Alexandria Marriott, courtesy of the University, was bathed in modern western luxury, including air conditioning, sit-down toilets, satellite TV and WiFi in every room.

Sarah was confused. Wasn't it Michael who had insisted on anonymity and secrecy? Here he was, announcing their arrival to find the remains of Joseph and his technicolor dreamcoat. That was going to remain as secret as Bill Clinton's extracurricular activities. Why didn't he just tell them that they were going into Sudan to thwart a biological weapons attack?

On top of that, who knew that Moses took Joseph's bones out with him when the Hebrews left Egypt? But, there it was, in the second to last line of Genesis in the Marriott nightstand, right next to the Book of Mormon and the Qur'an. Initially, Sarah thought that Michael's explanation was so ridiculous, he had to have had at least a little bit of prior knowledge. She should have known better.

"Sarah, it was clear you didn't have a game plan. And then it occurred to me that if we had a really sensational mission, we would be more likely to come out alive with world public opinion rooting for us. If we snuck in looking for some secret prize and disappeared, it would be too late."

"Michael, I don't think MC can protect us from our own stupidity. I don't even think *It* will try."

They met Ali Aswari and Mounir Elfar in the downstairs bar a short while later. Officially Egypt was a secular state, but even so, drinking by Muslims was frowned upon, as a violation of Islamic law. However, Mounir was a Christian, and Ali, a not so devout Muslim. They nursed weak Martinis and attempted to make small talk, but Mounir wanted details about their trip to Antarctica and the Nunavut territory. He then guided them on a tour of the antiquities and remnants of ancient Alexandria, a city more than 2000 years old. Named for Alexander the Great and designed by the Greek architect Dinocrates, it was one of the most beautiful spots on the African shore of the Mediterranean.

Ali had remained mute since their first conversation, watching every subtle movement of Sarah and Michael. He reacted to their conversation through the inflections of his lips, the thickening of his eyebrows and the occasional click of his tongue. He spoke abruptly. "My half-brother is expecting you. I will take you to him. Meet me at the Sudanese Embassy at one o'clock pm tomorrow. We must be circumspect."

"Mounir, have you ever met Ali's brother?"

He glanced nervously at his friend and then his eyes went to the floor.

"He was here, how do you say it in English? Incognito, once, with an Iraqi man."

Michael said to Sarah, "That would explain how you found Mounir, wouldn't it? We knew that we had a common acquaintance to the face in the vision and Ali wasn't it, so Ali's half-brother would have to have met Mounir for him to be a common acquaintance."

When they met the next day at the Sudanese Embassy in Cairo, they were immediately ushered into the ambassador's office. Egypt was a very important Embassy post, as the two nations shared a long border along the Nile River, yet the ambassador seemed to have nothing more important on his agenda than meeting with very minor celebrities. The ambassador gave his qualified support and arranged a meeting in Khartoum with the interior minister provided that all three traveled together. For the time being, Sarah and Michael had company again.

What we anticipate seldom occurs; what we least expect generally happens.

— Benjamin Disraeli

CHAPTER 20

The Hidden Cache

Sarah, Michael, and Ali arrived on the tarmac at the Khartoum International Airport on the last commercial flight of the day from Cairo. The orange desert sun had set over the Sahara several hours ago. The arid air was thick with the scent of pollen and the summer's grain harvest, a sharp contrast to the oppressive humidity of the fertile Nile.

A chauffeured car whisked them directly to Interior Ministry Rajoum's office. He had already been briefed by the Ambassador. Rajoum was a pencil-thin man who preferred finely tailored Italian suits to the ill-fitting garb of his political counterparts. His cheek bones protruded sharply from an unlined face. "Mr. Aswari, it seems a bit odd to find you here."

"Yes, Minister, I find it unusual myself. However, I am still a citizen in good standing, I believe."

"A citizen yes, but I am surprised to see you standing again on Sudanese soil." Rajoum forced a thin, lipless smile.

"Minister Rajoum, I remain a-political by alienating everyone equally, my brother, those of our tribal clan, and, of course, the Sudanese government."

"You risk your life by returning here."

"Mr. Seagal and Miss Baskin believe that they will find the bones of the prophet Joseph on Sudanese soil. Candidly, I am skeptical, but they have an excellent track record. It is in territory controlled by my brother and my tribesman. If I don't go with them, they will probably be shot as they attempt to make contact with my brother's forces. At best, they will be held for ransom, together with their prize, before they are permitted to leave. We believe that we have something to offer the rebels, in exchange for their safe passage into and out of the disputed area. That something is worth far more than their insignificant lives." He nodded deferentially to Sarah and Michael.

"And what would that be, Mr. Aswari?"

"Why, my life, of course, Excellency. They are even less fond of me than are you."

Sarah suppressed a gasp. Why would a complete stranger seventy-two hours ago be willing to barter his life for them?

"Minister, if you will provide us with a car, a radio and two hundred fifty liters of gasoline, we will make contact with the rebels and you can disavow any contact with us until it suits your purposes. We will be successful. Then you will be the lead story for all of the world's newspapers and internet news streams. You can announce each step of our progress to the world. You will be a hero to Christians, Muslims and Jews."

"Aswari, this is all too convenient. You show up here at my doorstep with these Indiana Jones types which will conveniently gain you safe passage back to your tribal territory. Even if I believe you, how do I know that you will not sneak out with these bones, just like in those movies?"

"You can keep our passports, Minister, and we will wire a small security bond into a Sudanese 'Customs' account. You will control our departure."

"You cannot pass through the disputed areas without both sides taking shots at you." Without Rajoum's magnanimity they were powerless. He waited until they came to the same conclusion.

"Government soldiers will escort you to within ten or so kilometers of the territory controlled by your brother. Then you are on your own, and I most likely will be rid of you forever." He proffered a Swiss bank account number. "Fifty thousand dollars. Each."

Ali responded quickly. "No. For all of us. That's all that is available right now."

"Pay the balance before we return your passports."

They shook hands.

On the street, Michael said to Sarah, "Well, there goes one exit strategy."

Before dawn, they were driven to where life in Khartoum ended and the subsistence existence of the countryside began. At the interface, marauding bandits waited to rob rural peasants on their way to market their wares or returning with their few coins. On a pock-marked two-lane paved road they rendezvoused with a five-vehicle convoy, where they were transferred into a battered ten-year-old Ford Crown Victoria with a soldier behind the wheel. His clenched teeth and flared nostrils spoke to the trio. Another soldier directed Aswari to the middle of the front seat with Sarah flanked by Michael and a lieutenant in the rear, his leg pressed against her thigh. They fell in behind a Soviet-era half-track, followed by several jeeps with another half-track bringing up the rear. They invaded the jungle.

Dense vegetation buffeted the car. Leaves the size of bed pillows blanketed the road and permitted only thin strands of the sun now high in the sky to penetrate the cloaking shade. They were surrounded.

Approximately fifteen kilometers before entering the disputed area, the three government soldiers that had been sharing their car with them retreated to the trailing vehicles. Ali slid behind the wheel.

After a time, Ali opened his window and waved the soldiers off. The convoy of five vehicles and thirty soldiers turned around where the clearing widened to a lane and a half and rattled away quickly across the uneven path. Aswari cracked the window to listen for the rat-a-tat-tat of semi-automatic weapons or the explosion from a rocket-propelled grenade. After awhile, he closed the window.

"At least there will be no senseless killing today on my account," Aswari said, exhaling audibly. "Regardless of the truth, at least in front of anyone but my brother, you must stick to your story. These rebels are fanatics. If they truly believe that you know of the whereabouts of Joseph's bones, then they will not kill you until you find your prize. After that, well, we'll have to improvise."

After several kilometers, Ali stopped the vehicle and insisted that Sarah and Michael wait in the ruts of the muddy road while he contacted his brother. Somewhere through the dense foliage were the rebels. Sarah, Michael, and Ali were easy targets. Ali motioned for Sarah and Michael to rejoin him and they continued.

"This car is heavily armored. My brother has sent out scouts to observe our approach. If the government soldiers depart peacefully from this area in another ten or fifteen minutes, my brother's soldiers will intercept us and escort us to their jungle camp," he said, still concentrating on shooting through the one lane tunnel carved from the overhang of vines and massive tree trunks that doubled as jersey walls.

It was a complicated situation in Sudan. Certain Arab countries supported the land grab and genocide effort of the Arab-dominated government, while other countries were concerned that their Arab brethren were gaining too much power in northeast Africa. The "others" had hidden the biological weapons in the territory controlled by Ali's brother, Jandra.

He had agreed to permit Sarah and Michael into the camp because he knew that the Janjaweed and the government would not attack if they knew that Sarah and Michael were in the camp. Jandra could exploit these human shields with impunity to send out nightly forays against his enemies.

With the government inevitably closing in on his hidden camp, this bought Jandra a few precious days to continue his fight against the government's covertly supported Janjaweed militia that had been terrorizing the locals. The government was attempting to consolidate the minority Arab and Muslim population's control of the country and wrest it away from the indigenous African tribes.

They bounced along in silence for several minutes. Finally, Ali spoke again. "My brother was in one of your visions?"

Michael said, "We saw someone whom we did not recognize and knew that he too, had visions. We originally thought that you might be that person. The vision sent us here."

"To find the bones of the biblical Joseph?" Ali asked.

"It has sent us on missions in the past. That's what led us to those other discoveries."

"I don't think that my brother has had such luck."

They drove for another several hours. At times, the jungle became so dense that the diffused light lost its battle with the canopy. They kept the headlights on and frequently swerved sharply to avoid low-lying vines and roots the size of garbage cans. They couldn't be lost but they also couldn't know where they were going. On the left, the jungle closed in so completely that even the air seemed trapped. Branches whipped at their doors. To the right they caught occasional glimpses of a rocky bluff overhanging an empty chasm below and a clear view of the blue sky trickled in from above. Unexpectedly, the car bottomed out with the oil pan and transmission resting on the ground and the wheels spinning freely above the ruts. They were stuck.

Sarah was sitting in the back. Aswari shut the engine and grabbed a roll of duct tape from the back seat. Michael and Ali taped their pants legs to their boots to seal out parasites. With the engine silenced, the more indigenous cawing of the four-banded sand grouse seeking a mate and whistling complex tunes, was occasionally drowned out by raucous responses from chimpanzees carrying on animated conversations high up in the branches.

Michael and Ali slid out through the driver-side door and went in search of a large branch to slide under the tires. The sucking thwack of their feet as they plunged in and out of the mud, weaving between the side of the car and the encroaching jungle telegraphed their movements. Sarah cracked the windows to listen for instructions and for relief from the stifling humidity penetrating the car. There was a hint of motor oil in the moist, sweet air.

Sarah watched them enter the foreboding jungle and disappear from view. She scrambled into the front seat and taped her pants to her ankles.

Sarah had always been the brave one when they were out in the wilderness, preferring the animals and bugs to the horny bastards of the big city, because she could seal one off with only duct tape.

She looked over the dashboard and saw the ruts ahead become swallowed by the jungle. As she became acclimated to the symphony, a distinctive noise stood out, the whoosh of running water. An overlooked narrow path had been hacked through the undergrowth and less dense hanging tapestry to the right. The rocky ledge she had glimpsed earlier was less than ten meters away. Arching over it in mid-air, she saw the multi-hued spray from a waterfall. The fall itself was hidden from view, but the rocky overlook projected ominously like the edge of a high diving board.

She sucked in air and grabbed the binoculars. Lying jumbled on the overlook she could see human bones, bleached from extended exposure to the sun. Sarah's imagination saw a tortured head screaming as the animals picked at his living flesh. Reality was dangling not a dozen feet above it, the frayed ends of a jute noose from which justice had been quickly dispensed and then abandoned to a carnivore.

The sound of semi-automatic fire broke her out of her trance. It strafed the rear half of the car. The bullets did not penetrate the armored doors, but perforated the thin sheet metal of the trunk. Sarah hit the floor of the car, shaking violently. She thought, *My cousin and Ali are dead and I am about to be gang-raped by men who haven't seen a woman for months.*

It grew still and after what seemed like minutes, Sarah's heart slowed and the music of the jungle slowly returned. She lifted her head up from the gritty floor, looked around and froze.

A spider with a golf ball body was inches from her right hand on the floor of the vehicle. It crawled lightly and quickly onto the back of her hand, tingling her flesh with its hairy legs and sending shivers up her arm to her back. It scurried along to the back of the car. Seeing no other carnivores and feeling nothing crawling down her shirt or up her pants, she resumed breathing, raised her head to the passenger-side window and screamed until there was no air left to expel.

A soldier and his Kalashnikov rifle was peeking in through the open crack at the top of the window.

The scream startled the soldier. He jumped back, leaving the muzzle of the gun hanging from the window. Sarah quickly opened the window and grabbed the muzzle but she didn't have nearly enough time. The soldier thrust his hand in and unlocked the door, but not before Sarah closed the window on his arm. He panicked until another soldier, one of obviously higher rank, stepped up next to him and pulled on the door handle, opening the door. A third soldier emerged from the dense foliage holding up a rather limply hanging Ali. He had been pistol-whipped.

The officer looked pleased. Through the front windshield, Sarah saw that several men had materialized out of the foliage with their automatic rifles pointed at the armored passenger vehicle. Next, a shoulder-mounted rocket launcher poked out of the woods and aimed itself directly at the car.

Finally, Michael emerged between two soldiers, blindfolded and gagged.

The most senior soldier, still holding the door, grabbed Sarah by the elbow and pulled her out, firmly but not roughly. Then a barrel-chested man emerged from the overgrowth on the left side of the road. Sarah gasped at the vision incarnate.

The man spoke to the others in a local dialect. They lowered their rifles and relaxed. He approached Ali warily. Ali had regained consciousness but still needed to be supported. He looked up at the taller man, eyes glazed and without recognition. At a nod from the barrel-chested man, Ali was released. When his knees began to buckle, the man pulled him up with a stifling embrace. Michael's gag and blindfold were removed, and Sarah and he breathed a sigh of relief.

Gingerly rubbing his head, Ali introduced Michael and Sarah, and then the four clambered back into the armored vehicle, with the big man behind the wheel. They followed a new convoy, this one controlled by the rebels, deeper into the jungle, and soon veered off the main path behind one that had been hidden by vines now pulled back by some of the soldiers.

"I now understand what would have caused my pacifist brother to risk his neck and return to his tribal homeland. I am in your debt, Ali," the big man said.

Ali nodded. In their youth, the half-brothers had borne a striking resemblance before Jandra's hairline receded, exposing deep furrows and his belt became lost under his belly.

Jandra spoke over his shoulder. "I am sure that my brother has told you that he is not welcome here. He has risked his life because of my visions. He realizes how important it is that I find others like me, who are able to see things in their mind but that are still real."

Michael said, "Do you know where your visions come from, Jandra?"

Jandra fixed his gaze purposely on the narrow jungle tunnel ahead. "No, they appear just after I have sex. But not always. In that blank space in my mind after an orgasm. If I was not always awake, and they were not always accurate, I would think they are a dream. And you? I assume you both have them? You are related, correct?"

"Yes and not then." Before Michael could continue, more soldiers magically took form out of the jungle and surrounded the car.

Jandra slowed the car and turned to them. "We will speak later this evening."

Sarah and Michael were shown to a tent constructed of stiff canvas on a wood frame. They found a wash basin with basic toiletries. The camp was an amalgamation of early African warrior, Vietnam-era surplus and Soviet Union relics. Most of the troops were bivouacked, but there were a couple of prefabricated, semi-permanent structures for officers' quarters and the armory. Nearby, a large generator throbbed noisily and spit out dark grey exhaust while providing power to a small air conditioner affixed to one of the more permanent structures.

Jandra summoned the three from their tent a few minutes later. They strode through the caked mud of the camp, eyed warily by the soldiers. It was difficult to pinpoint the soldiers' animus. Sarah and Michael's clean untorn clothing and new boots, the compromise to the security of their secret camp, granting quarter to the traitor Ali, and residual resentment of former white colonialists each seemed like adequate justification.

They entered a room in the most substantial of the prefab houses. It was illuminated by flickering electrical lights and a couple of kerosene lanterns. Tobacco smoke clung to the air and mingled with the sour stench of hours of pick-up basketball in the gym. The AC strained vainly to keep up. Three sides and the roof of the slimy structure were constructed of a corrugated cardboard paneling with precut punch-outs for windows. In place of glass, they were covered with milky sheets of sun-strafed polyethylene that let in a fraction of the light reaching the ground. The fourth side was an army surplus canvas, screwed to the other walls and bolted to horizontal wood studs that were staked to the ground.

Four men sat on folding chairs around a desk. All but Jandra hung unfiltered cigarette butts from their cracked lower lips, attached by dried spit. Jandra sat behind the desk. Sitting very erect opposite Jandra was a slender man whose mere presence in the room exuded authority. The other men slouched over deferentially.

Jandra beckoned them into the room, shooing two men off of canvas chairs he offered to Sarah and Michael.

"Before you sit down, I would like you to meet my most trusted assistant, Captain Mahmoud."

"Thank you, Colonel," responded the slender man in a practiced, unctuous tone. He rose from his seat to shake hands with Michael and Sarah. Like Jandra, he was dressed in simple green khakis, though on his epaulets he wore the double gold bars of an army captain. Everyone reseated themselves and Jandra continued.

"We were trying to determine how we may be of service to you, when we realized that we don't exactly know what you are looking for, or where you are going."

Michael said, "We believe that the bones of the biblical Joseph are not in Egypt, but are here in Sudan. We think we know approximately where they are."

Nervous laughter was stifled by the colonel's glare. The captain suggested, "Can you provide us with directions? We will be happy to send troops out to excavate them and return them to you here where you will be safe."

Sarah bristled. "We would certainly welcome your assistance, as we are strangers here. However, I think we have substantially more expertise in archaeological digs than your troops do. We want to exhume and preserve them, not chop them into firewood."

The captain bowed his head deferentially. "As you wish. The colonel has made it very clear to me that you are our guests," he articulated the last word derisively. "Approximately where shall you look for these old bones?"

"We don't know exactly. We understand that there is a labyrinth of caves about one hundred kilometers due west of here. We expect to find them there."

"Any cave in particular?" the captain asked.

"We memorized a map and then destroyed it. Possessing a written treasure map would be reasonably suicidal on our part. We also have a rough road map leading to the general cave area where the map we have memorized begins."

Jandra said, "Miss Baskin, Mr. Seagal, this whole mission of yours is suicidal. Those bones have been there for over three thousand years. Why don't you wait another five or ten before discovering them? At least that way, you will live to receive your much deserved accolades." The captain nodded vigorously.

"We are so close now. Why would we turn back? If you were to help us uncover such an amazing artifact, and then offer it to the world, you would add considerable stature to your cause. You would be recognized as freedom fighters that care enough about the treasures of their people to protect them for all mankind."

"We could also hold them and you for ransom. Your lives and the bones of Joseph could be worth a half dozen tanks. Those bones hardly make good weapons."

When the captain was absolutely certain the colonel had finished, he said, "I agree with the colonel." Ali began to protest but his brother put up his hand.

"That is only one of several alternatives. We will talk further in the morning. Mr. Seagal, you will sleep with Ali. Miss Baskin, your tent is accessible through your cousin's tent."

Sarah wasn't exactly sure how she was supposed to feel secure in a canvas tent.

Michael went into Sarah's tent for a whispered conversation.

"Sarah, these people will very happily kill us and not even remember it in the morning. They won't even bury us. We've hit a new low. Who was it who once said, 'Give me a natural disaster any day'?"

"We are safe for the time being because they are using us. They haven't raped me yet, or called you a cowardly weasel. Would you rather leave on the morning train?"

"No, ask them to call a limo."

Sarah said, "Let me give you some credit. That really was a brilliant idea about the bones in the cave. On the other hand, if you had lied and told them they were thirty kilometers in the opposite direction, we could have snuck off and destroyed the biological weapons while no one was looking."

"Right. And there are no guards posted around the weapons and we both know that we have no map to find the caves." He changed the subject. "What do you make of the colonel? Do you think Jandra knows why we are here?"

"If you were MC, would you tell Jandra we are coming and not tell him why?"

Michael thought. "Jandra clearly knows almost nothing about MC. Maybe MC's ability to communicate with him is much more limited. No way to tell. We won't know more until we get him alone."

Nine time zones, covering an audacious lie and a jungle confrontation within seconds of rape and murder made Antarctica seem like a ski trip to the Alps. A swamp leech had sucked out all of her emotions. Sarah began to keel over. "Tomorrow is soon enough."

Michael led his cousin to her cot. "Call me if you need me. I don't think the walls are soundproof."

Sarah opened her eyes abruptly to find Jandra and Ali standing over her. She bolted upright. "Where's Michael?"

The colonel put his finger over his lips and hers at the same time. The three crept into Jandra's office.

"I believe Captain Mahmoud has taken him, but he is alive."

Sarah's heart pounded. This time, Michael's obsession with getting some recognition was going to get him killed.

"How do you know?" she demanded.

"Because my visions foretold of your coming, and I could see that you and your cousin would prevail in your mission. I cannot stop you. But you must help me, Miss Baskin. I cannot compromise my cause," Jandra said.

"Then you know why we have come?"

"We have no use for weapons of mass destruction, and I have no desire to commit genocide on my countrymen, regardless of their tribe or religion. However, we need conventional weapons, food, and fuel to fight our war. When the Americans decided that terrorists were hiding in every Arab country in the world, one of those governments offered us conventional weapons, small arms, tanks, and artillery to keep their Arab brethren off-balance. We conceal their WMDs, in case they became the next targets of American imperialism. We don't know what we are storing. I assure you that my vision came well after those weapons had been hidden here. By then, it was too late.

"Our benefactors will turn on us if those weapons are destroyed. I think your suggestion that Joseph's bones were buried in those caves scared the captain. He realized that once you started snooping around, you would find the weapons. God does not look kindly on weapons of mass destruction. But I don't think that the captain fears God. He would kill you without thinking. However, he knew that I had guaranteed you safe passage and that this had to be something of great significance to get my brother, the traitor, back to his homeland. You piqued his curiosity. If he knew the whole truth, he would have shot all of you on sight.

"Sarah, you have no idea how much Ali has put at risk here. When I first became aware of your potential visit through one of my visions, I confided in my brother. We smuggled him out of Sudan several years ago, just before the Arab dictators started slaughtering our tribesmen. The elders wanted him to continue his education. He is a pacifist, but he is no coward. As a young boy, he saved his mother, sister, and two goats from a pack of hungry hyenas. He hacked one to death before the others ran off. He is here because of my visions and because he wants you to succeed. I allowed you here because like my brother, I would like to make sure that these weapons aren't used on innocent people."

He turned to his brother. "Mahmoud doesn't understand pacifism."

Ali said, "Coward, pacifist, and traitor mean the same thing to him."

"Where has he taken my cousin?"

"We are questioning some of his closest allies and assistants. We will know shortly. And then, we will retrieve your cousin, alive, and unharmed."

"You cannot harm him."

Jandra responded, "I have seen that you must succeed in your mission, but I suspect that you and your cousin bleed like I do."

He left the morbid tone. "Do you know where these visions come from? Unlike you, I am never told to do anything."

Jandra wouldn't even have begun to comprehend. "Jandra, we know where the weapons are. We have known all along. Michael and I have been instructed to destroy them. Our vision foretold that we would be forcibly separated," she lied, "although, I don't know why these particular weapons are so special."

Sarah then provided the exact location of the weapons, their descriptions and Jandra's security around them. When she finished, Jandra exhaled audibly. His shoulders fell.

"It would be simplest to kill you both now," Jandra responded.

"That wasn't the deal, Jandra," Ali interceded.

"No, and WMDs are not the bones of Joseph."

Sarah said, "If we die, you will no longer be able to send out your teams of saboteurs. I saw them leave last night. And everyone will know where the weapons are."

"How?"

"Because before I left I provided a sealed envelope to an attorney in the States as part of my will. He knows that this trip puts me in mortal peril. If he doesn't hear from me every ninety-six hours, he is to assume that I am dead. The next contact must be two days from now. Once he opens that envelope he will immediately hand it over to the American authorities. Then there will be a cruise missile strike on these caves, or perhaps an invasion, if they think that a missile strike will release the poison.

"There's a second copy on the university's encrypted server. It requires a retina scan to access. It is automatically programmed to be forwarded to federal agents and the press if I don't return to abort it within six days. If we were still alive, no one would have believed that we had knowledge of the biological weapons, but both of these documents link our death to the weapons. We have no political ambitions and no desire to impede your struggle. We, too, would like to prevent the intervention of American military might."

"Sympathetic words, but they don't solve our problem, Sarah. I am not sure where your cousin is, and I don't have the ability to destroy these weapons without destroying my cause. I don't think that's supposed to happen and if it does, I would prefer to be dead as well."

"And that, my brother, is why I am a pacifist."

"Jandra, not only your cause and the weapons are at stake, here. I am not sure whether these visions are a blessing or a curse to any of us, but our last vision made it very clear that whatever is in these weapons will destroy any and all victims' telepathic abilities, even if they are fortunate enough to survive the exposure. For whatever reason, these WMDs must be destroyed."

CHAPTER 21

The Imprisoned Guest

The fuzzy pictures drew into focus. The damp smell of a doused camp-fire penetrated Michael's skin. He was on his back, shivering on the cold ground with his hands bound tightly on his chest. A knot in his head acted as a door stop. The last thing Michael recalled was getting into an armored car in Khartoum with Ali, Sarah and some uniforms. He saw shadows of another familiar face.

Footsteps and voices grew louder, so he shuttered his eyes to invisible cracks and relaxed his body. Heavy boots were crunching on the tunnel floor. Someone leaned over his face with a flashlight.

"You're a moaner, Mr. Seagal. Wake up."

He knew the voice from somewhere. "I didn't ask for a wake-up call."

"Very funny," he said sternly, but a slight snort betrayed a sense of humor. "We don't get much sleep here. Open your eyes, please."

Two Africans, a very tall lanky one and a somewhat shorter one hovered over him.

"Are you hungry?" The taller one asked.

"Oh, room service. Now that, I could use," Michael said, looking for a way to get his bonds off.

"Sit up, please, and don't be such a wise ass." The man had advanced training in American slang rebukes.

At this point, Michael regretted not doing those ab crunches regularly. Try as he might, he could not sit straight up without the help of his hands. He entertained them by exhibiting the dexterity of a turtle as he rolled to his stomach, tucked his knees and then turned and plopped back down on his bottom.

The lanky one gave a coarse high laugh and spoke to the other man in an unfamiliar tongue.

The shorter one untied his hands and handed him a flat, coarse bread and a dirty bowl of tasteless gruel. Pieces of burned vegetables crunched in his mouth but stuck to his ribs. The shaking stopped.

The taller man asked, "Mr. Seagal, do you remember anything from last night?"

Michael looked at him suggestively. "Why? What did you do to me?"

"You're a funny man, Mr. Seagal. I meant, do you remember where you were, or any of the people?"

"Call me Michael, please. And no, nothing."

"I apologize. You hit your head. Do you know why you are here?"

"Hit my head? I was whacked."

"Michael, if you were whacked, you'd be dead now. Do you remember meeting Ali's brother, the colonel?"

"Who's Ali?" Michael's MC images were getting confused with his own.

"Now, you are lying. I am his second in command and the XO."

"Executive Officer?"

"Precisely. My name is Captain Mahmoud. The colonel had me bring you here."

"Thank you. That jungle weather was stifling. I assume we are in a cave now? It's a big improvement."

Michael thought quickly. He was beginning to test the captain's patience. Why was he here? The caves. Joseph's bones. The biological weapons. Where the hell were Ali and the colonel? He was a dead man.

The captain must have been reading his mind. "We believe that we are in the cave system where you say you will find the bones of the biblical Joseph. We would like to help you find them. Please give us some direction."

"Captain, since you came here as a passenger, while I arrived as baggage, I have no idea where we are. I would like to get my bearings and ask you a few questions before we start."

"Proceed," he responded in clipped military fashion.

"Why would the colonel want you to bring me here without Sarah? Why would you have to bushwhack me to do that? Assuming we are successful, what do you plan to do with me and the old bones when we are done? And if we are not successful, then what?"

"Kill you," and then he added, lest there be any ambiguity, "in either case. Michael, please appreciate my position. Normally we would kill you, or take you hostage immediately if you showed up in a hidden camp uninvited. For reasons of his own, the colonel views this situation a little differently. We have orders not to harm you. I obey orders, as I don't want to be shot. However, there are many people here who neither like nor trust the colonel's brother. They would be happy to see him dead."

"And now that he has gotten me here, and I see what he has gotten me into, perhaps I should agree with you."

"Humor while you're in mortal danger. Under other circumstances, we might become friends," he sighed. "We can go outside and figure out where you are, although I doubt it will help much."

"Why is that?"

"It's night time. We'll try in the morning."

"Captain, there are a couple of other problems." The captain seemed unsurprised.

"I am a science reporter, not an archaeologist. I would not know how to dig up and identify old bones any better than my dog. Worse, in fact. Miss Baskin is the scientist and that's why she's here. You invited the wrong guest, except that you probably should have abducted both of us. When Sarah and I came on this trip, we decided that, given the circumstances, we didn't trust *anybody*. And besides, the information we had was way too large for either of us to memorize all of it. As we told you and your colonel earlier, we each memorized half of the map to the caves of Joseph. I am useless without her," which Michael knew was true on many levels.

"So, you are saying that if I kill one of you, I might as well kill both of you?"

MC's omnipotency was now routinely falling well short of *Its* omniscience and even that made no sense half the time. He was on his own. "I prefer to think that there is no benefit to killing either of us."

"You would." He scrutinized Michael carefully. "I believe you, but I still want half a map to determine if it's really Joseph's bones that you are seeking. Regardless, this was your discovery. You must remember some of her half of the map."

"There's no way to tell. Miss Baskin and I split the map up like a puzzle. She has pieces two, four, six, eight, and ten. I have one, three, five, seven, and nine and there's complicated descriptions of directions and landmarks and the phases of the moon." He was improvising as fast as his lips could move. "You need us both. Why didn't you take us both, anyway?"

"The colonel and I both agree that it is much more effective to interrogate groups of prisoners individually."

"Prisoners? I thought we were guests." Obviously a little faux pas.

The captain put a gun to Michael's head and Michael began to cry.

Then, a wave of M'low Cloomian serenity overtook him. A subconscious vision that Michael never knew existed was revealed to him. The crying and despair stopped. Michael had a plan.

"Shoot me. It's only a matter of time anyway."

The captain smiled. "You are right about that, my friend. Your days are numbered."

"No, Captain, you are confused. I meant it's only a matter of time for you. Kill me and the colonel will hunt you like a dog."

His gun hand began to quiver. Not exactly the reaction Michael was hoping for. "Not if I prove that you came here looking for something else."

"Put your gun down, Captain. I haven't any idea what you are talking about, and I can't run away because I have no idea how to get back."

He tentatively lowered his gun and then frisked Michael roughly and thoroughly, pulling down his pants and ripping out the hems of his clothes.

"What are you looking for?"

"You will excuse me if we think that you might lie to us again. Back at the camp, you had said that you had a rough map to the cave area from our bivouac. Hand it over. You don't need it anymore. You are here already."

"Sarah has it. She reads maps better than me."

Mahmoud had undisguised contempt for a man that would entrust such important information to a woman. "Perhaps you are right. We shall wait until you and your cousin fail to find Joseph's bones. Then the colonel will kill you both."

As Mahmoud walked out, he yelled back, "We'll be back when it's light out."

They left Michael with a moldy, maggot-infested blanket, some sterilized water and a smoky kerosene lamp. Michael knew that it was very unlikely that the colonel would have permitted the captain to separate them, at least until the colonel was able to decipher his dreams. How ironic, Michael thought, the bones of Joseph, interpreter of Pharaoh's dreams.

The enigmatic captain spoke perfect English, was neatly groomed, and had an obvious distaste for these primitive conditions. Why take up the cause? Ambition? Empathy for his people? Money? Michael had his own concerns to deal with, like survival. He dozed off with the blanket in motion around him.

He was awakened by cool air rushing across the floor of his prison and being expelled into the night. A low pressure system the size of a hurricane was moving in and with that kind of air flow there had to be an opening big enough for Michael to squeeze through. He was getting desperate. Lost in the Sudanese jungle seemed no more serious than being lost in Wal-Mart, when compared to a bullet in the head. If his escape route was unguarded, he had a chance. For what, he wasn't quite sure.

Michael used the blanket to cover rocks and dirt he formed to look like his body and then followed the airflow deeper into the cave. The cave grew narrower and darker which of course meant that it was time for the kerosene to run out. Soon he could see nothing in front of him, not even his hand, so he felt along the side wall. Sometimes cool, muddy water ran down its surface. In many places it was highly irregular. At one point, He was feeling along at waist and chest height when a razor-like outcropping lanced his left arm and blood poured freely from the exposed flesh. He took a tattered piece of his shirtsleeve and covered the wound. It throbbed and his fingers and forearm began to get numb. He had probably nicked a nerve. He moved more cautiously toward the sweet outside air.

Michael never seemed to be descending more than a couple of feet. More often, he made a brief ascent. The air grew warmer and the tail wind increased. Without warning, the wind shifted and blew straight at him. He retraced his steps a few feet. He looked up and saw a halo. The wet walls of the cave reflected a yellow glow from a hole in the ceiling, probably ten or twelve feet over his head. A full moon smiled at him from the center of the opening.

Michael couldn't climb the wet walls. He sat down on his knees for a minute. The walls were too close together to squat further. That's when Michael realized that if he pressed his left foot and hand against one wall and his right foot and hand against the other, he could shinny his way to the top. It was not an ab-challenged exercise, but the walls were slippery and he wasn't sure that his left arm had the strength or that he could with-stand the pain. The cave narrowed as he moved upward and he now had only enough room to wedge his forearms against either side of the wall, rather than his hands while he released his feet and moved them up the wall. He continued to scrape his elbows along the walls as the inchworm process continued, the slippery mixture of blood and water making the process even more treacherous. Anything other than his army surplus boots and he would have slid to the ground and broken his ass bone.

He popped his head out of the hole and transferred all of his weight to his feet while he attempted to get a grip on the outside rim of the hole.

As his hands gripped the soft dirt, it came cascading down into his t-shirt and he felt his feet sliding down the wall. Desperately grabbing at the surface as his head disappeared, he caught a large root handle with his right hand and a secure rock with the other. He pulled himself up and then immediately lost the wall with his feet. If he slipped now, he would plummet nearly four meters, bouncing like a pinball off the jagged rocks. Michael rested his elbows on the outside ground. The earth around the tunnel opening held. He wriggled out with the rest of his body and lay quietly on the ground for a few minutes, listening for guards. A continuation of the stone tunnel wall rose to one side of him. Clouds were rapidly rolling in from the east, to cover the full moon.

He did a more thorough damage check. Other than his arm, there was no blood, but he was a black mess. He massaged the dirt between his thumb and forefinger. Black talcum powder. Coal. There must be a shallow seam running through the shaft he had scaled.

Raucous laughter, punctuated by the occasional moaning and scream-ing of female voices broke the stillness of the night. The men were hav-ing themselves a good time at someone else's expense. Michael couldn't afford sympathy. He was having more than enough trouble keeping him-self alive.

He scrambled to the top of the rocks, a good ten meters or so. From the overlook, the terrain matched perfectly with his M'low Cloom image. A fire hose undulated past his ankle and then disappeared. He grew light-headed.

The hill overlooked two soldiers guarding the entrance to his prison. A path led away from the entrance for a couple hundred meters and then split, with one way continuing into his M'low Cloom road map.

Michael circumnavigated the sentries and followed the memory map to the other cave. New growth was sprouting in the dual ruts that dead-ended at a small clearing which framed the other entryway.

A steel door with an airtight rubber seal had been fit into the cave's entrance, which projected out of a shallow hill. If he remembered correctly, once inside the entrance, there was a short steep decline and then the tunnel opened up quickly.

He knew that this cave had another access point. Hopefully, he wasn't going to find the opening shuttered with fresh concrete like the "build your own entrance" at magnetic north, because of MC's two-hundred-year-old memories.

The fitted steel back door was where M'low Cloom had left it. Over time, heavy vines had enmeshed it with tiny Velcro fingers and it had nearly succumbed to the jungle's encroach. Michael manually defoliated the door and found a rusted swastika haunting its face. He was suddenly hit with an epiphany from one of his visions. That was it, the personification of evil! But it wasn't relevant here. He knew that. He made a mental note to bring it up to Sarah if they ever saw each other again.

He tugged on the handle. The door scratched reluctantly across the ground, and then its rusty hinges would move no further. He squeezed his body through the crack and involuntarily groaned when he scraped his throbbing arm through the rusted flecks. A third of the distance toward the main entrance, several weak electric lights illuminated an area not much bigger than a child's bedroom. A rectangle of the room was cordoned off by fencing on three sides that was concrete anchored to the cave's wall on the fourth side. Sitting alone in the center of the secured area were two wooden pallets laden with steel cylinders. One pallet was missing a cylinder that had been rolled against the side wall. Michael walked slowly toward the weapons and his vision.

An airtight door stood ajar beyond the area of the stored cylinders and Michael could see that dawn was gradually adding golden rays to the monochromatic room beyond. The barking of slurred male voices, mingled with the pleading high-pitched screams of young girls resulted in a chorus of low nasal snorts from bovines disturbed from their tranquility.

The door beyond began to move, and Michael retreated toward the back door, straight into the chest of sinewy muscle that was the captain's assistant.

The captain strutted through the front door.

There was a brief foreign exchange with his attaché. The two men obviously disagreed about something. The captain barked a sharp rebuke and the man cowered and grew silent.

This time Michael's hands and feet were bound tightly enough to stain the cords red. The captain said, "Michael, my friend, you have found us a solution. You stumbled across our weapons cache. We have your solitary shoe prints into this secure room to prove it, and lots of witnesses. We don't wear expensive US issued army boots. Now, we will test them."

"Weapons cache? You're crazy. This cave is hiding the bones of Joseph, just like we said."

The captain pressed his index finger into Michael's wound and ground the rust particles deeper into his flesh. Michael writhed and sweat beaded on his forehead. He fell to his knees.

"Really?"

Through clenched teeth, Michael said, "Captain, Africa isn't the only place that AIDS is rampant. I certainly hope you don't have an open wound on that finger."

The captain pulled his finger away quickly and motioned to his adjunct who grabbed Michael roughly by his injured arm and dragged him through the door into the next room. He returned from the weapons room with a cylinder. He sealed off the room as he departed. Michael now found himself in a room filled with the true victims of this war. Michael's professional training pushed his own pain aside when he recognized the real story. Gaunt and tortured skeletons of human beings, some with filthy rags covering amputation stumps staggered into the cave under the constant prodding of their captors. Then came the dazed preteen girls, many with dried blood clinging their skirts to their loins, their childhoods brutally stolen. There were nearly twenty of them in all.

The captain turned back suddenly and smacked Michael across the face with his open hand, splitting his lip. More blood. "You, my friend, are having a big problem with reality. You know of nothing here but your belief that you will find the biblical bones of Joseph? This is not some bible legend, you damn fool. This is a war! While I was away attending the university in Nairobi, they slaughtered my whole clan, including my bride, who was here for a family visit. I will do anything to avenge their deaths, unlike your yellow friend Aswari!" He turned away again and hid his head in his hands.

Michael took a guess at the earlier debate of the captain and his subordinate. "What are your benefactors going to say when they find out that you have used these weapons for your own purposes? You have already been paid for storing them. You have food and arms to continue your struggle. You're a warehouse, not a deployment center. Killing me is one thing. Using them on innocent victims of war, a war for which these weapons were not even intended, will certainly get you killed, Captain, if not by your allies, then by your own colonel. It will avenge nothing." He tried to sound calm. These people around him didn't deserve this fate.

The captain released a shrill laugh that echoed deep into the cavern. "I watched our benefactors use these weapons on an Iraqi arms profiteer who attempted to double-cross them. These caves were fitted for just this purpose. These other people?" He looked at the men, "Casualties," and then at the women, "spoils of war. They will have never existed."

Mahmoud turned to a sergeant leaning on his rifle chewing on khat, the mildly narcotic stimulant derived from the leaves of an indigenous evergreen shrub. "Get these farmers' animals out of here and away from the lichens. This isn't a damn pasture. It's supposed to be a secure area and they're in here every day."

The sergeant called two other men over and they herded the seven animals out of the room. The oily pucker of an airtight hydraulic seal thrust the room into darkness. As soon as the doors were closed, he held out his hands to get one of the other people to untie him, but they were too afraid to move.

Michael heard a gas grill hissing. It was the delivery system to send the cylinder's contents airborne. He got up and attempted to move toward the back door, but a cloud enveloped him like a London fog. He began coughing. He fell and blacked out.

CHAPTER 22

Recovered

When Sarah and Ali woke just before dawn, Jandra was nowhere to be found. His third in command was at the edge of the encroaching jungle, barking orders. He spoke little English.

"Well?" Sarah asked anxiously.

Ali translated. "The colonel has personally assumed command of the search for your cousin. He departed the camp two or three hours ago."

"Ask him where the colonel went."

Ali translated the response. The man spoke nervously.

"He says that he is not supposed to tell us, but he believes the colonel has gone to the caves where he thinks he will find the captain."

"Ask him if that is the cave where the weapons are stored."

Ali gave her the finger, American style. "I'm serious, Ali. Tell him that I know all about them. Tell him they are behind a large steel door and that they are keeping prisoners in a cave nearby. I have visions."

Ali shook his head and translated.

When the wide-eyed lieutenant had finished, Ali laughed. "He says you are a witch and should be destroyed, but he doesn't have the authority to do so and hopes that you will remember he spared your life."

In each of the last two nights, the activity level in the camp had increased. A Janjaweed attack on the camp was imminent.

Jandra and a dozen men left their jeeps several kilometers away and approached the caves on foot. When the camp had been established, Jandra had personally located the permanent sentry posts. The first guard's perch was camouflaged high in the trees where he could surprise any attackers if his drunken snoring didn't give him away.

The colonel replaced the sentry with one of those in his entourage and continued a little less warily. The area was in squalor with broken liquor bottles, tattered women's clothing, and spent food cans. Jandra's men encircled the camp. He motioned for them to hold their fire while the colonel fired several shots into the air causing a small stampede of the oxen still wandering through the encampment.

Mahmoud bolted from one of the tents with his sidearm drawn. Others awoke with a start and fumbled for their weapons. When Mahmoud saw Jandra with the rifles of half a platoon directed at him, he lowered his pistol.

Jandra's jaws were the hinges of a steel trap poised to spring. His temples throbbed and he locked eyes with his subordinate. Mahmoud's men groggily stood at attention, a picture of slovenly confusion. Jandra broke eye contact first.

"The captain and I need to speak privately for a few minutes. Everyone who came with me is to replace and disarm the sentries. Secure the area. The rest of you, clean this mess and yourselves up."

Jandra handed the captain's weapon and his own to the sergeant he left in charge. They walked deep into the jungle, one committed to vengeance, the other to autonomy and obsolete humanitarian rules of engagement, but ultimately to the same victory.

"Mahmoud, why would you disobey me?"

"You are a naive fool. They will kill us. They have known about the weapons all along. Mr. Seagal found his way into the vault last night. He came in through a back door we didn't even know existed. If they don't kill us personally, then they will sabotage these weapons and the Janjaweed or the government troops will kill us."

"Mahmoud, it is you who are the fool. Isn't it odd that we keep moving our base camp to avoid detection, but this cave complex is never discovered and it has been here for what, more than a year and a half? As long as we don't carry out sorties from here, our Arab benefactors have declared these caves off-limits to the government and the Janjaweed. They use everyone to get what they want. It's no different than when they killed your wife. We are pawns of everyone.

"Where is Michael now?"

"I infected him. He is still in the exposure chamber. We haven't decontaminated it yet."

"You know we are prohibited from using these weapons. What were you thinking?"

"There were, ah, others, Colonel. It seemed more efficient and quieter than shooting all of these people."

"Mahmoud, I am not a fool and neither are these two Americans. If Miss Baskin does not make contact in the States within two days, there will be a cruise missile strike or a major military assault against this location. We will all be destroyed as will our cause. I knew that they were aware of these weapons before they got here."

"You will excuse me for asking, Colonel, but why did you reveal our bivouac's location? Why didn't you kill them and your traitorous brother immediately or forbid them from coming?"

"I have been able to carry out nightly attacks from our base with impunity, using them as human shields. We needed to be relocating anyway, but they bought us more time. If we didn't let them in, they would have just revealed the weapons' location to their government, the cruise missile strike would have been ordered and the result would have been the same."

The captain considered his mentor for a moment. He was a man of strong principles. This kind of pragmatic thinking was unusual. "There was another reason wasn't there, Colonel? Those visions you told me about once?"

The colonel was well aware of the captain's skepticism.

"This was the only way to salvage our cause. They didn't come here to compromise us, but to somehow permanently prevent the use of the weapons. Unfortunately, I don't see how they can do that without our benefactors finding out. We, and they, have to find a way to eliminate the weapons without retribution."

"Maybe we could just give them back?" This time Mahmoud made no attempt to contain his sarcasm. "Colonel, the only solution is to kill them."

The Colonel thoroughly described Sarah's fail safe method to assure the weapons were destroyed.

The captain laughed. "You *are* a naive old fool, Jandra. She is bluffing."

"Maybe. But are you willing to bet your life on that?"

"Are you willing to bet your life that she is not?"

"Fair enough. We will go back and clear out the cave now. If we find Michael alive, you will be executed for insubordination. If we find him dead, we will execute Miss Baskin and be done with it."

"No one survives that infection. But you," he said, "you survive either way."

"An excellent point. I will resign my command, and you may execute me with Miss Baskin."

Now, Mahmoud's honor was at stake. "You must announce our deal to the troops."

Jandra nodded in agreement. They nervously slapped each other on the back. As they walked back to the cave, Jandra said, "Remember the Iraqi arms dealer that was infected? You weren't around during the decontamination. He survived. We took him into the jungle and shot him. These weapons are not as foolproof as you think they are."

The sealed contamination area was disinfected with an airborne agent that destroyed whatever had been released into the chamber. Then, louvers on massive diesel powered fans exhausted the caves into the air.

As they unsealed the door, they were overcome by a cocktail of death and excrement. Jandra grabbed Mahmoud's elbow with a beefy hand.

"Come, my friend, let us see what is inside."

All of the men and young women were dead. Michael was on his hands and knees, his split lip swollen, dried blood and dirt caked around his mouth, chin and upper-arm wound.

The incandescent illumination cast concentration camp shadows on the corpses, and Michael slowly recalled the events of the last several days.

"Your men raped all of these girls and then you threw them in here to destroy the evidence. You're not warriors. You're cowards!"

Michael staggered toward Mahmoud, but Jandra blocked the way.

"There is no need. Mahmoud will pay." He ordered the hung over men to remove the bodies.

Michael whispered into Jandra's ear over the jet stream of air being exhausted from the cave. Jandra barked out orders to two of his senior militia men. They immediately returned to camp in one of the jeeps.

Jandra now turned to the assembled troops. "The punishment for Mahmoud's insubordination and for rape is death. Had this man not survived," he said, motioning to Michael, "I had permitted the captain to execute me for my poor judgment and leadership. I will treat Mahmoud the same way he treated his fellow countrymen and women. We will use these weapons once more, on Mahmoud. He will either suffer the same fate as his countrymen, or the same fate as this white man," Jandra said.

Late in the afternoon, Jandra's messengers returned with Michael's backpack. With the oxens' owners dead, Jandra gave orders to load several of them onto a personnel carrier to be transported back to the camp for a feast. Jandra sent Mahmoud's men back to the camp with the oxen, keeping with him a few of his most trusted men as guards.

The men arrived at the main bivouac with the oxen and Michael at nightfall. Joyous whoops of joy overwhelmed the camp as the animals were immediately slaughtered for the meal.

Ali pulled Sarah out of her tent. "They're back from the caves, and they've brought fresh meat."

It didn't take either of them long to spot the one white person in the short convoy. Michael was handcuffed and smeared with coal and blood, but Sarah reserved her shock for his complexion, a fiery sunset.

He smiled feebly when he saw them. The guard helped him out of the truck, unshackled him and transferred him to the lieutenant they had spoken to earlier. The two soldiers spoke briefly.

The lieutenant approached Michael in his most officious manner and stood at parade rest, hands clasped smartly behind his back. He spoke disdainfully to Ali who interpreted in first person. "The colonel has instructed me to allow you to use your phone and laptop, Mr. Seagal. Miss Baskin must immediately make a phone call and she is to be provided complete privacy in the colonel's headquarters. Miss Baskin, if you need electric power, please feel free to hook up to the generator." The lieutenant then saluted Sarah and Michael, scowled at Ali, completed a snappy about face and walked away.

Sarah's emotions were sapped. "Michael, this is not good at all."

He pursed his lips and pointed to the colonel's tent.

Ali said, "I will leave you alone. I hear there's a big party brewing."

In the tent, Sarah found sulfa drugs, antiseptic, and bandages. She cleaned her cousin's wound and held it together with sutures and steri-strips. It would have to do for now. At least they were current on tetanus shots. On the surface, Michael seemed unaffected by fatal doses of the pathogen, but he was the only human survivor. Sarah wasn't fully convinced that it was the same cousin sitting in front of her that she had seen three nights ago.

"Sarah, after all I've been through in the last two and one-half days, why was returning my lap top and cell phone the most important thing on their agenda?"

She recounted her warning to Jandra.

"Could you have concocted this story before they kidnapped me?"

"Michael, what are they doing with the oxen?"

"I don't know. Not exactly my focus after they released me from the cave."

"What do you mean, after they released you from the cave? Did you see them before they infected you?"

"Well, yeah. The oxen were eating lichens off of the cave walls."

"How many of them?"

"Seven, I think."

"Was this the first time they used this cave as an infection center?"

"No, Mahmoud told me that their benefactors had tested it in there before. What difference does it make?"

"I'll be right back."

There was a roar in the camp and Sarah rushed out of the tent door to see a freshly slaughtered ox being paraded around on a spit by six men. Others were building a bonfire in the center of the camp.

Sarah raced around the camp desperately seeking Ali or Jandra's lieutenant. She found the lieutenant first. "The meat is bad. Your men will get very sick! They mustn't eat it." She grabbed her stomach, doubled over and heaved.

Palms up, the lieutenant raised his eyebrows and turned his back on her, muttering, "Witch."

Then, she spotted Ali attempting to ingratiate himself by collecting wild herbs and spices for the feast. "Ali, these oxen were eating lichens in the cave where they exposed Michael. The animals have been contaminated by plants exposed to these pathogens. It's too risky."

"The animals seemed fine to me when they got back, Sarah. You are a very paranoid woman."

"Ali, I know this will sound really absurd, but do you remember the biblical story of Joseph? It started with Joseph interpreting Pharaoh's dreams about cattle and seven years of feast and then seven years of famine.

Michael and I looked up that story in the bible in the Marriott nightstand when we were in Alexandria. I had that dream last night."

Ali shook his head and walked toward the lieutenant. He attempted to explain the situation to him and then translated his response to Sarah. "The lieutenant told me to butt out. He said that if these animals ate the lichen and survived, then they must have special powers. All of the men want to eat from these animals, because they think that they can gain their immunity. I am afraid that I do not have a lot of credibility here, Sarah. He did ask me an interesting question, though.

"He said that if the oxen were afflicted, as you say, then Michael must have been even more severely affected, but he is alive and apparently unharmed. How?"

Sarah took a step back in surprise. "They want to eat him, too?"

"No. They are not cannibals, you stupid American tourist," he said with a twinkle. "They just wonder if he is any different now, as well."

Michael had approached unnoticed as they were talking with the lieutenant. "A very good question, and while I don't know the answer, I am not complaining about the outcome."

The bonfire light reflected in Michael's eyes, casting his face in a demonic glare. It had to be Sarah's imagination. She looked at Ali. No glowing there, but he recoiled from Michael slightly and she knew that he saw it, too.

She shook her head resolutely. "We can talk about that in a minute. Right now, we have to do something about these animals. I think something very bad is going to happen if the men eat them."

"Like what, Sarah?" Ali said. "Indigestion? Instant death?"

"I don't know anything else." Then she turned to Michael and continued, more softly, "But, it's consistent with everything so far."

Michael nodded.

The bonfire grew and the aroma of fat sizzling on the open fire permeated the camp. It seemed harmless enough. The meat crackled and browned and pairs of men took turns turning the spit. As blobs of fat dripped off of the animal, flames shot high above the carcass, carrying embers into the night sky and a roar would rise from the men.

The men in the camp had immediately wanted to pull out whiskey and hashish, but the soldiers that had just returned from the caves reminded them of Mahmoud's fate as a result of his men's disobedience and debauchery. They would have to settle for fresh meat. The lieutenant immediately redoubled the sentries around the bivouac's perimeter and doubled the ration for cigarettes and khat.

Ali left Sarah and Michael and they returned to the flimsy headquarters. Michael's orange-pink complexion had not faded and his pupils had dilated, completely consuming the normally bright green irises. They bored into her, probing her mind. She shifted in her chair, uncomfortably peeling her sticky bottom from the seat, even though the room was comparably cool.

"What happened to you in the caves?" She tried to sound calm.

Offhandedly, "Why, do I seem different?"

"Your eyes are a window into a place I've never seen before. Don't you feel different?"

He never took his pitch-black irises off of his cousin. "I woke up in total darkness. There were fans roaring nearby, where Mahmoud had imprisoned a number of tortured men, a gaggle of freshly raped women—girls really, and me."

It took him at least several minutes to sort through the mental confusion before he spoke again.

"Other than the fans, I heard nothing except for a man moaning. Then I realized it was me. I saw a light at the end of the tunnel, literally. Shadowy outlines took shape in the light. It was Mahmoud, Jandra and their entourage. Then bright lights came on pretty quickly."

Michael's eyes rolled into his head, revealing only the whites. When he spoke again, his voice was spectral. "I don't know what those pathogens are, but they have changed me. I don't know why I didn't die. Somehow my immune system immobilized them or maybe they just aren't poisonous to me. But I wasn't completely unaffected.

"It's my mind, Sarah. The world looks different now. M'low Cloom looks different. So many mysteries of life are coming into focus." His eyes returned to their normal position. He seemed less sinister now.

Sarah said, "MC's top priority is knocking out those weapons. But why? Because they don't work as intended, but kill selectively?"

"No. You got it right the first time. MC wants to assure that nature be allowed to take its course, and weapons of mass destruction don't meet that criteria. But, not because of some symbiosis with the earth or because *It* cares. The little monkey reptiles became extinct because they could no longer find enough mates to maintain their population levels. It's a big ocean and if the last two remaining male blue whales can't find the last three remaining female blue whales, then the blue whales are goners. MC wants to prevent telepathy from becoming extinct at man's hand."

"Collateral damage, collateral benefit. MC didn't know what would happen to those oxen, or to you for that matter. *It* was just lucky the way it worked out. You're alive and the oxen were a great example of the unforeseen side effects of WMDs on other life, in this case, lichens. Tomorrow, the unforeseen collateral damage could be from genetically engineered grain. But, how lucky were we and MC, Michael? That's a great blue whale story, but what if those little monkey reptiles died out because the diseases humans exposed them to left them sterile? You've been affected in more ways than you know. Your eyes, your skin. What else? Maybe you're sterile now, too.

"That's not possible."

Even as Michael denied it, he knew Sarah's theory made plenty of sense. The exposure *had* affected him somehow. But his exposure was unexpected, so MC hadn't foreseen it, either. MC needed his telepathic genes. He had to find a way to reverse the effects of the exposure before it was too late, and only MC would have a solution. He needed to communicate with MC again, but they had to do *Its* bidding if they expected *Its* help.

"Jandra is videotaping Mahmoud's symptoms from exposure to the pathogen. I think we can use the disease's progression to identify the agent online and then maybe destroy it without disturbing the packaging. As soon as his men get back here with the video, we can get to work."

They slept on Jandra's floor to await his return.

They were awakened by the barking of sharp commands to rouse the troops as the colonel approached the bivouac. Moments later came chaotic, anxious cries and then the door burst open. Blocking the doorway were Ali and Jandra. Jandra was a big man, even on a small day, but today he was larger than life. The halo of bright morning light diffused around the two men and blackened their faces while Michael and Sarah adjusted their eyes to the bright sunshine that entered with the blast of hot, humid air.

The last two nights had taken its toll. Jandra's shoulders drooped and his eyes were badly bloodshot. He had just executed his most loyal subordinate because of his brother and these meddling Americans. And he had returned to find his camp in an uproar.

Sarah said, "Jandra? Who's that, Ali? What's all the noise?"

Jandra answered wearily. "The men are sick. Tainted meat from last night's celebration, I suppose. Michael, I have your video camera here. I would be very grateful if you would take it and your cousin with you and give me a few moments' peace. See if my brother can help you find a solution to this mess you've created."

Sarah jumped up and quickly unfolded a cot standing upright along the wall. She laid her sleeping bag on it for Jandra.

In Sarah's tent, they methodically dissected the digital video. The visual symptoms, the vomiting, shaking, diarrhea, and rashes were easy. But there were also more subtle physical symptoms that would have been much better detected in person: chills, clamminess, fever, dry mouth, discoloration of urine and feces. Then they had to piece together the symptoms for a meaningful internet search match to a biological weapon.

Michael went to investigate the condition of the men. He wandered over to the latrines and found crowds of anguished faces doubled over and holding their stomachs. Few of them spoke English. The crowd around the latrine grew. The lieutenant that called Sarah a witch approached Michael.

He spoke in halting English. "Help us. Men very sick."

"How?"

"Don't know."

"Stomach pains?" Michael rubbed his own stomach.

"Yes, but," and the lieutenant pointed to his mouth and his rectum, "Goes in same as out."

"I'm sorry, lieutenant, I don't understand," Michael said, patiently.

"Meat in. Still meat out. Vegetable in, still vegetable out. Men get very weaker."

Now there was urgency in Michael's voice. "Lieutenant, I need to go see my cousin. I'll be right back. You take care of the men. If necessary, I will wake Colonel Jandra." He ran to his tent and returned with the Costco size of Pepto Bismol Maximum Strength and Imodium tablets. When they were gone, the men were on their own.

At Sarah's tent, they had finished reviewing the gory video of the sycophantic Mahmoud's torturous decline into unconsciousness and subsequent involuntary muscular movements. Ali was just getting online.

"Maybe this is the seven years of famine to which Joseph was referring," said Michael.

"What *are* you talking about?"

"The oxen, Sarah. This will sound too incredible, but the soldiers are shitting out completely undigested oxen meat. They have lost the ability to digest food, all food."

Sarah buried her head in her hands and started sobbing. Michael comprehended. Sometimes, MC visions were buried in their subconsciences and didn't appear until much later. Sarah had not dreamed about the biblical dreams of Pharoah; she believed that they were MC visions that had been reincarnated here.

Ali said, "This is not the time for recriminations. We attempted to stop them. The question is, how long will it last? And what can we do to help these poor souls?"

He said to Ali, "Probably nothing. Even if you keep these men alive with intravenous nutrition, some will probably still starve to death or die from dehydration."

"That's quite impossible, Michael."

Sarah, her elbows leaning on the table in front of her, her head still cradled in her open palms, nodded vigorously. "Some biological agents like anthrax naturally occur in soil and are absorbed by plants through their root systems. The lichens in the cave were infected when the cylinder was previously used and it just got in the soil and the lichens kept absorbing it. It appears that the oxen are just carriers and it got into their flesh. Your men ate the meat. Now they are afflicted. Apparently, their bodies have lost the ability to absorb nutrients."

"Sarah, do something. They may want me dead, but these are still my brethren."

As Michael said, "Ali, we have to tell your brother. Sarah, you keep working online," Jandra came exploding into their tent.

"What happened to my men?"

Ali spoke first. "We were just coming to tell you. Sit down for a minute, brother."

Jandra said, "We cannot tell the men. Keep searching for an antidote or some sort of treatment."

"Jandra, we will do everything we can, but some will probably die."

"How many?"

"I have no idea. Probably no one has any idea."

"Keep searching," he ordered and departed.

The genetically altered anthrax's progression was more rapid than the pathology for even the most virulent strains. Typically, death followed exposure to inhalation anthrax in about four days. The people in the caves, including Mahmoud, had been exposed, experienced symptoms and died within twenty-four hours. But, the mortality rate for the new strain may have been much lower than other strains with more clinical data, or it may have just been much lower for Michael. What's more, the progression rate of the genetically altered strain may also have varied more widely, with death coming to some in hours, while others might not show symptoms for weeks. Michael wasn't safe yet.

Michael and Sarah found Jandra pacing in his headquarters. Sarah asked, "How did these crates get transported to their current location?"

"Our Arab benefactors came in here almost two years ago. They knew that the UN was looking for weapons of mass destruction hidden within every country hostile to the United States. They would have preferred to send them farther away, like North Korea, I suppose, but they didn't know if they could get them back from the North Koreans when, as you Americans put it, 'the heat came off.' We are much easier to control because they have overwhelming military superiority to us, we are accessible over land and we need their conventional weapons. And who would look for them here? Arabs control the government so they could also protect the weapons from attack by our enemies. A marriage of convenience."

"Accessible over land. So they brought them in by truck?"

"A refrigerated truck. They tested it on their own slave labor when they got here and some of our prisoners, and like Mahmoud told you, it worked fine."

"There is really only one way to kill anthrax without opening those cylinders up, or injecting something through their seals. The bacteria we are dealing with are pretty sensitive to changes in temperature, so we are going to try to roast them."

"And no one will be able to tell?"

"Not for a long time. We won't heat the cylinder that was used on Michael, so that if they test it on site, unfortunately, that one will still kill people."

Michael said, "Colonel, when I was a prisoner, I noticed that the cave walls had seams of coal running through them. We'll need some diesel and gasoline to get a fire going that will be hot enough to ignite the coal in a controlled burn to raise the temperature to maybe a hundred ten degrees Celsius. That will kill all of the bacteria. After we vent the caves, it will look and smell like we were never there."

"Once we're done, we'll be out of here for good. A day or two, tops," said Sarah.

"As soon as it is dark, load up a truck with whatever you need. You have forty-eight hours and this camp is being dismantled."

"Jandra, one more thing, for the safety of your men and all the people."

"Yes, Sarah?"

"Those remaining oxen have to be killed, destroyed, incinerated. If they run loose and somebody else eats them, or worse, if they are able to reproduce and pass this affliction along to their offspring, well, who knows what the result will be?"

"Done. Neutralize these weapons and I hope I never see you again, particularly in my dreams."

Michael, Sarah, and Ali hurried out and Jandra summoned the lieutenant into his office to give the orders. The lieutenant exhibited none of the side effects that Sarah, Michael and Ali had been describing.

"Lieutenant, how are you feeling?"

"Fine, sir."

"You didn't eat the meat?"

"No, sir."

"Why not?"

"The witch, I mean Miss Baskin, knew all about what was stored in the caves. I knew then that she had the power to destroy us. I asked her to spare my life. She agreed. Then, when she came to me and nearly begged me to order the men not to eat the meat because it was bad, I knew that they would disobey me and there would be a riot. So, I told her the men thought that the meat had special powers from the lichens. The truth is, I just knew they wouldn't listen. But, I listened. She saved my life."

"You are a smart man, Captain."

Jandra sent sick men from his garrison to replace the sentries on guard at the depot.

Michael, Sarah, and Ali arrived in the middle of the night. They chloroformed the sick sentries and then they kicked on the generators. Michael went to collect the coal.

While he was gone, Ali and Sarah inspected the one stainless steel cylinder that had already been used. Stamped on the bottom was a manufacturer, model, and serial number.

"Your university or mine, Sarah?"

It took one call, two transfers within the engineering department at Sarah's university and a follow-up call thirty minutes later, to confirm that they would need a sustained temperature outside the cylinders of two hundred degrees fahrenheit for about two hours to sustain an internal temperature of one hundred thirty degrees fahrenheit for forty-five minutes, the required temperature to kill all of the more common AMES-type strains of anthrax bacteria. Hopefully, it would kill these as well.

Michael returned with several loads of coal and they worked through the night and into midday. They piled any vegetation that they found inside the cave atop the coal.

They started the fire around the cylinders as soon as it was dark and at sunrise on the third morning, they returned to the bivouac, only to meet Jandra driving toward the caves alone in the armored vehicle lent to them by the government. He told them that half of the sick men at the base camp were already dead, with almost all of the infected others beyond help. Only three out of nearly eighty appeared to be improving. It was a higher mortality rate than the naturally occurring anthrax strains. So, he had twelve, plus himself and the recently promoted captain left in his camp from those that had been around for the feast. A sortie had been out on a sabotage mission and had returned after the men had taken sick so they, too, were healthy. All totaled, he now had twenty-six healthy or recovering men under his immediate command.

He had Sarah, Michael and Ali's things with him. "We buried our dead soldiers and moved our camp to protect our cover." He handed them a package.

"I have recharged your batteries Michael. You three are ready to go?"

They nodded.

"You all look like shit," he said.

Jandra returned to his new bivouac and Sarah, Michael, and Ali headed to Khartoum.

CHAPTER 23

The Getaway

The rebels had land mined the jungle road back to Khartoum after their rendezvous with Sarah, Michael and Ali to keep from being followed. Jandra had made them a copy of the map showing the location of the land mines, but Michael still believed that hitting a land mine would have solved all of Jandra's problems.

They had no bones of Joseph to barter for their freedom and little time before the owner of the biological weapons got wind of their visit and became suspicious.

Sarah said, "We have another problem. The Sudanese government facilitated our entry into rebel-held territory and they have our passports. They are going to question us about the rebels before they permit us to leave."

Ali said, "Just me. They'll let you leave because you have American passports. They will arrest me on some trumped-up charges and interrogate me. I'd have been better off being shot by my brother."

"Didn't you suggest that to the interior minister when we met with him?"

"I am sure you'll agree that it's much easier to offer your life as part of a negotiation than to actually give it up. Has anybody ever told you that you have a very wry sense of humor, Michael?"

"Just recently, in fact."

Sarah swerved suddenly. What she thought was a snake, nearly as big around as the car tires turned out to be only a giant lizard, almost seven feet long. They continued on, slightly rattled.

Michael studied the dense jungle purposefully and said, "Aren't we near where Jandra ambushed us?"

When they first made their rendezvous, Sarah was oblivious to land-marks. It seemed like a different lifetime. "Probably. We sort of stampeded through here. I think we'll find it. Why?"

Michael said, "We will pick up that skeleton you spotted and claim that he was our quarry."

"*Who* will believe that, Michael?"

"We don't care, Sarah. This isn't a doctoral thesis. It's all about getting out of Sudan alive before someone discovers the truth."

"And when they attempt to hold me hostage to assure your return?" Ali asked.

"All we need is a distraction to get you out of the country and this is going to be it."

Seconds before a repeat performance, Sarah slammed on the brakes to avoid bottoming out the car again. The hanging vines of the jungle provided a ready transfer point for poisonous lizards, spiders and flesh-eating, bur-rowing parasites to alight undisturbed on unsuspecting heads and shoul-ders. They took turns whacking away with a machete, creating a swath to allow a simultaneous view of both the car and the waterfall. The jungle dead-ended at the rocks and a shear drop of over a hundred meters. An underground stream ejected from the rocks and, cascading from a ledge perpendicular to where they stood, sent a cooling spray up to their faces and cast a rainbow across the entire canyon. The green jungle and grey rock on the other side of the waterfall were visible only through a kaleidoscopic colored haze.

Scratch marks had been left by hungry animals on the bleached bones. "You'd better hope that skeleton was not female, or we are going to have to lose a real lot of parts, Michael."

Some of the body's 206 bones were missing, but Joseph wouldn't have survived intact unless you believed the Genesis version that he was embalmed and put in an Egyptian coffin.

The heel at the bottom of the horseshoe-shaped falls formed the back of a pitcher filled with crystal clear water, which rushed out of its mouth to the headwaters of the river on the opposite end. It was continuously refilled by the white foam of pent-up energy from both the falls above and the underground stream emerging from the rocks below their feet.

Michael pulled the binoculars hanging from Sarah's neck and he scanned the craggily falls inch by inch. Finally, he pointed to a particularly inaccessible ledge protruding from the falls.

"There, Sarah."

"What's 'there'?"

"See that sort of reddish igneous rock?"

"Kind of. So?"

He handed her the binoculars. "That's where we found the bones. We'll take some pictures and draw a sketch. The rainy season will make that area inaccessible for half the year."

When they finally departed under the heavy jungle canopy, it was already beginning to grow dark. Michael swung into the driver's seat and Ali fell asleep in the back.

When Ali's breathing became regular, Michael whispered to his cousin. "Something else has come up. I received an e-mail from Neil. He knows we're in Sudan. Not only is Lindsey worried about her investment, she's got him following us to see if he can find out where we got our leads from."

"It was only a matter of time, wasn't it?"

"It's a toxic combination. She's blinded by ambition and he is obsessed with exposing me as a fraud. If he succeeds, he's a dead man."

"Why, Michael?" Sarah was more than a little apprehensive. MC had no reason to kill Neil and she had never known Michael to directly harm anyone before.

"I know that we don't have a meeting prearranged, but *It* will come to me. *It* needs to meld with me and if Neil catches up with us during our next audience, he's going to become another Oishkipeh. It can't be helped."

"I demanded a rendezvous because I now know the who, what, where, when, why and how of MC. But I will also become sterile, and because MC needs my telepathic genes, *It* will have to use *Its* considerable knowledge base from throughout history to find some antidote."

Sarah couldn't believe what Michael was spewing. MC was not God. *It* could no more reverse historical events than foresee the future. Clearly the exposure to the anthrax had changed him, but only now did she even begin to comprehend the extent to which it seemed to have twisted his mind.

"You think you can summon MC and *It* comes whenever you call?"

"We shall see," he responded flatly.

Michael's pallor deepened again. She touched him lightly. He didn't respond. His body temperature was alarmingly high. His temperature and color seemed to change with his emotions, and right now he was all revved up.

"You're scaring the shit out of me, Michael."

"Sorry," he said.

"Where are we going now?"

"To Lisbon."

Further discussion was pointless.

As they approached the airport, Ali made return reservations to Alexandria via Cairo on a flight leaving in less than two hours.

They dropped Ali off at one end of the terminal and waited until seventy minutes before his departure. They confirmed that his flight was scheduled to depart on time, parked the car and then hiked to the decrepit security and customs counter at the opposite end of the airfield. Sarah and Michael identified themselves to the station head and asked if he might call Minister Rajoum to confirm their identities and get further instructions. As expected, the customs chief scoffed. Michael dialed the minister's cell phone directly from his satellite phone.

"Minister, it's Michael Seagal here. We are at the Khartoum airport in the office of your senior customs officer awaiting your instructions. You have our passports, remember? Officer," he glanced at the man's name badge, "Al-Ahmad should be commended for his professionalism. If anything, he has been a bit overzealous in detaining us, but what can be done in the world we live in today?

"We have returned with a significant find. We want to securely transfer it to you and then return to the United States. Can you have your customs people here assume custody of the contents until you arrive? Apparently our embassy has been looking for us and entering embassy grounds with Sudanese property would have been a breach of our agreement. They will be meeting us here within the hour and I would prefer to tell them truthfully that the car and its contents are not in our possession."

Michael turned to the head of customs. "It's for you. It's the interior minister."

The custom minister's obsequious tone told the story.

He took the phone back from the customs official.

"Excellency, could you please bring our passports when you come? We have transferred an additional hundred thousand dollars to cover the cost of security until we return. Please make it clear to your people that security of this treasure is their highest priority."

The panicked customs chief and nearly all of his staff followed Sarah to the car while Michael stayed at the customs counter awaiting the embassy official who arrived a few moments later and consumed the remaining resources of the customs office.

Sarah dawdled and flirted her way through the car transfer and reminded the customs chief that he couldn't leave the car unguarded and the interior minister might arrive at any moment. They relocated the vehicle to the customs office as an Egypt Air flight left the runway carrying Ali Aswari on his Egyptian passport. He had long since been lost in the shuffle.

With the car in protective custody, the customs agent saw no reason to detain Sarah and Michael who were now escorted to their departing flight by the embassy official holding replacement passports.

CHAPTER 24

Two Pursuits

Sarah and Michael deplaned in Lisbon from a turbulent flight through an electrified sky. Michael robotically walked past the motionless baggage handling conveyor, abandoning Sarah to the monotonous wait for their suitcases. Sarah crumpled against a building column facing the carousel. She complained lamely about the delay, but when she opened her sleep-deprived eyes, she found no one listening. Michael was near the exit door, his complexion an incendiary red. She sprinted over and lightly touched his shoulder. He was unresponsive, but even through his shirt she felt his whole body burning up.

He moved outside and stared into the sky, oblivious to the rain soaking his clothes and washing across his eyes. Sarah followed him into the rain and quickly retreated behind the automatic sliding doors. Cognitively, she was aware of nothing unusual, but when she stood outside, even for the briefest of moments, she sensed a M'low Cloomian presence. Someone was rapping on her subconsciousness, waiting for the door to open.

From the heated baggage claim area, she tracked her cousin through the window and kept an eye out for their baggage. The creepy sense of an MC presence departed. Michael returned quickly and she was pleased to see that his complexion had faded to lightly toasted sunburn. His pupils, though, were fully dilated again.

When they retrieved their bags, Michael spoke in a computer-synthe-sized monotone. "We have communicated, although there was much inter-ference. We are to meet with MC tonight in a remote area. I have a map. Come, we need to rent a vehicle."

Before she could respond, Michael was at the first rental counter. He went to several before he seemed satisfied. She couldn't stop him, so for the time being she would just tag along and keep her cousin out of trouble. Odd that the roles were now reversed.

They rented a high-clearance four-wheel-drive Range Rover. The rain stopped as they left the airport. As they drove away from the city lights, the sky cleared. Neither spoke a word.

Michael turned recklessly to the right. His cranial navigation system seemed to be kicking in. He gazed intently at the road ahead. About two hours outside of the city, he veered right again and departed the road.

Sarah couldn't stand his silence any longer. "Michael, I am hungry, I have to go to the bathroom, I've got my period, and I don't know where we are going. Would you or M'low Cloom like to fill me in? And could we please eat something before we completely depart civilization?"

He coasted to a halt on a sandy plain and spoke vacantly. "I'm sorry, Sarah. I was lost in navigation. This is the best I can do for a bathroom now." He motioned her to the plain. "We will have one more opportunity for food before we reach our destination."

She returned to the car several moments later and had only one foot in the car when he raced off again. Along the horizon, Sarah could begin to make out a small cluster of lights. With a sudden bounce from their seats, they hit pavement again. Sarah had lost all sense of direction, but from the salt-laden air she knew they must be approaching the coast. They passed through a lonely town of several dozen shops, a church and a two-room town hall. Bungalows and beach houses dotted the area. Michael slammed on the brakes in front of a dive shop. Scuba tanks and equipment were hung haphazardly in the dusty unkempt bay display window. Without hesitating, Michael broke the window in the front door, reached his hand in, and unlocked it from the inside. He grabbed two sets of filled tanks, along with regulators, slipped twenty one hundred dollar bills under the edge of the register, and departed.

He slid in behind the wheel again and said, "I paid for the tanks and the damage."

A gas station at the end of the street proved to be the only merchant open for business. They filled up the car, bought what food they could and moved on into the night. This time, Michael left the road in a more traditional manner, turning off onto a path that led straight up into the hills for a while and then across a treacherous rocky terrain. As they bounced along, Sarah looked off to her right and saw the moon shimmering over an angry sea. Soon, they and the moon were lost in fog and mist. Without warning, sulfur gas suffused the salt air and they gagged repeatedly.

Sarah turned to hitch up the regulators to the tanks and Michael stopped her.

"Don't put them on yet. MC says that we won't really need them until we reach our destination. Another hour, but the going will be slower. It needs to start raining again."

The tire ruts ended in front of a barrier and a large stop sign. In both Portuguese and English, a sign warned of toxic hydrogen sulfide gas and unstable terrain. Michael simply veered to the left and kept driving up the hill. Every time it seemed like the Range Rover lost traction and would slip off the road, Michael instinctively turned toward more stable ground and continued his ascent. Finally, when Sarah felt that she was about to be overcome by the fumes, Michael stopped the four-wheel drive and announced, "We are here."

There was nothing left to do but follow. They strapped on their tanks and scrambled down the side of the mountain to a promontory extending ten to thirty meters over the ocean. An unknown distance below, through the fog, the waves crashed against the cliff. When the cousins looked up to the craggy rocks from where they descended, they saw on the far right that the rocks overhung the plateau slightly, providing some protection from the elements.

Some distance from them on the promontory and back into the deep shadows of the overhang was a yellowish pool.

Sarah pointed. "Sulfuric acid?" Michael didn't respond.

Bubbles popped through the surface while raindrops made little symmetrical plinks and splashes in the liquid.

At first, Sarah walked tentatively and then crawled on her hands and knees to avoid sliding from the slippery rocks into the turbulent Atlantic below. When she looked into the ocean and away from the overhang it was pitch black, so she closed her eyes and felt, listened and sniffed her way across the rocks. The salty, wind-blown landing reeked of rotten eggs.

"M'low Cloom will come to us now," and Michael, for the last time, turned beet red.

No sooner had Michael uttered the words, then the earth seemingly shook with the declaration, "We are here."

This time there really was *nothing* there. No shimmering lights, no dead animals, nothing.

Michael was sitting on the ground now, his slicker tucked under his rear. Sarah followed suit. Soon the images started and she found herself lying flat on her back with her knees bent and the tank lying beside her. Next to her, Michael moved to the same position.

Sarah saw images of Michael in the cave in Sudan and saw the mutant anthrax infecting and killing all of the cave's inhabitants. Then she witnessed the agent's mutation of the oxen and of Michael. Michael appeared to die briefly and during that moment some of Michael's memories were shared with MC permanently. She was interrupted from her trance by Michael's audible screams. She wished that there was some way she could participate in Michael's side of the communications with MC.

When the telepathic-like communications started, Michael had immediately demanded an explanation from M'low Cloom of his survival in the caves. M'low Cloom had accommodated Michael and he was devastated. He had assumed that he was somehow unique. He was. The microorganisms in the comet had immunized him against the deadly effects of the anthrax. Otherwise, as the visions were showing him, he was no different than the bacteria's other victims. As MC choreographed the scene, Sarah might have experienced the same outcome from the exposure, but *It* couldn't be sure. Regardless, Michael's near-death experience in the caves had enhanced his ability to communicate telepathically with MC and had permitted the brief merger of his consciousness with MC. *It* had shared with him otherwise unattainable knowledge.

Their brains pulsating with the rapid transfer of information, Sarah and Michael confirmed that with normal evolution, a large slice of mankind would eventually adapt and communicate with MC at the level of Sarah and Michael—or higher. Some evolutionary paths to telepathy would become extinct because of other genetic flaws, but others and their progeny would survive, propagate, and continue their telepathic evolution.

Ever since he had been exposed to the anthrax, Michael had fancied himself the father of a new great race of human beings. In his mind now, though, he saw that many millions of people would eventually evolve the same telepathic traits as him. They wouldn't need to be his descendants. And they couldn't be, because he was irreversibly sterile.

Why couldn't more humans be biologically or chemically exposed and achieve the same results? Michael asked M'low Cloom.

Michael and Sarah witnessed the mass destruction of several million humans exposed to the genetically altered anthrax. And after the dust cleared, perhaps one hundred thousand or so walked away as survivors. And they saw that perhaps twenty of them were mutated like Michael, because they had the same telepathic DNA sequence of Michael to start with. But, like Michael, they suffered from a collateral side effect. They were all now sterile, but one, who had yet another mutation that preserved her fertility. And MC reminded them that part of Michael's metamorphosis was a result of his natural exposure to the microbes at magnetic north.

Michael wailed in despair and Sarah sat up. He was carelessly wandering around the plateau and flailing his arms in exasperation.

Michael pressed M'low Cloom further. He wanted access to *all* of MC's infinite knowledge. The response was ugly. Sarah and Michael saw Michael's brain explode. It didn't have the capacity. Sarah leapt to her feet. She saw the response, but wasn't privy to the question.

Michael knew that some living being had communicated the location of the WMDs and he wanted the ability to access MC's historical knowledge base while he was alive.

Michael was wrong. There was no living being. The Iraqi profiteer who had also briefly survived the exposure had passed on all of his knowledge of the WMDs when he had been shot in the jungle minutes later.

There must be another way, Michael demanded, "Yes," MC responded. "Mankind must wait passively on the sidelines for the eons of evolution to run their course."

Michael was rapidly slipping into insanity. Sarah was jealous of his ability to communicate as MC's equal. MC wanted Sarah to mutate to his level of communication and to share *Its* knowledge with her and not him.

Michael couldn't reconcile the trade-off of death for knowledge. "Aren't I communicating with all of these sentient beings now? I'm still alive." Sarah stood in the way. She must be destroyed.

The wind increased to a hurricane. Gulls and other birds that were flocking around the ledge had left to roost on higher ground. Sarah had seen this animal behavior before.

Michael seemed to be entirely detached from reality now. Sarah attempted to pull him away from the precipice, but he would not be distracted. Michael shoved Sarah away and she slipped on the slick rocks, sliding toward the crashing waves below. Michael wanted nothing more than for his cousin to be out of his MC communications permanently.

Deja vu. Sarah relived the tsunami in the Antarctic. It was not an MC image this time. It was her personal memory. Sarah felt around for hand and footholds and sniffed her way toward the rocky overhang and its acrid smell from the sulfur pool. She was just in time. A wave crashed over the edge of the promontory as a gust of wind knocked Michael off his feet. Michael's air hose was torn, and he was dashed against the rocks.

His body jerked involuntarily, his arms flailing wildly in all directions. His facial muscles contorted into the embodiments of emotion. He displayed the stone-coldness of anger, the smirk of loathing, the upturned mouth corners of a child's amusement, the joy of victory, and then the moist-eyed fear at seeing the dark cloud of death that had come to call.

Michael collapsed on the edge of the bluff and slid slowly over the side into the Atlantic.

Trillions of voices, in millions of languages, many beyond audible range, many communicating through electromagnetic radiation that Sarah couldn't begin to comprehend, now simultaneously called out to her. One emerged from the crowd above the others. "Save my body, Sarah. It's too late to save me."

In the MC image in Sarah's mind she saw Michael's body slipping into the violent ocean. His head slipped over the edge, his broken arm forming a noose around his neck, with his right hand reaching down the left side of his back. As the inertia of his torso moved over the side, his pants caught on the jagged rocks at the edge of the cliff and held him there.

Sarah's trance broke into reality and just as in her vision, there was Michael's body caught on the cliff. She jumped up and slipped and slid over the rocks to reach Michael's lifeless form. The rocks were a greased skillet and Sarah fell hard, the mouthpiece flying from her mouth. She felt around for it feverishly as she became dizzy, nauseous, and finally unconscious.

CHAPTER 25

Monkameleon and Sarah

Sarah emerged into a semi-conscious twilight. Her left elbow was plastered with pus. The ocean had merged with the downpour and soaked through her slicker. She lay with her eyes closed, waiting for the pain to subside. She began daydreaming. There was a cat caressing her ear with its dry sandy tongue. Musky wet fur wafted into her nostrils. Reality merged with soothing memories of Soufflé, the pet that captivated her youth. They were curled under her blanket in front of the fireplace. As she drifted back into unconsciousness, the licking became decidedly more real.

Her eyes flashed open. Sarah was pinned under a dead weight. Painfully, she hoisted herself up on her good elbow and found herself staring into Michael's vacant eyes.

The licking had stopped. She jerked to her left and froze.

Just as quickly, she defrosted. There was no threat. The lizard-like creature's thunderbolt tongue licked her in a blur. By the time she could flinch, the tongue had disappeared into its mouth. It wasn't Soufflé, but a yellow impregnable reptilian body with a broad vertical crocodile's tail. Its tiny eyes were a murky black with golden round buttonholes for irises. They were covered by a second set of transparent lids that opened and closed like the spiral lens shutter of an expensive camera. The animal closed its eyes and moved its head back and forth purposefully. It grasped the situation much more astutely than Sarah did. And it reeked of sulfur.

It offered human-like facial expressions from a monkey's face coated with fine brown fur that bled into the yellow reptilian body. Slowly and evenly, Sarah reached out to caress the animal that had returned her to consciousness and befriended her. The coating was not fur, but microscopic reptilian scales that grew to form a prickly facial coat.

The broad tongue flicked from the grinning face and licked her hand. The animal moved on webbed feet with amazing dexterity and gently pulled Michael's dead weight off her abdomen with its mouth and clawed front paws. Millions of little suctions covered the rear paddles. Sarah called it a monkameleon.

It all fit. These were the mysterious animals in their first vision that had either died or lost their telepathic abilities. Sarah had stumbled across another colony exposed by the low tide on Puget Sound, but now it appeared that it was no coincidence. The colony in Uzbekistan must have created the vault and left the sulfuric acid residue that burned her hand. It might also explain the animal carnage of their vision, if the sulfuric acid vapors were toxic enough. She'd mull that one further when she could think straight.

Their habitat must be so hostile to humans that no one ever knew they existed. They could have been flourishing in their own little environments all the way to the dinosaurs. Just like the coelacanths.

With a little tug on the arm from the monkameleon, Sarah sat up and immediately started gasping. Her regulator wheezed and the gauge showed empty. She realized that she had to get away from the toxic air and return to the SUV. The monkameleon disagreed. It sensed her respiratory distress and suctioned over to Michael's body surefootedly, barely touching the ground with its front paws, removed his tank and regulator and brought it over to Sarah. As soon as she had swapped it with her own, MC returned.

It projected the timbre of Michael's voice into her mind, for he was now part of M'low Cloom. She saw several monkameleons in the sulfur springs in Uzbekistan. Their coloring was slightly different. Where her friend here was yellow and brown, the central Asian variety were decidedly more orange and grey. They had carried the vault on a small cart with large soft wheels and using their front paws and oddly shaped digging tools, they had buried the vault there as their own little temporary bathysphere to survive in the inhospitable climate of their home planet's surface when they were away from sulfuric acid habitat. They were no different than the creatures thriving under the crushing water pressures and four hundred plus degree Celsius temperatures of the ocean's hydrothermal vents.

One of the monkameleons had been crushed to death while installing the vault. Sarah had seen the whole scene through that little creature's sentient eyes. His memories were added to all of the others that made up M'low Cloom.

They had cremated the monkameleon on the spot using some sort of flammable propellant. Sarah's little friend tried to explain the chemistry, but it was beyond her. However, she could see that the smoke contained an intoxicating drug that no animal could resist, which attracted at least some of them to the vault area. When air-breathing animals inhaled that drug in sufficient concentrations, all of their internal organs expanded rapidly, yielding the gory result that Sarah and Michael had witnessed. The translucent wall in their vision was to protect the humans and monkameleons from each other's toxic habitat.

Sarah wondered what attracted the dolphins to her at Puget Sound, but MC ignored her. As always, it had a more important agenda. While other, less sentient animals lower down in the animal kingdom continued to evolve and adapt their senses, bats with echolocation, and the mutant echidna with electroreception, for example, man had arrested his own evolutionary development.

In an alien faraway land, Sarah witnessed an image of today's earth fast forwarded to an advanced society that had no disease. Some of the masters of this land were forcibly sequestered and forgotten on a remote island in a forbidding climate. Meaningless time passed, but it appeared to be almost two hundred generations of these animals. The forgotten community was rediscovered.

The island colony had evolved incredible powers of electroreception, well beyond earth's primitive platypus and echidna. They had so advanced the ability to communicate with other animals via electrical impulses, that within years, the master species that had been their ancestors became their pets. Sarah realized that the only distinction between the subjugated pets and human "Planet of the Apes" slaves was that the pets couldn't be taught to speak the language in which their new masters communicated with each other.

The pets and the new masters' common ancestors had genetically engineered away all disease and with it, all hopes of further advancement. It didn't take a lot of imagination to realize that this was man's fate, already in progress. The notion of natural selection or evolution was irrelevant to MC. *It* just needed to assure that all of these dominant new creatures could communicate with MC, and natural selection was the only way to do it, because it made sure that the unintended, flawed side effects either became extinct, or at least became a dormant piece of the double helix.

And then Sarah understood what the evil was that they had seen in MC. It was Adolf Hitler's life. Other evils were there as well, but none were more deeply personified. Somehow, much of his life had been recorded or observed by another sentient being that possessed the prophesy gene.

Biblical prophets like Isaiah, Jesus, and Mohammed had the same telepathic ability and destiny to merge with MC as Sarah and Michael, which is why those biblical figures thought M'low Cloom was God.

Michael's voice was in MC and in Sarah's head. "Everyone who can engage in thought transference becomes part of M'low Cloom when they die. That's all MC is. There's no separate omnipotent, omniscient anything. It's not science fiction. It's just science. All of MC's thought and reasoning comes from the millions of intelligent telepathic lives dying every millisecond. They think, they make decisions and then they die, and those decisions become part of MC."

Quicksilver's Native American ancestors seemed to have properly interpreted the message. They viewed death as a logical consequence of life and made no attempt to change the course of evolution upon the planet, knowing that their acceptance of life and death would assure that their progeny somewhere down the line would evolve to merge into the afterlife of M'low Cloom.

The placid animal sat next to Sarah throughout the entire MC session. It seemed to be communicating with MC in the same manner she was. Behind it, two other monkameleons had emerged from the sulfur pools pulling a Gurney on low flat wheels that moved easily atop the rough terrain. The lemon-yellow tires deformed slowly as they rolled over rocks and branches and then gradually regained their shape. The contraption was only about one and a half meters long, more than adequate to carry a monkameleon lying on the coarse fabric stretched between two poles. Sarah could tell the three animals apart. Her earlier monkameleon companion motioned her away as the two little creatures gently placed Michael's body on the stretcher. Sarah rose to object, but her companion scowled at her and motioned off in the direction that she had come from in the SUV to warn her that company was coming.

They drove the Gurney over the sulfur pool from which they had emerged. Its wheels floated. On the other side, deep in the shadows, completely camouflaged, was a crack in the rocks that was inaccessible without drowning or being burned in the pools. Michael was gone and so were the monkameleons.

The monkameleon's electrosensory abilities allowed them to communicate, navigate, and hunt in their conductive sulfur springs and in the pea soup atmosphere by detecting electrical signals generated by the brain waves of other species, the same way sharks find their prey hidden in the sand. In the monkameleon, though, it was even more developed than in primitive sharks. While both sharks and the monkameleon navigated by detecting changes in the earth's magnetic field, the monkameleon could actually read the electrosensory cells and sense stress in other animals through changes in neural impulses.

The monkameleon hadn't shown up until Michael was gone. It seemed to sense that Michael might be too opportunistic and it didn't trust Michael to keep its secret. Sarah never was sure if Michael was serious when he said that they should trap some of the little monkey reptiles and sell them to a circus side show. Was that why MC had insisted that they "come alone or survive alone"? Because, if non-telepathic humans became aware of Sarah's or Michael's or even the monkameleon's abilities, they would certainly want to study and dissect them all.

Michael's brain had exceeded its human capacity, but then he had always pushed it to the limit. Sarah queried MC about life elsewhere in the universe that evolved *beyond,* but without telepathy. Now it was MC's turn to be purblind. Highly advanced life that developed without telepathy was invisible to MC. Sarah sensed fear in those memories. For about the thousandth time, *It* felt fear in Sarah. MC lauded her deductive abilities. In *Its* collective consciousness, the notion hadn't occurred to *It* that, hidden in MC's "blind spot" of non-telepathic creatures, there might be something more advanced that viewed MC as primitive.

Almost in mid-vision, MC disappeared, leaving Sarah alone on the promontory, watching the greying of the dawn.

CHAPTER 26
Neil Down and Take It

Sarah sat with her back to the ocean, the sky brightening ahead of her over the sulfur pit. The wheezing of her regulator reminded her that she was out of air and this time there was no spare. Reluctantly, she made her way back to the vehicle before her tank gave out. The monkameleons hadn't returned and Michael was gone. When she reached the SUV and saw Michael's Astros baseball cap, she broke down.

Two of the monkameleons re-emerged from the pit, shook themselves off and approached her. She looked into their eyes and they gently touched her arm with the back of their paws. A wave of meditation-like serenity relaxed every muscle in her body and cleared her head. Without warning, the yellow bled out of their fur scales and became more orange. They scowled at each other and then abruptly fled into the sulfur pit before Sarah could thank them.

Seconds later, Sarah could make out the faint rumble of a vehicle. Squinting, she saw wheels kicking up dust in the distance. Sarah had neither eaten nor drunk in well over a dozen hours and she had just lost her best friend. The visitor was irrelevant.

She slouched into the driver's seat and closed her eyes. The other car's tires ground coffee as they slid to a halt on the gravelly surface.

A paunchy man in his forties emerged and leaned toward the open window.

"Lindsey thought that you and Michael had taken millions of dollars and run out on her. Was it worth it? You look awful."

Sarah recognized the voice and attempted to thread her fingers through the seaweed knots of hair. She never even opened her eyes.

"And you've never even really met me before. Imagine if you had something to compare it to, Neil."

Her anguish moved Neil and he responded gently. "Where's Michael, Sarah?"

"Dead."

As she acknowledged it aloud, the suppressed emotions came spewing forth. She broke down and her body seized uncontrollably. Neil pulled open the car door and she fell into his chest, tear stains covering his grey sweatshirt. He awkwardly put his arms around her in an attempt to be a compassionate gentleman for the first time in his life, Sarah supposed.

When the crying subsided a bit and she started hiccoughing and wiping her nose on her own sweatshirt sleeve, he asked, "What happened?"

Sarah looked at him for a blurred moment through bloodshot eyes. Her mind went blank. She fell back into the car. It was a long while before she answered, but Neil waited patiently.

"Michael slid off the rocks and his hose tore. The air over there is a sulfuric acid cesspool. That's why we brought the tanks. He slid into the sea. I thought he might have gotten hung up on the rocks below, but he's gone."

Sarah realized that she was still holding on to Michael's hat and his belongings were in the back of the car. She couldn't stay in the Range Rover. She sat on the ground just next to the car. Neil went back to his car and returned with juice and granola bars. Sarah took them and looked at them unfamiliarly.

"It's food, Sarah. You eat it."

She smiled and mechanically peeled the wrapper. She nibbled slowly at the edges until her ravenous hunger took control and then she realized that she now had the ultimate alibi. If nothing else, it would save Neil's life.

"I know why you're here, Neil. Michael had been getting these leads from a source that he refused to disclose to me. It made sense for me to be his front because it would keep suspicion away from his source. He met with the source in various places around the world, and while I usually came along for the ride, I was never included in their little rendezvous, just hearing little secondhand bits and bites along the edges. They'd meet privately. We were going to meet his source tonight, but something went terribly wrong. The weather turned bad, so I guess *It* never came and I never found out who *It* was. This is one deep throat whose identity has just gone to the grave."

"Do you think it might still come?"

"And reveal *Itself* to me? No. I didn't understand *Its* need for anonymity at first and neither did Michael, but near the end we both did. There will be no *Primary Colors* tell-all at the end of this saga, so you needn't wait around hoping."

"It's almost a better story than Lindsey expected. Michael misrepresented his sources and he was the news. You claimed these discoveries for your own. What's it going to do to your reputation?"

"I can still take credit for the scientific analysis. The investigative reporter who risked and then finally sacrificed his life for the truth is the story. You'll still get your story from Nunavut, and my cousin will posthumously get a Pulitzer."

The authorities detained Sarah a couple of days while they perfunctorily dragged the shoreline for remnants of Michael's body. To Sarah's surprise, Neil remained a perfect gentleman.

Sarah woke in the middle of the second night to close the windows in her cottage. The salt air should have been therapeutic, but for a Midwestern girl trapped only two days ago on an ocean outcropping with her dying cousin, the reminder sent chills up her spine. She dragged a comforter to a wooden chair on the front porch to watch the sun rise. Exhaustion overtook her and she dozed off. She bolted upright at the squeak from Neil's screen door as he emerged from his cottage.

"Jet lag?"

"Yeah," he responded. "Too much traveling. You?"

"Just a lot on my mind."

"I can imagine," he soothed.

"Neil, I can't go back yet. Michael left one piece of this puzzle that we still haven't fit into place."

"Your cousin is dead, Sarah. Your family…"

"It's about my family. They'll understand, and maybe there will be some small measure of closure."

"Do you want company?"

"That's very dear of you, but I'm all right. And this is going to seem so foreign to you. I mean, it won't make any sense. Hell, it doesn't even make sense to me and I can assure you that it has nothing at all to do with our discoveries, Michael's leads, or any possible future discoveries."

"Then why the secrecy? Take me along. I can stand another day or two on my expense account. Where to?"

He finally caught a glimpse of the disarming smile. "A cemetery, for starters."

The car plowed north on the windy mountain road. Sarah opened up a little to relieve the awkwardness. "We are heading to Bragancas near the Spanish border. Some of Michael's ancestors on his father's side are buried there. We are related on his mother's side. His mom is my dad's sister. On his dad's side, Michael's great-grandmother's maiden name was Cruz. She was apparently born here in about 1900 and was sent to the US to be raised by relatives. They died and she ended up being raised by a distant cousin of one of her parents who was in a childless marriage. We don't know much else about her, but I figure that a visit to one of the parish priests, assuming he understands some combination of your Spanish and mine, could lead us to some lineage or perhaps even her parents' graves. When we transferred here in Portugal on the way to Sudan, Michael insisted that if we ever survived this trip, we would find their graves on the way back. One of us survived, and I need to keep my promise. Jeez, I forgot something. I'm not even sure what language they speak on the border. It's probably Portuguese." She looked at him hopefully.

He shook his head. "Sorry."

As they headed deeper into the mountains and farther from the twenty-first century, the fancy galvanized guard rails along the switchbacks gave way to chipped, painted wood barriers designed to rein in a runaway horse-drawn wagon, not a car. Next, the asphalt surrendered to tightly packed dirt and gravel, occasionally serrated by wagon wheel tracks that slowed the pace and challenged the suspension. Finally, they emerged in another century that was home to a grand cobblestone parade route into the town square where the center of life was a granite fountain with a green oxidized copper flute pumping clear spring water into a drinking trough shared by the town's children and animals. Watching from a hilltop over the main square, a large stone church dating from the fifteenth century, according to the cornerstone, dwarfed the nearby market buildings and town hall. The Virgin Mary promised safe passage for all who entered the doors under her outstretched arms.

As Neil and Sarah parked the car next to the entrance, the belfry came alive with the naked sound of the church bell. It rang once.

"Lunch is over. Let's hope siesta hasn't begun yet," Neil said, in a hushed tone.

"I probably should have asked before. Are you Catholic?"

"Not me. I'm not much of anything. My mother dragged me to one of those unitarian universalist churches growing up. Can't say much about my religion, but I do have a soft spot for gospel music. How about you?"

"Well, maybe a little bit."

The parish church building was typical of most medieval constructions. It possessed the requisite choir, nave and transepts which formed a structure in the shape of a cross. Parish churches throughout much of Christian Europe maintained the most reliable records of birth and death on all the inhabitants of the parish county back to its earliest recorded settlement, or in this case, its subsequent conversion to Christianity.

The brothers of a local order were housed in an accessory building to the rear of the church. Rather than enter the church, Neil and Sarah wandered curiously around the side of the building that abutted the ancient cemetery. It spanned the eons. The earliest readable date on the granite tombstones said 1529 AD. Names and dates on the softer and older limestone markers had been eroded away like washable ink on paper caught in a thunderstorm. It had run together, faded and in some cases, altogether disappeared.

Monks and brothers of the friary worked meticulously in the cemetery as they strode by. They looked up and stared briefly at the peculiarly dressed Americans, abruptly averting their gaze back to the cemetery gardens.

Neil said, "Helluva greeting, don't you think?"

"Maybe they can't or don't speak."

"Ya think?"

A frail, heavily bent man glided over to them from a remote portion of the cemetery separated by a thigh-high black iron fence ornamented with sharp spears alternating with inverted hearts.

"Si, senor, senorita?"

"English?"

"No. Sorry."

"Spanish?"

"Yo comprendo. Mejor portugués." Better Portuguese.

With Neil assisting, Sarah began in broken Spanish. "I am looking for birth records of a woman born around nineteen hundred. Her name was Anaisa Cruz. I am not sure of her parents' names. They sent her to the United States when she was five or six. She was the great-grandmother of my cousin."

The little man's eyes widened rapidly and just as quickly narrowed warily. Then, he pursed his lips and put his finger to them thoughtfully. He was nearly bald except for a triangular wisp of long gray strands hanging halfway down his forehead. He had sad eyes and thick bushy white sideburns that curled in tufts around his ears, keeping them nearly hidden.

He motioned for them to follow him and he shuffled down a path into a cool dimly lit brick building. He lit several kerosene lanterns and began poring through dusty tomes clucking his tongue as he went.

Forty-five minutes stretched into an hour and a half. Neil and Sarah had seen power lines run into the main chancel area of the church but they clearly had not been extended to the accessory buildings.

"How old would you say he is, Neil?"

"I don't know. He's got to be pushing seventy-five, but who knows, he could be a tough sixty or a very well-preserved ninety."

"Oy!" He shrieked. Without warning, he grabbed Sarah by the hand and dragged her unceremoniously across graves and through an opening in the wrought iron garden fence. He babbled in another language until he reached a double gravestone of Joao and Judith Cruz, the parents of Anaisa Cruz. He pulled her down to the ground and wiped the dirt away from the bottom of the gravestone. Then he dug a stiff corn bristle hand brush out of the folds of his robes and swept and scraped with a small screwdriver until an inscription appeared that had been hidden just below the soil line..

Cristãos ✡ Novos
Born Joseph Cardozo and Judith Ruach

"Oh, my God."

"So what, Sarah? Michael's great-great-great grandparents were Jewish? Lots of Jews hid their identities in Spain and Portugal because of the Inquisition. If they didn't, they would have been burned at the stake."

"You don't understand, Neil."

The monk articulated, and Sarah started shaking. He wasn't speaking Spanish or Portuguese, yet she understood him, even better than she understood the locals in Rabat and Lisbon. She started counting on her fingers and stopped at five.

Neil looked at her in disbelief. "That's not Portuguese, is it?"

By now, tears were pouring down her cheeks as she nodded and hugged the man. He, too was crying.

"He's my fourth cousin, by marriage anyway."

"Your cousin? I thought we were tracking down Michael's family?"

"We were. Michael's great-great grandparents were Crypto-Jews. This man is Brother Antonio, Michael's great-grandmother's first cousin, who converted to Catholicism. Years ago, he took it upon himself to protect and honor the lives and memories of his Jewish brethren. He has spent his life maintaining the Nomos Christies section of the cemetery."

"But how is he your cousin, and how do you understand him? What language is he speaking?"

"My great-grandparents, Shprinster and Zvi Cardozo, I'm named after her, came to the US with their daughter Rachel. Soon after they arrived, another child, my grandfather Anthony, was born. Anthony and Antonio are namesakes of a common grandfather, Abraham. We didn't know exactly where my great-grandparents were from and if they told my grandfather, he never told us. But my grandfather and grandmother used to talk to each other and my great-Aunt Rachel and sometimes even my mom, in Ladino. They spoke it routinely in our house until both grandparents died when I was six. After that, my mom used to speak to her sister in Ladino whenever they didn't want us to understand them. My grandmother and grandfather were from different countries. I think her native tongue was French, but they both spoke Ladino. I can't speak a word of it, but I guess I still understand it."

"So you and Michael are related on both sides of your family?"

"Uh, I guess so. My other siblings are from a different mother than me. My dad's first wife died. Throughout our whole lives, Michael and I could read each other's minds, I mean really read each other's minds, in a way that neither of us shared with our own or the other's siblings."

Sarah had barely finished talking when the friar magically produced a small shovel from within his robes and continued digging at the tombstone. There, below Joao Cruz and Judith Cruz's names were the names of their fathers in Hebrew. Judith Cruz's father, born Baruch Kohn in 1865, had died in 1925, according to her cousin Antonio. He had an older sister, Antonia Julie Kohn who had fled the hamlet for fame in the Viennese theater in Austria in 1880. He gave her some coal and a large piece of paper to rub over the tombstone's chiseled inscription.

CHAPTER 27

Blue Genes

An excited phone call from Sam interrupted Sarah's work in the lab. So far, they had found what they expected. A naturally occurring vaccine against the black plague and a fungus that could make a big dent in global warming by naturally breaking down CO_2 and sequestering the carbon in rock, while excreting modest amounts of light sweet crude oil as a by-product. MC had no idea about something that could be so significant to repairing the damage that humans had done to their habitat. It was simply a collateral benefit. And MC didn't care at all because *It* had nothing to do with telepathy. The irony was MC's tunnel vision on *Its* agenda only proved *Its* point about letting nature take its course.

How could they replicate the fungus' properties outside the cave at magnetic north? Every time man introduced an invasive species to control an out-of-control plant, animal or compound like CO_2, there were always unexpected disastrous consequences. Snakes were never indigenous to Hawaii, but they were introduced to the island by hitchhiking in airplane landing gear or escaping their pet prisons and then they destroyed whole species of ground nesting birds.

And there was still the original concern. Which of the many toxins in the cave that hadn't yet been identified would abandon the comet and follow magnetic north on its brief migration in the next several weeks, possibly unleashing a pandemic against life on earth? At one time, that would have been the only question for Sarah to answer. But now, she had the opposite concern. How could she assure that nature would be allowed to fulfill *Its* destiny?

Sarah returned to her work. On the screen of her computer were coded sequences of partial DNA strings of several animals, a shark, a bat, and the monkameleon. Hair/scale samples had returned with her from her brief contact with the animal on the promontory.

It was astonishing to Sarah that the trait possessed by many prehistoric marine mammals to hunt through sand and navigate by the earth's electro-magnetic field was now limited to most sharks. That portion of the DNA double helix was virtually identical on the monkameleon, though completely dissimilar to most of the other mapped portions of the shark's DNA.

A boy in his early twenties popped in without knocking. Sarah kissed Michael's baby brother Brian on the cheek and brought up two different DNA strings on the large computer screen. One was Michael's and the other was her own.

"Ready?"

"Do we have to do it this way, Sarah?"

"Pricking your finger? You're a bigger baby than your brother. I need to compare your DNA to Michael's and mine and I don't want to get an incomplete code. I'll tell you what. I'll go first."

She drew several drops of blood into a tube. Her cousin grew pale, thrust his hand in her direction and looked away.

Brian left and Sarah pulled up a third DNA strand and laid it over Michael's and her own, which were a nearly perfect match. The third one was a poor match, but still substantially better than the one labeled "background population." It was the DNA of Jandra.

The temptation was nearly irresistible. Sarah could select a mate that would offer her children unlimited evolutionary opportunities. Or perhaps that opportunity belonged to Michael's brother and her half-sister. Sarah couldn't banish the dark thoughts from her head of genetically engineered thought transference. Was it the same irresistible enticements that ultimately killed her twin cousin or was it just scientific curiosity? In either case, the path led backward up the cladogram shared by telepathic and electroceptive creatures like the monkameleon and Sarah.

One other thing troubled Sarah. She studied the family tree on the screen which completely connected her lineage to Michael's. Was it possible? It didn't take the search engine long to discover the connection. Antonia Julie Kohn was Antonie Julie Kohn, the mother of Hermann (Herschmann-Chaim) Steinschneider, born in Austria in 1889. He grew up to become Erik Jan Hanussen, Hitler's infamous Jewish clairvoyant who was murdered by Goebbel's henchmen just a month after Hitler came to power. It was his witness to Hitler's rise to power that was now vested in MC's memories. He, too, had possessed the prophesy gene.

Seagal - Baskin Family Tree

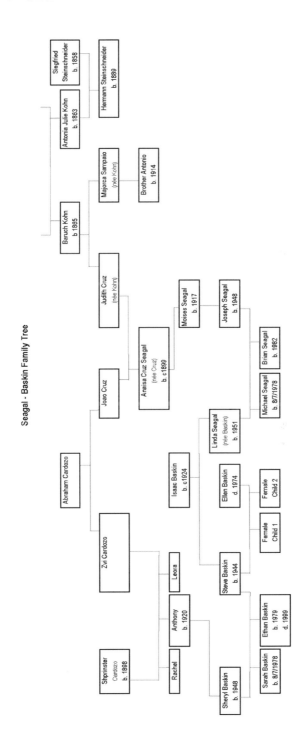

Made in the USA
San Bernardino, CA
05 November 2012